The Dharma Expedient

the dharma expedient

NEVILLE SARONY

Vajra Publications
www.vajrabooks.com.np

Published by

Vajra Publications

Jyatha, Thamel, Kathmandu, Nepal

Tel.: 977-1-4220562, Fax: 977-1-4246536

e-mail: bidur_la@mos.com.np

www.vajrabooks.com.np

Distributed by

Vajra Books

Kathmandu, Nepal

ISBN No. 978-9937-506-86-1

Printed in Nepal

For Tania

This book is a work of fiction, describing a possible future in Nepal. At the date of going to print there has not been a communist or military coup and since 2008 Nepal has functioned, in its own idiosyncratic way, as a lively republican democracy the inwardness of which has baffled observers whilst leaving this beautiful country's remarkable people merely a little puzzled. The characters in the following pages bear no resemblance whatsoever to actual living people but owe their existence to the imaginative functioning of the left hemisphere of the author's brain.

Contents

Calcutta

16th February...sometime in the future

"And now, ladies and gentlemen, Princes Restaurant is happy to present the ever-popular Angela and Dolly in their Dance of the Seven Veils!" Jimmy's right arm threw itself out in an expansive gesture that would have stopped the traffic if he'd been on point duty. "Angela and Dolly!"

The already dim lights were faded to extinction, leaving the restaurant lit only by the table candles. Jimmy's introduction, delivered in a Goan version of an American accent, was throttled by the crash and wail of the band which faded into tom-toms as the two scantily clad Anglo-Indian girls, fixed smiles verging on the grimace and skins shedding a light cloud of baby talcum, threw themselves into a routine that must have been choreographed by a spider with St. Vitus Dance.

At the bar, Max pondered, not for the first time, that none of the bar stools enabled one to see the floor show. Not, he readily conceded, that it was really worth watching, yet its very shoddiness had a compelling quality about it. The dancers were so embarrassingly amateur that they unwittingly burlesqued themselves. Looking around the room he observed that only a couple of fat lechers were paying attention as the shaking and wriggling that passed for entertainment became increasingly frenetic. Not that they were bad kids, he thought, just a couple of *chee-chee's* with a micron of talent, pretty faces and trim little bodies. Momentarily he checked himself for using the pejorative term for Anglo-Indians. It was too easy to lapse into the bad old habits. Oh! What a far cry from the political correctness of New York and London. He permitted himself a derisive internal laugh. Could anything be further removed from the lunacies of the politically correct world than this relic of a bygone colonial age? Of what comfort would it be to an ageing Angela or diseased Dolly if it deprived them of a regular income, no matter how small. They also knew that it introduced them into a wider world of social contacts than their shrinking community would offer them and by this tenuous route, a potential escape from the imprisoning cycle of pregnancy or prostitution or both. Even marriage within that same community held little attraction. All the brightest young men had long emigrated to Australia and only the outstandingly beautiful stood a chance of breaking out of the stifling downward spiral.

In his mind's eye, Max saw the handful of old Anglo-Indian women who still hung around the outskirts of New Market looking for a tourist to latch onto. In a curious way, despite the legions of destitute and homeless Bengalis that were synonymous with Calcutta, these old women were, in his mind's eye, the most pathetic sight in this vast and architecturally leprous city. In their shapeless frocks, dhobi'd into a nondescript colour, their casteless eyes set in comparatively light-skinned but drawn and wrinkled faces seemed to see nothing. They clung to the very fringes of a lost dignity so that they would address you as 'Sir', not 'Sahib', so as to distinguish themselves from the indigenous beggars whom, in this delicately structured social hierarchy, they still looked down upon as 'natives'. Max was sure that those adventurous foreign souls who still visited Calcutta thought that they were Europeans who had simply fallen on hard times. Now, that was a thought that struck far too close to home for comfort.

He took a long pull at his rum and coke, draining it down to the ice cubes. The comforting aroma settled briefly in his nose, displacing the musty staleness of the air-conditioning. The familiar stimuli to his senses of taste and smell were suddenly inhibiting, almost claustrophobic. He caught the barman's eye.

"Another rum and coke please, Charlie." Charlie was as Indian as a *chappati* but affected a Christian name. He also wore a perpetual look of wounded pride. An uncomfortable thought prompted Max to check his wallet just in case he had insufficient with which to pay his bar bill. A quick calculation told him that after tonight he'd be down to his last few hundred rupees. The 'Christ! What am I doing?' thought battled with the alcohol blunted senses and the anodyne lost. With disturbing clarity he knew that whatever he was doing, it wasn't enough and that if he didn't get off his arse and organise something in the next 2 or 3 days, he might well join the old ladies around New Market. It was remarkably easy to persuade himself that he was being overly self-critical. Yet that had to be set against 7 months without either work or income. The anger rose in his gorge like an acid reflux – Nepal's new Maoist-Leninist Front government had robbed him of his home, his business, his whole way of life. Incredibly, the extremist communist movement, as though totally oblivious of the worldwide trend, had captured the polls and immediately set about taking all private sector business into state control. Foreign investors had been the first targets and within a remarkably short time of taking power, he and his partner had made the metamorphosis from affluent owners of the Trans-Himalayan Travel Corporation to asset stripped members of the unemployed. After all the years of work they had put in to developing a sophisticated tourism industry for the erstwhile Himalayan kingdom, ploughing back the profits and betting on the long term benefits, now the Jungle Lodge, the Hills 'n Rivers Trekking & White Water Rafting Group, the domestic airline had all been 'localised'. Grand larceny was never grander than when done by governments. Since the Front's philosophy was that wealth-creating entities were the sole preserve of the state, they had no compunction in refusing even to discuss compensation. When Chuck had raised it with the minister for industries, the diminutive politico's eyes had burned with the anger of the zealot faced with an unrepentant heretic.

"Compensation? Compensation?" His voice had invested the word with the alchemy of a disease. "You peoples have exploited our birthright...our Nepalese mountains and rivers and toilers." He had risen from his chair behind the aircraft carrier size ministerial desk and his fingers quivered as he pointed at them alternately. "Now you come here like thugs," he pronounced it 'tugs', "in the night to demand payment for your crimes against the Nepalese working peoples, I am thinking to cancel your visas, right now!"

"Bullshit..." Chuck began to explode but Max motioned to his partner to shut up and opened his hands wide in a gesture of indulgent acceptance. If they were expelled now, they would lose any prospects whatsoever of salvaging anything. He set his face in an earnest expression and spoke quietly in Nepali.

"*Muntrisahib* we have worked primarily for Nepal, we invested all our personal assets and neither of us has ever taken one *paise*[1] out of the country. Truly we may look like foreigners but our hearts are pure Nepalese." There was an electric silence as the words sunk in. Almost as suddenly as his rage had flared up, the minister's face changed, replaced by a crafty half-smile.

"Ah! Colonel Devlin, one must not be forgetting your famous fluency in our language."

Max permitted himself a half-smile of acknowledgment.

"So, your Nepalese hearts will be glad to donate all this work to the re-building of our country, in our struggle to repair the damage of all the previous corrupt rulers." He extended his arms towards them inviting a triumphal handshake. Max had recognised at that moment that all was lost but the inertia of survival prompted him to accept the man's hand which also managed to convey the message that the meeting was now over. Instinctively, he knew that Chuck would refuse to shake hands. Forcing a smile, Max turned his face towards his partner and spoke softly:

"He who fights and runs away..." He watched reason fight with emotion across his friend's features.

"For you." Chuck's eyes flicked towards Max seconds before he reached forward to grasp the minister's hand.

For the next 2 months they had tried to negotiate a deal which would have enabled them to continue to run the corporation as salaried employees, then as unpaid executive directors, anything to prevent it being destroyed by incompetence and nepotism. The talks collapsed when the newly-appointed board of directors served them with notices terminating their positions as joint managing directors and blank mandates for them to sign, addressed to the banks and cancelling their authority to operate the corporation's accounts. Chuck had gone berserk having just returned from a meeting with the American ambassador.

---

1 A unit of currency representing 100th of a rupee.

"Asshole told me that we were big boys and should have known better'n to trust everythin' to a pissant little country run by a bunch a cockamamie priests. When I ask't him if this was the best he was gonna do for a US citizen an' ex-Vet, know what the asshole said?" He paused for effect rather than a reply. "Hell, Doc', this is off'n the record but my orders is to pussyfoot around with these fellas 'til they run outta steam. Ain't no way ah'm goin out on any limb for jes one guy whose big enough an' ugly enough to fend for hisself."

Max and Chuck had argued fiercely with each other over whether to sabotage the aircraft and set fire to the Jungle Lodge. Recalling how he had fought to dissuade his partner from doing anything which would be immediately traceable to them, the way Max now felt he would have had no compunction about throwing the spanners into the aircraft engines and igniting the first match. And so it had been, that one American ex-special forces veteran and doctor of anthropology together with an Irish ex-major of the Royal Gurkha Rifles found themselves unceremoniously shorn of 12 years of work and achievements.

The bitterness had cankered away within him over the intervening months leaving an unhealthy appetite to root out the burning sense of outrage, something simple but savage to mollify the unpropitiated anger.

The clarinettist's reed gave up the unequal struggle with a dischordantly wet squeak, interrupting the less than euphonious accompaniment until the trumpeter had a misguided stab at carrying the melody.

Max caught Jimmy's eye and squeezed his face into a wince of pain. The maitre d' smiled and shrugged his shoulders. No matter what the situation, that particularly negative Asian expression 'What to do?' whether articulated or inferred, seemed to face him on all sides. Here in Calcutta, in Chuck's graphic description 'the colonic zenith of the asshole of the world', merely to survive was to triumph. He looked into the dark brown liquid of his glass and it stared back at him, yielding no secrets of its own. His thoughts turned to the muddy waters of the rivers in Karnataka where Chuck had managed to land the CEO's job in an American consortium's hunting and fishing lodge. A good friend, he had offered Max employment as general manager. Max was too honest with himself to ignore the fact that he would make a poor 'company man'. Being his own master had, with all its shortcomings, lodged too deeply in his psyche for him to abandon it. He was pretty certain too that the Karnataka operation would not have supported both of them in any event and he would be financially beholden to his ex-partner. Right now, however, with 2-month's back rent owing, an unsecured overdraft which was already way over his limit thanks to an accommodating Irish bank manager in London and the inexplicable last minute cancellation of two Himalayan expeditions which he had been asked to organise, independence looked like a luxury he could no longer afford. His efforts to raise cash or backing to replicate the Nepal venture in India had both foundered when the potential backers both wanted too large a slice of the action and would not relinquish executive control of the proposed operations to him. Though the British Raj had departed the Indian subcontinent more than half a century ago, Indian entrepreneurs whilst recognising the need for specialised expertise in international tourism operations, still harboured unconquerable suspicions, as though a new imperialism was to be founded upon a breed of expatriates. Scratch many an Indian businessman and just below the veneer lay an unreconstructed *Suraj ud D'aula.*

This line of thought was interrupted when he caught sight in the bar mirror of two familiar figures behind him, Prakash bulking a head and shoulders over 'Woody' White. He turned around to face them on the bar stool. "I might have known you two bastards wouldn't leave me in peace for long."

"Jimmy!" The Indian pointed at Max, his voice booming over the music. "I thought I gave strict instructions never to let this degenerate in here again?" Jimmy grinned back and gestured helplessly before placing his forefinger against his lips and pointing to the dancers who were fast approaching the *moment critique* of their routine. Max managed a smile that barely reached his eyes.

"Remind me to have you blackballed from the Bengal Club."

"Whilst you're blackballing people, how about a lifetime ban on those two from ever appearing here again?" Woody flicked his head towards the dancers.

"Unemployment is no bloody joking matter." Max could not disguise the feeling behind his words. Quickly he added, "I reckon that this may well be *my* last appearance at the rate things are going downhill."

"Balls!" Woody laughed at him. "The day you're on your ucksters, as you would put it in your usual decorous way, I'll give up drinking. So, what'll you have?" Woody exuded success. Momentarily, it served only to heighten Max's sense of failure. The Englishman had wheeled and dealed from nothing to a backdoor into the cornucopia of the Indian IT world. In 10 years, he'd gone head to head with some of the best in the business community, outsmarted the Armenians, pared the Marwari's closer to the bone than they believed possible and beaten the Scindi's at their own game. His operating ethic that every transaction had to show a profit informed every aspect of his life, not just his business dealings. It contrasted starkly with Max's intuitive approach. It had certainly not been hard financial reasoning that had led him to sink his commuted army pension, terminal bounty and all his savings into the little business empire in Nepal. The mental image immediately conjured itself of his capital and the fruits of his labours being frittered away by Kathmandu's current political masters. Though one could not make a silk purse from a sow's ear, the Front's litter had been provided with the silk purse, free, gratis and for absolutely nothing.

"Stop feeling so bloody sorry for yourself," Woody chided. "Let's have a bite at The Taj, or have you eaten?" Max shook his head in reply. "Then let's go. Ivor'll fix us up with something special, this place's kitchen has gone to the dogs."

"What I like about you Woody," Prakash put his hand on the Englishman's shoulder, "is that you'll fix yourself the bridal suite come judgment day."

"How d'you like that?" Woody turned to Max for support. "It's like an Armenian calling a Jew tight-fisted. Have you no respect for my legendary ability to conjure up triumph from disaster?" Max was disinclined to join in the banter in his current mood.

"I think Rudyard Kipling had it about right when he described triumph and disaster as imposters."

"When you two silly buggers have finished, shall we go and eat? I'm starving." Prakash turned and began to walk away. Max felt uncomfortable knowing that his friends would insist on paying for everything. He'd seen it happen to others but even now found it hard to come to terms with the reality now that it was his turn. A special personal panic began to palpate his guts, flat broke in Calcutta! Doubly appalling in the world capital of poverty. Like an emetic spasm it reached up into him and blanched his innards. Instinctively, he clung to the short-term *placebo* of his friends' company.

They walked out of the air-conditioned vacuum of the restaurant into the limpid yet febrile Calcutta night. He could not recall a time when the smells, the touch of the heat, the way it collapsed the fabric of his clothes against his skin had failed to fascinate him. Its languorous embrace drew him in with a post-coital torpor. They got into a waiting taxi, Max and Prakash sitting in the back and Woody squeezed beside a vicious looking Sikh riding 'shotgun' beside the driver.

"God knows what we want a taxi for!" He laughed. "Still we might as well sit tight now we're in." Max and Prakash groaned in unison at the laboured pun. "*Achha, Sardarji*, Taj Hotel *chalo*."

It struck Max that he would not have cared to embark on a lengthy journey with the driver and his 'assistant', a pair of thin, malevolently bearded Sikhs with ill-bound *pagaris* who muttered to each other throughout the short journey, furious at having lost their place in the taxi queue for an uneconomic fare.

The heat laden night air was sucked in through the open windows and clung to him as the decrepit Hindusthan ambassador bumped and lurched protesting and unsprung through the treacle and charcoal richness of West Bengal's capital city. They came to an angry halt and Woody fished some exhausted looking rupee notes out of his shirt pocket. The driver gave the money scant attention but managed to acknowledge the healthy tip by an expressive hunching of his shoulders before he blew his nose delicately into his fingers through the open window before wiping his hand on the trailing end of his pagari. They were still climbing out of the taxi when one of the regular pimps began to hustle them.

"You liking nice girls in room, Saheb? I bring soon, Yes? Very clean, no dirty AID's *beebees* and special price for you Saheb." He kept it up until they stepped into the foyer of the hotel and the impressively liveried doorman bore down on the entrepreneur. Max often exchanged a little ribald banter with the man but tonight he lacked the spirit. He had a size-10 predicament in a size-8 brain. The old conviction that, come what may, he would somehow fall on his feet had suddenly come face to face with the handful of rupees in his pocket.

"Major...?" The young Anglo-Indian receptionist called out to him from behind the desk. "There's an email attachment for you, sir.

Came about an hour ago." Courtesy of the hotel management, he had all communications sent to him at The Taj. It was more impressive and a great deal more reliable than his rooms at Jenny Christiansen's which had neither broadband nor WiFi. Max tore open the envelope and recognised Chuck's corporate logo above a Karnataka office address. Written with Chuck's habitual economy of words, it took a few seconds to sink in.

'Old Buddy, you have a VIP Thai client, Mr/Dr(?) Sutape Sukhum arriving Delhi on flight TG 655 ETA 0035 Sunday 29th who wants you personally to meet him to discuss a Himalayan project (details unknown). The guy's a very serious type, bit of an oddball but I guarantee he's not a time waster. All arrangements made for both of you to stay at Intercontinental, inclusive airport limo transfers. I have sent PTA to Indian Airlines for your flight CAL/DLH. The guy is talking serious money so be sure and get your ass over there in time.

'Keep me posted. Good luck!'

He had to restrain a surge of renewed confidence. Rescue missions came in all shapes and sizes and the road to independence was paved with serious money. A ticket out of Calcutta at this particular moment felt like Cinderella's glass coach.

"Judging by the look on your face, your last surviving maiden aunt has finally popped her clogs, leaving her entire estate to her favourite nephew in recognition of the example he's set the world for clean living." Woody was unashamedly peering over Max's shoulder trying to read the email. He refolded it back into the envelope and pushed it into his jacket pocket whilst the flush of relief refuelled his resilience.

"Once again, the gods nail the rug firmly beneath the feet of their favoured sons." He permitted himself the grin that had been struggling to get out. "To the bar, gentlemen, and on this auspicious occasion that even includes you Prakash, my over-pigmented friend."

"Get stuffed!" The Indian grinned.

"What? Like all those poor bloody animals on the walls of your grandiose outhouse?" What Max admired about Prakash was not only his natural generosity of spirit but his earthy sense of humour. The erstwhile Maharaja of Udai Deo was an anachronism, one of the furnishings of a bygone era that time and a succession of egalitarian Indian governments had failed to wash away. In his mind's eye, Max always pictured him in one of the sepia-tinted photographs that lined the rooms of his princely apartment in Alipore.

"The impoverished Irish gentry are well known as the world's greatest authorities on lavatories. This, you see, is because the amount of alcohol they consume requires them to pass copious amounts of urine in public toilets, privies, outhouses and suchlike where their family mottos are to be seen engraved upon doors and walls. You, my dear Max, are no exception. But as, despite all that, you remain a true gentleman, I shall accept your kind invitation."

Max savoured the recently absent luxury of shared laughter and led the way to the bar. He let his mind speculate on the future. If the fee was particularly generous, it could be sufficient to provide the seed money to get one of his schemes underway. He assumed that Sukhum Sutape, whoever he was, had been making enquiries and Chuck had sold him on Max's unique talents. Chuck had always been the marketing genius, leaving him to manage the operational aspects of the business. Thank god for Chuck's continuing high profile in the travel industry, something which he, self-evidently, had to concede he did not have. But there was still something a bit out of the ordinary, after all, he had had his ear finely tuned to the bush telegraph and there had been nothing remotely connected with Thailand that he had heard of. Still, he reflected, there came a time in every man's life when even the most prudent refrained from asking who actually tolled the bell? The fact that it tolled for him was more than sufficient for his immediate needs.

New Delhi

28th February

A late February night in Delhi demands an overcoat. Max was embarrassingly aware that apart from its classic military cut, his 'British warm' was decidedly over retirement age. The aftermath of an invasion of white ants into the lapels and epaulettes contributed little to his sartorial elegance. He would have to dispense with wearing it before meeting the client. He shivered slightly in anticipation, both at the prospect of being cold and also a little in nervous tension.

He watched some incoming passengers emerge, appearing almost to stumble out of the international arrivals terminal straight into the car park where they stood, momentarily anaesthetised by their first raw contact with Mother India. Their baggage trollies were seized by porters whose faces, swaddled against the cold night air, immediately conjured up visions of brigands. Simultaneously, a hustling swarm of small boys began to importune them.

"Taxi, Saheb?"

"This way, Memsaheb."

"You want private taxi? Where you going?"

"Meter wallah, OK! OK! This way."

Tugging at the trolleys and fighting amongst themselves, porters, urchins and bewildered passengers moved like a swarm of bees with sections peeling off and then rejoining as it moved towards the taxi rank. Max smiled to himself, comfortable in this familiar tatter of the subcontinent's rich fabric. He still had time in hand so he headed for the airport restaurant and ordered a sweet *lassi.* Sipping the whipped and chilled buttermilk he reviewed the events of the days since he'd received the email. Chuck had followed up with a much fuller attachment letter in which he explained that a contact in Bangkok had approached him on behalf of a Professor Sutape of the Queen Sirikit Institute of Buddhist Art. Apparently, the Professor had asked that arrangements be made for Max to meet him in Delhi to discuss a Himalayan expedition. Fifty-thousand rupees had been wired to Max's bank account to cover initial expenses and the fee was US$1,500 a day plus all expenses, payable wherever he wished. It was not quite the king's ransom he had hoped for but he contented himself with the thought that he could probably renegotiate it. Moreover, it was not even a firm commitment yet, a *possible* expedition was not a bankable proposition. What had rather surprised him was to discover that it had not been on Chuck's recommendation but that the client had sought him out specifically. In these circumstances, what puzzled him somewhat was the failure to identify the objective of the expedition and, even more to the point, its destination, assuming that it had a destination. He could see no good reason for not disclosing such details when so much hinged on them. The probability favoured Nepal which was his area of greatest expertise even though he had mounted every description of trek and expedition along the entire Himalayan Range. More particularly, the current state of emergency ruled out Kashmir and the Afghanistan imbroglio did likewise for the Hindu Kush as did the tribal and ethnic unrest along the Assam/Naga hills. The Chumbi Valley between Sikkim and Bhutan was a permanent no-go area so far as the Indian Government was concerned, that whole area was one vast military encampment. Bhutan's tight control over tourism made it highly unlikely and that left only Nepal and Sikkim. Assuming, as Max did, that the Buddhist Institute's interests lay in some academic aspect of that great religious movement, Nepal as the birthplace of *Gautama* the Lord Buddha himself, seemed far and away the most likely candidate. As against this conclusion, the meeting was taking place in Delhi despite the fact that there was a daily direct flight from Bangkok to Kathmandu. What had, to all intents and purposes, been a bloodless revolution in Nepal had frightened off many of the foreign tour operators and without that revenue Max reckoned the new government's financial pips had begun to squeak. World Bank and IMF support had been frozen and despite all the usual expressions of fraternal love and ideological support being broadcast from Beijing, China had enough potentially disastrous economic problems of its own without having to prop up a bankrupt Nepalese administration and incur the ever-ready wrath of New Delhi. The wry thought struck him that political pragmatism in Kathmandu was not dead even though it may be going through a period of post traumatic stress disorder. Nor, given Nepal's extraordinary faculty for developing political hybrids, was it a simple case of communism versus capitalism or east against west. It was, as the government-owned *Rising Nepal* daily newspaper blazoned under its title, 'An awakened perception of historical horizons', and, as Max reflected, if you could make head or tail of what all that meant, you're a better man than I am, Gunga Din. Some of the horizons that had been rudely skewed included the American Peace Corps, British Voluntary Service Overseas, the entire US Aid extravaganza and the sugar, tobacco and brewery factories whose foreign personnel had all been given 24 hours' notice to quit. The UNDP had been left in no doubt as to the ethnic and political acceptability of their expatriate staff, known locally as the 'yellow, black and red rule'. The USIS Library had been vandalised with such monotonous regularity that its director had been evacuated back to Washington with an acute case of *cannabis tremens*. On the principle that good diplomacy is self-effacing, the British had an uninterrupted record of success. A succession of lack-lustre terminal posting ambassadors whose main claim to fame in Whitehall had been their gutless sycophantic vacuity had created the very apotheosis of such a diplomatic policy. Indeed, had it not been for their courageous refusal to be bested in the annual 'Best Embassy Garden' competition, her Brittannic Majesty's envoys, not so much plenipotentiary as extraordinary, would have passed totally unnoticed.

Max's eye fell on the little gold kukri-shaped cuff-links just visible beyond his jacket sleeves. He wondered how Deepraj was faring? The ex-Gurkha soldier from his own battalion whom Max had employed as a personal butler-cum-driver and general 'Man Friday' had been busying himself in various Calcutta markets trying to locate the sort of equipment that they might need if this meeting proved fruitful. So dependable was the Gurkha that Max realised, not for the first time, that he had a tendency to take him for granted. In all the years that he had been in Max's service since they had left the Army together, the tough, undemonstrative man had been a five foot four inches tall marvel of pragmatic loyalty. The son of a Darjeeling Himalayan railway engine driver, he had taken to the Army like a duck to water, his remarkable ability to adapt to whatever circumstances he faced had been a godsend on countless occasions and all carried out with a mischievous grin, especially when doing something that bordered on the illegitimate. He could and did turn his hand to anything, some of which Max thought it best not to enquire about too closely, especially recently when cash had been tight.

"Thai International Airlines announces the arrival of its flight TG 655 from Honolulu, Tokyo, Hong Kong and Bangkok." There was a muffled roar audible inside the restaurant as the ex-Thai airforce pilot thrust the 747-400's engines into reverse thrust. Max walked slowly through the departure terminal, picking his way around the recumbent bodies of world travellers and latter day hippies of almost every nationality, colour and description, sex being the most difficult feature to distinguish amongst the flowing hair, unisexual robes and the often emaciatedly thin limbs, their drug pallid faces buried into their pathetic bundles of luggage, an ineffective defense against the mosquitos which successfully defied the air conditioning system. Little honeysuckle, much bindweed he mused. He began to wonder how their parents reacted to the lives these children had chosen. A thin girl of no more than 17 or 18, whose gaunt face, framed against long soft brown hair that swirled around her throat struck him as quite exquisite. He felt a need to reach out and help her, a feeling that died upon the moment with the realisation that he could barely help himself. If he had married, he wondered, would his son or daughter have been amongst this flotsam and jetsam? Or would he or she have rebelled against the unstructured would-be Renaissance man of the east whose children they had the misfortune to be and elected to become lawyers, doctors, investment bankers or one of those other stress filled passages to material success? All in all, he acknowledged, it was better that no one should be dependent upon him. Inevitably, his mind reached back to Kimmie and the love that they had shared, the future that they had planned together when the world looked younger and bright with hope. The hit and run driver in Hong Kong had smashed into her slender frame leaving her beautiful face untouched but massive internal injuries to which she quickly succumbed. The years had only dimmed the grief. Time healed the gaping wounds but left intractably unyielding scars on the heart. No one had reached him since then. Perhaps, he reflected for the umpteenth time, the invisible carapace that he had developed as a protection against emotional hurt had deterred other women from attempting to breach his defensive mechanism. He shook his head slightly in a conscious effort of will to close off this fruitless backtracking.

Walking slowly, he made his way out of the busy departure terminal and walked through the maze of parked cars, empty security boxes and occasional dejected looking palm trees towards the complex of featureless buildings that disgorged the new arrivals. He draped his overcoat around his shoulders and clipped his expired Delhi airport pass to his breast pocket. He had spent nearly 9 months based in Delhi three years previously and most of his old contacts were still around. It always impressed the clients to be met within the airport precincts rather than outside. Pushing his way firmly through the crowd around the exit from the customs hall, he waved to the Punjabi Rip Van Winckle of the Delhi Police who guarded the door.

"Not out with the girls tonight then, *Bapu*?"

"*Nahi, nahi, Saheb*." The old man grinned, displaying a set of teeth like a Shetland pony. "*Mahin burra lohg hei*."

"I'd lay fifty to one you're not too old!" Max chaffed back. The guard waved an admonitory forefinger to and fro whilst cackling with laughter then with a wave of his hand, he motioned Max through.

So far so good. He walked on. Ahead of him he could see various European passengers pushing trolleys and being waved through whilst the Indians were putting their luggage on the customs inspection desks ready to be exploited. Standing a little back from the cavernous main hall in a position from where he could see all the customs channels he studied the arriving passengers. He had a well developed eye for distinguishing one Asiatic from another.

The crisp white uniforms of the customs officers created oases of apparent efficiency in the vast emptiness of the customs shed where the passengers and their luggage looked incongruous, like so many misfits at a Mad Hatter's tea party. He caught sight of Bina, the Thai Airways ground manageress, as she guided a distinguished looking Asian man of medium height, his close cut dark hair revealing distinguished streaks of grey. Bina saw him and smiled: 500 rupees well spent. Max walked to meet them, taking in the details of his potential client. Forty to forty-five, he guessed, casually but smartly dressed in a white roll neck sweater under a Lacoste blouson, facially he had the patrician features that made some Thais look almost European. The eyes, Max noted were steady and revealed nothing.

"Professor Sukhum?"

"Colonel Devlin?" They shook hands. Max was a little surprised to find himself promoted, true, he had held temporary rank as Lt. Colonel when commanding the Jungle Warfare School in Sabah but had reverted to his substantive rank on taking early pension. Well, at this stage, anything that counted in his favour was worth keeping.

"Thank you very much, Bina." He smiled appreciatively and she gave a little cock of her head.

"Any time Max. See you around. Enjoy your stay, Professor." She raised one hand in salute and turned away. Max caught the look on Sukhum's face which conveyed an impression that he guessed at a closer relationship between Max and the attractive Indian manageress.

"Strictly professional, Professor." Max allowed a slight *mou* as he spoke. "Please give me your passport." He handed the document and customs declaration form over to the unsmiling official who had watched the exchange.

"You are having any computer, DVD or electronic gifts for any peoples?"

"No. Just personal effects, clothing and so on." Max noted the American accent.

"The Professor is on a short business trip, staying at the Intercontinental." Max indicated the solitary suit carrier. Turning the pages of the passport, the officer spoke without looking at them.

"And getting VIP welcoming, isn't it?" He returned the passport and flourished his chalk imperiously, leaving that day's cryptic sign for the gate sentry. Max acknowledged the salute from the uniformed janissary and shepherded his guest out of the building. A sturdy Punjabi boy appeared out of the shadows and seized the suit carrier causing the Thai to step back momentarily.

"It's OK. He's one of ours." Max reassured him with a wry grin. The deft administration of several kicks to the shins and a vicious elbow kept at bay those of the boy's colleagues who tried to get in on the act. The limousine's doors clicked shut and Max leant back, another swift, clean and uneventful arrival satisfactorily accomplished.

"I was warned that Delhi Airport could be a sonofabitch." Max was mildly amused by the incongruity of expression on the lips of a man he had taped as a reserved South East Asian academic. "Do you always handle things as smoothly?"

"We try, Professor, we try. The odd trick of the trade here and there…" He let the matter trail off leaving Sukhum to draw his own inferences.

"I think we may need quite a few of those in time." The Thai half turned towards Max. "I have been travelling almost constantly for the last 24 hours and I'm pretty well tuckered out. I'd like to get my head down and start afresh in the morning. But I'd appreciate it if you would bring me up to date with the present political situation in Nepal, your standing with the authorities there and so on, if that would not be too tedious." He twisted his head forward suddenly as the car swung madly out of the oncoming traffic lane just in time to avoid a truck coming towards them. "Provided that we survive that long."

"*Asti! Asti!*" Max commanded the driver. Hunched over the steering wheel, the man managed a quick backward smile whilst turning cloth ears to the instructions. *Plus ca change plus c'est la meme Bhose* one of Woody's more memorable observations on life in India sprang into his mind. So, he had been right, Nepal it was. He felt a fresh surge of confidence.

"I'll do my best but it will take a little time to give you the full flavour."

"Well, I've paid for the ticket, now roll the movie and run the credits real slow." Max found himself amused by the contrast between the Professor's appearance and his verbal style. As Max painted in the background and added in the details, Sukhum began to ask questions that revealed an insightful grasp of the Himalayan political scene. He began to suspect that the object of this exercise was so that his prospective employer could assess him rather than receive an educational briefing. It was not until they were outside the doors of their adjoining rooms and out of earshot of anyone else that Max heard, with welcome relief, the words that set him at his ease.

"Clearly, you are our man, Colonel. I have little doubt on that score. Tomorrow we will get down to details."

"Thank you, sir." There was little that Max could think of to add at that point.

"Goodnight to you."

"Goodnight, Professor." As he closed his door behind him, Max felt the first rush of exhilaration. He looked at his watch but recognised that it would be several hours before Bina came off duty. Pity.

New Delhi

1st March

The telephone's intrusive ringing penetrated Max's REM sleep.

"Yes."

"Good morning, Colonel." Max looked at his wristwatch, 06.30.

"Good morning, sir."

"Breakfast beside the swimming pool in half an hour?"

"Make that ten past, would you, Professor." He wanted sufficient time for a swim before he faced breakfast.

At 07.10 precisely Sukhum walked through the glass door and walked along the poolside to join Max at a table set up for breakfast. Only one other table was occupied and that at the far end, where the sun already bathed a triangle of space. Max had deliberately chosen a table in the shade of a palm tree, conscious of most South East Asians' aversion to the Caucasian obsession with sitting in the direct sun. A busboy took their order, his starched white shirt and trousers a striking contrast against his almost black skin. Sukhum wasted no time with pleasantries.

"I hope that the financial arrangements for this meeting are to your satisfaction?" He barely paused for a response before continuing. "Assuming that you accept the assignment, your expenses will be met in full and I trust we can agree your fees." It was a statement rather than a question. "I suggest we leave these details in abeyance till you have the whole picture."

Max gave a slight nod.

"From what you told me last night, I take it you are still sufficiently *persona grata* in Kathmandu to arrange trekking permits for a party from my institute to make an expedition to eastern Nepal?"

"When the MLF Government took power they banned all trekking and mountaineering despite the loss of revenues that that caused. After things settled down a bit, my partner and I approached the minister of tourism and the foreign secretary to try and get some limited trekking allowed. We badgered them for a few weeks but eventually abandoned our efforts when our corporation was 'localised'. Since then, a Japanese botanical expedition in the eastern hills and an Israeli study group surveying farmers' co-operatives in the far west have been granted permits."

"Japan and Israel were the first to recognise the new regime weren't they?" Sukhum surprised Max with the detail of his political knowledge.

"Yes and Japan signed a very beneficial loan agreement which helped them to meet government expenditure in the absence of IMF funding."

"And the Israelis?"

"It's my guess that the Israeli military mission gave the Nepal Army paratroopers their anti-monarchical indoctrination. The MLF had to neutralise the military top brass so as to get a free hand for their cadres to work the electorate."

"So there's a political *quid pro quo*?"

"Precisely." Max nodded. "I think we may have similar leverage through Thai International Airways. Their decision to maintain daily schedules, despite the dramatic reduction in traffic, has put them in particularly good odor." Sukhum nodded slowly. Max continued. "When Indian Airlines cancelled their flights immediately after what the Indian Government regarded as nothing short of a *coup*, it put enormous strains on Nepal. They have always been particularly sensitive about being land-locked and the Indians play this card for all it's worth. Relations with India have hit rock bottom. They always were mercurial, the love-hate relationship with their southern 'Big Brother' is a continuing paradox, they emulate Indian fashions, watch Hindi films and listen to their popular music but they're hypersensitive to their political and economic domination."

"Yes, New Delhi isn't loved by any of its neighbours, big or small." Sukhum smiled briefly.

"And with the Chinese star in the ascendant, Kathmandu will be on the lookout for destabilising interference plays." He paused momentarily, not quite decided whether to pursue this line if it was likely to curb the Thai's enthusiasm for his project. He decided to be candid. "There's good and bad in all this." He watched Sukhum's face for any adverse sign but pressed on. "On the one hand Kathmandu's xenophobia will be at a high setting, on the other there is likely to be a disproportionate friendliness to those they see as supportive of the regime. Can you get your embassy to put in a good word for you?"

"Consider it done."

"The local Thai International manager will be on the Board of Airlines Representatives which is chaired by the secretary for tourism. I think that would be the most influential route in."

"OK," Sukhum nodded agreement without hesitation. The man had to have influence in Bangkok to be this assured. The concern that niggled in the back of Max's mind was whether this political clout could be peddled so as to include the presence of one maverick Irish entrepreneur in the deal. It was all very well knowing the ropes and being a one man 'Lonely Planet' guide to Nepal but it had not sufficed to salvage his own corporation. Anxious lest he reveal his own desperate need to secure the contract, Max ploughed on quickly.

"Of course, a hell of a lot will turn on the precise nature of the project that you have in mind."

"I expect that you know that outside Tibet, the greatest source of the iconography of the Mahayana school of Buddhism is to be found amongst the ethnically Tibetan and Tibeto-Burman communities in Nepal?"

"The inhabitants of Lo-Mustang, the Manangi's and especially the Newars." Max counted them off on his fingers.

"Quite. But systematic pillaging of temples, *chortens* and simple shrines in the more readily accessible regions of Nepal has provided the subject matter for the major art auctions by Christie's, Spinck's and the other major league players in London, New York and Hong Kong. One has only to visit Paris' Musée de l'Homme to witness the extent of this devastation of a rich religo-cultural heritage. And all this against a background of governmental prohibitions on exportation." There was an intensity behind his words that Max had not previously noted. A contained anger. "My institute has been fighting what amounts to commercial sacrilege for many years but, until recently, we have been restricted in what we could do by a shortage of the green stuff." Max stifled a yen to grin at the momentary lapse from the academic into the vernacular.

"Thanks to the generosity of some individuals and organisations, particularly the Smithsonian in Washington, we now have the possibility of cataloguing the major works with the objective of mounting a campaign to return them to their original sites. If they come back onto the international art market we could even bid for them."

Max checked an impulse to suggest that there was more than a hint of the poacher turned gamekeeper about the Smithsonian's interest but the piquancy of the situation amused him. At this stage in the discussions, he reminded himself, he knew precious little about Sukhum's connections and he didn't want to offend him with a careless remark. He shared the Professor's animosity towards the art smugglers, too many of whom had enjoyed the sanctity of the diplomatic pouch to spirit the beautiful artifacts of Buddhist iconography out of their proper homes and into the world's art museums and auction houses. It was important to let the man know that they shared a kindred concern.

"It's a pity it's taken so long to get something done. I'm afraid most of the horses have already bolted."

"Too goddamn little, too goddamn late."

"But still worthwhile."

"The purpose of our project is to carry out the initial survey, locating and identifying the reliquaries, great and small in the primary and secondary areas of Buddhist culture in Nepal and Sikkim. We hope to build a series of catalogues which will eventually be worldwide but we have to start in Nepal, the greatest repository of all. You understand, this is because the Newar craftsmen of the Valley of Kathmandu have been the traditional creators of the vast majority of these works of art throughout the history of our religion. A thousand years of inspirational creativity in stone, wood, precious and base metals, not to mention the exquisite *thangka's.*" Pausing, he allowed himself a self-deprecatory smile. "More to the immediate point, we have to convince our sponsors of the worth of spending their dollars. Forgive me, I quickly get carried away once I'm into my subject." He drained his coffee cup. "We'll go up to my room and I'll show you our maps of the regions of greatest importance and therefore, their greatest interest to us. You will have to advise us about accessibility, geographical and climatic conditions…anything which bears practically on the logistics."

Max was concerned that there was too tacit an assumption that the necessary permits would be a minor hurdle. "I think you'd better hold hard a bit, Professor. What you have in mind is way out of the ordinary. You're not climbing mountains or collecting plants or butterflies. More to the point, I don't need to consult your maps to know that you want access to regions of Nepal where the Kathmandu government's writ has never run strong, historically. My guess is that they will need a great deal of persuasion before they allow foreigners into areas where the people are culturally and genetically dissident." Sukhum's facial expression indicated disagreement. Max held his hand up, palm forward, gently preventing interruption. "These regions have a long tradition of opposition to whoever holds the nominal reins of power in Kathmandu, ever since King Prithivi Narayan Shah founded the current dynasty in the 18th century, the Rana Maharajas, the Nepali Congress Party, no matter who, Kathmandu has a chronic sensitivity to allowing outsiders to lift the veil." The potential problem he was not going to articulate was the even greater whimsy governing the acceptability of westerners. Despite having sold himself as 'the acceptable foreigner' it was far from certain that he would be allowed to lead the expedition into the farther reaches of the country. Within the Valley of Kathmandu there were still enough friendly faces at the middle and lower reaches of the administration to secure him access to the politico's and their appointees at ministerial secretary level. Beyond that it was untested ground. Still, he reasoned, without so much as a backward glance at modesty, no one else around had his expertise, these people were buying the best man in the business. If he could engineer it carefully enough, he could finesse a decent profit out of it even if the expedition never got to the jump-off point. He would argue the moral toss with his conscience if and when he could afford that luxury.

"We can count on full diplomatic backing." Sukhum spread his hands out, palm down in a gesture signifying that all the problems would be smoothed out. "I have assurances of maximum co-operation from our Ministry of Foreign Affairs. Our ambassador here will see me at 12 noon today." He signalled to the busboy and signed the check. "Let's go look at the map."

The maps were already spread out on top of the dressing bureau, each inside its own 'talc' overlay. Sukhum pointed to the eastern sheet and his finger traced a line through the villages of Melung, Phaphlu and Dingla.

"Each of these places looks like a convenient base from which to trek up into the Bhota Kosi, Dudh Kosi and Arun valleys, respectively."

Max gave a slight nod. He was very familiar with them, each at about ten thousand feet.

"The first phase of research would aim to cover the temples and chortens in these three valleys."

"How much time have you allotted for this first phase?"

"Twelve months."

"Mmm..." Max imbued his response with a thin layer of doubt. "I'd say you were more than a little ambitious in your time scale." He scanned the map for any other marks or signs which would indicate areas of interest. Keeping his eyes on the greens, browns and blues of the cartographer's palette, he continued. "You can allow yourselves a maximum working period of seven to eight months between the end of one monsoon season and the beginning of the next."

"What if we have to work through the monsoon?" The query struck Max as odd. He couldn't see why a project such as had been outlined to him would be under the sort of constraints of time that would demand working outside the normal trekking season.

"Well, if you're prepared to cope with rock and soil slips big enough to bury whole villages, rain so heavy it weighs you down and leeches taking up residence in every orifice in your body...yes. You could." He ignored the little warning light that cautioned against pursuing this. "But why on earth would you want to do the survey in such impossible conditions?"

"Just the unvarnished information, Colonel, without the commentary." Max promised himself to heed the marker buoys in future.

"I apologise." His words hung a fraction too heavily, waiting for absolution. He pressed on in hope of restoring the atmosphere. "You can work safely until the monsoon actually breaks. Pulling back to base during the early rains wouldn't present a problem."

"When does the monsoon break and how long does it last?"

"It varies each year. Safely, I'd say to the middle of May, maybe the end. You could chance another week closest to Kathmandu." He pointed out the Bhota Kosi on the map. "Particularly if you worked the lower reaches of the Tamba Kosi." Back on safe ground again, he felt his confidence returning as he spoke of the world he both knew and loved. "Conditions deteriorate alarmingly quickly. Work in the valleys further east would have to stop by mid-May at the very latest. This assumes that our airlifts of men and materials are from the all-weather airstrips at Kathmandu and Biratnagar. Even then we'd be subject to low cloud closing down Biratnagar which doesn't have any radar guidance system. Failing that, all time schedules would have to be advanced by two weeks." He did a quick calculation. "We should have more than adequate time to get it all set up for a start in early September."

Sukhum was leaning over the map, listening. Still bending forward he turned his head towards Max and spoke quietly.

"I intend to complete the pilot survey before the next monsoon breaks."

"Impossible." Max shook his head. "Even when I had a fully operational organisation on the ground and the route to the Everest Base Camp looked like Coney Island on the 5th of July I wouldn't have given any guarantees." He could tell from the imperturbable expression on the Professor's face that the message was not getting through. "Look, sir, what have we got? Twelve weeks? I'd have to recruit a team, engage porters, beg borrow or steal the equipment we couldn't carry in, organise transport, square away the authorities for permits which God alone knows whether this bunch will even consider giving us and…" He hesitated momentarily, calculating whether to add the rider. "I'm going in cold." There, it was done. Miracles, as the saying went, took longer. Maybe he'd blown it with candour. Old habits died hard. Too many good folk had been conned into believing that there was 'no problem' in a land where the devil shopped for problems of every hue and size.

It was one thing to be down on your luck, quite another to abandon all the principles once held so dearly. He realised that he was already abandoning the mercenary approach he'd adopted only minutes earlier.

Sukhum stared at him in silence. The look on his face was that of a patient man waiting to be told one valid reason why he could not do that which he intended. Max obliged him.

"I know these people." He let that thought sink in. "They have a genetic system of delay and procrastination that takes the Nobel Prize for blind bureaucracy. I wouldn't even be prepared to put good money on you *starting* in September!" The Professor's level of silence reached a crescendo.

"Colonel, if this was a war and I was a General who ordered you to carry out this mission, there'd be no room for idle speculation, you'd just go do it." All of a sudden the mantle of committed academic dropped away and there was no mistaking the unvarnished authority. Max had known one or two senior officers in whom he'd recognised that same faculty for the instantaneous gear shift in personality. But in their cases it had seemed a natural transmogrification. This was... eerie. He recovered his mental composure.

"With all due respect, Professor, it isn't, you aren't and I won't." As the words tumbled out he knew he had to correct the impression that he was making. "What I'm trying to say is that with the best will in the world, I can't hold out a snowball's chance in hell of getting this done for you and that, for what it's worth, is the God's honest truth." With the same startling speed, Sukhum's manner reverted to the quietly serious courtesy of his other *persona.* He even managed a gentle smile as he put his hand on Max's forearm.

"Colonel...it's my turn to apologise." The smile broadened. "It was a silly analogy and you were quite right to resent it. Come." He turned and led the way out onto the balcony, inviting Max to sit opposite him. "You see, I have become so deeply committed to this project that I think I may have lost all objectivity."

"I'm sorry too, Professor..." His attempt to meet the Thai halfway was cut short.

"No. The fault is mine. I..." He gave a little hand gesture of self-criticism as he cast around for the words. "...bought the dog but decided to do the barking myself."

Max gave a shrug of his shoulders. In truth he wasn't sure how to manage this situation any more. He judged it prudent to let the man put the train back on the rails in his own way.

"Colonel Devlin, in my work, research is about 85% of the job. I took the liberty of researching you before setting up this meeting. Quite apart from your remarkable professional knowledge and expertise in this part of the world, I felt that you have qualities which could prove invaluable to our project. Chief amongst these qualities is your reputation for refusing to give in to adversity."

"Alternatively it might be classified as the innate stubbornness of the Irish."

"It's the *yin* and *yang* or different aspects of the same coin."

"Yes, well, given time, sir, given time." Quite out of the blue, a line from a poem by A.E. Houseman lodged in his mind,

They carry back bright to the coiner the mintage of man.

With an imperceptible chill, the next lines came to him clearly:

The lads who will die in their glory and never be old.

There was little profit in having his ego massaged, much though the months of failure longed for a little verbal therapy. He would be 38 this July and it struck him that his glory days were now behind him. Cranking himself up for a fresh start began to feel more demanding. He took temporary refuge in a little professional flim flam.

"I could take your money and bolster you up with cautious optimism. I could promise to do my utmost, which I'd do in any event, and I'd probably deliver on most of the preparatory aspects of the job. But when I failed, and note I say '*when*' not '*if*', I'd be beyond reproach and the richer for it to boot. You, on the other hand, would be poorer in pocket and given the extent of your commitment, a sadder but none the wiser man."

"Unless I researched the wrong man, you wouldn't short change me." He leaned forward and Max could almost detect the effort of will to curb a growing impatience. It was in the tautness of his body position.

"Nor am I so naïve as to think that it will be easy." He pointed his finger at Max. "But that's one good reason why I want you. *I* intend that *we* shall make this work." He saw Max about to interject and his hand shifted from pointing to signalling him that he had not yet finished.

"Wait on Colonel, wait on." He leaned back and took a deep breath before inclining forward again. His voice, if anything, grew softer but increased in intensity. "I had to fight like hell to get these funds allocated. I staked my reputation and promised to have the pilot survey's model catalogue ready by the end of the year. Our sponsors made it a condition of releasing the balance of the funds that I keep to this schedule." He pronounced it '*skedule*'. "If we fail, the whole goddamn project fails and my chances of getting it reactivated will be zilch. I can't allow that to happen." The words had been spoken slowly and eked out with weighted deliberation. The effect was like creating a cold spot in the early morning sunshine that bathed the balcony.

"D'you see?" Less a question, more a punctuation, Max found himself nodding gently. One part of his brain said the man was a religious fanatic but another part was engaging neurons of enthusiasm which Max thought had atrophied with disuse.

"I hear what you say about it being too late and all..." Suddenly his face creased in a conspiratorial smile. "I guess almost every aspect is an unknown quantity but..." He leaned forward and tapped his finger on Max's knee as he ticked off his points. "...for the time being we have a substantial budget...we have my unshakeable conviction and right now, that includes my faith in you." The smile remained fixed, willing Max to agree. With the same abruptness that he had felt the atmosphere chill moments earlier, now he sensed the heat. But there was an added dimension, as if he was a silent spectator of an event in which he was participating but over which he had no control. Whatever it was that touched him, a part of the old imaginative spark reignited. In the face of the old plangent cynicism that had doggedly clung to his steps there had remained a perversely residual hope of salvaging what amounted to a lifetime investment in Nepal. It was not, he knew, the balance sheets or the physical assets of the commercial enterprise, underlying it all was a commitment to a people both in time, spirit and space. When he spoke, he couldn't be sure which Devlin it was, the old, a new or some leprachaun invested stranger. He heard the words but wondered who the mad bugger was who uttered them.

"If I agree to take this on, it will be on those terms, what I mean is to succeed no matter the price in terms of money and human effort." Not *would,* he heard his voice, but *will.* He acknowledged to himself that he had already committed. Why indulge in further deception… who was he fooling, certainly not himself? Forget the motives, in any event did they matter in the overall scheme of things? Judgment, wisdom, caution…all had been thrown out of the window of his mind. It was the *banshee* that now dictated to him. He heard his father's words, 'What Irishman can resist a folly?' Folly indeed, but who was to say that it wouldn't work, apart that is from his professional judgment but that stern taskmaster had been unceremoniously defenestrated.

Sukhum's face bore a curious combination of gravity lightened by something in his eyes that Max couldn't quite define, more than mere hope but less than triumph, or was he fooling himself when deep down a still small voice whispered that he had been outmanoeuvred? Was this what was meant by Oriental inscrutability?

"There's no question that we'll succeed." There it was again, that certainty in the face of the odds, strangely unacademic, more spiritual. "It has to." Sukhum stood up and extended his hand. Now there was unmistakeable animation in his expression. "I am in your capable hands, entirely." As he returned the firm handshake, all Max could think was 'Shit, and I'm in the hands of a fruitcake.' But if this was so it was a case of folie a deux with himself as the deuxieme.

Gartok – Western Tibet

2350 hrs 1st March

The interior of the detection unit trailer was cold, despite the banks of computers and signalling equipment that whirred softly. Apart from the emergency lighting set in the roof, the illumination came from console screens and the back-lit displays of frequency ranges. Comrade captain Wang Changsheng needed a cigarette to ease the tension in his body but smoking was prohibited inside the unit. He checked the digital wall clock for the 10th time. If the clandestine signal maintained its usual schedule it should go out about now. Dangerously close to being on time but always subject to the habitual Tibetan lack of punctuality. How he hated being stuck in the middle of nowhere, in this nothing region full of stinking stupid lice-ridden clods, always mumbling their incomprehensible prayers preaching love and understanding but reserving an unfathomable hatred towards their ethnically superior Han administrators. It would take another hundred or more years to so intermingle the races as to breed out their distinctly primitive racial characteristics. Pity the poor immigrants from Fuzhou and Guangzhou who had 'volunteered' to be the pioneers of ethnic, cultural and political change in this savage land. All they would get for their troubles would be hybrid progeny whose pure Han genes had been corrupted by this strain of prehistoric aboriginals. The transmigratory programme begun under the late great Deng Xiaoping and now being accelerated by the collective leadership in Beijing as a means of heading off unrest as unemployment bit deeper into the motherland was headed nowhere. Was he too, headed into a professional *cul de sac?* No, he comforted himself, his technical skill was respected by his military superiors as was his political commitment by the party cadres. His current team, put together over the last five years, he knew to be acknowledged as the best anti clandestine counter revolutionary detection unit in the PLA. They had enjoyed phenomenal success locating 73 secret radio transmitters operating along the border in Xinjiang and nearly a dozen along a two hundred mile corridor opposite the Taiwan straits. He had been selected to watch the traitors having their brains blown out immediately following brief trials conducted by military tribunals. He just could not understand why they bothered with the ritual formalities of a quasi-judicial process.

A tiny corner of his mind nagged him. All the high tech IT equipment he had under his command also enabled him to hack into transmissions from Taipei and the US Pacific Fleet's telecommunications network. He pictured them working in their smart air conditioned units, exchanging the latest technical developments and scanning the internet both professionally and for leisure. There were times when he felt frustrated by the budgetary constraints that forced him to use outdated equipment when the enemy had access to the latest and the best. The thought process brought him back to the job in hand. There had been a great furore over the escape of the Karmapa Lama and he guessed that Beijing had been embarrassed that it had been achieved so easily. Now they wanted blanket communications coverage of Tibet and that had led to the identification of what he was quite sure were clandestine signals operators who were somewhere in a vast area of largely deserted terrain in the broad triangle between India, Nepal/Bhutan and Amdo province. His unit had been working at it for nearly two weeks now but all they had established was this unidentified electrical 'signature' which appeared every alternate night at about this time. His immediate superiors at divisional HQ in Urumchi doubted whether it was anything other than an electrical glitch, Colonel Xiao Xiean had suggested it was a wild card being thrown off an American surveillance satellite but the man belonged to the Tang dynasty in terms of communications knowledge. Wang knew he would be proved accurate. More than anything else, it was the fact that the clandestine signaller was using a frequency hopper which made it almost impossible to identify in the first place and had proved beyond the technical expertise of the PLA to break. He had been lucky to pick it up at all and now he wanted as many contacts as possible to establish some sort of data base to send to the mainframe in the Shanghai Communications Centre. The one break had come as a result of an intuitive guess that he had made after Colonel Xiao's stupid contribution. There was just a possibility that the communication system was somehow linked to the surveillance satellite system. Division had given him the schedules for the American tracking satellites and there seemed to be a correlation there. At least it had narrowed down the focus of their search to a time band. He swung his swivel chair round to face his 2i/c Lt. Su Zhou.

"Give me the visual on the international frequencies." The monitor screen showed that all the propaganda frequencies had been jammed. Silencing the BBC and VoA was a party requirement. Wang wanted them left undisturbed in case the clandestine operators were 'riding' on their frequencies; sometimes the party hacks lost sight of their priorities. With the remaining frequencies divided up between his separate sub-units and all the best operators hunched, tense over their monitors, he was as poised as he was ever going to be to lock on. The software for the computers that they were using had been 'hacked' off a US aircraft carrier that had paid a courtesy visit to Hong Kong after the bombing of the Chinese Embassy in Yugoslavia. A PLA communications wizard had penetrated the carrier's firewall and lifted the entire programme out of their system. The Americans must have been incandescent with rage but having just restored Sino-American relations on a layer of thin ice, they were not about to jeopardise it all again over their own incompetence. Wang settled comfortably in front of the bank of monitors that now used the liberated software to give him a visual read-out. He adjusted the earphones to shut out any ambient noise.

"Yes!" The triumph in the exclamation came simultaneously with the movement of Mingming's arm as she manipulated the joy-stick on her console. He caught it in his outer left field of vision.

"B Two." He commanded into the mouthpiece mounted on his earphones. Immediately, two more monitors picked up Mingming's. This was the critical stage, would they track the signal as it 'hopped' frequency? He could hear the curious pitch of the signal and then it was gone. His eyes roamed the monitor bank for a lock as the search engines roamed the frequencies looking for the distinctive profile. On the periphery of his vision the digital clock tripped one second…two seconds…

"Ah!" A grunt from the operator beside him coincided with his ears picking up the signal only to lose it within the time that it had taken to register it.

"Open." The command was superfluous, all the operators were back scouring the frequencies. The atmosphere in the trailer was so tense you could have bounced on it.

Gone.

He knew it but refused to acknowledge the fact. The fuck-your mother signal had gone again. He tore off his headset, his lips were compressed so thinly his mouth barely moved as he spoke to the co-ordination operator.

"Run it back and project it onto the co-ordinates map." The man's unusually long fingers caressed his keyboard and the visual image was superimposed over the map of the region. "Give me a zoom from our position." The fingers played their tackety tune again and the screen sprung out towards them. No sooner had the picture stilled than Wang could tell that they had not had sufficient imprint to allow the frequency search tool to reach out far enough. The faint rings blinked emptily back at him, they had caught nothing. The co-ordinator said nothing. He knew what his commander was thinking and judged it prudent to maintain radio silence.

"Commander?" Su Zhou had a diskette in his hand. "I've downloaded all the material. Shall I send it to Urumchi?"

Wang thought for a moment. He didn't want to advertise failure to the idiot Colonel Xiao. This was sensitive stuff. If he bypassed his immediate superior he could be disciplined. On the other hand, if he sent it back to Shanghai to his mentor cadre, his political loyalty would be beyond question and it would be processed on the mainframe that much faster. The pragmatic answer proffered itself without a further thought.

"Yes…and give me a further copy." That one would go back to the mainframe by his own means of communication. His instincts told him that this whole operation was a can of political worms and he had no intention of becoming a sacrificial scapegoat. Just because they had despatched him to this, the remotest posting from the centres of power and influence in Beijing and Shanghai, he would not be deflected from his ambition which was...well what was it? He looked around at the anxious faces of his subordinates; amongst all these very capable people only he knew where he was going. Limitless, that was his ambition. Whatever the significance of this particular operation, nothing would be allowed to hinder the inexorable rise of the star of Wang Changsheng and it would certainly not be these Tibetan bumpkins with their antiquated smoke and bells, blowing long horse farts on their absurd horns.

Raxaul – On the Indo-Nepal Border

"Jesus wept!" He said it to himself, softly, like a bad ventriloquist practising whilst trying to maintain the semblance of a friendly smile on the rest of his face. Self-control, that was all that he required he reminded himself forcibly. Reaching forward slowly so as not to startle the man, he picked up his passport and turned it right way up in front of the sub-inspector of border police.

"I think you'll find it easier to read this way." He smiled at the same time wondering whether even this might have been a phrase too far. The official nodded sagely, his eyes drifting up to meet Max's before returning his attention to the passport. Holding the document in both hands, he turned the pages slowly, drinking in the whole page advertisements that passed for visas for India and the inconsiderate centering of the much smaller Nepalese visas which occupied a whole page with a quarter page's data. He placed it face down on the desk causing Max's hopes to flicker upwards, then with studied application he scratched his crotch with one hand whilst excavating some troublesome materiel from his nostrils with the fingers of the other. Max's eyes roamed the careworn, utilitarian office furnishings of the gloomy room. He offered one or two helpful suggestions.

"Pen?" He unclipped the Cross ballpoint from his shirt pocket at the same time that the thought crossed his mind that this may not have been a sensible gesture. Officials like this one would have been well aware of the value of such a writing instrument. Happily, this was refused with a vague wave of the hand that had relieved his crotch whilst the other began an unchoreographed search through the dust laden ledgers on top of the desk.

"You have car?" The question was posed without so much as a glance to interrupt the nameless quest.

"No. I have a *dandy* waiting outside." This produced another silent nod. Max decided to try a little empathy. "*Inspector Sahib, Ap kya chayeh?*" The enquiry provoked no response at all but Max sensed an almost imperceptible rise in the temperature of activity. Now, each of the registers was picked up and relocated to a fresh site on the desk top. The capacity of these remotely posted officials in India to perform every movement as though under water was a constant source of wonder to Max. True, this was Bihar, a state noted for the insensate cruelty of its police officers rather than a recruiting ground for rocket scientists.

Max twisted in his chair to look through the open doorway and check on the pony-drawn *dandy* and its driver. It was difficult to tell which of the two looked the most forlorn: the poor bloody pony, tossing its head negligently towards the insects that burrowed into the threadbare hair stretched tightly across its ribs or the distressed pile of collapsed humanity whose form was only distinguishable by reference to the *dhoti* clinging to his skeletal loins and the voluminous *pugaree* wrapped around his head like soiled bandaging. Max's eyes took in the sandy coating of thick dust that made the sickly palm trees look like props in a third rate production of Desert Song and then marched ineluctably across the surface of what passed for furnishings in this room. He looked up and watched the ugly dark brown ceiling fan contributing its mite to the mood of utter futility by turning at a rate slow enough to allow the flies to hitch a lift on its dirty blades. Shrugging off the suffocating slough of futility, he turned his attention back to the policeman, chancing his all on the improbable prospect that his labours would, at the least, have begun. Two flies were executing lazy zimmelman turns between a variety of landings on the heavily oiled hair and a khaki uniform that had repelled the attentions of a hot iron.

"Ah!" In the near silence of the darkened room, it came out as a *sotto voce* grunt of almost rude effrontery. Wrestling to remove his hand from his trouser pocket, the official extracted a pair of wire framed spectacles that would have met the Gandhi seal of approval, unfolded them carefully and wound them over his ears with the gravity and deliberation of an elder statesman about to deliver a momentous pronouncement. Thus sighted, he recommenced his perusal of the pages.

Max knew that if he was to cross the border into Birgunj on the Nepalese side in time to catch the late afternoon flight from Simra to Kathmandu, he would have to jolly this joker along somehow without upsetting him.

"*Inspector Sahib...?* He smiled at this man whom, he was convinced, was indestructibly bent on thwarting his plans, then firmly but gently he removed the passport from the long brown fingers and flicked quickly through the pages until it reached the stamp of his last entry into India. Pinching the intervening pages between finger and thumb he turned his wrist over to show the front of the passport which showed his full name. This sleight of hand yielded a soft gleam of recognition in the man's eyes. Max offered up a silent 'thank you, God' that he still had the elaborate old style Eire passport, the dumbed down claret coloured Euro job would never have the same effect. Gratification continued apace as he watched the slender brown fingers extract an ancient fountain pen from under the flap of a breast pocket in the uniform shirt.

"May I?" He asked as he picked up the completed embarkation card from the desk top and held it at a convenient angle in his free hand. With painstaking deliberation, the data in the documents was transcribed into the register. Watching a process that could have changed little in its essential character over the last 150 years, Max wondered whether he had, perhaps, tempted fate by taking the overland route? He acknowledged that circumstances had more or less dictated this course. He certainly could not have waited for a seat on the hopelessly overbooked *Rastriya Nepal Airlines Corporation,* RNAC for short, an acronym better known to its unfortunate customers as 'Rastriya Nepal Always Cancels'. He cast a surreptitious look at his watch, so as not to draw attention to it. Watches were prime material for sharpening the interest of the less than zealous Indian official. Just after one o'clock and he still had the reverse side of the ceremony to observe on the other side of the border, then on into Birgunj and the

RNAC office, provided there was a seat available...provided there was a flight. He had a visa, courtesy of an old friend who was currently first secretary at the Nepalese Embassy in Delhi, despite which he was apprehensive about his likely 'official' reception once back in the land he once thought of as home. Still, he'd hedged his bets as best he could and the land route was by far the lowest profile he could adopt.

He watched the long dark fingers write and having writ, run out of ink. Precious minutes ticked away as the pantomime of filling the pen and the search for something to remove the inevitable excess that had spilled over onto those same primordial digits was played out. The backyard of his mind was busy recalling something Rudyard Kipling had written. Now, there was a man who had real insight into the essence of the subcontinent. It came back with haunting accuracy:

Now it is not good for the Christian's health
To hustle the Aryan brown,
For the Christian riles and the Aryan smiles
And he wears the Christian down.

The rest of it eluded him save for the last line about 'the end of the fight is a tombstone white'. Such perspicacity at moments like these served only to reinforce the sense of folly that anyone in his right mind would embark on such a venture. As he watched the pen leaving enuretic puddles of ink across the page of the register, only to be spread thinly by blotting paper that looked like leftovers from Curzon's viceroyalty, it occurred to him that even Kipling may not have been moved to his customary pithy wit in such a situation.

"Acha. OK." These gloriously mis-matched words were accompanied by that waggle of the head that was the ubiquitous Indian expression to signal that all's well and one may proceed, albeit it was something of a favour.

"Thank you, *Inspector Sahib.*" He shook the man's hand. There would always be another time and Max was a firm believer in long term credit. It felt good just to leave the gloom of the immigration office and step directly into the sun. The *dandywallah* unfurled himself so that both *dhoti* and *pugaree* assumed their rightful positions on his frame, then sleepwalked to his perch on the front of the cart.

"*Jaldi!*" Max urged him on briskly "*Jaldi eh!*" The pony stumbled into a trot that carried them across the railway lines and over the border into Nepal. The weather was hot and beginning to turn a little humid. The tops of the mountains, some 25 miles to the north, were obscured by white clouds that lay like a duvet over the peaks. The majesty of those hills, only 8,000 feet high but rising precipitately off the plain was uplifting. If one kept one's eyes on the mountains, the shenanigans of the infinitesimally tiny people lost their impact, reduced to molecules of no significance in such a context. Still, he hoped that the cloud base would not descend any lower and prevent the flight from taking off.

By the time that he arrived at the airfield he was nursing a painful headache. With only minutes to spare, the mounting tension had resulted in a severe right sided muscle spasm in his neck. There was virtually no wind but the cloud base was definitely lower. Would the flight come or cancel? He approached an RNAC official holding a business-like clipboard.

"*Aunchha ki aundaina?*"

"*Kooni?*"

Well, there you go. Ask a silly question get an even sillier answer. An untidy knot of passengers stood looking towards the north. The usual mix of travellers, all the women in the traditional *gunnia-choli,* the colourful print of the ankle-length wrap-around skirt and high neck tie-across blouse joined by a cummerbund wound around their waists and into which they stuffed their little money bags. It seemed to him that fewer men were wearing *daura surwal*, though most wore the little flower pot shaped cap as a last gesture to a dying tradition. Sensing rather than seeing the mood of general poverty, he did not relish the prospect of having to spend the night in Birgunj, a town whose hospitality extended to unhygienic doss houses. He was about to renew his endeavours with the RNAC official who had offered him neither information nor courtesy when the siren suddenly started up. Its wail, such an anomaly in this pastoral setting, galvanised a couple of cowherds into spastic action as they chased cows off the landing strip. With barely a low buzz of warning, there it suddenly was, appearing as if out of nowhere and descending rapidly as the waiting passengers clapped in relief.

Max had mixed feelings about it. For a 15-minute flight, it was, nevertheless, possibly one of the world's most hair-raising when the clouds lay as low as they now did. From time to time the impenetrable curtain of cloud that lay across the portholes would part, momentarily, revealing the peaks of the mountains, stark in black and green and threatening as they drew the flimsy bug of an aircraft down into their magnetic field. Max could feel the malevolence as they reached up, trying to dash the pitifully thin-skinned craft against their unyielding surfaces or pitch it down the crude pock-marked scarring of landslides. The relief as the cloud slipped itself around them, the peaks drawing back like the fingers of some occult power, was only replaced by barely controlled rising panic as they flew blind. His hands gripped the fragile arms of the seat as he hoped to God that the RNAC pilots had lost nothing of their skill, that they'd judged the heights correctly and that the instruments were working. For someone who had once owned an airline, even a one-aeroplane airline, he was the paradox, the man who would never conquer his ungovernable fear of flying.

"*Ayo!*" A Nepalese across the aisle from Max leant in front of a small boy and pointed out of the porthole. The cloud had cleared and as the aircraft banked he caught site of the Kathmandu Valley. He turned to look out of his own side as the last wisps of dirty white slipped past and the aircraft levelled out and suddenly, there it was. Everyone who came to Kathmandu eulogised their first aerial impressions. Dictionaries had been combed for fresh superlatives. Max just drank it in, renewing an old familiar acquaintance which combined the strange mixture of spiritual and aesthetic. He had long ago given up on looking for words to encompass the indefinable. Each time was as the first time.

The sun shone, illuminating the late maize which contrasted with the greens and the red-brown soils through which the dun-coloured roads ran like a simple neurological system. As the aircraft descended, the haphazard clusters of terracotta brick and tile houses collected at the nerve-ends. The mystery of the haff-like construction of the valley floor struck him yet again, like miniature canyons carved out and left high and dry after the rivers had dried up. Perhaps, he mused, there was a geophysical truth in the legend of how the Buddhist giant Manjusri cleaved the surrounding mountains with his sword and drained the lake that had filled the valley thereby fulfilling the prophecy of Siki Buddha that it would be 'a delightful abode for those who dwell in it and a sweet place for pilgrims'.

He watched as the plateau on which the Israeli construction company had ironed out the old Gauchar Airport to create the Tribhuvan International Airport, rose up to meet them. With the gentlest of bumps the Nepalese pilot set them down and Max's heart beat began to respond to the normal tug of its governors.

The drive from the airport to the Subarna Hotel afforded him an opportunity to savour the mood of the place. Once it had only been a question of driving around whimsical cows and the occasional water buffalo, now every motorcyclist was an incipient Mad Max, bus drivers drove their ill-assorted and battered tin coffins with a manic disregard for anything else on the dusty roads. *Plus ça change*, he thought. He wound down the window and let in the inimitable smells. The once extraordinarily clear air, now seriously polluted, streaked from time to time by the smell of a charcoal fire burning, sweet shops wafted out the aroma of the sticky-sweet curd confections cooking in oil. As they passed the junction to Baudhanath his sense of smell sought out the old rancid butter on copper and brass that he associated with the Tibetans but his nostrils filled with the sharp sweet stench of freshly sawn *sal* and *seesaw* in a furniture maker's yard. He associated it with the thick sweetness of cannabis rising from the clay bowls of the artisans' pipes. He drifted off into a reverie of recollections. The cacophony of motor horns and the puttering of hundreds of motorbikes with which the valley's drivers punctuated their progress broke into his thoughts as they navigated their way past the gates to what had been the Royal Palace at Narayanhity. The tall gate piers still bore the work of some mad confectioner who had drizzled concrete icing over their peaks and Nepal Army sentries still stood on guard.

"Who lives in the Narayanhity Palace now?"

"The Rajmentri." The taxi driver had shown little interest in his passenger for which Max had been thankful. His monosyllabic responses had been enough. Pretending ignorance, Max spoke in English.

"Rajmentri?"

"Our president." It was said in a non-committal tone which gave no clue as to the man's political allegiance. "Madan Bom Malla." He added as if an afterthought. So, Max thought, the new regime had elevated the old Nepal Congress Party warhorse to provide the 'Front' element in the Maoist-Leninist Front Government.

The taxi swung drunkenly across the pot-holed road and into the herring-bone patterned brick driveway of the Subarna Hotel, its classic façade a portico of columns supporting a classic Ionic pediment all of which concealed a labyrinth of corridors giving onto spacious, if somewhat utilitarian rooms. It's as genuinely Doric as Bombay duck, he thought, but it's still my idea of Nepal.

The Newari girl at reception was pretty, pert and rather beautifully proportioned. He spoke to her in Nepali and her smile widened. Max took an instant fancy to her. Apparently Subarna himself was not in but had left a message to say that he would return tomorrow and to make himself at home. Checking in, there was a slight feeling of letdown that he could not share the pleasure of his return with an old friend. This feeling was reinforced when the receptionist apologetically drew his attention to a notice that directed all foreign nationals to observe the curfew from 9 pm to 6 am.

"I'm very sorry but what to do, I even hear that they have shot some foreigners caught out during the curfew." She added. Max noted that despite her apparent disapproval, she obviously regarded it as fairly normal. He noticed a little wooden signboard with a slip in card announcing that the duty receptionist was Ambika Shrestha.

"What time do you go off duty Ambika?" The smile she gave him managed to convey both 'I'm not that kind of girl' and 'I'm happy you asked'.

"10 o'clock."

"So, do you have a special pass that let you travel in the curfew?"

"No. I have quarters in the hotel compound." She laughed lightly. "Subarna Shrestha is my uncle."

"Ah." Seducing his host's niece might not be such a brilliant idea. Still, she was still smiling and he couldn't think of a warmer welcome. But not tonight. It was already quite late and he decided on a simple curry from the hotel kitchen and an early night.

Whatever else had changed, the Subarna's cullinary standards had been maintained at their legendary lows. Even in death and a warm marinade of spices, the elderly chicken leg put up a spirited resistance to both fork and knife. Fortifying himself with three double measures of Kukuri rum, Max retired to a celibate bed and passed the night in troubled dreams.

Max's taxi turned off the metalled road and onto the broken brick driveway. Though the driver nursed it gently along the narrow approach, the mica-laden dust still rose up in puffs beneath the wheels. The first flush of pride as he saw the signboard for the Trans-Himalayan Adventures Corporation (Pvt) Limited gave way to anger and bitterness. He was not a vengeful man by nature but by God they really had tried his patience. Even in the few short months that he had been away the place had been infected with that peculiar indifference that Nepalese government officials reserved for everything they touched. It was the reverse of a Midas touch in which everything turned to dross. The flower beds that used to welcome visitors like a proud housewife's colourful new apron now wore neglect like an old tart, succumbing to the raddling of time. Every window ledge and flat surface wore a thick coat of dust and despair.

He paid off the driver and stepped out into the early morning sun. Skirting the empty offices, no one would have been there at this hour of the morning anyway, he headed for the living accommodation. He rapped against the wooden cross member of the fly screen, causing dust to spring off the wire mesh.

"*Ko chha?*" A woman's voice preceded a handsome girl with the strong features and friendly eyes of a *Sherpini.*

"Is Jamsung Saheb in?"

"He's gone out." She shook her head.

"D'you know where?"

"*Huzoor,* what is your name?" She cocked her head slightly to one side, it was a friendly enquiry.

"I'm Devlin."

"Ameee…!" She clapped her hands across her mouth, her cheeks shining like a pair of tail lights. "Huzoor is my husband's Saheb." Then quickly she added, "Ong Chu." Max's heart lightened at the mention of his old Sherpa *Sardar*'s name. Sliding back the bolt, she opened the fly screen and beamed a welcome. "Come in, please." Turning her head she called to an unseen maid. "Maia!" Max smiled to himself, some things never changed. Almost every female servant in the Kathmandu Valley was named Maia. As she gave instructions for tea, a small bundle of shaggy off-white hair ran into the corridor and began to bark excitedly before springing up and hurling itself at Max.

"Hello Tigger. How's my little bugger then?" Max held the Lhasa Apso whilst it licked his face frantically. Leaving the dog behind had been another wrench but he knew that the heat and humidity of Calcutta would not have suited it. He followed Ong Chu's wife down the corridor. "Please don't trouble. I take it your husband's out as well?"

"He's with Jamsung Saheb, they're both at the *Chyeea Dhokan*. She led him out onto a balcony where everything was regimentally neat and clean. Old habits died hard and Ong Chu's living quarters stood out in marked contrast to the office accommodation.

"Where is it, this *Chyeea Dhokan*?" By way of reply she grinned from ear to ear as she giggled.

"They call it 'Max's Place'." She obviously saw the joke and could hardly contain herself as she gave him directions. "It belongs to Jamsung Saheb and my husband runs it for him." She put one finger to her lips and lowered her voice conspiratorially. "But don't tell the chairman, Saheb." She nodded towards the offices. "There's no business and so he tells us that there's no money for wages. But he still expects them to work. What to do?" She completed the circumstantial equation neatly.

Now that he knew that both men were not only still around but together and nearby, Max could hardly contain his impatience to see them. He downed the cup of tea as quickly as courtesy would permit, then thanked her.

"We'll meet again soon." She called out the traditional farewell as he climbed back into the car and headed back onto the main road. So, Ong Chu had taken a new young wife. Well, we all need the warmth of human consolation he observed to himself before abruptly shutting off that line of thought.

'Max's Place' turned out to be an imaginatively designed and decorated bistro-style restaurant, hardly the smoke-blackened indigenous tea shop that he had been expecting on the strength of Ong Chu's wife's description. He pushed open the half-glazed door and paused to take in the simple but effective décor. The theme of black and white was cleverly relieved by a series of recesses in the walls in which Buddhist and Tantric sculptures were softly lit. The one dispensation to colour was a life-size holograph of the Dalai Lama mounted on the rear wall, but what a dispensation, Max thought with a smile. The overall effect was calm and inviting.

"How do you like your place?" The powerfully built figure with classic Tibetan features, high cheekbones, long triangular face and wide, smiling mouth, strode towards him. "When did you come, Man?"

"Jamsung." Max swung his arm up to meet the high-five greeting. The Tibetan's Americanisms had been adopted following a six-month training course he'd attended to qualify as a river guide in Colorado.

"I think you've done me proud, my friend." Max's arm swept around, taking in the restaurant. "But a trifle politically dangerous wasn't it, naming it after a foreigner?"

"Who gives a damn?" There was an intensity in the booming response despite the smile on his lips. Jamsung lowered his voice. "And anyway, it *is* your place." He seized Max's hand and gripped it in a firm handshake seeing the puzzle in the Irishman's eyes. "Jamsung and I 'liberated' some of the more expensive aircraft spare parts and sold them back to RNAC. Since we could only get paid in rupees, we decided to invest the proceeds in something which you could enjoy when you returned. So," he opened his arms in a wide embrace. "It's all yours."

Max was at a loss for words. He was saved from having to work out an appropriate response by the entrance of Ong Chu. The compactly built Sherpa, hair cut *en brosse* and immaculately turned out in white shirt and black trousers hurried forward.

"Max Saheb!" The welcoming grin split his face from ear to ear. Max stood his ground, aware of the man's propensity for overenthusiastic greetings but a yard away from him, Ong Chu came to a sudden halt and snapped to parade ground attention. Despite the closeness of his relationship to Max, the Sherpa had never abandoned the deeply ingrained habits of military discipline within which he had soldiered, chiefly as signals sergeant in Max's battalion. With an equally sudden transition, he relaxed and they seized each other's hands in a double grip. For this brief moment in time, Max was back in the milieu he loved best with men in whom he trusted as completely as they did in him.

Jamsung indicated a table. "Coffee?" He gave the order and then turned back to Max, a look of concern on his face. "You don't need to be told how good it is to see you back again but..." He hesitated a moment. "I think you should know that there's no real prospect of any compensation. This..." He took in their surrounds with a short gesture of his arm. "...is all that there is to show for all your years' of work in Nepal." His voice conveyed not only sorrow and despair but it was informed with a sense of apology as if in some way he was responsible. Max reached forward and put his hand on his friend's shoulder.

"Let's not dwell on it. We've all lost out. I think I knew in my heart of hearts that there'd be nothing to salvage." He leaned forward drawing the other two into a confidentiality, their heads slightly inclined towards him. "No, I've come to organise an expedition."

"But Saheb..." Ong Chu began, only to be interrupted by Jamsung.

"Max, unless it's the Shanghai Ladies' Climbing Club, forget it." He shook his head dismissively.

"Not quite." Max outlined the project to them. Though he spoke in the measured tones he fell into whenever giving a briefing, he found himself waxing enthusiastic. "Why not?" He reminded himself, they would be paid well and who knew, despite the government's previous attitude, a successful expedition involving a friendly, no, for friendly read 'fraternal' he corrected himself, Asian near-neighbour might re-open doors? He found himself buoyed up by the simple ingenuity of his immediate plan.

"If we channel the whole operation through Trans-Himalayan, the government benefits financially. Surely that's going to tempt them into giving approval?"

Jamsung's facial expression didn't reflect a shared enthusiasm.

"The managing director of Trans-Himalayan is Harihar Bhandari. You remember him, he was director general of the National Trading Company?" Max nodded thoughtfully. "Wasn't he pathologically hostile to foreigners being involved in anything in Nepal?"

"That's the one." Jamsung shook his head slowly. "He'll never co-operate."

"Well, he's a fine bloody choice for an organisation whose principal business is dealing with foreigners!" Max felt the old anger surging back. "I'm sorry, I know it's not your fault...but it's typical Kathmandu *snafu*."

"Max, I'm with you all the way, you know that. If you can get the trekking permits, you could bypass Harihar and do the rest from your own resources." Ong Chu nodded his emphatic agreement.

"OK." Now he could disclose his trump card. "We can rely on a powerful diplomatic request from the Thai government. We'll finesse Harihar with the foreign secretary, that should keep the little bastard in his place." He smiled in anticipation of putting the man down. It turned out to be a dramatically shortlived triumph.

"The foreign secretary is out of the country for 10 days." Jamsung said it in tones that carried the weight of his own regret, a regret Max interpreted as tinged with a feeling that whatever Max set his hand to with the current political regime was condemned never to find its feet.

"Shit!" The disgust in the constantly bad hands he kept being dealt kept his temper on the shortest fuse. "The delay...we can't afford it." As he spoke the words, he heard himself advising others about the systemic procrastination that was as much a part of Nepal as the timeless Himalaya. As if to rub a little salt into the wound, Jamsung gently upbraided him.

"Max...Max...this is Nepal. Remember?"

"I know, you're right." Max exhaled resignedly. Jamsung leant forward a little to emphasise the earnest of his concern.

"It was always bad, but now..." He broke off, his hands opening a little as if to contain the small coffin of despair. "The country is still bitterly divided. The government has little control in the eastern hills where the *Kiranti* alliance is defiantly strong. The Army's loyalties are split so that they have to rely on the paratroops, the armed police and the armed students' organisations." He paused for a moment, then added: "I hate to have to tell you, but Harihar is the president of the ASO's."

"We christened them the arseholes organ, just for you Saheb." Ong Chu chipped in with a grin.

"Arseholes or not, they do most of the MLF's dirty work, and I mean *dirty.*" Jamsung's forehead creased with concern. "You remember that series of attacks on foreigners in Kathmandu that started a couple of years ago?" Max nodded silently.

"Well, everybody put them down to a vicious streak in the Manangis who had a reputation for that sort of thing but it turned out they were the ASO's 'wet work' operatives." As if he had suddenly become aware of the icy water he was pouring on Max's plans, Jamsung equally suddenly made a constructive enquiry.

"What's your timescale?"

Max couldn't be sure whether the enquiry was to assess the enormity of his folly or a genuine attempt to measure its practicability. When he spoke, his voice had lost its enthusiasm.

"We have to get a small party up into either the Bhota Khosi, Doodh Kosi or Arun valleys and give them a good clear two to three weeks before the monsoon breaks." With a short gesture of impatience he added. "Just to make it easier for us, we won't be told which valley until later."

"Crazy!" Jamsung said flatly and slapped the top of the table with his palm. Coffee spilled into the saucers. "Sorry." He grinned at them, robbing the moment of the anger they all felt building up.

"The Sherpas can be organised now and stood by. All the old team will jump at the opportunity to work with you again Saheb." Ong Chu contributed. "But we'll need a STOL aircraft and we might have difficulty getting the CAA to authorise our flight plan. Any other aircraft wouldn't be a difficulty, with no tourists worth talking about there are lots of them lying idle. But a STOL poses problems. It has military connotations." Max had guessed correctly that men and basic equipment would not be the problem but the Short Take-Off and Landing aircraft was essential to enable them to access anywhere without difficulty. Once he had that up his sleeve, if necessary he could set up three separate teams and despatch them to the alternative destinations ready to move out as soon as the expedition members arrived. No, it was the government and its directly-controlled agencies that posed the real threat. The Civil Aviation Authority had been relatively effective in the past but in the current climate, everyone would be looking over their shoulders, afraid to do anything that might expose them to instant dismissal by an administration fed on suspicion and guided by irrational whimsy. Perhaps the key would be found in a non-governmental organisation?

"What about the Israelis...and the Japanese?" He added as an afterthought. "How'd they get into their expedition areas?"

"The Israelis walked in." Jamsung provided the instant answers. "What would you expect from them, they never take the easy way if there's a difficult alternative. The Japs brought their own, a Mitsubishi version of the Twin Otter, very nice piece of kit." He paused for effect before adding. "Naturally, they made a present of it to the 'friendly people of Nepal'." He smiled ironically. "Even then, it took them about four months to get clearance to bring it in."

"I take it that was before they decided to make a gift of it?" Max added his small mite of cynicism.

"What d'you think?" Jamsung gave a dismissive twist of his head.

"How many clients, Saheb?" Ong Chu held up his right hand ready to count out the fingers.

"Six."

"Special equipment?"

"No, nothing special. A load of photographic gear I expect."

"Mm..." The Sherpa was thinking aloud. "If we carry all our own food, except for fresh vegetables, use all Sherpas instead of porters, it will be more expensive but..." He gave a little upward move of his head as if inviting anyone to contradict the inference that this would solve most of the logistical problems. Max felt an ember of his doused enthusiasm begin to glow a little.

"I don't think the expense is a real problem."

"We'd still need a STOL aircraft and flight plan authorisation." It did not escape Max's notice that Jamsung had dropped the 'you' for 'we'. The faintest of smiles ghosted around Jamsung's mouth and eyes.

"We'll just have to find a way, won't we?"

Lhasa – Tibet

Despite all his years of study in China, his medical degree from Shanghai Institute of Medicine, not to mention Beijing's expression of trust in him by appointing him Tibetan governor of Lhasa district, Kalsang Lhawang registered with satisfaction the fact that he still thought of 11 o'clock in the morning as 'the hour of the snake'. Even more satisfying and apt to have such a thought in the ante-room of General Fei Yisheng, head of the PLA security in Tibet and the *de facto* ruler of the Tibet Autonomous Region of the PRC.

A tall door opened on the far side of the room and a uniformed Chinese staff officer beckoned him forward.

"Enter! Dzongpen. Enter!' Use of his Tibetan title was the tiniest sop to his native culture in a cynical programme aimed at wiping out the distinct Tibetan identity. Not for the first time, his medical training caused him to wonder whether the General suffered from retained testes, the high-pitched voice that emanated from the mass, barely recognisable as a human being, occupying a space almost equal to the width of the desk behind which he sat. Whatever it was that supported the giant water-balloon of flesh clothed in a sweat-stained uniform was a physiological mystery. A hand with incongruously long, slim fingers indicated a chair in front of the desk and he sat down, unable to remove his eyes from the excuse for a face. He noted the particularly narrowed angle of the eyes, together with those long digits which made him a prime candidate for *Marfan's* disease. An acute glaucomatous attack would be excruciatingly painful and might, just might, put this dreadful ogre in Kalsang's professional hands. He savoured the un-Hippocratic satisfaction he would derive from announcing 'Oh dear, General, such a tragedy, had you come earlier I could have saved your sight. As it is...' His unprofessional thoughts were interrupted as the tiny orifice that seemed disproportionate for such a huge animal began to move. The blubbery little lips moving like those on a ventriloquist's doll in an illegal imported movie he had once seen as a student.

"You must excuse me for not getting up to greet you but..." The long fingers on an arm that looked like an elongated bed-roll, made an eloquent upward flick, compassing his enormous girth and the obviously complex mechanics involved in such a manoeuvre.

"Please." The Tibetan matched the frugality of unspoken matters. A pulsating wheezing accompanied by a slight tremor of the massive head indicated that the General was laughing.

No, Kalsang thought. I won't excuse your deliberate lack of courtesy, not that it makes a grain of difference. You never move for me, I never complain. These are the conventions and I shall continue to observe them so long as I have to. Instead, he smiled.

"I understand that you wish to discuss something of importance?"

"Yes, yes." The sounds were a sibilant mush as though every word required an excessive effort of will. "A most unfortunate situation..." He broke off, leaving the words hanging in the air and without an accompanying gesture of his hand. The physical immobility lent the words a threatening coloration. Kalsang wondered whether he was being tested to see if he would volunteer a response which would reveal some guilty knowledge. He was, he felt, a trifle too old a hand at this game to be drawn so easily.

"Situation?"

"You haven't heard, Dzongpen?" The slight emphasis on his title carried a hint of incredulity.

"If the General will kindly inform me what situation he refers to...?" Two could play this game.

"Khambas!" The great mass of adipose tissue jerked and the word was uttered more like a spit. Kalsang watched with fascination as a froth of saliva dribbled down the fold of chin.

"What about them, General?"

"The Khàmbas here in Lhasa, in your area of responsibility."

"Ah." Kalsang nodded his comprehension. "I have had them arrested by the municipal police. Neither of them had identity papers." He wondered whether to add 'either' but took the risk that the General's intelligence was not comprehensive enough to have discovered that the guerillas had also been armed with Russian-made automatic pistols. If he was wrong, then he'd have to feign ignorance. He looked at the narrow folds out of which the angry corneas glared. If a *ho tei* was capable of looking malevolent, this, he felt, would be its incarnation.

"How did they get so far inside the municipality without being stopped? Khambas are prohibited from entering Lhasa district." Kalsang breathed a tiny draught of relief, it looked as though his gamble had paid off. Not a time for taking additional risks, he warned himself.

"Yes, indeed." He adopted an air both apologetic and concerned. "A regrettable lack of alertness by the police in the outlying areas." He kept his criticism deliberately vague, he had to try to prevent anyone being penalised. He felt again his anger at the lapse in security, if only the men had not got drunk and drawn attention to themselves in an area which was frequented by PLA soldiers, all would have been well. "I have instructed the chief of police to institute an immediate investigation."

"They will be handed over to divisional intelligence for interrogation." There was an implied criticism in his failure to hand them straight to the PLA's counter insurgency unit, the standard protocol. If he couldn't think up a compelling reason for not doing so, both men would have to die.

"They are being interrogated by the police district investigator's department, General. You have often commended the work of police captain Dorji." There was no appreciable change in the glare beneath those fat lids. "I don't wish to sound in the least critical of our central officers..." He deliberately allied himself with the centre. "...but if we are to make headway, do you not agree that one Tibetan will get more from another Tibetan than someone from outside? You have often stressed the importance of integrating loyal members of the Autonomous Region into the command structure." He had to choose his words carefully to 'shine the shoes' of this obscene but powerful man. At this geographical remove from Beijing, General Fei had a virtually untrammelled authority. If he could not dispose of this problem easily and without arousing suspicion, he certainly could not afford to jeopardise his own position for the sake of two irresponsible couriers. Lamentable though it was to hold their lives so cheaply, he recognised the essential truth that without a ruthless determination to see it through, the Tibetan people would never realise their goal.

"You remember how much trouble we have had with these people before. As you rightly say, they have to be tricked into revealing what they know, all the beating in the world simply seems to harden their resistance. Captain Dorji is anxious to retain your high opinion of him." This, he felt, was about as far as he dared push it. He watched and waited for the response.

The incongruously long fingers appeared to play an invisible keyboard *larghetto*. The rumble of the worn bellows that did service for the man's lungs, laboured to draw breath through his nostrils and recycle it through his mouth, fighting its clackety way over his teeth and spilling out through the blubbery lips.

"You learned well in Shanghai, Dzongpen." The phrase was uncomfortably equivocal. Kalsang felt the urge to add a little perspective.

"I am eternally indebted to the Central Committee and to the late and lamented comrade Deng Xiaoping for giving me the means and the opportunity to serve." He looked directly into the shadows of the folds, searching out and holding the man's eyes.

"Most kind of you to have taken the trouble to visit me, Dzongpen." The interview was over. Typical of the man's style, there would be no direct response. What was left unsaid was for Kalsang to interpret, at his own peril. He rose from his seat and gave a stiff, short bow from the waist.

"Whenever I may be of assistance, General." He turned and walked carefully out of the room. An instant flood of relief coursed through him as he heard the door closed behind him. One day, and he offered up a short prayer that it would not be soon, the Chinese general would stop fencing with him. Deep inside the bulbous head atop that grotesque body there was a mind as penetrating as the iced wind across the Changtang plateau.

General Fei watched his aide close the door behind the Dzongpen.

"Bring me those intelligence reports." The staff officer opened a metal filing cabinet and extracted three manila files.

"Do you trust the Dzongpen, General?"

"I trust these Nanyang Tibetans less than the ones who never left this savage region." The fleshy folds of skin prevented his face from forming facial expressions. With Fei, it was all in the eyes and the voice. Contrary to every other facet of his physiology and features, the high, almost girlish tones of his spoken Mandarin were soft and sibilant. "Whilst he is Dzongpen, I have him where I can keep him under surveillance." He aligned the three files in front of him like a blackjack dealer.

"Now, let us see what you learned at the intelligence evaluation centre." The forefinger of his right hand extended itself, pointing at a 45° angle. "First, we have the flight of the Karmapa Lama, a deceitful young man to whom we should never have entrusted the responsibility." A second finger shot out. "Then we have the disappearance of that decrepit reprobate whom they call abbot of Shadung, together with a confirmed sighting of him at Dharmasala. All these monks are forever plotting when they are not mumbling their hocus pocus and gulling the congenitally backward Tibetan peasants." "Thirdly," another finger joined the previous two, "we have reports of Topgye Sey, the Khamba counter-revolutionary leader being recognised in Amdo province. And," he paused and a fourth finger shot out, "we have unlocated and unidentified clandestine radio transmissions in the area between Dharmasala and Gartok." He shook out the little finger with its long curling fingernail that curled back towards his palm. "Finally, we have Khambas without identity papers appearing here in Lhasa itself and our precious Dzongpen does not wish us to interrogate them. Do you detect a relationship between these four matters, tell me?"

The long fingers resumed their reflex position and began to play, *prestissimo*, the three soft pads augmented by the click of his nail.

Kathmandu

A little after 10.30 am, the taxi drove in through the open compound gates of Trans-Himalayan. Max noticed there were no cars in the parking spaces. He exchanged a good natured banter with the driver over the exorbitant charges for waiting then walked into the house-cum-office. The fly-screen banged against the wooden door frame and Jamsung came out of the general office.

"He hasn't arrived yet. He's a Big Man, remember?" He added with a slight smile. Time and Bhandari waited for no man, Max thought.

"Come in and wait in here with me." Max entered the sparsely furnished room whilst Jamsung despatched a small Nepalese boy to fetch two teas.

"Want to hear some good news?" Max allowed his satisfaction to show. "RNAC are going to charter us their Twin Otter."

"Great!" Jamsung spoke the word but it didn't come out with the enthusiasm he had intended. His mood was tempered by an intuitive foreboding of nothing good. He was a man who had learned to rely on those intuitions. In this instance it required little in the way of prescience: an imminent meeting between Max and Bhandari was incapable of auguring favourably. Max, however, had proved obdurate and would not be dissuaded. Now he was pointing towards the map rack on the wall behind Jamsung's head.

"I think we'd better have the trekking maps for Rolwaling, Everest and Khumbakarna Himal." With his back to the door, Max failed to see the short thin figure that stood, momentarily framed against the corridor before walking in and regarding him with as much malevolence as his pebble-lensed glasses would permit. Max did recognise the rude form of address that could only have been directed towards him.

"What's this?" Not even "who?" Max thought, he was already at the lowest level of honorific. He turned, waiting for Jamsung to make the introduction.

"Huzoor, this is Colonel Devlin, the founder of THAC," Jamsung added for good measure, "and your predecessor." Almost as soon as he uttered the words he knew it had been a mistake. Max smiled politely and stepped towards Bhandari, his hand outstretched. He noted the silver cap badge with *devanagari* script initials for the ASO over a kukri which he wore on his Nepali *topi.* Bhandari's hands remained clasped behind his back and Max allowed his own hand to drop to his side, determined not to let himself be riled by so obvious an insult.

"I'm very happy to meet you, Bhandari-ji." He adopted an apologetic tone as the thought occurred to him that he ought to protect Jamsung's position. "I hope you didn't mind me making this appointment through your deputy here, but I wasn't sure that my messages were reaching you."

The eyes behind the thick glasses watched him like a goldfish up against the side of its bowl. Without a word, he turned around and began walking out of the room. Just as he reached the door and without looking behind him, he said curtly, "My office is this way." He stressed '*my*'. "Come." Max was beginning to feel annoyed at the man's deliberate rudeness. They had been speaking in Nepali, Max using the respectful honorific, was entitled to be similarly addressed but Bhandari used the familiar form, an intentional put-down. He followed the man down the ill-lit passage and into what he could not rid himself of thinking of as 'my' office. Once inside, Max felt rather than saw the difference. Without the many small items with which he had personalised the room, his pictures, his presentation *Kothimoora* kukuris and the framed and signed photographs of celebrities that had been Trans-Himalayan's clients, it looked and felt utterly forlorn. Dust coated the empty bookshelves and the green glass lampshade on the old reading lamp that he had forgotten to take with him had been cracked by some careless hand. It occurred to Max that the neglect somehow sharpened the evocative atmosphere, reminding him all too forcibly of what he had been deprived of. He looked around for a convenient chair and pulled one across so that he could sit facing Bhandari over his desk. Rather than risk more gratuitously offensive remarks, Max decided to make the running.

"I would like to engage the services of THAC on behalf of an influential Asian client who will pay rack rates for everything that you provide." It was always wise to get the money side out in the open at the earliest opportunity. He had noticed that Bhandari was wearing a nearly new pair of Gucci loafers. Greedy little bugger's bound to want to cream off as much as he can, he thought. Surprisingly, his opening gambit failed to yield any response. The silence began to hang a little heavily so he decided to press on.

"I've been asked to organise a small survey expedition to be headed by Professor Sutape Sukhum of Bangkok's Sirikit Institute of Buddhist Art." He put a glossily composed project brochure in front of Bhandari, carefully avoiding the man's hands that were spread lifelessly along the opposite edge of the desk. As he outlined the expedition's objectives and enthused over the benefits to the company, Nepalese cultural artifacts and the revenues that numerous people would share in, he studied Bhandari's face for some positive reaction. The man's silent, expressionless features stared back at him through the goldfish bowl glasses. Wondering whether he had been less than generous with the sycophancy, Max waxed quite eloquent about the personal prestige that would enure to the managing director of Trans-Himalayan and how it would appear to have been the results of all his own endeavours.

"As indeed it would." He added quickly lest the man misinterpret his words. "Effectively, you would facilitate the whole project." Since the man was a powerful political figure, it made sense to put some stress on that too. But try as he could, Max couldn't think of a political angle that made any sense. The man's rude impassivity was getting to him. He wondered whether an outright offer of a bribe might not be the only way through, then checked this thought. If Bhandari could be bought, Jamsung would have briefed him expressly on this. He decided to close his presentation with a succinct summary.

"Look, Huzoor." If he had to play to the man's inflated sense of self-importance, so be it. "Actually, we would be paying your corporation for the hire of some equipment and the services of some of your Sherpa *sardars* and cooks. We'd be hiring three complete trekking units, using only one but paying for all of them for the whole expedition time. It's a great deal now, isn't it?" This was offered more as a statement than a question. The silence in the room was broken only by the sound of a lorry with a noisy engine labouring past the compound wall. As the lorry noise receded, the silence in the room grew louder. Max was on the point of wondering whether he was supposed to just up and leave when Bhandari shoved the centre bar of his spectacles up onto the bridge of his nose so that the goldfish stared out even more large and vacuuous.

"Trans-Himalayan's equipment and personnel are not for hire to outside persons or organisations." Max was more struck by the crass perversity of this remark than its significance for him. If outsiders couldn't hire their services, there sure as hell wasn't anyone in Nepal who wanted to. Forcing himself to remain civil, he managed a smile and shook his head.

"No. Of course not. I think I expressed myself badly. On behalf of Professor Sukhum I am applying to you to mount the expedition." What the hell, he thought. So long as they got their permits, it didn't matter who took the credit for organising it.

"All applications to Trans-Himalayan must be made at least three months before the commencement date of any expedition or trek." Bhandari's voice lacked any inflexion, it reminded Max of the disembodied recording from an automated weighing machine. "Each application must be accompanied by a sponsorship letter from the Nepalese Embassy in the country of each member of the party." It was as though Bhandari had not listened to a word he had said. Max felt the heat begin to rise in a flush up the back of his neck. Still he refused to let his anger get control.

"We appreciate the usual procedures but, as I explained, we don't have sufficient time to follow through all the steps. Since you don't have any other treks or expeditions on your hands at present, surely it wouldn't inconvenience you to waive the usual requirements?" In his anxiety to push through with the project, he fell into the trap of not thinking several steps ahead. Bhandari was already there and it stirred the first intimations of animation.

"The procedures that I have laid down are not to be abandoned just like that." He waved his arm in a short peremptory gesture of dismissal. "This is not your corporation any more, we have rid ourselves of foreigners here, milking our country for their personal benefit." The goldfish bulged huge behind the glass and Max listened with growing dismay as the man got the bit firmly between his teeth.

"How do you know what treks we have in hand?" His accusatory eyes swung towards Jamsung who stood silently just inside the doorway. "Have you been stealing in to look at our books?" Bhandari picked up a plastic ruler and his knuckles turned white as he curled his fingers around it. How ironical, Max thought, he's actually trying to contain his anger too. This was getting neither of them anywhere, fast. He'd have to try a different tack.

"Huzoor, that is all past history. I am happy to know that I was able to give something of value to Nepal. That's why I'm here, because you're the head of the best organisation there is for this type of operation. If you could see your way to accommodating us, personally I shall be very happy but much more important, it will cement the new administration's relations with Thailand."

As he spoke, Max saw, out of the corner of his eye, the small Nepalese boy who had entered quietly carrying a cup of tea which he proceeded to place in front of Max. Simultaneously, Max saw the potential gloss that could be put upon this innocuous gesture. Picking up the cup and saucer, he moved it across the desk top towards Bhandari. He smiled at the boy and said. "This is the director Saheb's."

Too late. Bhandari's voice was authoritatively angry.

"Who ordered this?"

"Jamsung Saheb."

"Take it away!" It was said in a tone that brooked no room for disagreement. The boy leant forward hurriedly and picked up cup and saucer, spilling some of the contents as he did so. Max could only wonder silently at this extraordinary denial of the most basic Nepalese courtesy. So common place a tradition of hospitality that one was never asked, tea was automatically served. The man had not merely disregarded the book of custom and etiquette, he had tossed it out the window.

"You come here and order my staff around as if you still owned the place, telling me what I must and mustn't do. You, a foreigner!"

He put a special dollop of vitriol in the last word. The mutant's voice had given way to semi-hysterical xenophobia.

"*I* am in charge here. This is *my* office, *I* am managing director and *I* say what shall and shan't be done. *My* corporation will not be helping you. If these Thai people want to use our services, let them apply to me in the usual way, using the proper channels."

Max had been building a head of furious steam which he had kept shut down. The safety valve blew.

"I'll tell you what you are, you piece of dung, you're a receiver of stolen property, *my* property. You're sitting at *my* desk behaving in a way that no self-respecting Nepalese would dream of. You talk of *your* services. The only services you can offer are by exploiting the Sherpas, cheating them out of their retainers, men with more guts and ability in their little fingers than you have in your whole body. You're in charge?" He gave a derisory laugh. "You couldn't organise a poke in a whorehouse. You're the dog that wallows in its own shit." He was on his feet and was suddenly aware of Jamsung tugging at his arm. It was too late to salvage anything now, he'd blown it. It was all he could do to restrain himself from reaching over the desk and hauling the man up by the lapels of his jacket to give him a damn good shaking. But his anger had provoked a joyful wrath in his protagonist.

"Aha! Now we see the great *burra-saheb* when he cannot give orders any more. Well, I will guarantee not only that you will not be getting any equipment or services from Trans-Himalayan but also that any expedition that you are involved in does not get trekking permits. Now you will learn who is in charge in my country!" In his heart of hearts, Max knew that he ought to have kept a rein on his Irish temper. But it was more than a morning's frustration and goading that had broken through. Whilst mentally blaming himself for his intemperance which had doubtless cost him the expedition, he was justifying it too. He walked towards the door then turned to look at the little man who was visibly shaking with hate.

"One more thing, director Saheb..." He spoke in English. "Go and fuck yourself." He had the presence of mind to ignore Jamsung and walk straight out of the building into the forecourt. The taxi driver rose from where he had been squatting beside his vehicle.

"Let's get out of here."

It was late evening when Jamsung caught up with Max. He found him sitting alone at a table in the Soaltee Hotel's bar. He wore a grim look of self-reproach and the glass of beer stood barely touched. His expression lightened fractionally when he caught sight of the Tibetan.

"What'll you have?"

"At these prices? I'll split a beer with you." As he sat down opposite Max he nodded towards the glass of beer. "Perhaps you ought to order something a bit stronger."

Here it comes, Max thought, they've cancelled my visa.

"RNAC regret that they have no aircraft available for private charter after all."

"Damn their eyes." He found a few more colourful phrases inviting unpleasant carnal invasions of the airline's body politick before stating the obvious. "They've been got at by that prick."

"What did you expect?" Jamsung spoke wearily. "His cousin-brother, Gopi Raj Bhandari is minister for transport."

"Ah!" Max slapped his forehead with his open palm, disgusted with his own improvidence more than anything else. "I just saw red and said the things that I've been suppressing over the past months."

"You'd have been better keeping them suppressed a bit longer." All that Max could manage was a grunt of agreement. Jamsung managed a rueful smile. "I think I can buy the equipment from one or two of the shops in Thamel, they'll be only too glad to trade, the lack of tourists has devastated business in the area."

"Better get the best kit available...and make sure it looks bright and clean."

"Agreed. Incidentally, I forgot to tell you, Deepraj has arrived with your Range Rover. He's fixed himself up with a berth at the Subarna."

"Well, that's one bit of good news." There was more than a measure of relief to know that his personal comforts would now be catered for.

"Max! When did you come?" A tall Nepalese dressed in an impeccable *daura surwal* stood beside the table with his hand outreached.

"Damoo." They shook hands and the newcomer slid into a vacant chair as they exchanged pleasantries. Damodar Rana had been in the foreign ministry, with a bit of luck he might still be. A small breath of hope lifted Max's spirits. "What are you doing now?"

"For my sins, I'm chief of protocol. I was just here seeing a visiting state guest into his accomodation." He laughed lightly. "I don't have to ask what you're doing. You've been fluttering our Nepali dovecotes ever since you arrived."

"The Bhandaris?" Max managed to look sheepish.

"Who else?" The protocol chief looked around him before leaning forward to draw their heads in. "You may, unwittingly, have gained a powerful ally on the council of ministers. Tej Singh Mishra. He has the most influential portfolio of economic development and there's a long-standing feud between him and the Bhandaris. If I were you, I'd adopt a low profile and let him battle it out for you. Most of the political appointments are rewards for past favours. Between them, the Bhandaris have exhausted their quota of goodwill and Tej wants to get shot of both of them because they've put the brakes on his plans to revive the tourist industry. My advice is sit tight and you'll win in the end."

All this news was reassuring except for the sitting tight bit. In Nepal, this could take months. Nonetheless, he was grateful for the information.

"I appreciate your advice, Damoo. My problem right now is that I'm up against a deadline for an expedition and I really need whatever help I can get, especially over the trekking permits for my clients. I know the foreign secretary is out of station but is there anyone else in the ministry who could bring some influence to bear?"

Rana's expression remained non-committal. "I'll see what I can do…but this is going on way above my head. Remember Max, everything runs on Nepali time." He looked around him once more before getting to his feet. "Watch your back, Max." He shook hands with both of them and they made *namascar* to each other before he turned and left.

"It looks like stalemate." Jamsung pondered his beer. "These power battles are business as usual in Nepalese politics, everyone trying to get their hands on sources of wealth. They give their parties different names but most of them are as ready to change allegiance as a professional footballer, so long as the transfer fee is high enough. It wasn't so bad when they were just playing politics, grabbing their share of the slush money from the big international aid projects and the overseas RNAC GSA contracts but now that none of this is available, it's power for the sake of power...and they've begun to bump each other off in the name of Marxist-Leninist purity."

Max shook his head. "It could only happen in Nepal. Whilst the rest of the world is struggling to throw off all the ideological evils of communism, Nepal is rushing to welcome it in with open arms."

"Not really." Jamsung countered. "There are a handful of genuine ideologues but the majority is still playing the old Nepalese political game of pass the parcel. Selfish greed is the only philosophy that they genuinely embrace." He frowned. "But this time it's got a lot more serious. Madan Bom Malla is just a figurehead. The various factions within the ruling party are vying for the support of the police and the army, they're the ones who ultimately hold the reins."

"But I thought the paratroops had thrown in their lot with the MLF goons?"

"They did." Jamsung nodded. "But the rest of the army is chafing at the bit. Traditionally, they were always seen as the last line of defence for the king. If other members of the royal family hadn't dragged the palace down in the eyes of the populace, the army would have protected His Majesty...after all, he's still a reincarnation of Vishnu and religion is still a potent force throughout the entire country. Some of the younger career officers want to restore the monarchy because they feel their futures will be more secure."

"But whilst this is all going on or, more accurately, not going on in the time-honoured Nepalese way, our timing is going all to cock." Max scratched his head as he spoke.

"Don't do that, Max!" Jamsung's peremptory tone startled him.

"What?"

"Scratch your head at night, I've told you before, it's bad luck."

"Oh God!" Max rubbed his scalp with his open palm as if it were an eraser. "What more can go wrong anyway?"

"Lots. Think about it. Despite all the problems, we're still making some progress. Ong Chu should get back from Lukla tomorrow with some of the lead Sherpas. He sent me a message that he'd contacted Nyima and Tsering. The rest will be here by the end of the month. Equipment isn't a problem, we can have our choice of everything that's available, and that's pretty much everything if we have the money."

Max began to feel a trifle uncomfortable. Whilst he railed against misfortune and let his temper run riot, Jamsung was being as practical as ever. The Tibetan tapped the table with his forefinger.

"We can dispense with acclimatisation treks by taking longer over the early part of the journey. If we need more men, as soon as we know which route we're taking, we can switch some of the best Sherpas over from the alternative teams and have them join us at predetermined rendezvous."

Max wondered what on earth he'd do without Jamsung's steady approach to problems. From his perspective, it was a challenge like any other challenge that the mountains threw up. The Tibetan poured the last of the beer into their glasses and raised his.

"Well, here's to Tej Singh Mishra and the success of the expedition."

"I'll drink to that." Both men drained their glasses. Max looked at his watch. "It's 7.45. Just time for a quick bowl of *thukpa* at your, I mean *my* place." He grinned. "Then beat the curfew and to bed."

An hour later, Max left the restaurant and walked the short distance to where the taxis usually waited outside the Annapurna Hotel entrance. There were none in sight and he began to wonder whether it had been a mistake not to call Deepraj to come and pick him up. He checked his watch, wondering whether the taxis disappeared well before the curfew began. Concerned lest he run the risk of breaking the curfew he was about to stride out for his hotel when a figure stepped out from between some parked cars.

"Taxi?"

"Yes." The Nepalese pointed across the wide expanse of Durbar Marg and as he did so, Max saw a car's headlights come on. It was facing towards him, parked in the driveway leading to the Yak & Yeti. He was gratefully relieved as they crossed the road together.

"You'll have to be a bit quick or we'll be stopped by the police."

The Nepalese grunted something unintelligible. He wondered whether to repeat himself but as he looked at the man it struck him as incongruous that anyone would be wearing dark wraparound sunglasses at night. Sometimes it was difficult to make a lot of sense of what Kathmandu people wore, fashion dictated the strangest of habits. Still, he couldn't recall seeing anyone wearing dark glasses after dark, especially if they were driving. Kathmandu was arguably the worst-lit capital city in the world, even when all the lamp standards were working. A sixth sense made him look behind them. Two shadowy figures appeared to be hurrying to catch up with them. He looked towards the taxi and saw two of the doors opening. Kathmandu odds. He registered both fear and disgust at the same time. He felt for his keys in his trouser pocket and rearranged them so that the pointed ends would protrude between his fingers if he clenched his fist. Desperately short of a defensive weapon, his eyes swept the immediate area for a length of wood or iron. Nothing. He slowed his pace down to try to take sufficient stock of his position. Suddenly remembering the coins in the pocket of his bomber jacket, he slipped his free hand into it and grasped a handful. Out in the open they could surround him and attack from all sides simultaneously. It had to be something solid to get his back against but the nearest thing was a concrete gate pillar, almost 10 feet away. He was still walking forward as though unaware of what was afoot, he knew he had to exploit the situation with a surprise move. Take out the nearest man. Remember the basics. Without pausing in his stride he half turned to his left and brought the key fist up hard and fast into the man's throat. The half-turn was what saved his head from a crushing blow that landed on his right shoulder as one of the men behind him struck down with some sort of crude wooden billet. His shoulder went momentarily numb but the one who had taken the blow to his throat had gone down. He sensed rather than saw someone coming in at him from his rear. Instinctively he stepped back and doubled over. It was a good move, his assailant's impetus carried him straight over Max's back and he landed heavily on the road. Seizing the moment, Max threw himself towards the pillar and shouted with all his might as he did so.

"Jamsung! Jamsung!" A body jarring blow to his thigh knocked him back against the pillar as a face presented itself no more than two feet in front of him. He smashed his right fist straight into it and was rewarded with a scream of pain as he twisted the key ends against the flesh. Someone had grabbed hold of his jacket collar from slightly to his rear. He drove his right elbow sharply backwards and heard a grunt of pain as he connected with something. A heavy kick landed against his ribs sending him staggering away from the pillar. He felt liquid running from his forehead down into his eyes and knew that it was blood even though he hadn't felt anything hit his head. His mind was still working objectively and it told him he'd been knifed. That meant he had to get his jacket off if he was going to fend off whoever was wielding the knife but he needed a respite to do that and his attackers were not intent on giving him one. The one with the length of wood was coming at him again, the billet raised over his head in a two handed attack. He waited for the blow, watched it coming and twisted as he saw the man's arms dip slightly before bringing it forward and down in a chopping action. His body reacted more slowly than he'd anticipated and the billet caught him across the shoulders as he grabbed the man's hair and yanked his head down onto the fist loaded with coins. There was a satisfying crunch as the face took the brunt of the blow. The adrenalin was coursing through him and he managed to kick the man in the groin as he fell forward. Then the lights in Max's world went out.

He knew he was awake and alive. The sickening pain in his head told him that much. He wanted to slip back into sleep, anything to escape the combined effects of the pain and the nausea that was rolling up in his stomach. He opened his eyes slowly, fearful as a child of what he would see. It was dark and he feared that he was still in the street and breaking the curfew. As his eyes adjusted to his surrounds, he realised that he was in his bedroom at the Subarna. The curtains were drawn and a dim light was cast through the partly open doorway to the adjoining sitting room. He tried to lift himself up only to gasp with pain and sink back as the pain intensified across both frontal lobes. He panicked as he felt he was about to vomit and instinctively didn't want to throw up all over himself. He shut his eyes and moments later he had drifted off again.

"Saheb? Saheb?" He recognised Deepraj's anxious voice. Then another, less familiar voice he struggled to place.

"Max...can you hear me, Max?" Unwillingly, Max opened his eyes. The face leaning over the bed towards him was a friendly neurosurgeon whom he associated with several uninhibited nights drinking. The name drifted back into his consciousness, Joshi, Dr. Joshi. He started to speak but his lips weren't responding and the sounds were incoherent. The doctor put a cool restraining hand on his forehead.

"Don't try to talk, just rest. I'm going to give you another shot to keep you under for another 24 hours."

The '24 hours' registered on Max's pain dulled brain. He tested the threshold of the pain by moving his body a little. It was not good, but the relief at being able to move at all encouraged him to make the effort to speak.

"What day is it, Doc?"

"Thursday. But never you mind, just rest. You took a great blow to that thick skull of yours and I really need to do an MRI or at least a CT scan." Each revelation was a fresh jolt: he'd lost a whole day and now Joshi was talking about brain damage. It felt as though he'd been inadvertently disinterred.

"Jamsung?" His voice was a rusty croak.

"I've sent him home to rest." Joshi sounded a bit impatient. "He stayed with you all through the night and all today. I told him if he didn't get some sleep he'd be no use to anyone and you'd be relying on him when you came round. I told your man Deepraj the same thing but I might as well have saved my breath." He shook his head in mock despair.

"How does a man as unlovable as you inspire such loyal friends?"

"It's my Irish charm." Max felt the urge to smile but even this seemed to fill his head with a metal net of pain. He felt himself blanch and the strength he had summoned suddenly evaporated. He couldn't recall ever having felt quite as bad this before. Perhaps, this time, he'd done himself some real damage. Better to know than lie here letting his mind exhaust the undesirable consequences.

"Doctor?"

"Yes, Max?" Joshi was absorbed in the task of taking his blood pressure.

"Have I…you know…" Having embarked on it, Max shied away from a blunt question that could yield an equally blunt response. "How bad is it?"

"Well…" He was wrapping up his stethoscope inside the sphygmomanometer box. "That great heart of yours is still beating like a drum, nothing wrong there and your pulse is strong and steady." He broke off the top of a glass phial as he talked. "Your reflexes all seem normal but I still want to get some film of your head." He paused and smiled. "If I can find a scanner that can penetrate your skull." Max wasn't sure he was in the mood for bedside humour.

"I'm going to keep you under observation for another 24 hours. If you don't develop any untoward symptoms, I think you'll prove the strength of matter over mind."

"Well, what symptoms do I have at the moment?" Even asking the questions was proving an effort. Joshi pressed the hypodermic plunger sending a tiny spurt of clear liquid into the air.

"As a friend of many years' standing, I can testify to your imperviousness to alcohol and moderate physical punishment. As a doctor, my provisional diagnosis is a moderate to severe post-concussional syndrome. I'm not troubled about the cuts and bruises, that one on your head is superficial, they're always great bleeders, in case you were worried." He pushed the needle into Max's forearm with a remarkably gentle touch. "The symptoms you are experiencing are those with which you should be familiar as a card carrying member of the drunk squad."

"Thanks a lot." Max managed to inject some sarcasm into his voice. He wanted to add something about superficial wounds but his brain wasn't up to verbal sparring. Joshi's joking manner did not appear to be masking any serious underlying concern and Max knew that if he could have felt through the pain, he would have been relieved.

"You can save some of that sarcasm for those who don't know you as well as I do." The words were spoken harshly in marked contrast to the gentle manner in which he raised Max's head off the pillow and helped him to down some pills. Within minutes he had fallen asleep again.

The girl from the reception desk lay under him, the sweat of their bodies gave their skin a sheen which oiled the rhythm of movement. Her long dark hair spread savagely across the pillows. Her mouth was pressed against his with an urgency that made their teeth slide raggedly across each other...then, with a growing detachment Max began to perceive that he was awake and alone. He peered at his watch only to discover that it wasn't on his wrist. Turning his head towards the bedside table he could see the small digital travelling clock, 4.54 am. A sense of frustration had replaced the eroticism of waking and the dream wisped away. It dawned on him that the pain was no longer filling his head. Afraid lest it be a mere momentary relief, he moved his head carefully against the risk of precipitating a flood of excruciating pain. He registered slowly that his eyes were fully open and that the early light of dawn wasn't hurting. No photophobia, that was positive good news. He lifted his head slightly off the pillow, suddenly aware that he was not alone. His eyes quartered the room, anxiety flooding back then just as suddenly he relaxed, Ambika was asleep in the armchair, a pashmina shawl draped across her shoulders. He lifted himself up, aches but no pain. Carefully, he moved himself until he was sitting on the bed with both feet square on the floor. A few muscles complained at having had to work and the bruises made his movements stiff but as he tested himself he was satisfied that no bones were broken. He did a few stretches, wincing a little when it hurt but gathering confidence as he tested himself. His movements woke her up and brushed her hair out of her eyes and enquired anxiously.

"How do you feel, Huzoor?" He realised that he must look like a derelict drug addict, three days' growth of beard and a pallor to match, doubtless, but the sight of her cheered him immensely.

"A bit battered...but surviving. What are you doing here?"

"Uncle told me to watch over you whilst your *naukur* took a rest." That made him laugh inwardly, Deepraj would be mortified to be described as his servant.

"You're very kind but you'd better get along and catch up on your sleep." She rose out of the chair pulling the shawl closely around her then reached and laid her hand gently on his forearm.

"I'm really glad that you're not badly injured or..." She left the option unspoken. Suddenly conscious of her hand still resting on him, she withdrew it swiftly.

"I'll come back later to check on you." All of a sudden she was in serious nursing mode. "I think you should sleep now." Her serious mien was even more alluring, then the door closed behind her and she was gone. Now he knew what he needed, no more damn sleeping. Pulling on a bath robe, he slipped out into the fresh morning air. The swimming pool was deserted as he'd anticipated. Shrugging off the robe, he lowered his naked body into the pool and let the water take the weight before pushing off and swimming underwater. He guessed that it was how a fish would feel, being returned to the water, the sense of a returning strength in the silent world. The sun's rays lit up half the pool and he swam in and out of the dark and light water letting his mind wander as it would. After about 15 minutes he decided it was enough for a start and climbed out.

As he walked back into his service apartment he almost bumped into Deepraj who was carrying a large cup of coffee out of the kitchenette.

"Good morning, Huzoor." The Gurkha grinned. "I guessed where you'd gone and was bringing you some coffee."

"Thanks." Max added. "Can you pour in a slug of rum?"

"Saheb?" Deepraj's face acquired a frown of concern.

"Rum, in the coffee."

"Really? What about the medicine?" The coffee shook a little as he nodded towards the little packets of pills beside the bed.

"Best medicine there is. Put some in, there's a good man." In reality, the swim had brought back the aches and he'd decided to miss out on the pills. He held the cup and saucer whilst Deepraj poured the rum out.

"You look much better Saheb, but…" He touched the side of his head with his free hand. "Your head?" Half-serious, half-joking, it caught a little of Max's own concerns.

"I'll take it easy today."

"Breakfast?"

"*Geelo roti.*" As an afterthought. "Have we got some decent flour?"

"Huzoor. I got some from the hotel kitchen." Deepraj's foraging skill was one of the qualities that made him so invaluable. The butter-heavy Nepalese pancakes required a good quality flour if they were to taste their best. Whilst breakfast was being put together, he returned to worrying about the expedition. Battered or not, there wasn't a lot he could do to forward their plans. Jamsung and Ong Chu had got the logistics under control, the devil, as always, was in the detail and the particular detail was the trekking permits. His reflection on these problems was interrupted by the arrival of Dr. Joshi who smelled the alcohol on his breath.

"Max, you're incorrigible. You know that booze and barbiturates are a dangerous cocktail."

"OK, I'll give up the drugs."

"Not until I say you may."

"Now you sound like one of those God-bothering missionary quacks."

"Rubbish! You know very well that I'm a product of Oxford and Tommy's and like all the great London teaching hospitals, we had our close encounters with the demon drink." He stuck a thermometer in Max's mouth. "That'll shut you up for a few minutes. Incidentally, you shouldn't disparage the missionary doctors, they used to do a great job when they staffed the Shanta Bhawan Hospital."

Max removed the thermometer from his mouth long enough to reply. "But I prefer my medicine without a tongue lashing from Luke 3, verse 27."

"Put that back and don't be disrespectful." The doctor finished his examination and only then did he remove the thermometer.

"You didn't even look to see if I have a temperature!"

"Tricks of the trade, Max, tricks of the trade. Provided your brain scans give you a clean bill of health, you appear to have made a suitably miraculous recovery."

"You make it sound as though we should have left him to the tender mercies of his attackers." Jamsung joked from his position in the doorway. The doctor waved his stethoscope in greeting as he packed up his bag.

"Try and keep him off the *raksi* will you?" He shook his head in mock despair.

"Did I ever tell you what a lousy patient you are?"

"Without fail, Doc. Bye." The doctor raised his hand in a loose salute as he disappeared through the door.

Jamsung recounted the events as he had witnessed them.

"As soon as I heard your shouts I guessed what had happened. I told you not to trust to luck as far as Bhandari is concerned."

"You think it was his goons?"

"Without a doubt. But we'll never prove it. Thank God I called on some of the boys to follow me. I think it was the sight of the cook's meat cleaver that frightened most of them off. We weren't in time to stop you getting clobbered by the big guy with the pickaxe handle but the cook must have almost severed his arm and he left a lot of blood behind." His expression changed from the obvious enjoyment in retelling the saga to one of concern. "In future, one of us will stay with you."

"D'you really think that's necessary?"

"Don't you?"

Max screwed his face up in recognition of the inevitability of Jamsung's precaution.

"Join me for breakfast?"

"No thanks. I'm on my way to the airport to meet Ong Chu and the Thangboche Sherpas. Frankly, I can get a lot of the logistics done faster and without nosy questions if you aren't along as my shadow." Despite a sense of being superfluous, Max realised that it made sense.

"Rest. You're going to need your strength." He put his hand on Deepraj's shoulder.

"Get rid of the *raksi.*"

"Huzoor."

"Seriously."

"Huzoor." Jamsung sighed. The Gurkha and Max were inseparable. He knew he couldn't break the symbiotic unity of the two men. He just hoped that Deepraj would realise that, for once, Max ought to take his medicine. He walked out thinking about the wider ramifications of this thought. He wondered whether despite Max's tenacity, he might not have to admit defeat on this one.

Tingkye Dzong – Tibet

The monastery thrust its many storeys into the night sky. Darker than its background, it had an air of lofty permanence coupled with that curious capacity of some religious structures that suggested that it had been there forever. Occasionally, a yellow tinged terracotta light would flicker and burn like an incandescent pore on a grim face. From where the group of Khambas stood, the sleeping giant seemed both to be within arm's reach yet beyond scaling. They had been motionless in this position for nearly 2 hours, listening and watching.

High up on the left hand side of the monastery, a sharp white light, quite distinct from any others, flicked on and off in a staccato pattern. The Khamba chief's lieutenant touched him on the arm at the same moment that he saw the light himself. He acknowledged the touch.

"I see it, Gojo-la." Provided that the Chinese had not discovered their plan and forced Gyalwa to disclose the signal, it was safe for his party to enter the monstery. The Chinese had never attempted to lay hands on the Dalai Lama before he fled to India. But things had changed dramatically since 1959. Gyalwa Rinpoche was the High Lama of the Kagyupa sect and to Tibetan Buddhist eyes he was due a reverence little short of that owed to the Dalai Lama himself. It was no longer certain that any of the Lamas were inviolate, in fact the trend was the opposite, especially since the Karmapa Lama had taken flight early in 2000. Now the norm was even more savage cruelty meted out to all their holy people, both monks and nuns. The only thing he felt he could count on was Gyalwa's silence. Yet within him he also knew that all men had a breaking point. But Gyalwa was a Rinpoche, capable of letting his spirit transcend his physical body, leaving behind the pain and watching it as if in a fourth dimension. It was a faculty of what they knew as 'The Third Eye'. It had been necessary to involve others too and in these troubled times no Tibetan could be trusted as a true patriot at face value. He whispered in Gojo's ear.

"Leave a couple of lookouts here. The rest of us will go up to the monastery." The younger man dipped his head gently in acknowledgement.

Despite the signal, they advanced cautiously up the broken track to the main entrance. Several times he called a halt so that he could listen and allow his senses to feel the air. His intuition was his keenest defensive mechanism. The only noises to break the night were an occasional dog barking or growling in the distance. As they reached the great main entrance door, a small grate in the wall opened. They froze against the walls. A lone figure advanced slowly but deliberately until he could see that it was the High Lama himself.

"Topgye-la." The Khamba chief bowed his head in response. Never since 1959 had he prostrated himself before any of the Lamas. It was not a lack of respect but a heightened sense of personal security. There was no way that he could afford to put himself in a vulnerable position. His body bore an ample testimony of scars to witness the narrow escapes of the past, he could not afford to take unnecessary risks. The Lama beckoned him to follow, turned and re-entered through a narrow door that lay behind the grate. Topgye pointed to one of his men to go first, Gojo followed, then he ducked under the low lintel. No amount of caution was too much.

Once inside, they passed down a narrow stone corridor which brought them out into a great courtyard. Crossing the courtyard in silence, his eyes quartered the surrounding walls, peering into the corners cast in almost impenetrable darkness. A faint suggestion of light silhouetted a monk who held a door open for them, then they began to climb a series of flights of stairs and disorientingly long corridors. Topgye hated the feeling of passing through uncharted territory. His sense of direction was uncannily accurate but without a picture of the structure in his head he found it unnerving. Now the red-yellow light of butter lamps in small recesses in the walls gave way to fluorescent tubes hanging by their flex from the ceiling and casting harsh light onto the dark faces of the men as they strode forward behind their leader.

Round yet another corner and another monk holding aside a curtain across a doorway to allow them to pass inside. By the time that they had all entered, there was little space left. The room itself was lit by butter lamps and their aroma filled the room. The light was cast in close warm pockets so that the ceiling was all but invisible. One end of the chamber was dominated by a huge statue of Chenrezig, some 8-foot high, it was surrounded by prayer wheels and brocade drapes. Laid out on a low table before it were silver butter lamps and small porcelain tea cups filled with water. He heard the murmuring of several of his men telling their prayers. After the chill night air, the warmth made him feel a little drowsy. They were very high up in the monastery, that he knew. Errant draughts blew through the wooden shuttering causing some of the lamp wicks to stutter.

"You are 15 in number?" The Lama asked.

"Seventeen. Two men are on lookout on the approach road. They can be called as soon as we are ready to leave." He studied the Lama's face now that he could see him clearly. The skin was drawn back against the facial bones and despite his age seemed remarkably free of wrinkles. The eyes, that was what he remembered, still young and bright. The Lama spoke softly.

"Our last meeting was when you were with the party accompanying His Holiness to India. I remember you well...one Khamba can always recognise another."

"Holiness." Topgye had indeed forgotten that they were both of the same clan. Perhaps he should have guessed it in the light of the Lama's reputation.

"Do you feel sleepy?" The Lama was smiling.

"Yes, Holiness." He sniffed the air. "There is something in the incense...I don't recognise it but I know it's there."

"You are observant." The Lama nodded. "We add a little opiate which is concealed by the incense otherwise it would be instantly noticeable. Many times the Chinese soldiers have searched the monastery and many times they have entered this chamber. The effects of the drug soon make them lose interest and their enthusiasm is dulled." He was still smiling, enjoying the success of his simple ruse. Topgye smiled his appreciation.

"Come." He turned and signalled to the two monks whose hands were hidden behind the brocade draped around the base of the statue. Quite slowly, a large bronze panel seemed to detach itself several inches from the back. The monks now seized the panel and tugged it clear. A draught of fresh air disturbed the heavy atmosphere in the room. Leading the way, the Lama stepped onto a low platform and then over the threshold of the opening. He shone his torch so that Topgye could see there were narrow spiral stairs leading down inside the statute and below it.

The Lama spoke softly to Topgye. "If the Chinese had spent more time in the study of Gautama Buddha instead of condemning our religion and destroying our monasteries, they would have learned that our most treasured icons contain the living heart of our spiritual beliefs." He laughed gently and Topgye smiled politely without understanding what the man was saying. He reminded himself that he was a man of action and had no time for monkish riddles.

The stairs spiralled steeply down and gradually the low, bubbling reverberations of the monastery's monks at prayer began to fill the air, bouncing back off the walls. The bubbling gradually became a great seamless rumbling monotonal chanting that seemed to beckon them into the very bowels of the earth.

"It is the ventilation shaft." The Lama gestured towards a tin duct that ran up the side of the stairwell. Topgye felt as though the Lama had read his thoughts.

The steps ended before a low arch that gave onto a long, wide stonewalled chamber barely high enough for them to stand upright in. The proximity of the roof gave him a feeling of claustrophobia and a disturbing sense of the enormous weight of the monastery over their heads. Again it seemed as though the Lama was psychic.

"We are not under the monastery here but beneath the western courtyard. The doors..." He paused and indicated some wooden gates set flush with the walls, as tall as the room itself and some 5 to 6 feet wide. "...open onto a ledge outside the monastery wall. I have had the mules brought immediately outside so that your men can load them directly". He gestured to some nondescript bundles of what appeared to be covered in tired looking fabrics. "Each load has been prepared so that that it will fit straight onto the animals' backs, they will only require to be secured."

"We are grateful, Holiness." Topgye ordered Gojo to organise the loading. He sat down on a bundle covered with a blanket of sewn sheepskins and motioned to the Lama to sit beside him. The Lama spoke as he eased himself onto the makeshift seat.

"When I was a young boy and before my discovery, I too wanted to roam freely across our lands as you do. The life of the nomadic warrior seemed wonderfully romantic to me then. Of course, it was the only life I knew. My father was not a cruel man, he never killed anyone though he did rob many." He interrupted his narrative and smiled in a deprecating manner. The Khamba chief nodded slightly, his face impassive. "If he had had to face the life that you have, especially in these terrible times, I am sure things would have been very different." He paused and Topgye watched the old man's face drift out of focus as he became lost in recollection.

"He was thrilled when I was declared to be a reincarnation, particularly of such a high divinity. Both my mother and father came here to live with me in the monastery in the beginning. But gradually he began to chafe at the loss of personal freedom and the ritual of our ordered lives. He told my mother he was bored but I sensed that he longed for the old wandering life yet didn't want to remind me of the carefree childhood that I had lost so abruptly. At first he began to leave for periods of time that grew longer and his visits became less frequent and much shorter. Eventually he told me that our destinies were distinct and that each of us must follow our own path nor look behind us. I knew that he was taking his final leave of me. He took my mother with him and after that I never saw my parents again." Topgye felt rather than heard the distant loss in the Lama as he told his story, his soft musical voice accompanied by the gentlest of rustling as he fingered the amber beads around his wrist. So, he thought to himself, despite his great wisdom and the discipline of his order, he was still the familiar of human frailty. Yet he also sensed that there was more than a personal message in the Lama's words. It was the holy man's way of instilling into him an important part of the duty with which he had been charged. His mind made a quick logical connection to the families camped on the western approach to the monastery, awaiting the return of the menfolk. The women and children, his joy and equal burden. He spoke softly but firmly, intruding into the Lama's reverie.

"The rest of our party will be in added danger from now on. I have never been happy about this part of the plan." The Lama's face registered a subtle change as his mind refocused on the present.

"You have come a great distance. These last days should hold no fears for you. We have consulted the oracles and all the signs augur well for your journey through our land." Topgye was tempted to ask what the oracles said about a journey beyond the land of snows but he contented himself with his customary doubting pessimism.

"But so far and no trouble at all?" He shook his head. "I wonder whether our luck will hold." The Lama put one hand on the Khamba's arm and his voice was sad as though he could not credit such disbelief in one so committed.

"It is not a question of luck. It is your *dharma*. So many of us have returned to our land to make this journey possible. Do you really believe that our endeavours would be futile in the face of such a momentously favourable augury?" Topgye struggled with his conscience in the face of the old man's unquestioning trust in his dharma. The Lama could not bring himself to even countenance failure. He allowed himself an inner sigh and mentally shrugged off his apprehensions. He was the fearless leader, the one who inspired with his daring attacks on military convoys and isolated PLA units. The one who kept the guttering flame of physical resistance from being snuffed out. Here he was, sitting beside the spiritual head of the Tibetan resistance movement within their land. Together, theirs was a sacred duty, the sword and the spirit. But his resources were pitifully inadequate when ranged against the inexhaustible power of the PLA.

"I have fought the Chinese for so long and I have learned to respect their military skills. Though they are the lowest of all men since they have no religion, I often wonder why it is that they have such strength when they lack the wisdom of our teachings?"

"In their world, you are a great leader of men, Topgye-la." The Lama felt inside his robes and produced a small book, its covers worn with use. He pressed it into the Khamba's hand. "My own book of the verses of Milarepa. Please keep it and study the words whenever you feel that you are losing your way on The Path."

Topgye knew the customs of his people, knew them yet had ignored them for many years, always justifying it to himself on the basis that his life allowed no time for such metaphysics. He did not even have a prayer scarf to give to the Lama, the most basic yet personal of gifts to demonstrate respect. He stood up and cast his eyes quickly round the room, noting that his men were still busily engaged in removing the final loads. Then, swiftly, he went down on his knees and bowed low before the Rinpoche. No words were spoken or necessary. As much as the Khamba chief knew of the High Lama, so the latter knew of him. The Lama recognised the significance of this gesture for what it was. He began to recite from the Tibetan legend of the Beginning:

Northward lies Dra Minyen, blessed but wordly land
Where all beings are born with wealth,
Destined to lead their lives in peaceful leisure.
But that seeming happy land is land of the unpleasant voice,
That speaks Death.
Land without religion.

Topgye had risen to his feet and pushed the little book into the folds of his *bhaku*.

"All will be safe in my care." As he spoke, Gojo joined them. "Go and bring in the lookouts."

"I will send a monk soldier with one of your men, he can guide them to rejoin you at the foot of the hill."

Topgye nodded agreement to Gojo then turned his attention back to the Lama.

"What will you do now, Holiness?"

"I will return to our Order's temple in Kalimpong to unite our followers." He paused before adding. "I shall also be able to celebrate the success of your mission."

They walked out onto the ledge where the loaded mules were now standing silently, only the steam from their nostrils moving in the cold, still night. The men were all positioned for the march, some holding the lead reins lightly, the rest split into two groups to cover the van and the rear. Topgye noted it in silence, pleased with their discipline. He had handpicked every man for this mission and they were validating his judgment. He cast his eyes up and around. The night sky was heavy with darkness, clouds obscuring both moon and stars. The timing of this phase had been determined by the Lama and his planning had been immaculate.

"It is time." He uttered the words softly to Gojo and the young lieutenant moved out along the line, his ghostly wake precipitating a chain of reactions. Topgye saw that they had all swung up into their respective saddles before he took the reins from Gojo's hand and mounted. He leant forward and lifted up an Aksu assault rifle, folded the stock closed then slung it over his shoulder before concealing it under his sheepskin coat.

"*Lha Gyalo*!" The Lama said softly. Topgye raised his hand in salute and squeezed the mule's flanks, driving it forward and down the slope. Yes, indeed, he thought, Victory to the gods. Then, he allowed himself a little irreverence, Victory to Topgye Sey.

Gojo nudged his mule alongside until the animals' flanks were rubbing against each other. "I heard Gyalwa Rinpoche say that he recognised your face." His features looked puzzled. "But you shaved off your moustache and all your hair before we left Amdo, just to change your appearance. How did he know?"

Topgye grunted a reply that he knew would take the younger man a moment or two to grasp. "When you are as holy as he is, then you know everything. Have you forgotten everything you were taught?"

Momentarily, the puzzled expression remained on the young man's face before it split into a wide grin and both men laughed quietly.

"In 1959 I was young and my head was full of foolishness. I had no moustache but I shaved off all my hair because I thought it would help me to ride faster." He waved his open hand at Gojo to ward off any further disbelief. "What I say is true. I was really only a raw youth but I knew I was the fastest horseman, even then. I was very serious about these things. When the war started, I forgot all about racing and concentrated on fighting. Then I grew my hair and moustaches long, sacrificing speed for a frightening appearance."

Gojo scratched the back of his head, pushing his sheepskin cap forward.

"I never know when you are telling me the truth or just joking at my expense." He said in mock complaint.

"When it matters, I don't joke, eh?" The young man took in the hardness in his chief's face, despite the disarming smile. He would never really know this man whom he admired so much. Yet what did that matter, he chided himself. Just to ride with him was the height of every Khamba's ambition. To be selected his second-in-command on this, the most important task undertaken by his clan was something that he had yet to come to terms with. So much responsibility. He shook his head silently. He, Gojo Dawa had not sought this position. He had been chosen.

It was the hour of the hare. The little caravan was busy with preparations for departure. Topgye held a bowl of steaming butter tea in the cupped palms of his hands, warming them against the raw cold of the dawn air. He watched the women packing up the cooking vessels, kicking the dying embers and retrieving the partly burned yak dung and pieces of dry azalea to kindle the next fire. A woman's voice shouted, catching his attention. His eyes picked up the running figure of little Dondhup and the same young woman was hurrying after the boy telling him what she would do to him unless he came back. The boy turned his head and chuckled at his mother as she caught up with him. Tashi Yangzom's face, animated with mock anger then laughter was strikingly beautiful. Even now, with wisps of loose hair blowing across the broad sweep of her forehead and a dark smudge on her cheek where she had managed to leave some charcoal from a cooking pot, the unkempt only seemed to enhance the line of her fine, sensitive nose and high cheekbones in perfect symmetry with generous lips.

"Tashi-la has the graceful beauty of a gazelle, even in these rough surroundings." Gojo's voice interrupted his thoughts. The lieutenant had also articulated a concern that had begun to nag at him. This was supposed to be a nondescript caravan. Nothing about it should mark it out as any different from a hundred others, not even the rare beauty of one of its womenfolk. He grunted in response and walked over to where she was putting an inverted fur hat on Dondhup's head.

"Tashi-la." She looked up at him and smiled. "You are too beautiful." She reacted with a puzzled look of amusement.

"I pay you no compliment. Your looks are a danger to you, Dondhup–la and everyone in the caravan." Her face took on a serious concern and her body appeared to sag a little. "We're drawing closer to the mountain passes into Nepal, the militias and the PLA patrols will view every Khamba caravan with suspicion. A very attractive woman will give them another excuse to prolong their search, you know what these pigs are like." The significance of his words struck home and he could see that she must be wondering what this was all about. She tugged on her son's hand, pulling him close against her side. Topgye reached forward and gently pushed the boy's hat a little lower on his head.

"I don't want you to worry about it, just remember to keep your face averted when we bump into their patrols. Wear your hat low on your brow, like I have set the little one's." His chin indicated the child. "Try to look down, never stare them in the face, there's really nothing else that you can do but it should work." As he spoke, he bent down and scooped up a handful of ashes from the dead fire and moistened them with a few drops of his tea. "But you could look dirtier." So saying, he lightly smeared some of the ash paste onto her cheeks and across her nose and chin. He stepped back to view his handiwork. Ironically, it struck him that it actually made her look more attractive. He shrugged his shoulders. "Don't worry, if the pigs get too close to you, we'll create a diversion, otherwise we'll have to fight them off." He made a joke of it and she held her free hand against her mouth, palm outwards as she laughed, her eyes merry above her fingers.

"If you had left some hair on your head Topgye-la, you could have cut some off and made a moustache for me!" She laughed at her own joke. It also gave him an idea.

"Gojo!" The young lieutenant strode across to where they stood.

"Have you got a spare travelling *bhaku*?"

"Yes, Chief."

"Good. Get it and give it to Tashi Yangzom." He faced her as he continued. "Take off your *chuba* and wear the *bhaku* instead..." He felt a fleeting embarrassment and added, "...or put it on over your *chuba*...or something." All three were looking at him inquiringly. "A good-looking young man is better than a beautiful woman." He turned and walked away to hide his momentary sense of discomfort. This was ridiculous, the great guerilla leader feeling awkward with a woman... yet she was the loveliest woman he had ever seen. Behind him, Gojo and Tashi looked at each other then towards his retreating back before they began to giggle. He didn't know if they were laughing *at* him or at the idea. Tempted to turn back and tell them to hurry up, he decided against it. It was unlikely that there would be much to laugh about in the coming days.

They reached Chushar in the late afternoon of the following day, just before the hour of the bird. One of the older men was despatched to hand over the papers to the militia post whilst they led their animals into the courtyard of the little town's principal merchant. Topgye rode in and dismounted onto the cobbled floor in front of the wooden stable building. A servant took the reins and motioned to him, respectfully, to follow him inside. His personal bodyguards stationed themselves automatically, one in front, the other behind and in this order they entered the stables.

Once inside, it took a moment or two for his eyes to adjust to the gloomy interior. He made out the familiar bulk of the merchant, an old acquaintance.

"Topgye-la." The man's voice wheezed. He'd long had trouble with his throat. The Khamba greeted him formally.

"I'm afraid that it is not safe for you to stay here tonight." He could see the anxiety in the man's eyes. "Make camp outside the town."

"It's a bit late for that now, isn't it?" Topgye was irritated by the merchant's obvious fear for himself.

"There is a Chinese officer here with the militia. I have also heard that all Khambas are being detained and questioned."

Topgye turned to one of his bodyguards. "See if you can stop our papers being delivered to the militia post. Run!" To the other man he gave orders to halt the unloading and to send Gojo to him. Both men were gone even as they received their orders.

"Why was no one posted on the road to warn us? You knew we were coming." He let his anger out between his teeth. The merchant's face screwed up in dismay, partly that it should be thought that he had let the Khamba chief down but also because the grip on his shoulder at the neck was hurting him.

"No! Topgye-la. I did not know. How could I know, you sent no message?"

"Because Geljen Dawa came through this town a week ago and warned you." Topgye's voice was low but the words carried heavy menace. The merchant shook his head violently.

"No! *Goon 'ch soom*! None of your men have passed this way for months, I swear."

Topgye stared into the man's eyes and judged that he was telling the truth. The significance of what he was told had him worried in earnest. If Geljen hadn't reached Chushar there was real cause for concern. He'd certainly been to the monastery at Tingkye Dzong so where had he disappeared? The only safe assumption was to assume the worst. No Khamba was safe travelling through Tibet these days. Did that explain the presence of the Chinese officer in Chushar?

"How long has the Chinese been here?" He released his grip on the man's shoulder and the merchant rubbed his neck whilst looking offended.

"Since the day before yesterday." The timing reinforced his fears. He took the merchant's hand and gripped it firmly, apologising and thanking him for his help. As he walked out of the stable door he almost bumped into Gojo coming in with his bodyguard.

"What's up?"

"I think the Chinese are onto something. Geljen hasn't been here, that probably means they have him."

"But he doesn't know more than that we are travelling this way." Topgye observed a strict need-to-know discipline that he had been taught as a young geurilla by a CIA field officer in Mustang years ago.

"There's a PLA officer with the militia, he arrived two days ago."

"*A-ksay!* I see." Gojo turned towards the gates to the compound as though expecting to see them thrown open at any minute.

"We are ready to leave right now." He began to stride towards the waiting men and women.

"No." Topgye's voice was firm. "We haven't time. We should just behave like any other caravan. We've been through this routine countless times. There's nothing to give us away provided they don't examine the skins of butter too closely and the weapons are well concealed. Pass this on to everyone quickly and quietly."

"What about the ammunition?" Gojo enquired. Topgye reacted with the first thought to enter his mind.

"Put it in the feed bags for the mules. Get some of the stable lads here to fetch some fresh feed, then hang the bags over the mules' heads."

Within minutes the last bag was being hung over a mule's head but only just in time as the compound gates were thrown open unceremoniously to admit the militia brandishing their old type 56 AK Avtomat Kalishnikova rifles. The militiamen were almost all Chinese immigrants unable to find employment elsewhere. Lazy and ill-disciplined they rarely posed much of a threat but this time they had a PLA officer accompanying their quisling Tibetan commander.

The older Khamba who had taken their papers to report to the militia post was standing next to the Tibetan officer who was translating to the PLA officer. It was their usual defensive posture, they were only poor nomads carrying their butter for sale in the western Changtang. The man was a seasoned performer and was doing a convincing job to Gojo's eyes. Certainly the Tibetan officer appeared to show no great interest in yet another party of filthy nomads. Not so the PLA major. He was pointing in various directions and issuing crisp orders directly to the militiamen who began searching the mule packs. Gojo allowed his eyes to find Tashi-la and noted with satisfaction that it took some time to sort her out from amongst the men and women who were standing around mutely observing their belongings being thrown negligently onto the ground. He became aware of the Tibetan officer approaching him.

"Who is the caravan leader?" The question was barked at him and accompanied by a shove to his chest. The ineffectual Tibetan was throwing his weight around to impress his Chinese superior. Gojo allowed his muscles to relax and pointed to the man who had gone to report to the militia post.

"The old one." He let his tone suggest that he had no respect for their 'leader'. The PLA officer was now standing between Topgye and himself, staring from one to the other. Gojo let his head drop forward a little so that his eyes avoided looking directly at the Chinese.

"Uurrgh!" It was a rolling stomach churning noise as someone close to him began to retch violently. His head turned automatically towards the sound and he was astonished to see Topgye bent double, his body heaving as it was racked by the spasms. His mind panicked. Here they were, in peril of being discovered and Topgye's reaction was to vomit in fear. Hard on the heels of this thought he recalled the briefings that the Khamba chief had given him before they had embarked on this journey. Two thoughts jostled for primacy in his mind: his chief's capacity for spontaneous invention and the guiding principle, 'When in doubt, do nothing until the situation resolves itself or its resolution occurs to you.' As he stood there taking in the scene, it dawned on him that the rest of the Khamba guerillas appeared not to have reacted other than to shrug their shoulders as if disowning any association with the obvious drunkard who couldn't hold his liquor. The older Khamba talking continuously to the Chinese, bowing his head respectfully and describing the hardship of their journey and complaining about the merchants who paid so little for their butter. The Chinese officer appeared to be ignoring the pleas but he suddenly spoke in broken Tibetan.

"What's the matter with him?" He pointed at Topgye.

"Him?" The Khamba screwed his face up in an expression of disgust. "He's a worthless drunk, sir. Just another burden that I have to bear in this worthless caravan." The PLA officer walked over towards Topgye's doubled over figure and kicked him in the buttock with his polished leather riding boot. This appeared to act as the stimulant for more convulsive retching. Then, as he caught his breath for a second or two, he turned his flushed face, eyes almost completely closed, in the direction of the Chinese and recommenced another deep bellied train of retching, the spittle dripping down from his open mouth. The PLA major stepped smartly back, obviously aghast at the prospect of being hit by flying vomit.

"Why do you let this piece of dung accompany you?"

"Sir, he is my wife's brother, you understand." He opened his arms wide in a gesture of captive despair, the inflection in his voice suggesting that as one man to another, the Chinese would understand. But the Major had lost interest and was now prodding the grease discoloured bags hanging over the nearest mule's back.

"Butter?"

"Yes, sir." The older Khamba flourished the bundle of papers in his hand. "We have our trading permits here, sir."

The Chinese officer reached forward and snatched the short bladed *choopi* from the Khamba's waist belt. The older man began to cringe away but stopped when he saw the Major's purpose. Thrusting the point of the blade into two of the butter skins, the Chinese pressed against the bag until the heavy yellow fat began to ooze through the slits. The older Khamba pressed his palms together in supplication, his voice weary with anxiety.

"Sir, this is our livelihood. How shall we survive if our goods are spilt?" The PLA officer threw the *choopi* onto the floor.

"You and your caravan will remain here until I authorise you to proceed." He signalled the Tibetan militia officer to call off the search and strode ahead of them out of the compound gates, a small group of local Tibetan oglers parted to let him pass, bowing deferentially. The militiamen trooped out, one or two of them having stolen something for themselves. The gates closed behind them and one of the Khambas put his eye to a crack in the wood. After a minute or so, he turned away from the gate, his face cracked in a wide grin.

"Gone."

Topgye wiped his mouth with his sleeve and clapped the older Khamba across the shoulders, grinning broadly.

"Well done, Yishi. Well done. We made a great team." He gave a friendly wave towards Gojo. "Even had our young lieutenant worried for a moment, I think." He turned back to Yishi. "What chances our Nanyang lord and master with the friendly boot recognised Topgye Sey, the notorious bandit chief?" The older man put his hand on his hips and roared with laughter.

"You were disgusting chief!"

Gojo felt a pang of discomfort that he had ever doubted Topgye, even for a second. He realised too that these men had fought and survived together for years and that he had a long way to go before he could earn the respect that they had for each other.

"Gojo?" Topgye's voice startled him. "Where'd you hide the radio set?" In the last few minutes before the militia had arrived he had had the responsibility of concealing their hi-tech radio communicator. He walked over to where three mules were tethered. Behind them was a mound of fresh droppings, still steaming in the cold evening air. Scrabbling away the top layer, he unearthed the oil-skin bag in which the transmitter was housed. Topgye stood with his arm around Yishi's shoulders.

"Mule shit! Tremendous!" He walked forward and gave him a playful punch in the chest, then put his arm around his shoulders and turned him to face the entire caravan, his face suddenly grown serious.

"The next time you allow a Chinese to kick me in the arse, I'll line you all up and kick each one of your miserable arses!" Their laughter dissolved much of the tension of the previous minutes. Yishi pointed at Topgye's face.

"Chief, you looked absolutely disgusting!" The laughter redoubled and Topgye and Gojo exchanged grins.

In the militia post, the Chinese officer was trying to telephone his regional commander at Shekar Dzong. The land lines were of poor quality and the switchgear in the exchanges was ancient and subject to frequent breakdowns. It was several hours before he made contact and given the lateness of the hour he had to be rerouted through to the commander's quarters. He apologised for inconveniencing him and explained the reason for the call.

"And you say they are Khambas?"

"Yes, Comrade Commander. They don't look any different from any of the other nomadic traders but..." He paused, still a little unsure of his uncertainty. "...I just have this feeling." There was a pause and the line crackled and hummed alternately. The commander's voice came through indistinctly, the sound ebbing and flowing.

"Known guerillas?" He guessed the question.

"None that I recognise. I am carrying the latest photographs of wanted counter-revolutionaries from command intelligence but none of them looked like any of those we are looking for." He was a little troubled that he had not spent sufficient time comparing their faces with his file of criminals. The incident of the vomiting drunk had offended his fastidiousness and cut short the inspection. "Shall I let them proceed or set up an interrogation procedure?" There was no immediate response and he could not be sure that the line was still open.

"Commander?"

"Yes, I hear you. Keep them there until I give you further orders. I will communicate with the Lhasa command centre tomorrow. Goodnight, Comrade Major." The line went dead. He lit a cigarette and enjoyed the sense of relief at having passed the problem on to his superior who, it was apparent, was doing the same. That was the name of the game if one were to survive, especially if one wanted to be posted out of this appalling country with its sullen, hostile inhabitants and equally hostile environment. As far as he was concerned, they could keep it. The Tibetans added nothing to the image of modern China. He would have to give orders to the useless Tibetan militia commander but he was probably off somewhere getting drunk on *chang*. He brushed some cigarette ash off his uniform jacket and wallowed in self pity. The matter could be attended to in the morning, the filthy caravan was certainly going nowhere in a hurry.

Kathmandu

The week had toiled by, unfruitful and frustrating, the only leavening had been the brain scans which confirmed that there was no serious damage. Physically, he now felt restored to fitness. An old Nepal Army friend arranged for him to exercise a horse in the early mornings and each evening he increased the number of lengths of the swimming pool that he swam. By Wednesday evening, he owed a significant part of his sense of well-being to Ambika. She had continued to show genuine concern for him after the attack and had taken to bringing him cups of coffee and tea at odd hours. An inadvertently close physical brush caused her to fall against him and with his arms around her it had seemed a very natural progression for their faces to touch and they kissed. She was warm and soft and sweet and he couldn't recall the last time he had allowed himself to give way to physical passion. The previous two nights she had slept with him, slipping out of the bed just after dawn. His erotic recollections of the night were interrupted by Deepraj walking into the room.

"A lot of mail has arrived, Saheb." He put a fat package of letters he had collected from Max's post box together with a bundle of emails collected from the hotel's mini-business centre. Max began to go through the emails from Bangkok. The most recent contained confirmation of the Professor's ETA and flight number. The letters all bore signs of having been opened and resealed clumsily. He guessed that the intelligence officers who were checking his mail were indifferent to him being aware of their activities. He shook his head in resigned amusement. Why they bothered when all the important communications came via email was beyond him.

"You look amused." Jamsung had walked in through the open door. Max explained his thoughts on the efficiency of the Nepal intelligence bureau.

"I see." Jamsung gave him a quizzical smile. "You see the funny side of the strangest things. Most people in your position would be enraged at having their mail tampered with."

"It's one of my more endearing qualities. Humour in adversity." He paused, some things didn't pass the cultural barriers, but that did not inhibit him. His Nepalese and Tibetan friends shared their saws and sayings with him and he, in his turn, never left out what he was thinking just because he believed it might be beyond their knowledge. "Have you ever heard of the opera, Pagliacci?" Jamsun shook his head slowly. "It has one of the most beautiful and popular pieces of music ever written and it's centred around a clown whose personal life is an emotional disaster but he has to go on smiling and making people laugh. I'll play you the music next time I have the opportunity." Momentarily, he felt the swell of depression overtake him. Recent experience had taken a larger toll of his life than he wanted to recognise. The fact that he no longer had a place that he could think of as home where he could surround himself with the music and books and pictures that, for all their ephemeral quality, added substance to him, dragged him down. In his head, he could hear Pavarotti singing *Nessun Dorma*.

"Well, you'll be pleased to know that most of our Sherpas are currently feeding their faces on *dhal bhat* over at the restaurant." Jamsung's voice had broken into the train of thought that was lowering his spirits.

"Ong Chu?"

"He split them into three parties rather than have a large number all travelling together towards Kathmandu. Anything out of the ordinary attracts unwelcome attention these days. He phoned me on his mobile to say that Hans Fischer, the WHO pilot was going to fly him, Nyima and Tsering on Sunday. Those two are here but they said Ong Chu had something else he wanted to fix before returning."

As usual, Ong Chu had used his initiative wisely, splitting up the Sherpas. Nowadays though the mobile phones made life so much easier, communicating with far off Namche Bazaar was not yet a doddle. Physical travel across the great Himalayan Range was still quite a formidable enterprise and messages tended to be hand carried.

"I'd been thinking of getting the Sherpas fixed up here, you know, four to a room to keep the expense down. But that business of avoiding large parties being noticed makes me think we should let them disperse to their relatives."

"I agree. I also called the WHO office just before I came. They're expecting Hans Fischer back this morning at around 12. Do you fancy going out to the airport to catch him? "

"OK. Action, the great panacea against depression. Wasn't that supposed to be the watchword for Renaissance man?"

The little aircraft suddenly seemed to materialise in the sky as if conjured up by a gifted illusionist. It occurred to him that he had never actually seen an aeroplane flying over the southern range of mountains that bounded the valley on the most used approach.

It landed and taxied towards the apron in front of the UNDP hangar. Well before they reached it, Max was delighted to see that the three passengers climbing out were his lead Sherpas. For all their quiet courage on the mountains, they had a flare for the theatrical. All three had adopted a swaggering gait as they walked towards the Range Rover, their gear slung over their shoulders, all grinning madly from faces burned to a dark hue by the mountain sun.

"*Dheelo bhayo, Saheb*!" Ong Chu greeted him.

"Yes, you are bloody late. What happened?"

"This simpleton..." Ong Chu jerked his thumb towards Tsering "...didn't want to come until he'd got married."

"What?" Max feigned horror. "I didn't know he was still unmarried."

"Well, he is now and this one has a face like a yak at sea level." Nyima, a good head and shoulders taller than Tsering added his contribution.

"*Hut*!" All four feet six inches of the little Sherpa squared up to Nyima.

"Better leave him alone." Ong Chu said resignedly to the big Sherpa. "We have to have someone to throw across the rivers if the bridges are down."

Max realised he was unlikely to get any sensible answers to his questions in their present mood. He was sufficiently distracted to be about to walk off towards the Range Rover when he remembered why he'd actually come. Turning back towards the aircraft, he saw Hans tinkering with something on the undercarriage.

"*Morgen* Hans. Thanks for bringing the Sherpas in." The Swiss smiled his greeting, wiping his hands on a piece of rag before shaking hands with Max.

"*Wie gehts* Max? I heard you nearly got killed by the local Gestapo." He eyed Max quickly. "But you're looking great!"

"Just the advantage of a thick skull." Max gave a deprecating toss of the head. "Actually what I wanted to ask you, is there any chance of you doing a little private flying for me, properly paid for, of course."

The Swiss absent-mindedly continued to wipe his hands on the rag and shook his head. "Sorry, Max. Even if I get overdue, I have the civil aviation gorillas on my back. You know I would if I could but…" He opened his palms in a gesture of hopelessness. "What to do? What to do? They only allow me to fly because their entire mountain health programme is funded by WHO."

Max had expected this reaction. He persisted. "If you just happened to make a slight detour and drop something over the side, I don't suppose anyone would ever know would they?" The Swiss looked as though he was about to say yes but instead he put his hand on Max's arm.

"You know, you are a mad fellow Max, perhaps that is why I like you." He laughed. "If you see me in the Soaltee Bar and you happen to leave a bottle of whisky near my elbow, I don't suppose anyone would know about anything, would they?"

"But I thought it was me that you liked, not whisky?"

"Oh, I just like you better after a drink."

Deepraj took the Sherpas on to their respective lodgings and Max sat down with Jamsung and Ong Chu to review their arrangements. They had several plates of pork *mo-mo* dumplings and bowls of soup on the table. Max juggled his papers carefully, trying to avoid the soup dripping onto them, then finished up with grease stains on the corners.

"Haven't had such good *mo-mo* for a long time," he said appreciatively.

"What'd you expect in *your* place?" Jamsung smiled through a mouthful of dumpling. "Turning to serious matters, though, have you decided whether you want me to come on the trek or not?"

Max had been putting off making this decision but now was as good a time as any to decide. The absence of any formal organisation in the valley was the determining factor.

"I think I'd hoped to work it out so that we all finished up on the actual expedition. But the way things are here, we have to have a reliable base in Kathmandu. With you here, I shall feel that my back is secure. Added to that, it should keep your position safe, whatever happens on the political front." Jamsung gave a little dismissive movement of his hand.

"That doesn't worry me too much, but once you're underway, especially as we don't even know where you will actually be going, you never know what you may need. In my semi-official position I can probably get things done." The fact that they both agreed on the wisdom of this decision reinforced Max's view that it was correct.

"When do we leave?" Ong Chu's pertinent question was a rude intrusion on the false sense of progress that Max had constructed for himself. Nor did he want to chance fortune's arm by assuming it was 'when' rather than 'if'. Ong Chu was unaware that they still had no permits.

"The permits haven't been issued yet."

"*Arey!*" Ong Chu's incredulity was unforced. "Why?"

Max did his best to explain in as brief a fashion as he could. When he got to the bit about the split in the council of ministers and the critical role of the police, Ong Chu interrupted him.

"My middle brother is a policeman." Max dismissed the information in his own mind. Some junior-to-middle ranking police officer was not going to be of much assistance. However, Jamsung's eyebrows lifted.

"The clever one?"

"Yes." Ong Chu's grin managed to convey both pride and a touch of 'I'm not such a dummy'. "My wife's seen him, he was transferred here recently but he and I have been so busy we haven't seen each other yet." Max decided to kill the subject.

"Unless he's a deputy inspector general or something, I can't see that he'll be in a position to help us." The fact that he had only recently been posted to the Bagmati district suggested that he would still be finding his feet, not that he would have a network of contacts.

"He's a senior inspector." Ong Chu's pride was unqualified. "He was recruited by the DSP traffic division when you were here before." There was the outside chance that if the DSP was friendly, he would be a useful addition to their armoury, especially in the absence of anyone else. There was only one day left before the Professor arrived and Max was beginning to feel a sense of desperation creeping into his thoughts.

"Look, do you think you could ask your brother if he could arrange for me to meet this DSP?" As an afterthought he added, "Suggest the Police Club, preferably sometime today." Ong Chu gave an affirmative flick of his head.

"Saheb." He looked at his watch. "I can ring Police Headquarters and see if he's there now." Max began to slide out of the bench seat to let Ong Chu out.

"You do that." As Ong Chu started to walk towards the office, Max called out, "Ask him what the DSP's favourite drink is."

"Bribery and corruption, neat." Jamsung murmured.

"No. Just oiling the cogs of the wheels of co-operation." Max threw back.

"I suppose you'll want me to go and buy a bottle of black market Red Label or something?" Jamsung managed to look pained.

"I'd rather hoped you'd volunteer."

The day was breaking tolerably well so far. Perhaps it augured favourably even though he could not see how it would all work out. When in doubt, follow your nose.

Jamsung was making notes on a millboard.

"How are we going to keep in touch with you once you take off? These mobile phones don't work up in the mountains." Max had the answer pat.

"The Professor is bringing in an Insat phone. It'll reach you from anywhere." At least that was what the promotional literature said. Max had reservations about all radio communication equipment after his experience with the SAS in Afghanistan. This line of thought was interrupted by Ong Chu's cheerful voice.

"Six o'clock at the Police Club, Saheb. I'll go with you and introduce you to my brother. He says Johnny Walker Black Label."

"Well done." Max allowed himself the luxury of a little hope. Ong Chu was beaming broadly.

"And Saheb…"

"What?"

"The DSP."

"What about him?" Ong Chu's smile spread from ear to ear.

"He's not a DSP any more." He paused, watching the look of disappointment that crept back into Max's face.

"He's a DIG!"

The Police Club
1800 hrs

Lakpar, Ong Chu's brother, led them through the lofty club restaurant to a table close to the bar. Their passage provoked interested stares but Max kept smiling back at the inquisitive faces. The room had more the atmosphere of a large canteen than the sort of ambiance he associated with a club. He noted that it was exclusively male, the level of conversations remarkably subdued save for the occasional short laugh or a voice raised in animation.

The brothers were remarkably dissimilar in appearance, so much so that he wondered whether they were actually cousins rather than brothers. Within the average extended Nepalese family, most males tended to refer to each other as 'brother' irrespective of the true familial link. Facial features and physical build aside, Lakpar had the warm, easy hospitality of the Sherpa, overlaid with that invisible uniform of reserve that seemed to be the psychological apparel of policemen all over the world. Over the first round of drinks, the brothers brought each other up to date on their respective fortunes. Max was on tenterhooks, anxious to get a profile of Lakpar's mentor before the DIG arrived. Over half an hour had passed and he had yet to discover the man's name. It was a delicate situation in which he was beholden to Lakpar but by the same token, Ong Chu ought to have realised what their objective was and also been more cognisant of the pressures of time. They were so deeply into family politics that it made it awkward to interrupt.

"And you know *Phupu*?"

"Which *Phupu*?" Max saw Lakpar's eyes suddenly switch to looking over his shoulder and he turned to follow the direction in which he was looking. A stocky figure in civilian clothes was bearing down on their table. Lakpar sprang to his feet.

"Who've you got here, young'un?" The voice was slightly gravelly but not unfriendly.

"General Saheb." Lakpar stood rigidly to attention for a second before relaxing and making *namascar.* Max stood up too.

"This is Colonel Devlin." Max and the General formally namaste'd to each other and then shook hands. "And this is my eldest brother." All three were now on their feet.

"Sit down, please." The General spoke in English and pulled a chair from an adjacent table but turned it around so that he was sitting with his hands resting on the back of it. Lakpar spoke in Nepali, indicating Max and addressing him in the high honorific.

"He speaks fluent Nepali, better than I do in fact." He grinned.

"Well, none of you Sherpas speak proper *Khas Kura*." The General laughed at his own joke. Turning towards Max he questioned him bluntly but politely.

"Are you ex-British Army Gorkhas?" Max was pleased to note that he had reverted to Nepali.

"Yes. I left a few years ago to start a new life in Nepal."

"I have heard your name, many times. But we simple policemen don't get the opportunity to meet the big shots." Max wasn't sure whether this implied criticism.

"Well, General, if you include Big Shots who trekked and rafted with the Sherpas and river guides and then worked long hours in the office doing the paperwork and took out only enough for his simple living expenses, then I could fit your description." Even as he spoke, he felt this conversation was not getting off to an auspicious start.

"Trans-Himalayan?"

"Yes, General Saheb." He decided not to mince words with the man. Since all the senior posts in the police were in the gift of the politicians, this man had friends in high places. The only question was on which side of the political divide his loyalties fell.

"My corporation and all my assets were taken over by the new government. I was the told that my services were no longer needed."

"Really?" It was less a question than a conversational punctuation mark. The man was a canny bugger, not to be drawn that easily.

"Actually, I'm surprised that we haven't met before. I suppose you must have been posted to different anchals?"

"Probably." This, Max felt, was bloody marvellous. Every opening gambit he tried flew like a lead balloon. He couldn't even take refuge in offering him a drink since he was the guest. He was grateful that he had decided against bringing the bottle of whisky with him. Clutching that between his knees whilst labouring through this excuse for a conversation would have been an acute embarrassment.

The DIG looked at Lakpar.

"Does he know where I work?"

"I don't think so, Huzoor." The General looked Max square in the face.

"Do you know where I work?"

"No, General, not specifically."

"Bom Mahal."

"Ahh…I understand." Max let out a soft breath as comprehension dawned. It was unlikely that they would have met since the General worked in the police intelligence organisation.

"So you must be the deputy inspector general of the PIO." Max searched the man's face for clues. He was smiling but was it the smile on the face of the tiger?

"You know I am in the secret police and yet you expect me to tell you a secret."

Here goes, Max thought. In for a penny in for a pound.

"Why not, General Saheb? You must know everything about me." The half-smile became a full grin.

"*Arey*! You want to question me? That's my job."

"Only to get the answer to my question." Max grinned back. The General nodded.

"Yes, I am the head of the PIO so you'd better watch your step or I might have to arrest you!" It sounded like banter but Max still harboured niggling doubts about where this was all leading.

"Well, since you know all about me, you know that I am a law-abiding foreigner."

"I can take you to see two young men with very badly scarred faces who would tell a different tale, if they told the truth which they can't afford to." The smile was still intact but he still couldn't discern what lay behind the words. Might as well push his luck.

"Well, that is interesting. Do you happen to know whether they have a friend with a makeshift baseball bat who's almost one arm short of a game?"

"I have a pretty good idea who he is but he's gone to ground."

"Frankly, I'd far rather get to the man who organised it."

"That's playing dangerous politics."

"Yes, I understand." Max shrugged his shoulders. The General was staring him straight in the face, his expression giving nothing away. Max looked him straight in the eye. The thought occurred to him that he'd over-reached himself and shown his hand too soon. The General's eyes shifted to Max's glass.

"What are you drinking?"

"Kukuri Rum and coke." A hovering steward was summoned and the General pointed at Ong Chu and Lakpar who both declined the invitation.

"I have to go on duty shortly, Huzoor." Lakpar rose and stood momentarily to attention. Ong Chu slid back his chair and made *namascar.*

"I only got in from Lukla this morning." He smiled and added, "My wife is waiting for me." The General waved them both off before pointing directly at Max.

"We shall sit and talk, you and I." The brothers left and drinks were ordered. It seemed to Max that the General had relaxed somewhat now that they were alone.

"Where did you serve?"

"Iraq and a tour with the SAS in a number of bush fires around the world including Afghanistan." The General stood up and turned his chair around, sat down and took off his Nepali *topi.*

"I was a soldier too, before I joined the police. Nepal Army, *Purano Gorkha* Regiment."

"I hear it's the best."

"We think so." The man's face came alive as he spoke of his army days. They began to swop reminiscences and discovered that they had probably both been in Mozambique at the same time when the

General was with the Nepal Army contingent of a United Nations peace keeping force.

"Will you eat with me?" He was beckoning a steward over as he asked the question. "Only simple Nepalese *dhall bhat*, almost as good as army style, but you're used to that." He ordered without waiting for a reply, taking Max's smile for an answer. It was a safe assumption.

"Now Max, you drop the General business, my name's Mani." The neat rum he was drinking was warming the relationship.

"How long have you been DIG?"

"Six or seven months. I was posted out of intelligence as DSP traffic, then after 18 months, the inspector general promoted me back to run the PIO. He was an ex-Nepal Army man too, Bhim Thapa." His eyes took on a distant quality and his mind appeared to have wandered off into some private territory. Max judged it wisest to wait him out in silence.

"There were a few of us, ex-soldiers in the police. We tended to look after each other." He paused again and Max noted a different look in his eyes.

"We weren't able to help him, though."

"How come?" The General took his time, as though he was assessing whether or not to confide in a comparative stranger.

"You were a soldier, I was a soldier." The drink was beginning to loosen his tongue. Max nodded silently. The General's voice dropped into a lower tone of confidentiality and he leant across towards Max.

"Straight after the revolution, that's what it was, don't fool yourself with all this democracy crap, he was replaced as IGP and posted as consul-general to Shanghai. They didn't trust him, you see. He was old school, wouldn't have any truck with the corrupt bastards who kept on coming to power whilst they all played musical chairs with the National Assembly." He tapped the table top with two fingers, quietly emphasising his words. "He was His Majesty's man. True to his salt and potentially very dangerous to the new crowd." He looked about him cautiously, obviously anxious not to be overheard. "They couldn't buy him off and they knew that he commanded the loyalty of the bulk of the police."

"So, he was sent out of harm's way," Max contributed.

"Oh yes. He's out of harm's way." The General looked grim and spoke softly. "He's dead."

"How come?"

"That's the mystery." He opened his palms wide. "They said it was his heart but he was as strong as a bison with no known health problems." He cast another quick look around in a manner that Max found faintly comical in its theatricality. "But some of our present leaders are in bed with the Chinese." Further elaboration was interrupted by the arrival of their food. The General began to heap large quantities of *dhall* and chicken onto Max's rice.

"Let's eat."

The General began to eat with his hand and Max followed suit.

"I see you're a genuine Nepalese." It was said with approval.

"Others don't think so and they're the ones who are holding up the trekking permits for my Thai cultural group."

"I can organise your permits, don't worry."

The next bit was tricky. Max had to identify his opponents so that the General would know where the trouble was coming from. By the same token, he obviously regarded himself as influential and might think that Max was not sufficiently impressed. Past experience had taught him that many Nepalese could be disproportionately sensitive about their relative power in the scheme of things.

"I suspect that Harihar and Gopi Raj Bhandari are behind the spoiling operation."

"Those two pricks?" A grain of rice shot across the table from the General's mouth. He waved his arm in a dismissive sweep. "They're nothing." There was nothing equivocal in this reaction, Max noted with growing satisfaction. However, the apparent ease with which the General was ready to dispose of two very powerful political figures did give Max cause for concern. It sounded too easy.

"I heard that the council of ministers is worried that the whole of the army isn't behind them, there just aren't enough paratroops to keep the lid on so they rely on the armed students organisation. That puts Harihar Bhandari in a pivotal position of power doesn't it?"

"Prick!" This was accompanied by a shake of the head. The General hailed a steward and pointed to their glasses, indicating a refill. Max looked at his watch.

"Oh shit!" It was four minutes to nine.

"What's the matter?"

"Curfew. I won't get back to my hotel in time."

"*Hut terigar*!" He laughed. "No problem. I'll take you back."

"Thank God for that."

"No. Just thank me." He laughed at his own joke. "Eat up, don't worry." The immediate cause for concern having been resolved, Max's mind switched back to the unresolved problem. Aside from his contemptuous dismissal of the Bhandaris' influence, he hadn't come up with a positive solution. It was also very much in his mind that it was the rum talking and that by tomorrow the expressions of soldierly solidarity would have faded.

"You probably think I'm just another nice Nepali who gets pissed and makes promises he either won't or can't keep."

"No, no, Huzoor." It was too close to the truth for comfort, however.

"We old soldiers should stick together."

"I'll drink to that."

The General asked for the bill and it was brought with a remarkable show of deference by the senior steward. As they walked out through the tables, the officers began to rise out of respect only to be waved back into their seats accompanied by friendly exchanges. Irrespective of anything else, it was clear that he commanded both respect and moreover, what struck Max as genuine affection, by his subordinates. Once in the police officer's Toyota Land Cruiser, the uniformed driver drove them swiftly through the deserted streets, the police checkpoints waving them through with salutes. It was all very impressive but Max was now worrying about how to broach the subject of the permits again. He directed the driver to the entrance to his service apartment entrance.

"Thank you, Mani Saheb. Will you come in for a nightcap, I have some Black Label?"

"I thought you'd never ask." The General slapped him on the knee. Max felt a sense of relief that he had bought himself some extra time to work on him. Four stiff measures later, he decided it was now or never.

"Can you suggest who I should approach to get these permits pushed through?"

"Give me the names of your clients, here..." He fumbled in the pocket of his windbreaker and produced a small notebook. Opening it at a blank page he pushed it across to Max. "Write them down." He slumped back into the easy chair and watched as Max wrote. "You're right, I am pissed." He took another swig of the whisky. "It'll cost you another bottle of this excellent Black Label for my old friend General Arjun Singha." His voice was slurred but his eyes remained focussed. "We can't let an opportunity to screw the Bhandari pricks go by." He grinned. "When did you say your people arrive?"

"Tomorrow."

The General took another long drag on his near empty glass, spilling a little of it down his shirt front as he waved the glass at Max.

"Had enough." He gave a short grunting laugh. "I've had enough of your whiskey and we've had enough of these cocksucking politicians." He took the notebook that Max passed back and stuffed it into his pocket.

"I'm sure you can find a good home for this. I'll get another one for General Singha." Max smiled and handed him the half-empty bottle.

"*Tik chha* Max Huzoor. Call me tomorrow afternoon." His face became studiedly serious. "This's just between us, OK?" He grabbed Max's hand and held it firmly before repeating, "OK?"

"Of course."

They walked an unsteady course out to the waiting vehicle and driver. The General hauled himself into the front passenger seat and wound down the window.

"Don't forget, call me tomorrow." If anyone was likely to forget, it would not be me, Max thought.

"Goodnight, Max Huzoor."

"Goodnight Huzoor."

Max watched as the Toyota, bearing Max's sole hope of salvation embalmed in 70% proof Scotch whisky, disappeared, inviolate, into the curfew.

"Max?" She put her arms round him from behind.

"Mmm?" His mind was still churning over the meeting and the prospects of it yielding a positive outcome.

"Are you in trouble?" The anxiety in her voice was palpable.

"No. Why?" He laughed, clasping his hands over hers.

"That was a policeman."

"A friend, at least I think he's a friend." He turned around, still in her embrace and kissed her forehead. He sensed that she was hesitating and let her decide whether she would continue.

"It's not safe to trust policemen." It came out as barely above a whisper. He squeezed her against him and spoke softly into her hair.

"You may be right...but I think this one is a good one." He was betting the farm on this man, he had to hope that his instincts were sound and that Maniprasad's memory survived the whisky.

Chushar – Tibet

Topgye had not been unduly concerned when their travel papers had not been returned to them the morning after their arrival. Caravans such as theirs would be expected to spend a few days in the trading town striking bargains for their butter. No word had come by the mid-afternoon and in the early evening he had sent Yishi to make polite enquiries. The older Khamba had returned wearing a look of concern.

"I didn't see the Chinese, only the local militia commander. I don't think there's much love lost between those two but he just shrugged his shoulders when I asked about our papers, useless fart." He spat onto the floor with an emphatic nod of his head.

"Bribable?" Topgye asked.

"I guess so. His uniform is in poor shape." Yishi screwed his face up in momentary concentration. "Funnily enough, his shirt was unbuttoned at the top and I could see a string of prayer beads hanging around his neck."

"So, he's a believer."

"Seems so."

Topgye decided to wait until the following morning. He ordered them to eat well, drink a little but make it look like a lot. A sober band of nomads would stand out like a sore thumb.

By the following morning there had been no further developments. Yishi was despatched again, this time carrying a gift of a little silver and bronze *gau*. Though small, the god-box bore a very intricate design of auspicious symbols in the silver front surrounding the little window through which a tiny terracotta *Bodhisattva* could be seen, wedged in with a remnant of prayer scarf. Yishi returned within the hour, minus the *gau* but still looking troubled.

"The Chinese has been talking to his regional commander in Shekar Dzong but the only instructions the militia has been given are to retain our papers and hold us here."

Topgye decided to confer with his officers. A watery sun cast short shadows in the thin, cold air as they squatted beside the stable, a worn and greasy deck of playing cards spread meaningfully between them. Nothing would appear out of the ordinary, even to an interested observer.

"If we leave here without those papers we're on the run." Restating the obvious was as good a place to start as any. "If we can put enough distance between us and our pursuers before they realise we've gone, we have a slight chance of resuming apparent anonymity. We have replacement papers, so the loss of the ones we've been using is not a problem in itself."

"But disappearing from here will send its own signal, the game will be up." Gojo articulated the real problem. Topgye nodded.

"Yes, but not the whole game. If worst comes to worst, we'll split up as agreed. You'll come with me and our passengers." He pointed at Gojo, a grim little smile on his face. "And you, Yishi, will lead the remainder of the caravan in a diversionary tactic." The older man's head bowed slowly in acknowledgement. "I want to avoid a fire fight if I possibly can, it would bring their counter-terrorist forces out against us and our strategy has to be deception, not a pitched battle. The stakes are too high." No one spoke, their situation was dictated by their circumstances.

"Timing is even more critical now. We can't stay here much longer otherwise we risk compromising the rendezvous." A creature of habit, he searched the skies and sniffed the air. "We will have to contend with the snows as well."

High over their heads, a hawk glided smoothly, its keening reminding Topgye of the loneliness of their lifestyle, both hunter and hunted. He took heart from its appearance, the hawk was his personal talisman, embodying the qualities he most admired, grace, speed, patience and ruthlessness in the attack.

"We cannot allow others to deprive us of our room to manoeuvre and my face is also a liability. To linger only increases the risk of detection." He picked up a few cards and immediately discarded one with a flourish.

"We must assume that Geljen has been taken, that means our original route is compromised." He threw down another card.

"We will have to obtain yaks from a fresh source after Shakyetang, we can't rely on the mules over the passes. And...." He threw down the last card in his hand. "We need ponies to fight from."

Gojo flicked his head towards the stables. "Our host has a number of good-looking Mongolian ponies."

"Yes, I saw them too." He gave the matter further thought before looking at Gojo.

"Check them over, see which ones are not fit and remember to leave them behind."

"With the ponies and the mules, we could avoid having to get yaks. That would mean we could avoid all the larger towns. We'd have to take one of the lower passes, perhaps Pepti though it would limit our choice of route." Gojo floated the suggestion.

"Uhuh." Topgye shook his head. "Flexibility is essential. We need the ponies to fight from and the yaks to carry the loads, the mules are not as sure footed at height but they give us speed before we start our ascent. I have a relative at Kharta Shika who can supply us with yaks." He looked around them. "Pepti is a possibility but we may have to go by Chabuk or Rakha, what do you say, Yishi, you're the authority on these passes?"

"Chabuk is our traditional route, the one they will expect us to take once they guess where we're headed. If we have to split as you suggested, I could take the main party over the Chabuk. I suppose we can't leave all the other women and children here? "

"No." It was unhesitating. "They're our best cover." To Gojo he said. "Take whatever provisions you need from the merchant's store. Get the women to prepare some hard *tsampa*, we won't be lighting cooking fires for a couple of days. We leave at the hour of the hog. Everyone get as much sleep as they can, there won't be much of that either." He lifted his head in a short movement towards the living quarters. "Yishi, call our friend." They sat in silence until Yishi returned with the merchant. He squatted down with them and absent-mindedly picked up some of the cards, examining them in a semi-concentration. Topgye sensed the man's nervousness.

"So, they haven't returned your papers?"

"No."

He spoke quietly, both to reassure and confide. He had decided on their route but decided to keep it to himself out of an abundance of caution. This man would be a weak link in the chain and looking at his face as he smiled nervously at them, Topgye changed his mind about asking for the merchant's help.

"You have risked enough already, brother. When we leave, we will tie up you and your family to deflect suspicion falling on you. I'm sorry but there will be inevitable repercussions." The merchant continued to look uncomfortable but he was quick to thank Topgye.

"My wife has cooked a great pot of *shetuk* for you."

"I thank you." He rose and the others followed suit, going about their individual tasks.

Topgye wandered over to where Tashi Yangzom was washing some clothes in a crudely coloured plastic bowl, the soap froth reaching up her forearms, her *chuba* hanging down from her waist where she had shrugged herself out of it. He could see that her hands were not accustomed to being exposed to the raw elements, they looked soft and unworn, unlike the coarse chapped hands of the other women in the caravan.

"Should you not leave this work for one of the servants to do, Tashi-la?" She turned her head towards him whilst still plunging the clothes into the water.

"Then I would stand out from the others." She paused and smiled at him. "I'm sure I remember you saying that such behaviour would be dangerous." He laughed and she laughed right back at him, her teeth slightly parted, eyes challenging him to refute her logic.

"We leave tonight, at the hour of the hog." He looked around for the boy. "It will be hard for you and little Dondhup-la." His face resumed its more serious mien. "Remember to act like a man." Even as he said it, the absurdity of this lovely woman having to conceal her all too obvious femininity struck him. She brushed away some wisps of the dark hair that had escaped from the braided plait and fallen across her wide brow, leaving a trail of suds that, momentarily, caught the rainbow hue of the sun. Even when doing the most menial of tasks, she managed to make it seem graceful and wholly appropriate that she should be doing it. Her attention had returned to the washing but she started to sing softly to herself. He recognised it as part of the song of *Milarepa* to the huntsman:

To strive for happiness hereafter
Is more important than to seek it now.
The time has come for you to rely upon a teacher,
The time has come to practice Dharma.

He nodded his head gently and walked away from her towards a sun-filled corner of the courtyard where some Lhasa Apso puppies were stretched out, their little pot bellies full of food, rising and falling as they breathed in the aroma of the straw on which they lay. His back against the wall, he slid gently down until he too was seated on the straw. He took out the little book that Gyalwa Rinpoche had given him and found the song. He read it over to himself, his lips moving silently, seeing her face in his mind's eye as if she stood there reciting it to him.

A shadow fell across the page.

"Chief." He looked up, irritation springing but checked when he saw it was Gojo.

"They have posted guards at the compound gates."

"How many?"

"Eight that we can see. They may have others hidden out of sight."

"Unlikely." Topgye shook his head. "They're not that subtle."

"They look like men from *Ba,* Chief." Yishi joined them. "Armed with AK-56's."

"*A-kstay!*" Topgye snorted his disgust. "They've lived so long under the Chinese yoke in that province they're no better than the Han bastards."

"But worse than the worst Tibetans." Yishi threw in with a declamatory gob of spit against the wall.

"Keep a watch on them. There should be at least one change before the hour of our departure. If local men relieve them, we will simply silence and disarm them. If they are Chinese or these *Ba* bastards, they may not be so fortunate." He despatched Gojo to organise the surveillance then turned to Yishi.

"Find the merchant's wife. She is a proud woman and not given to the compromises her husband makes. Give her a fair price in gold for all the ponies and provisions that we will take. Tell her to say nothing of this to her husband until we are long gone. He will not have to manufacture his anger and grief at losing so much when the Chinese question him." He gave a disparaging short laugh. True patriots were getting very thin on the ground.

"By tradition and inclination we rob and steal. But not from our friends, eh Yishi? Not in these times."

Banepa – East of the Kathmandu Valley

"About another hour, Professor." Max turned his head to answer the question. Deepraj swung the Range Rover yet again on the road to Dulikhel and Max enjoyed the familiar way that the vehicle clung to the road despite its high centre of gravity. Pressing himself against the passenger door, he turned half on towards the clients and studied their faces.

The Professor maintained his impassivity, almost to the point of uninterest in his surroundings. The five other Thais talked amongst themselves, occasionally staring out of the window and pointing at something that caught their interest. Their conversation lacked the animated chatter that he was accustomed to hearing from clients as they climbed higher into the foothills of the Himalayas.

"Thank you, Colonel." They had dropped into addressing each other by their respective titles and Max was perfectly comfortable with this. The Professor leaned forward a little.

"I take it that we contour our way around these endless hairpin bends until we reach our destination?"

"Dolalghat, yes." Max thought he heard a tinge of impatience in the man's normally steady tone of voice. "If you find it boring or uncomfortable swaying around in here, it'd be as well to remember that we will abandon our transport from Dolalghat, from there on we'll be on foot." He said it with a smile on his face, intended to disarm any sense of dissatisfaction.

"I'm looking forward to that." The Thai summoned a smile and Max relaxed as the man leant back and said something to one of his companions. Thai was not a language that Max had any knowledge of and the Professor's companions spoke little to him, though their English appeared to be adequate.

His mind wandered back to the days ahead and he tried to imagine how they would fare on the trek itself. It was a routine he invariably observed at about this juncture in any major trek. The physical capacity of each of the clients, their character and general disposition, how they got along with their fellow trekkers, their attitudes to the Sherpas and the mountain people they would come in contact with en route; these were the questions that he had learned to ask himself, taught by some of the great Sherpa *sardars* that he had been involved with in the past. The old hands had laughingly christened him '*Super Sardar*' when he had started to lead the prestigious expeditions himself. He'd been careful not to dispossess any of them from their jobs, always taking a lead Sherpa with him as his number 2. No matter how much character assessment he did pre-trek, there were always a host of little problems that manifested themselves along the way. Some of them not so little, he reminded himself.

Of one thing he was confident, these men were physically in excellent shape. Indeed, they were the fittest looking bunch of academics he'd ever seen, a far remove from the reedy, cloistered pedants he had imagined in his mind's eye. Failing an untoward accident or altitude sickness, they would be able to accustom themselves to mountain trekking in no time. He had made his usual arrangements with Dr. Joshi and a not so usual arrangement with Hans Fischer to fly the doctor out in case they needed an emergency casualty evacuation.

Ambika caught his eye and he found himself reviewing the last few days. Despite the sudden breakthrough thanks to the efforts of the deputy inspector general that had produced permits *and* visa extensions, it was extraordinary that RNAC had continued to deny him any air transport. On second thoughts, perhaps it was not so extraordinary in this land of paradoxes. He allowed himself the luxury of a moment of self-congratulation at what they had achieved in so short a space of time. Setting out on any expedition always gave him a sense of euphoria but he deliberately dampened it down. It would have been good to share his feeling of well-being with the Professor but his professional sense of self-protection guarded him against giving a client an insight into his thoughts. Better to stick to the tried and trusted confidantes. He spoke to Deepraj in Nepali.

"Thais are all supposed to love chillies. D'you fancy adding a few of those evil little *akashi's* into tonight's *dhall bhat*?"

"Perhaps." A slow grin spread over the Gurkha's face as he wrestled with the steering wheel. There was a quick exchange of glances with Ambika who had caught on to what they planned.

They reached Dolalghat just after midday. The Range Rover pulled up alongside a small mound of equipment against which some of the Sherpas were lolling, drinking tea. Jamsung waved in welcome.

"We've got some light refreshments here for you all." He waved towards a small camp table and folding chairs. "Your last taste of civilisation before the mountains swallow you up." The Thais nodded and smiled appreciatively as they settled themselves into the chairs. Max took Jamsung aside and pointed in the direction of the track that they would take.

"After all the problems that we've been through to get this little show on the road, it ought to be straight sailing from here on, but I have a nagging doubt in my gut." He shook his head then took a sip of the hot coffee Jamsung handed him. "I can't put my finger on it, it's just a feeling." Even as he said it he questioned whether he should have articulated it at all. Jamsung was an inveterate worrier and he would have to hold the fort in Max's absence too. The Tibetan was silent for several seconds, staring off into the hills that rose around them wearing their aura of ambiguous invitation. When he spoke, he continued to look up towards the distant horizon.

"Yes, I've felt it too." The two men stood in silence, sifting through their thoughts. Jamsung spoke first.

"I can't say for sure…it's just the odd thing, here and there. You know how we usually spot the potential troublemaker or difficult ones." Max gave a low grunt of acknowledgement. This was no exact science and the mountain people had highly developed instincts, some might say over-developed but it was a faculty that frequently enabled them to avoid landslips and sudden deep fissures opening in the glaciers. They were a deeply superstitious people who endowed nature with all the characteristics of human beings allied to the limitless power of the gods. Max had learned to respect their intuitive abilities to read people and situations. Jamsung continued.

"You know the one that you nicknamed the Baggage Master?"

"The big guy?"

"Yes. He not only refuses to be separated from his equipment but he's forever checking it. He's already offended some of our people who think he's afraid we'll steal his kit. He's the biggest and the surliest. I'd watch my step there, if I were you."

"Point taken."

"Your professor man." His voice held a thin vein of anxiety. "He's so quiet and polite, you'd think he wouldn't say 'Boo!' to a goose. But when you suggested taking a commercial flight down to Biratnagar and then trekking up from there, he wouldn't even let you finish, cut you off in mid-sentence, nor did he explain why."

"Oh, I don't know. I rather take to him. He plays straight with us, he's already banked our fees for the estimated length of the expedition into my account in Frankfurt." Whatever minor reservations Max had about the man, he had to set them beside his actions and these spoke creditable volumes.

"After all, he's paying well, he's entitled to call the tune."

"True." Jamsung's reply lacked conviction.

"Anyway, from here on it's just another trek, no different from countless others we've handled. If anything goes wrong, it's unlikely to be our fault and that's the way I'm going to play it." He turned and faced his friend.

"In fact, I'm rather more concerned about you. You have to go back and face the music. I wish we'd made better arrangements for communications. These Motorolas won't operate at the sort of ranges we'll be at. That means using the Intersat and having to operate from the Trans-Himalayan transceiver."

"Don't worry about me. If things get difficult, I'll remove the transponder and tell Bhandari it needs servicing. He knows zilch about the technical stuff, I can blindside him on that then I can rig a small dish behind the restaurant."

"I'd be happier if you could arrange that sooner rather than later." A further thought occurred to him as he spoke. "We've got a pretty good Nepalese Army liaison officer, he's accompanied us on some treks in the past. I could 'borrow' his radio equipment from time to time if you can take out one of the old sets."

"Khadga's a decent guy but he won't go up into the heads of the valleys with you, he'll stay at your base camp then you won't have any comm's at all if the Motorolas don't work and I haven't got the Intersat on-line." He put a reassuring hand on Max's arm. "You know, we've been handling problems so often that now we see them even when they're not there. I suggest we just get on with our jobs. The politico's are too busy fighting each other to bother with small beer like us and you've obviously found a powerful ally in your DIG friend."

"OK." Max acknowledged resignedly. "But I still wish you were coming with us."

"We agreed I'd stay behind and watch the shop." He consulted his notebook. "The transmission schedules will be every morning at 05.30 hours. I'll give you an error time of 10 minutes. If you don't make the schedule, I'll shut down until the evening schedule at 19.30 hours. Four days running without contact and I send Fischer out for an aerial sweep."

"Highly elaborate and efficient, Sunshine, but a trifle unnecessary." Max clapped him on the shoulder. "Come on, we'd better be going." So engrossed had he been with these last-minute details that he had forgotten that Ambika was there. A little sheepishly, he turned to face her. They had said their intimate farewells in private and he had not been in favour of her accompanying them to the drop-off point but she'd asked and he couldn't refuse her. He smiled and lifted his arm in a loose salute then turned back to the worries of the expedition so that he failed to see the tears start into her eyes as she watched his back walking out of her life.

Ten minutes later Jamsung watched as the party swung steadily along the trail. Ong Chu had selected personal Sherpas for each client. Apart from Max and the Baggage Master there was little difference in the relative heights of Sherpas and clients. What really differentiated the Thais from the Sherpas was their gait. The Sherpas held back from time to time, breaking their natural rhythm whilst the Thais tried to establish a comfortable walking pace, shrugging their shoulders in the harnesses that Max had insisted they all wear from the outset.

He shaded his eyes as the line of figures began to climb higher, walking into the sun. It was a 3-hour trek to Dumre where they would meet up with the rest of the party but those three hours would really test their legs. If Max forced the pace as he said he would, the clients' legs would feel like putty this evening.

He turned away and climbed up into the Range Rover, then headed back towards the capital.

Lhasa

"Who is this Captain He Hua?" General Fei put one hand over the mouthpiece of the telephone as he spoke to his staff officer.

"He's second-in-command at Shekar-Tingkye district command. Shall I get his file, General?"

The great mass that was the military governor of Tibet moved in a familiar way to signal that the file should be brought, instantly.

"He insists that he will only talk to me." The blubbery lips conveyed both a sense of injured dignity simultaneously with curiosity. He removed his hand from the mouthpiece.

"You are addressing Fei Yisheng." There was a pause as this registered with the caller.

"I regret that I should have to trouble the Comrade General..." The voice was hesitant. General Fei's stertorous breath filled the tenuous link of air between them. "My commander left HQ six days ago for Chushar in the Tingkye district. I heard nothing from him for two days, so I communicated with the militia post there." Growing in confidence as he was uninterrupted, Captain He retailed his story.

"I was told that Major Li had reported a Khamba caravan and my commander went there to investigate himself." He paused, uncertain whether the silence signified censure or approval. "I...I learned that the Khambas left without their travel papers on the night of the 25th. They killed several *Ba'anese* militiamen to effect their escape. From what I gather from the senior militia officer remaining at Chushar, my commander has gone in pursuit of these terrorists."

A clattering noise, like a sack of bricks being dragged across the ground prefaced the General's reply. His lungs bore woeful testimony to the base quality of the Chinese cigarette industry.

"Your major is relieved of his command as of this moment." The General made short, effective cutting motions with his hand that communicated to the staff officer that the paperwork should be done. "You will assume command, Captain He, pending the arrival of one of my staff officers."

"I understand, Comrade General Fei." There was both relief and the first hint of self-congratulation in the man's voice. "There is another matter I wish to mention, sir."

"Yes?"

"A Khamba was picked up by one of our patrols on the Tingkye Dzong-Chushar road, some days ago. He was brought to Shekar Dzong for interrogation."

"A name, what is his name?" General Fei was piecing the jigsaw together, his mind seeking out the missing pieces.

"We think his name was Geljen Dawa."

"Was?"

"Unfortunately, he died under interrogation by my commander before we could get any useful information out of him."

"Did you learn anything useful at all in this incompetent exercise." Now the voice carried a cold threat.

"No, nothing, Comrade General." The junior officer's brief moment of confidence evaporated in the chill of the response.

"Why were we not informed of the arrest of this Geljen Dawa?" General Fei raised his eyebrows in a silent question to his staff officer who shook his head slowly in response.

"My commander..." The man's voice stopped as the mucous in his mouth dried up.

"Yes?"

"My commander had hoped to deliver a full report after the interrogation. When it failed..." Captain He was committed now, he'd sold his senior officer down the river, best make a good job of it. "He decided to say nothing and just dispose of the body."

"Very foolish of him." The words failed to reflect the anger behind them. "And very wise of you to bring this matter to my attention." Might as well give the man momentary face. His failure to report earlier on his commander's ego-oriented deception would cost him too.

"This will serve as a lesson to you, Captain He, not to emulate your ex-commanding officer whose desire for personal triumph blinded him to his duty." He allowed what, in his terms, amounted to a measure of warmth to soften the message but the deliberation with which he enunciated the words carried it starkly along the telephone wires. He Hua felt distinctly uncomfortable between the shoulder blades. He'd sold out his immediate superior but it looked as though he'd sunk himself in the process.

"Comrade General." It was meant to convey the idea that no such thought would ever cross his mind but it hung empty and hollow on the wires.

"I need hardly say that to you, Captain, since you have acted correctly." He was tempted to add 'but far too late' but discarded it as unnecessary. The man would shortly find himself posted to Xinjiang. Instead he simply replaced the telephone receiver.

"Alert the regional commands to this band of counter-revolutionary terrorists but make it clear that I don't want them stopped. I want to know where they're going and why?"

"Do you want aerial reconnaissance?"

"No. Let them think that they have given us the slip. That will give them a false sense of security. Concentrate on the access routes to India, ignore the Chumbi valley and the Sikkim passes, the military defence positions along that area will be sufficient deterrent. Even if they bypass our patrols, the Indian Army is under strict orders not to allow Tibetans to cross over. New Delhi is anxious not to give us an excuse for another armed confrontation, they're in enough trouble harbouring that treacherous Dalai Lama and his pack of running dogs."

He was intrigued. There was something in the wind, if he could but catch its true scent. The physical area of his command was massive and desolate, but a caravan could not just disappear. The main problem he faced was the poor quality of the officer corps posted to the Autonomous Region. Regarded as a punishment posting, it attracted the dregs that the good units wanted to be rid of. And he had them by the bucketfull. He could ill afford to be without his immediate aide but he was one of the few that he'd been able to pluck out of the intelligence command in Shanghai.

"I think you'd better go to Shekar Dzong yourself. Take my helicopter. Don't tell them you're coming."

"General." The staff officer permitted himself the ghost of a smile.

"And be back by tomorrow morning." He pushed the files on his desk a few inches away from his hand. "Take these with you."

His mind had already switched back to the broad canvas his mind was busy working on, etching in a few pencilled details here and there, experimenting with a dab of paint where he felt safe to do so. His long fingers arched like a spider's legs over the edge of the desktop and began their silent playing, *allegro*.

Yarsa – No. 2 East Nepal

2nd May

"We're at about 8,000 feet now. Look over there." Max pointed towards the distant range, majestically silent and so much more multi-dimensional than any full spread pull-out in a National Geographic magazine. The difference was that here, on the ground, you could sense the awesome power contained in the peaks and troughs of those mountains. If a lapsed Catholic like him could feel it, how much more did it impact upon the Sherpas who worshipped the gods that dwelt within them. He dragged himself back to his role as tour guide.

"Those two main peaks are Melungtse and Gauri Shankar, both over 23,000 feet, or 7,000 metres if you prefer." The Professor stood silently beside him, letting it all sink in. He had photographed people and village scenes with the same frenetic enthusiasm that consumed all the first-time visitors but he seemed content just to let the lens of his eye capture the mountains. Max was impressed, it was a sign of a rare spirit, a wisdom that usually took several trips to acquire. In one sense he was not altogether surprised. The Thai was remarkably sensitive to people and places, careful not to offend and alive to the smallest of things. When they had first come across the giant rhododendron in full exotic bloom, he had sat and examined its florid magnificence for several minutes before saying anything. Then he had turned to Max and said that it seemed to evoke the very spirit of Nepal, its extravagant colour and perfection in a landscape both wild and untouchable. He had held the bloom in his hand, observing that it was larger than he'd ever seen and though he held it, his hands could not enclose it.

Going through the hill villages or passing Nepalese on the mountain tracks, his attitude was markedly different from the charitable paternalism that characterised the Caucasian traveller. It had dawned on Max that the man respected these people.

"It almost seems a sacrilege to walk on the mountain tops." The Professor stared out at Gauri Shanker as he spoke.

"The Sherpas believe that the gods dwell within them. They always leave small gifts at the chortens to propitiate the deities onto whose homes they know that they are trespassing."

"Yes, I know."

"Their beliefs," Max had been on the point of saying superstitions then corrected himself, "are contagious. I can't escape the feeling that the mountains demand a human sacrifice when they feel that they need to remind us of their power. The people who inhabit the foothills live with the constant fear of landslips and the ultimate wrath, earthquakes. The mountain gods exact retribution in absolutes of death and destruction, there are no half-measures in their playground. The consequences leave you with indelible experiences of the destructive power pent up within this vision of unequalled beauty."

Both men fell silent, each reflecting on the supra-human aura projected from the fissile giants.

"Mountains do not sleep, Saheb, they watch us." Ong Chu's careful English broke into their thoughts. He squatted with his back to a boulder, smoking a cigarette held between cupped hands. The Professor looked towards him.

"Yes..." He gave a slight tilt of his head in acknowledgement. "It would be wrong to speak of them as sleeping giants."

Max looked at his watch and Ong Chu rose at the silent signal.

"We must move to reach the village before dark." He turned and walked towards the Sherpas who were shrugging themselves into their packs. Max fell in step beside the Professor.

"I'd like to talk about the programme on the way down."

"I wondered when you'd ask me." The Professor smiled behind his sunglasses. "You have been most patient, Colonel, your years spent in these mountains have imbued you with an Asian perspective, we would characterise it as the wisdom of the east."

Max laughed. "Not so much wisdom, I'm lazy by nature and it's too much effort to worry at something when you know you're unlikely to get an answer."

"We've made very good time, have we not?"

"Yes." Max swept his arm around the party. "You're all much fitter than I expected. You got your mountain legs faster than most people." He paused, wondering whether to lay it out plainly now that he had the man's ear. He opted for the opportunity.

"We're now part of the way back down the Bhota Kosi valley." He indicated towards the other Thais. "Your assistants have done a fair amount of photography and so on but we can't keep to this rate and still beat the monsoon. The Dudh Kosi valley is likely to prove much more interesting because of the Sherpa influence. Outside the Kathmandu Valley, this brings the Buddhist culture much further south. If we take the northern route we could be in the Dudh Kosi valley in about four or five days at the outside if we really motor on." The track narrowed suddenly, forcing them into single file. He motioned the Professor to go ahead of him and fell in step behind him. "It's pretty rough going up there and the Buddhist culture villages are thinly spread whereas the southern route is rich in chortens and temples." With his back towards him, Max couldn't tell whether he was making any impression. The Professor always heard him out patiently but by now he was beginning to get accustomed to his advice being courteously ignored. Nevertheless, it was beginning to niggle.

"We'll return down the Bhota Kosi valley and proceed by the southerly route." The Thai spoke with quiet authority.

Max made a mental note to qualify his unspoken criticism. "I think you'll find that's the best course." He had the urge to justify his advice. "The northern areas are far less likely to be pillaged because they're less accessible. We can cover them at a later date without the risk of missing much."

The Professor nodded in silent agreement. They both fell silent as they concentrated on the downward path. Max had warned them all to beware of neglecting to take care on the downhill gradients. The track wound down between twisted junipers whose roots criss-crossed the path whilst the sun burned down with that unique intensity that it acquired at higher altitudes. The soft thud of their boots on the packed soil created its own mesmeric rhythm. It was times like these when a man could easily lose himself in his private thoughts.

The gradient eased off as they contoured along a stretch of track that gave Max a view of the lead Sherpas strung out ahead of them, already putting distance between themselves and the clients.

"If we spend the same amount of time on the shrines in the Dudh Kosi valley as we have here, how long will we be there d'you think?"

Max was tempted to ask how long was a piece of string but he restrained himself.

"As I said, there's a great deal more for you to catalogue there, at a rough guess I'd estimate at least twice as long." This advice was received in silence. Having achieved a small measure of success, Max felt it was worth giving him unequivocal advice. Try as he would, he couldn't escape the notion that the Professor had his own agenda and would pursue it regardless of anything Max told him.

"Professor?" He deliberately waited until he received an acknowledging wave of the hand. "I have to tell you, you just can't hope to complete your studies in the three valleys before the monsoon breaks and drives us out of the hills." This had the effect of getting the man to stop in his tracks and turn to face him.

"I get the feeling that you think I'm exaggerating the difficulties, no, let me rephrase that, the *impossibilities* of carrying on once the rains come. Well, I'm not." The Professor turned to look out across the valley as he spoke.

"I have a good idea of how our study will proceed now. The work in this valley has been invaluable, thanks to your first-class organisation." He turned to face Max now. "I'll let you know whether we decide to complete our studies in the Dudh Kosi or Arun valleys within the next few days. I have to discuss it with my team first but I promise to put your mind at ease, very soon." Though he spoke softly, there was a touch of what Max read as mockery in his voice. It caught him on the raw. He fought down the impulse to respond tartly. What the hell? He thought, the man's paid the money, he's entitled to choose how he wants the trek run. If they went up the Dudh Kosi the Sherpas would be happy, a chance for some of them to go home and for all of them the prospects of seeing friends at someone else's expense. If they had to go up into the Arun they'd be permanently drenched if they maintained the sort of schedule they'd been following to date. He turned behind, looking for Ong Chu who was bringing up the rear party. The Sherpa was catching up on them fast. When he saw Max stopped on the track he broke into a loping run. By the time he'd joined Max, the Professor was already 20 to 30 yards ahead. They walked down together, keeping their distance from the client.

"What are the signs of the monsoon, d'you think it'll be early or late?"

Ong Chu took off his woollen ski cap and scratched his head. "My feeling is that it'll be early, Saheb, but..." He put his cap back on, pulling it over his ears. "...according to Nyima, it'll be late and Saheb always says that Nyima's right!" He grinned. This was an old trekking game they played about the weather, often taking bets on it. Max always deliberately bet heavily against Nyima so that there was a healthy sum in the end of trek kitty for the Sherpas to spend on an end of season party, or, as he wryly conceded, a drunk to last them until the beginning of the next season.

"OK. Then let's hope Nyima's right again, for our clients' sake." Ong Chu's face took on a serious expression and he dropped his voice.

"Saheb, the *Siam-ko* Saheb doesn't understand our mountains, you must explain to him."

Max gave a resigned shake of his head. "I've tried, several times. Either he can't or won't understand, I suspect it's won't. He's just told me that in a few days he'll choose which of the two remaining valleys he'll complete his studies in."

"What to do, Saheb?" Ong Chu shrugged his shoulders, turned away and shouted playful abuse at the Sherpa carrying the camp cooking range. "Your mother could carry that faster, you legless goat."

"At least I know who my mother is." The other Sherpas joined in the laughter as the two men ribbed each other. Max relaxed in the familiar atmosphere these mountain men created.

They had reached the camp a short distance outside the village of Yarsa just as the gloom turned to the darkness and before the moon had risen.

Max felt hungry and the aroma from the cooking pots sharpened his appetite. The Sherpas had lit a fire to lift the slight chill off the night air and the whole party now sat around it. The Thais had taken to the rice, dhall and simple vegetable curries, the whole given a cullinary boost by the combinations of herbs and chillis supervised by Ong Chu. Max loved eating in the mountains, the food always tasted that much better than even the same dishes cooked in the most sophisticated kitchens. Allowing a discount for the hunger developed by physical exertion and a bit more for the psychology of *al fresco* dining, from a scientific basis the only two items of difference were the water and the air. No matter, he concluded for the umpteenth time, there was a special zest to the food and he relished every mouthful.

"Saheb." Nyima was trying to attract his attention. The big Sherpa was shaking one hand, his fist closed and tipping his head slightly towards Captain Khadga Malla, their liaison officer. Max recognised the signal and set about putting it into effect. He looked towards the Professor who was sitting next to Captain Malla.

"Have you ever seen the Nepalese game of *Cowrah*, Professor?"

"No. Is it something I ought to know about?" The seriousness of the enquiry prompted Ong Chu to choke on his food as he tried not to laugh. He'd seen Nyima's original signal.

"Well, it's a fascinating aspect of indigenous culture." Max delivered this with a totally straight face. "But..." He paused and looked straight at Khadga Malla. "It's a form of gambling and officially all gambling is forbidden to Nepalese except during the festival of Holi." He waited for a response from the liaison officer.

"After dark, I think I'm entitled to be off-duty, aren't I, Colonel?"

Max managed to maintain a serious demeanour.

"Yes, Khadga Saheb. And it would be a pity to deprive our guests of some local colour." He looked back at Nyima.

"Yes, Huzoor?" The look on the Sherpa's face was all innocence.

"Have you got any *Cowri* shells on you?"

The Sherpa began to make a great pantomime of searching through his pockets.

"Yes, oh yes, Saheb. I picked them up after my son had been playing with them, just before I left." With a minor exclamation of triumph he took his hand out of his pocket, opened his fingers and displayed the little conch-shaped shells in the palm of his hand. "Lo! I knew I had them somewhere." Max hoped that the Professor had not picked up that Nyima was only days into his married life.

"What are the rules?" The Professor was showing a genuine academic interest, blithely unaware that he was being used as an excuse for some illegal gaming. One thought worried Max a little. Thais were renowned for having short tempers. If they lost heavily, as they were almost bound to do, it could lead to some bad blood. Max instructed Nyima in Nepali.

"Keep the stakes low, very low." He emphasised.

"Huzoor." Nyima managed to keep a straight face. Max spoke to the Professor.

"Well, to be truthful, I never did really understand the game. It's a bit like Craps, if you've ever seen it, instead of dice they use the little *Cowri* shells that Nyima has in his hand. I think the best thing is to watch whilst they play and explain the rules as they go along. You'll pick it up. Oh, and don't be surprised if there's a great deal of shouting, that's also part of the game."

Nyima, Ong Chu and Tsering sat at three sides of a rough square that they marked out on the ground. To Max's amusement, Nyima, with his customary disregard for authority invited Captain Malla to play at the fourth side of the square. To his credit, the Nepalese army officer accepted the invitation.

Within a short time, various of the Sherpas had grouped themselves behind each of the players and the game was underway with great shouts of encouragement and whoops of delight by the winners and jeers by the losers. Ong Chu was deeply engaged in mischievously instructing the Professor and the other Thais into the mysteries of the game. Whatever the true purpose of the exercise, Max had to admit that the visitors were being given a real insight into the Nepalese way of life. It had all the frenzy of a cock-fight without the blood and savagery. The Thais, Max noted, were all totally enthralled by the play and were soon casting bets on different players.

Max sent off one of the Sherpas to get a couple of bottles of rum and the atmosphere warmed with Sherpas and Thais now bound up in the excitement of the game. He was glad that Nyima had suggested the session, it had served to take some of the stiffness out of the relations between the clients and the Sherpas. Keeping the stakes low had also avoided the risks of ill feeling that gaming losses usually engendered.

After a couple of hours, Max decided that a little discipline needed to be restored. He ordered them to finish the game after the current series of throws. There was the usual amount of ribald objection to this arbitrary intervention, encouraged by the effects of the rum. Despite which, his orders were obeyed.

As the winnings were being divided up noisily, Ong Chu came and sat beside Max. He'd given up his playing position to one of the other players halfway through the game.

"The Baggage Master has gone, Saheb." It was said quietly, both men staring into the dying embers of the juniper fire. No one could overhear them over the playful banter of the dispersing players. "I saw him slip away. He didn't go to his tent, he went to the *Siam-ko* Saheb's tent, then came out carrying a metal brief case." Ong Chu pronounced it '*briff kes*' and it was a second or two before Max remembered seeing one amongst the Professor's personal baggage.

"He looked a bit *looki-looki.*"

"What d'you mean, what'd he do?" Max was accustomed to the vague use of language by the Nepalese, it was better to tie them down to a more precise description.

"He paused by the tent and looked towards the rest of us, as though he wanted to be sure that he'd not been seen. In fact I wouldn't have noticed him but I'd just gone to take a piss. I told Laptsering to follow him but to keep out of sight." Max wondered whether Ong Chu shouldn't have consulted him first but he acknowledged that the Sherpa's great merit was his ability to act on his own initiative. Anyway, Max trusted his judgment.

"Where's Laptsering now?"

"He hasn't come back either." They sat in silence, Ong Chu smoking one of the sweet smelling *biri* and Max sipping at his hot rum. Eventually Max spoke.

"What is it about the Baggage Master that you don't like?"

"He never laughs, doesn't smile, hardly speaks to us at all. He's suspicious of everything we do." Ong Chu paused before adding. "He's *anyajati.*"

Max laughed softly. "Well that doesn't say much, does it? I'm *anyajati* too."

"No." Ong Chu was quietly emphatic. "You are one of us, Saheb."

Max struggled with the mysteries of the forces of good and evil. For the hill people, life resolved itself into a relatively uncomplicated equation; there were good folk and bad folk and the worst of the bad folk were evil. The hills were populated by a people for whom the old Shamanic beliefs held ultimate sway, more powerful than the formal religions of Buddhist or Hindu, the *jäkri* was far and away the most influential figure in their unsophisticated society. He could bring the forces of black or white magic to bear on people. Max had witnessed a *jäkri* cure a man when all modern western medicine had failed. Whether or not he believed in the power of the *jäkri,* Max respected their psychic gifts. Ong Chu was a *jäkri.* It would have been rank foolishness to ignore his sixth sense as he'd learned to his cost in the past. If Ong Chu differed in his assessment of someone, they had agreed to differ until the Sherpa was proved correct.

From a purely objective perspective, Max had noted how the Baggage Master had kept a strict control over the Thais' personal equipment. Once or twice he'd been on the point of intervening when a Sherpa had innocently made to pick up an item of personal equipment and the Baggage Master had shouted at him angrily in Thai. But on each such occasion the Professor had intervened, calming his team member and quietly apologising to the Sherpa. Max's people, as a matter of habit, always assisted clients, carrying their personal equipment for them, knowing how the mountains took their toll of the unversed climber. With this group, however, they had quickly learned to let them carry their own loads, unaided.

Apart from Jamsung's initial note of warning, there had been no pre-arrangement between Max and Ong Chu to keep an eye on the Thai as a potential troublemaker. Every trek had to be watched for the eccentrics and misfits who could get on the nerves of their fellow trekkers but the ones who upset the Sherpas were the ones they disliked most. They were the ones who could wreck even the best organised expedition.

"More rum, Saheb?" Nyima came and squatted beside them.

"No thanks. I've had enough." Ong Chu just shook his head when Nyima proffered the bottle towards him. Nyima caught the mood of disquiet. He looked from one to the other.

"What's up?"

Ong Chu told him. "I've seen him go off on his own like that, sometimes the *Siam-ko* Saheb goes with him." He looked at Ong Chu. "Why'd you send Laptsering after him?"

"He's so secretive, what's he got to hide?" Ong Chu retorted defensively.

Max listened to the two Sherpas discussing it and let their anxieties roll around in his head. He wished now that he'd not had quite so many tots of rum, it was a time for some clear thinking. The Professor himself was still in the camp, he'd seen him go to his tent and the light from the lamp in the tent cast his shadow against the walls as he moved about inside. As he watched the soft light, he decided that events were being blown up out of proportion. Irrespective of his own and Ong Chu's assessment of the Baggage Master there was really little that the man could do out here in the Himalayas. He was off his own territory but in theirs. So long as he did nothing which would compromise the expedition in the eyes of Nepalese officialdom what he did in his own time was his business. He decided that he'd raise the topic with the Professor in the morning, he'd have the night to formulate a diplomatic way of broaching the subject.

"How long have they been gone now?"

Ong Chu looked at his watch and cupped his hand around the face to catch the phosphorescence on the dial.

"About half an hour."

The three of them sat in silence for a while, the soft sound of the juniper embers breathing out their softening glow. Max broke the spell.

"I'm going to sleep. I'll hear what Laptsering has to report in the morning." The Sherpas rose as Max got up and walked away, then they resumed squatting beside the fire. Max could hear them talking softly as he zipped himself into his sleeping bag. He couldn't make out what they were saying and he fell asleep almost as soon as his head touched the ground.

"Saheb…Saheb."

He dragged himself out of sleep. Deepraj was shaking his shoulder, a torch in his free hand. Max focussed on his watch and saw that it was 4.20.

"What's up?"

"Ong Chu told me to wake you up. He's gone out with Nyima and Tsering to search for Laptsering."

"What about the big Thai, the Baggage Master?"

"He's back Saheb." Max had a sudden presentiment that this did not augur well. The cold of the pre-dawn mountain air hit him and he shivered.

"Make some tea."

"Huzoor." The Gurkha crawled backwards out of the tent and Max pulled on a heavy sweater as he tried to sort things out in his mind. His gut reaction was to wake the Professor and interrogate the Baggage Master. This would mean admitting that Laptsering had been sent out to spy on them. In the mountains it was not uncommon for people to come to grief and lie injured for hours before anyone happened on them. As he thought of this, he virtually dismissed it from the range of possibilities. Laptsering was as sure-footed as a mountain goat, young and agile. The chances of him losing his footing and falling were too remote to bear worth considering for a moment. By the same token, Ong Chu was not a panic merchant but he knew his Sherpas and it was standard procedure to search for someone who was overdue. Max let the various possibilities run through his mind, there were many more natural hazards in the hills than were appreciated, from snakes to bears and leopards not to mention the sudden landslips on narrow trails. Yet try as he would, he couldn't quiet the suspicion that nothing good was going to come out of this. If the Baggage Master felt like communing with nature, there was no better place to do it than on the side of these great mountains. Like the lungs of a somnolent giant, they lent the illusion of movement to the Himalayan night. He'd done it himself, more than once, when faced with crises in his life. Staring out at the darkened, portentous sky, momentarily disenjoined from the soil on which one stood, the inner spirit acquired an existence quite discrete from the substance of mind and body. Though he had never learned the art of meditation, he knew, intuitively, that this was the separation of the life force from its gravitational tent pegs. The crude force of reason broke his line of thought, the character of this particular man had nothing even mildly suggestive of a contemplative inclination. Reason resisted his will to hear that the young Sherpa had had a minor accident. Intuition was full of foreboding and reason gave way to it. He made himself snap out of this unproductive speculation.

"Deepraj!"

The Gurkha stuck his head around the fly-sheet.

"Huzoor. The tea isn't ready yet."

"Did anyone speak to the Thai after he came back to camp?"

"Who knows?" It was an uncharacteristically discourteous response, uttered with obvious impatience. Max sensed that the atmosphere had infected him too. He opted to ignore it, silently upbraiding himself for asking questions that he should have been up and about asking those most likely to know.

"OK. Put a big *kitlee* on the fire, the others will be thirsty when they get back."

"Huzoor."

Max turned on his Coleman lamp and kept his sleeping bag wrapped around him whilst he gathered his thoughts. It had to have occurred to Ong Chu that as Laptsering was following the Thai, it would be important to know what route he'd taken. That would be the obvious direction in which to search. On the other hand, if the searchers had questioned the Baggage Master prior to setting off, not only would he know that someone was missing on the mountainside but he'd have to be a damn sight more obtuse than Max judged him to be if he didn't put two and two together. Max began to feel annoyed that Ong Chu had gone off without telling him first. Now what the hell was he supposed to do? Wait for them to return or wake the Professor and start some serious questioning?

He rolled out of the sleeping bag and pulled on socks and boots before crawling out of the tent into the raw early morning air. The fire glowed with the lonely warmth that only an early morning fire can. Deepraj loomed up out of the darkness and handed him a mug of tea, steam rising off it and creating a psychological pocket of warmth. He wrapped his hands around the mug and sipped the hot, sweet brew. There was another fire a little distant, close to the Sherpas' tents, shadowy figures hunkered around it, the low glow illuminating a false cupola over their heads. The sense of unease filled the void surrounding the pockets of warmth.

"Shall I wake up the guests?" Deepraj pointed with his pursed lips towards the tents housing the Thais.

"Uhugh. Wait a bit."

Max hunkered down and poked impatiently at the fire with a half-burned twig. He watched the little flames spring into life, dance slowly across the burning sticks, then flicker off and on, fibrillating spastically before they died or flared up again. His eyes were drawn inexorably into the red aura at the heart of the fire.

He sensed someone approaching even before he heard the soft thud of footfalls from behind. Deepraj rose to his feet.

"Tsering's here, Saheb." Max pushed himself up off his haunches and turned to face the Sherpa.

"Ong Chu wants you to come, Huzoor. We've found Laptsering. *Khasio.*" The Sherpa had used one of the most ambiguous words in the Nepali vernacular. Max willed it to mean 'fallen'.

"Is he alive?"

"Uhugh." Tsering shook his head.

The prescience he had felt since being woken had proved accurate. Max experienced a momentary chill of nausea. In his mind's eye, the little Sherpa's face laughed mischieviously and resolutely resisted a mask of death.

"How far away are they?"

"About 20 minutes." Silently, the other Sherpas had surrounded them and soft questions and answers were traded between Tsering and his clansmen.

Max turned to Deepraj. "Fill a flask with some hot tea and rum then stay here and keep an eye on things. But don't wake the guests. I'll do that when I get back." He caught Tsering's arm lightly. "Drink some tea first, then let's go." He detailed two of the Sherpas to fetch a mountain stretcher and come with him. Tsering swallowed the tea greedily then the four men turned and left the camp without another word spoken.

They half climbed and half slithered down the loose soil of the hillside below the track to where Ong Chu stood beside a juniper bush. Max saw the bundle of clothes, boots and one hand that he registered, reluctantly, to be Laptsering's body. Twisted in an unnatural repose, one leg was caught behind the knee, wrapped around the partly exposed roots of the bush.

"I haven't moved him, Saheb." Ong Chu's voice sounded a little hoarse and carried all the conflicting emotions of sorrow, anger and responsibility.

"But you're sure he's gone?" Max knelt down beside the body and felt gently along the neck until he located the carotid artery. The skin had been deathly cold to his touch and he'd known what his eyes had already told him before he verified that there was no pulse. The young man's face, caught in the ugly sharpness of Ong Chu's torch, bore no expression at all, neither surprise nor pain, nothing. From the angle of the head and neck to the body, it was patently clear that his neck had been broken. Gently, Max made to turn the young man's head until it lay in a less grotesque position. As he slid his hand beneath the head, his fingers became sticky wet. He withdrew his hand, knowing that it was blood even before he saw the dark streaking in the torchlight. The ground around the bush was soft soil and the short grass that grew at these altitudes.

"Point the light here." He indicated the woody stem of the bush and felt it with his dry hand. Dry. He patted around the base of the bush and cast about him, searching for a rock or boulder against which the dead Sherpa's head could have struck. Nothing.

"Where's Nyima?"

"Searching." Ong Chu directed the torchlight up towards the track from which they had scrambled down.

"What for?"

"Did you ever hear of a Sherpa who fell off a track as wide as that when he was sober?" Max gave a non-committal grunt by way of reply and unscrewed the flask, pouring out a mug of the rum-laced tea. They began to discuss the logistics of recovering Laptsering's body. The priority was to try to get it back to Pang Boche where his family lived. In the midst of these discussions a soft fall of soil heralded Nyima's return. His face was rigid with anger.

"I'll kill him, *sala*!"

"Not if I get to him first." Ong Chu's voice was almost devoid of emotion and that much more chilling for that. Max let the two men give vent to their feelings, Nyima cursing and spitting to emphasise his words and Ong Chu, mouth clamped in a grim line, nodded silently. Pouring a mug of the laced tea for Nyima, he waited for him to start drinking before he spoke.

"Whatever our suspicions, we don't actually know that the Thai killed him..."

"I know...I know!" Nyima interrupted. Max was all too familiar with the phenomenon of a Nepalese with his blood up. This was going to be very tricky to handle and the mere fact of the dead Sherpa's broken body crumpled at their feet added to the drama of the occasion. He spoke with quiet but firm authority.

"Listen, both of you. I think you're probably right." They both nodded fiercely. "But all that we really know is that Laptsering followed him out of camp. The Thai came back and Laptsering didn't." He could see that Nyima was about to interrupt again. He held up his hand, palm outwards, signalling him to hear him out. "What we found was Laptsering having fallen from the track, apparently." He stressed the last word. "His neck broken and a wound on one side of his head which may have been caused by the fall." He could see the impatience mounting in their eyes as they heard him out.

"No one saw what happened." He paused to let that sink in. "We can't even be sure that the Baggage Master came along this track or as far as this, can we?" He looked hard at Nyima as he asked this semi-rhetorical question. His reasoning was having as much impression on them as a rubber hammer on a rock face. The time for rational analyses would be after they had slept and the sun had risen. Right now, he had to keep a grip on things before one or more of them went back and killed the Thai. He abandoned the softly softly approach, in favour of a parade ground manner despite the fact that it went against the grain. Using the last four digits of Ong Chu's service number, the traditional mode of address in a Gurkha battalion, he relied on deeply ingrained instincts.

"5049."

"Huzoor." It was a reflex reaction and Max noted the stiffening of the shoulders.

"Take charge of returning the body to Pang Boche in double quick time. You and Nyima tell the other Sherpas no more than that we found Laptsering like this and that it looks as though he fell off the track and broke his neck. Nothing more. Is that understood?" It was more command than question.

"Huzoor."

"Saheb…" Nyima started in but Ong Chu stopped him, speaking as he would have to a child.

"You heard the Saheb's orders. Now, you and I have a lot of work to do." He suddenly changed into Sherpa dialect and Max could only judge what was being said from the tone of their voices and the expressions on their faces. He let Ong Chu handle this situation and called the other two Sherpas over, telling them to load Laptsering's body carefully onto the stretcher for the return journey to the camp. As they struggled with their load up the steep incline, he heard Ong Chu tell Nyima to take over the responsibility. It was a practical method of dealing with the big Sherpa's repressed anger. He seized the handles at the bottom end of the stretcher and urged his companion on and up. Max guessed that Nyima would not relinquish his hold on the stretcher until they reached camp. It would tire him out and the process would absorb a good portion of the pent-up spleen.

As they walked back ahead of the stretcher party, the cold light of dawn lifted the pall of darkness that had masked the terrain and contained their emotions. Max felt doubly drained and as the sun rose, casting its early morning shadows of warmth and cold, the beauty of this spectacle was lost on them.

They trudged on in a companionable silence, neither sharing their thoughts with the other. Whatever action he took now, he had to guard against precipitating a further crisis. He reasoned it out for himself. Assuming that they were correct in their suspicions, why would the Thai murder Laptsering? What on earth had he been carrying the brief case for? Whatever it was, could hardly warrant killing an innocent, albeit inquisitive Sherpa. There would have to be an official report by Captain Malla but Max knew that the Nepalese police were a long way out of the league of Sherlock Holmes and Hercule Poirot. The answer lay in the briefcase or whatever it was, though what could conceivably warrant killing an over inquisitive Sherpa was beyond Max to imagine. One thing was for sure, he'd find out.

Ong Chu maintained a dignified silence as the little cortège picked its way back. The silence was infectious. In his heart of hearts, Max knew that this was the one man who could keep the lid on the whole disaster. Sooner or later he'd have to confide in him and plan a course of action. As his eyes took in the dejected set of the Sherpa's shoulders, he realised that it would have to be sooner rather than later. For the immediate future he'd have to employ stick more than carrot, yet it went against the grain to maintain this artificial barrier between them, the bond between them demanded a great deal better than blind obedience. When Max finally spoke, his own voice sounded a little unfamiliar.

"Ong Chu?"

"Saheb?"

"Trust me on this one, eh?" Their eyes met and Max recognised that the old soldier's discipline had subordinated his lust for revenge. At least for the time being.

By mid-morning they had made all the necessary arrangements, by which time Max could see that both Ong Chu and Nyima were as emotionally drained as he felt in himself. Deepraj, dependable as ever, had organised food and insisted that they eat. All three sat in the sun, not that they had an appetite but each recognising the inherent wisdom of a square meal, they dutifully swallowed it down. Max sipped his coffee then set the mug down on the ground.

"I spoke to the Professor and asked him why the Baggage Master had taken a brief case out of camp last night." Ong Chu looked up and stopped chewing. "He says that they've been developing some of the film they've taken so far and that the reason he leaves the camp is to avoid being disturbed by over-inquisitive people who could inadvertently ruin the negatives." He paused before continuing. "Frankly I was disinclined to believe that they were using old technology, I've seen at least two digital cameras."

"Did you ask to see the film or this portable dark room?" There was a derisory contempt in Nyima's tone.

"I didn't have to ask, he produced them for me. They've got the equipment alright and a fair quantity of developed negatives."

"How do you know that he showed you the case that was carried out of camp?" Nyima persisted and Max let him pursue his line of questioning, glad of the opportunity to deal in facts rather than speculation.

"I don't. Not for certain." He looked around him to make sure that their conversation couldn't be overheard by any of the Thais. "But I don't want to let them think that we have more than a vague feeling of unease about things at the moment. As we get higher up into the hills, we'll be in the heart of our own territory, they'll feel more disoriented and we'll find a convenient opportunity to search all their luggage. In the meantime, if any of them leave the camp at night, Ong Chu and I will follow them."

"I want to go too, Saheb." Nyima, Max was heartened to note, had abandoned his earlier truculence and was now seeking authorisation.

"I understand. But Ong Chu and I are old hands at this, we're unlikely to be spotted and anyway, I'll need you to take charge of the camp whilst we're gone." The big Sherpa seemed to accept this with decent resignation. "Speaking of organisation, will you go and check with Captain Malla if he's accompanying the body or staying with us."

Nyima gulped down his tea, got up and left without another word. Max spoke quietly to Ong Chu.

"We'll have to keep any eye on Nyima. I think he's likely to engineer a quarrel."

"Huzoor." Ong Chu nodded agreement. "Incidentally, there are two other Sherpas who are *Lahori.* I think they served together in 2 RGR's Recce company so they'll be up to following our guests without running the risk of being seen."

"Good. Brief them generally but don't be too specific and try not to give the impression that there's a link between Laptsering's death and our interest in the Thais' activities." Ong Chu nodded and carried on eating. Over the lip of his mug, Max caught sight of the Professor heading towards them.

"The *Siam-ko* Saheb is coming over here." He warned Ong Chu softly before inviting the Professor to join them.

"No, thank you, Colonel. I have just eaten. But I would like a few minutes of your time, if it's not inconvenient?"

"Be my guest." He indicated a camp stool.

"I realise that you have had a great deal on your mind with this tragic incident, but I thought you would want to know that I have decided to make the Arun Valley the main focus of our research, until the monsoon breaks."

"I'm grateful for that but it looks as though you'll have to rethink your plans. Laptsering's death will delay us whilst the formalities are commpleted. We were in trouble with time before this happened, as you know, now…well." He shrugged his shoulders.

"I've already given it all the thought necessary, Colonel." The response was stiff. "We shall press on to the Arun without delay." Max got the message loud and clear. He who paid the piper called the tune, but he found both the decision and the manner in which it was communicated offensive in the circumstances. It goaded him into an unguarded reaction.

"I appreciate that this project is important to you, sir. But a young man is dead, a delightful young man who made his living in these mountains, either climbing them or guiding the unwary visitor. Apparently, he fell off a track some 2 feet wide, frankly that's like the Champs Elysèes to a Sherpa. I don't think Captain Malla is satisfied about it and for myself, I'd like a great deal more information." As he spoke he watched the Thai's face register annoyance then concern before it visibly softened. When he next spoke, his tone had changed, now he sought to persuade where a moment or two earlier he'd tried to compel.

"Of course, of course. I've already asked Captain Malla to send a signal to our embassy in Kathmandu. I have made generous provision for the young man's family." He leaned forward, his face earnest, his hands palms uppermost. "But, surely, accidents in these mountains are not that uncommon. There is little or nothing that we can do to help the authorities." He removed his sunglasses and looked Max in the eye.

"Isn't it more important to press on now, to make his death have some significance?"

There was no doubting his earnestness and, Max acknowledged, it was a persuasive approach. However, what swayed him was the knowledge that the only way he'd get to the bottom of the mystery was if the expedition continued and the party stayed together. Nonetheless, it was not without a sense of unease that Max decided to comply with the request. He lingered thoughtfully before inhaling deeply and compressing his lips.

"Alright, Professor." He acceded grudgingly. "I'll speak to Captain Malla and see what can be done, though I cannot promise you a result."

"Thank you very much, Colonel, I knew I could rely on you to arrange it." He stood up and walked away.

Despite the earlier condolences, Max had the impression that his current employer was indifferent to the death of the Sherpa, as though it were just another hurdle to overcome. Moreover, he was uncomfortable with his own ambivalence. He questioned whether his agreement to press ahead if possible was consistent with paying proper respect to the dead man or whether he was motivated by a personal quest to succeed? He threw the dregs of the tea onto the fire and stood up. The hard reality was that he could not afford to allow sentiment to overrule practicality.

Dingla – The Arun Valley

"If you can't get a pig, get a few decent looking chickens, not those scrawny bloody *pahari* birds."

"Huzoor." Ong Chu smiled.

"Oh, and see if you can get some *tongba,* as much as they'll let you have." The smile remained and Max was relieved. It was the first that had appeared on Ong Chu's face since Laptsering's death.

"Take Nyima with you but for God's sake don't let him get at the *tongba*, I want to be sure there'll be some left for the rest of us." The smile broadened into a grin. As Ong Chu walked off to find Nyima, the Professor came over.

"Now that we're here, I'd like to make an early start so that we get to the head of the valley as soon as possible. That way we can complete the work and return ahead of the rains."

"Well, that depends on a lot of factors, sir: provided the monsoon doesn't break early, provided the Sherpas are still willing to break their backs to get you all up there quickly." Max gave a slight inclination of his head towards the Sherpas' tents, his eyebrows raised quizzically. "Provided that the high altitudes don't slow you and your colleagues down."

"You need have no worries on that score, we'll match whatever pace is set."

Max shook his head. "I know you're all physically fit but, believe me, Professor, if the Sherpas want to, they'd leave you all standing." He noted what he thought was a glint of irritation in the Thai's eyes, so he smiled in an effort to ease the slight tension. "Do you propose to work your way up or start at the head and work down?"

"Work down from the head of the valley."

"That's your best plan." Max nodded his agreement. "But I very much doubt we'll complete everything before the rains hit us."

"Do we have to wait for Captain Malla?"

"He did us a big favour by taking over responsibility for tidying up after Laptsering's death. I promised him we'd wait here until he arrived." Max looked at his watch. "He may even be here already, he was going to try and fly from Jiri to Tumlingtar, just south of where we are now." The Professor stared out at the shallow ravine that ran between the two flanks of the hills between which they were encamped. Max looked away to let the man digest what might yet prove a further obstacle to his plans. A slight flurry of movement at the base of a juniper bush no more than 20 metres away caught his eye. He stood up to get a better look and this broke the Professor's thought train. Max spoke in a whisper.

"Look." He pointed towards the bush. "Just to the right of that area of exposed rock, d'you see the bush?"

"Yes." He caught on to Max's whisper and spoke softly. "What is it?"

"I think it's a blood pheasant. Very rare, very beautiful...yes, there it is now, see it?" Both men stood in silence as the game bird stepped delicately into full view, its crimson breast feathers gleaming in the sun. It stopped and then cocked its head to one side, listening before suddenly hopping forward, spreading its wings and taking off, veering away down towards the floor of the ravine.

"Beautiful, simply beautiful." There was a genuine wonder in the Thai's voice as he followed the bird in its flight. It was almost as though he'd dropped his guard of single-minded efficiency for a moment and Max felt a sense of relief to find that he had the capacity to appreciate the rich bounty that the flora and fauna afforded the traveller in the hills. A minute later the moment had gone.

"If Captain Malla hasn't arrived, how long will it be before we can go on d'you think?"

Max lifted his arms skywards. "Who knows Professor? He could hitch a ride in an army helicopter and be here in a couple of hours or he may have got caught up in the cat's cradle of Nepalese bureaucracy and be away for another week or so. Worst-case scenario is that we'd have to abandon the expedition and get out before we got washed away." The Thai considered this for a moment or two before he spoke again.

"According to the time scales we discussed, you say it will take us eight days to reach Honggaon?"

"Everything being equal, yes. But, as I told you, we won't be allowed to go further north than Hatia. To be frank, even that is closer to the Tibetan Border than foreigners are normally allowed to go. Usually, we'd have to stop at Lamobagar Gola, 12 miles from the border. Captain Malla told me he'd turn a blind eye to the extra day's journey. He's being extremely co-operative, I think the least we can do is wait for him."

"Yes, yes, I see that but..." Max found himself increasingly intolerant of his client's habit of blindly ignoring the careful explanations for delays that were completely outside either control or anticipation.

"No Professor!" He ran his fingers through his hair in a gesture of irritation. "I'm afraid you don't see." He paused then spoke with measured deliberation. "We will wait for Captain Malla."

This was the first time that Max had stood his ground rather than reluctantly accommodating his client's demands. He wondered what effect it would have on the Professor. He didn't have to wait long.

"You're right, Colonel. We'll wait." He smiled and this made Max feel a little uncomfortable at the uncompromising attitude he'd adopted.

"I'm sorry if I sounded a bit sharp there, sir, but I do have the overall responsibility and you hired me for my judgment as much as my experience. As a matter of fact we're organising a small party for tonight, I think everyone deserves a break before we set off on this leg of the expedition. I think this will be our last opportunity until we complete the trek."

"I think that's a very good idea. I have felt the strained atmosphere since the death of that unfortunate young Sherpa at Yarsa." Yes, Max thought to himself, you'd need to have the sensitivity of an armadillo not to have noticed it. But to the Professor he volunteered a suggestion.

"Perhaps you could talk to your colleagues, sir, and ask them to make an extra effort to get alongside the Sherpas. I know they'll appreciate it."

"Of course I shall." He nodded vigorously and Max added silently, 'And we'll be getting alongside all of you.'

By 8 o'clock that night the unspoken hostility that had settled uneasily over the members of the expedition appeared to have been dissolved in a sea of food and *tongba*. Max allowed himself to relax a little as the clients and the Sherpas seemed to be mixing without restraint. The *tongba* was particularly good, hot and quietly potent as it settled in the stomach. There were early signs that the Sherpas were warming up to start singing, a couple of the double ended *madal* drums had appeared and some sporadic rhythms were being tried out.

"This *tongba* is very good, Colonel." The Professor sat beside him, sucking the hot liquid up through a bamboo straw. "It's made from millet, isn't it?"

"Fermented millet. This is a particularly good brew." Max smiled at one of the Sherpa's who topped up his 'mug' of *tongba* from a kettle of boiling water.

"I think Ong Chu has a special drink for you. He got hold of some *raksi* in the last village we went through. I don't think you'll have any difficulty keeping warm with some of that inside you."

"What is it?"

"It's a distilled rice liquor, not unlike a raw vodka to look at and taste but about 200% proof."

"I'd like to try a drop." As they spoke, Max's attention was drawn to the sound of someone coughing and spluttering. He looked across to where the Sherpas and the other Thais were laughing and shouting. One of the Thais was making a face as if drawing in air with difficulty. He could see Ong Chu with a water bottle in his hand. The remaining Thais appeared to be enjoying the discomfiture of their comrade.

"I think one of your colleagues has beaten you to it." He waved his *tongba* container over towards the others.

"My friends seem to be accepting the challenge." The Professor observed with a laugh. The Thais were holding their mugs towards Ong Chu who was pouring out generous libations of the colourless liquid from the water bottle. Max shouted across to Ong Chu.

"How about some for us?"

"Huzoor!" Ong Chu grinned and poured a generous measure into the Professor's proffered mug, a distinctly smaller amount into Max's. His expression became a little more serious.

"It must be drunk slowly, Professor Saheb, it can burn your throat."

"That's seriously good advice." Max added. The Professor gingerly tipped the mug and sipped. His expression changed as the neat alcohol caught his breath and he struggled to conceal its effects.

"It's…most interesting." The words were uttered little above a whisper but Max gave him full marks for having retained any power of speech whatsoever. He touched Ong Chu's sleeve and pointed behind him. "I think the serious drinkers want some more." Ong Chu took a quick look towards the group of Thais and Sherpas some of whom were raising their mugs in a clear signal that he should return with the bottle. Max tapped him on the elbow.

"Are we going to have some dancing?"

"Will a *maruni* do?" Ong Chu grinned and walked back towards the others.

"What's a *maruni*?" The Professor had recovered his breath and his curiosity.

"Amongst the hill people it's still considered bad form for a girl to dance in public, there's an inevitable connection drawn between dancing girls and whores." As he spoke, the high timbre notes of the *madal* began to ring out, a little exploratory at first and then strengthening into a confident pattern of drum phrases, *tung-ta-tat-taa, tung-ta-tat-taa*. Deepraj had it slung around his neck, the fingers of both hands tapping out the rhythms at opposite ends of the cylinder.

"Traditionally, one or more of the good-looking young men gets dragooned into dressing up in women's clothes and dancing the girl's role. Some of them remind you of what their mother-in-law looks like but others really look the part." His mind turned back to the *naatch* parties in the battalion when he had been a very young officer and the genuine anxiety he had harboured about the patent bisexuality inherent in these dances. The epiglottal trill that heralded the arrival of one of the least feminine looking Sherpas dressed as a traditional Sherpini girl was followed by a roar of approving laughter and suggestive jokes as the *maruni* went through a coquettish dance sequence. Max chuckled as he clapped and remarked to the Professor. "He may be ugly but he's a damn good dancer."

It wasn't long before the Sherpas had beguiled one of the Thais to partner the '*Sherpini*' to added roars of laughter from the onlookers, fuelled by the expressions of discomfiture on the Thai's face. Soon everyone had joined in the dancing, Max felt the warmth of the *tongba* spread through him and he was soon adding his voice to that of Deepraj and the Sherpas in the same old hill songs that Gurkhas had been singing for generations. He stepped his way carefully through the whirling figures, the men with their arms stretched out at their sides like great windmill sails and the 'girls' with their arms reaching forward in the familiar beckoning of the strumpet. He smiled with a genuine sense of pleasure when he noticed that the Professor had joined in and was emulating the dancers with studied care.

Max stepped out of the swaying figures and picked up his *tongba* container. Ong Chu joined him and they both looked on with amusement as one of the Sherpas gave a frenetic exhibition of solo dancing, what Max privately labelled as a fornication quadrille. Every move of the hands and body carried an unequivocal sexual nuance. Without taking his eyes off the dancer, he asked quietly.

"How are things?"

"OK, Saheb." Max stole a quick sideways glance at the Sherpa's face and noted that he was still happily engrossed in the entertainment. His enquiry, he was reassured to note, had not resurrected the silent brooding of the last few days. He decided that this was as good a time as any to test reactions.

"The Professor wants to get up into the head of the valley quickly. What shall we do?"

"I think we're going to risk getting very wet, even if we start now. I don't want to be up there when the heavy stuff starts to loosen the rocks and the landslides begin."

"Right." It was what Max had wanted to hear. Now he knew what to do. "We'll give Captain Malla one more day, then if he isn't here, we'll leave a couple of Sherpas behind and take the main party up the valley."

"OK, Saheb." They stood watching as the combined effects of the *tongba* and *raksi* worked their alcoholic magic on Sherpa and Thai alike, the effects indistinguishable.

"I'm off to bed." Max announced quietly.

"Good night, Saheb." Max half turned to walk away when Ong Chu's hand caught his sleeve. "Saheb?"

"Yes?"

"We're still going to watch the Baggage Master, aren't we?" *Raksi* or no *raksi* there was a chilling sobriety in this half-question, half-announcement. Whether or not it was the *tongba* speaking, the words simply came to Max's lips unbidden.

"Bet your life on it."

Hatia – North of the Arun Valley

"*Chha* Saheb." Having delivered his message, the Sherpa waited for fresh instructions. Max sent him down the track to join the main party. Standing next to Max, the Professor pressed him for the information the Sherpa had brought from the village.

"Does he say that the police post is manned?"

"Yes." This was what Max had hoped to avoid. A little luck at this juncture would not have gone amiss.

"We can't get round the fact that once in the village we'll have to produce our permits to the police. Once they see them, they'll insist on detaining us there until soldiers or more police can escort us back within the area that we're supposed to be in." The Professor promptly voiced the thought that Max had carefully pushed to the back of his mind.

"Can we skirt around the village without coming to their attention?" His words formed spurts of steam in the fast freezing air. Max rolled back his sleeve and checked his watch.

"You don't give up trying, do you, sir?" He had to smile as he said it, the man had an endearingly irritating determination and a correlative disregard for the consequences.

"Well, can we, Colonel?" He persisted.

"We'll have to wait until dark." He looked up towards the contrasting panels of a sky fired by the setting sun and the impenetrably dark shadows on the reverse slopes of the mountains. "In another 45 minutes or so. In the meantime, I'll send two of the Sherpas to scout out a route for us."

"Excellent." The Thai clapped his mitts together in satisfaction. "You have a natural aptitude for overcoming obstacles, I knew it." Max felt that he was only the incidental benefactor of the Professor's shrewd judgment.

"When we get back, after this is all over, I don't think I'll be given another opportunity for hurdle hopping in Nepal." His words went unnoticed as the Professor walked away from him.

The scouts were despatched and the rest of the party, which had been travelling as one unit since they'd left Lamobagar, found some shelter from the icily penetrating wind behind some rocks. Max called out to Ong Chu.

"Brew up!"

He could feel the sweat on his skin beginning to chill as the wind found its way through the loose joins between his clothes. He told Deepraj to get him a sweater out of his rucksack and he advised the clients to do likewise. Even after he shrugged himself into his sweater and got the padded jacket back on, his skin seemed to solidify.

The darkness welled up from the floor of the valley to their left and clung to the sides of the mountains. Ong Chu worked his way around all the Sherpas, securing their loads and strapping down any loose gear so that it would not jangle and attract unwelcome attention. The ex-army Sherpas helped out and those without military experience grinned at each other, caught up in the lure of the illicit. Max found himself somewhat ambivalent; he shared in their good humoured attitude towards what had become a totally illegal expedition but he worried about their prospects of getting through undetected. He walked amongst them, double checking their pack straps and giving off a reassurance he didn't truly share.

"Don't you little buggers start making any noise once we get underway or I'll cut your bonuses!" They responded with quiet good humour, draining their mugs of hot tea.

They put in nearly three hours of hard, silent trekking between the police post at Hatia and their night stop. During the last hour a freezing mist had descended and enveloped them in its eerie, silent, texturelesss shroud. Now the flames of the cooking fires melted holes in the mist. A darker shade of grey materialised into a shape in the vapour. It wasn't until the scarf swathed face was inches from his own that Max identified Ong Chu.

"If he chooses tonight to go, we'd better follow him together, Saheb."

"If." Max emphasised. "I hope like hell that he doesn't. I'm cold enough as it is without having to crawl over the side of this mountain." Ong Chu gave a sympathetic grunt.

"Who's watching them now?" Max enquired.

"Deepraj. Nyima's getting your food."

It was during the bustle of drinking and serving more helpings of hot consommé that Deepraj came up quietly to where Max and Ong Chu were sitting.

"Saheb, one of the clients has just left camp carrying something."

"The Baggage Master?"

"No, Saheb, one of the others."

"You keep watching the Baggage Master but don't follow him if he leaves camp." Max and Ong Chu rose and followed Deepraj until they reached a narrow track where Max told Deepraj to go back.

The mist had lifted a little but they could barely see more than a couple of yards in front of them. They walked in silence in Indian file, straining their eyes and ears for sight or sound of anything ahead. The mist not only shut down most visibility, it wrapped their quarry in silence.

Ong Chu reached behind him and put his hand on Max's forearm, lightly but firmly indicating that he should stop. As they did so and the sounds of their clothing as it brushed against itself also stopped, Max caught the merest alien noise, a rhythmic squeaking. Ong Chu leaned in close to Max's head and whispered into his ear.

"It's the leather handle on the case." Max nodded silent acknowledgement. They resumed their tracking, stepping with even greater caution, trying to catch the tell-tale sounds ahead whilst keeping their own movements to a minimum so as not to confuse their ears.

The squeaking became more distinct as they gained on him. The mist had begun to thin more rapidly and suddenly they were almost on top of him. Max had to steel himself so as not to bump into Ong Chu. Both of them were startled that they'd got so close without the man sensing that they were right behind him. They froze lest the slightest sound alert him to their immediate presence. The Thai stopped and Max's heart pounded so loudly he thought it must be audible at this distance. However, the man stepped off the track to the right. Max felt the faintest breath of an icy wind on the exposed part of his face. If they didn't get into some sort of cover quickly the mist was liable to lift suddenly, exposing them where they stood. Again, it was Ong Chu who spotted a small *chorten* of piled stones and pointed to it silently. It was about 15 feet away from them on the flank side of the track. Max guessed that there might be a shallow rain water depression running in the angle of the hillside to the path. The problem was that if the man turned round now, he was bound to see them. They inched their way towards the makeshift cover, scarcely breathing. Once on the *chorten's* blind side, they eased themselves down into a squatting position. Even so, Max realised that at least one of his shoulders protruded beyond the sloping edge of the piled stones.

Relying on the sheer unlikelihood of anyone being close by, he peered slowly around the edge of the *chorten* until he could see the Thai. The man obviously suspected nothing because he made no effort to conceal his actions. Max could see that the briefcase opened out into two separate components with electric cables linking the two halves. The Thai was now extending a horizontal telescopic aerial with a mini directional dish wired to one end. Max withdrew his head a little and tapped Ong Chu's shoulder to catch his attention. He made a questioning expression with his eyes. Ong Chu cupped his hands around Max's ear and whispered.

"Satellite communication transceiver."

The mist had now lifted to such an extent that only the colour of the night separated them. They watched as the Thai busied himself with the aerial and the transceiver. They could even see the illuminated LCD screen. Max was finding his position acutely uncomfortable. Chosen in haste, he now had time to regret it, especially as there was no indication of how long all this was going to take.

The Thai consulted his watch and then appeared to be depressing buttons on the equipment. Suddenly they heard sounds as if some weird musical instrument was playing a snatch of a Maurice Jarre cyberscore. It lasted for no more than 10 seconds. This was followed by another snatch of the same type of music but this time for only five seconds and at a slightly lower pitch than the first sequence. Seconds later there appeared to be a repeat of the first sequence. The LCD screen went blank and the Thai started to pack up his equipment.

It was time, Max decided, to find out what the hell was going on. He turned and looked at Ong Chu. The movement was enough to cause the Sherpa to look back and Max gave a quick twitch of his head in the direction of the Thai then stood up. His voice cut strangely through the night air, booming unnaturally loud in his ears.

"Leave that equipment where it is!"

The Thai was startled and sprang away from the transciever as he rose from his squatting position. But this was a momentary loss of control and he recovered into what Max recognised as a martial arts defensive posture as he watched them approach him. Max spoke to Ong Chu in English.

"Collect up that stuff." Ong Chu gave a soft assent and advanced towards the equipment which lay just to the left of where the Thai stood.

"Do not touch! Do not touch!" It was a peremptory order and the Thai's voice conveyed no sense of fear. Ong Chu paused for a second then continued forward. The Thai took one step towards him, changing his stance slightly. Max didn't like the look on the man's face and barked out a sharp command.

"Stand back! Do as I say!"

Ong Chu reached the transceiver case and started to bend down when the Thai appeared to explode into action, striking Ong Chu on his jaw with a forearm smash. Max heard the sound of the bone cracking as Ong Chu gasped, staggered a few steps then fell to his knees, his hands reaching for his face. The totally unexpected brutality of it shocked Max into an instinctive reaction.

"You bastard!" He cast around him for a weapon to level the odds against the expertise of his opponent who now stood in a threatening posture facing him, his arms tucked loosely against his side but reaching forward. The base of the telescopic aerial was close to his foot. Keeping his eyes fixed on the Thai he bent his knees at the same time as his fingers reached out until they closed around the cold thin metal above the spiked base. Not knowing how much force he would need, he put his entire body weight into yanking it out of the ground and in one continuous movement he whipped it up and down in a violent slash that evaded the Thai's defensive arm movement and opened a long thin gash across his face running down from beside his right eye across his cheek and down to his chin.

"Stop! Put that down, Colonel!" The voice cut into Max's consciousness and seconds later he identified it as that of the Baggage Master. He couldn't see the man but the sound came from his left rear. Ong Chu made a groaning noise and his eyes flicked a warning. Rage had made Max impervious to anything but the immediate focus of his attention. He took another whipping crack at the Thai as the blood seeped down the open side of his face but though he winced as the aerial cable bit into his forearm, he managed to ward it away from his head.

"Next time, I shoot you!" The Baggage Master's shape loomed into Max's peripheral vision and he registered that the man was holding some sort of firearm, pointing the end of the barrel directly at him. At this distance, he could hardly miss and his aim was rock steady. Max recognised both the tone and the stance of a professional soldier. He turned towards the advancing figure, his anger barely contained.

"This time you'll have to push two of us down the mountain, won't you? You murdering shit!" He was breathing more heavily now as the tempo of the situation upped another notch or two. "That'll take more explaining than you can muster, shithead!" The Thai stared at him with a remarkable impassivity before he spoke, his words slow and to Max's ears infuriatingly emotionless.

"We must all return to the camp…now." He shrugged his shoulders dismissively. "But…people fall off these mountains sometimes."

There was something Kafkaesque about the whole situation. Max could not help but contrast the controlled coolness of the Thai, a race legendary for its explosive temperament and his own almost uncontrolled fury, an ex-army officer with years of experience of combat. In the same moment that he made the comparison he knew that he had to reverse the roles if he was to recapture the initiative. Keeping a wary eye on the wounded Thai who was busy staunching the flow of blood down his cheek, he knelt down beside Ong Chu who held his jaw in both his hands. Even in the darkness Max could see that his face had taken on a greyish pallor.

"Don't try to talk, I think your jaw's broken. I'm going to get you to your feet and fix a temporary sort of splintage until we can get you to a doctor."

"Speak in English, Colonel." The command came from almost beside him.

"I'll do what I have to do just as I choose to do it." He didn't even bother to look at the Thai as he spoke. "We have two men here who both need medical attention. We get them back to camp first." He unzipped his down jacket and shrugged out of it before peeling off his sweater. He began to take his shirt off when he felt the muzzle of the Thai's gun against the back of his neck.

"You do what I tell you." Moved by a curious sense of disorientation, Max ignored both the gun and the words and continued removing his shirt.

"Do what you like, fellah, but you might try to use your brain more and that substitute for your cock less. Nobody's going anywhere or doing anything until we get these casualties back to camp." He folded his shirt into a makeshift sling and as he did so, he felt the muzzle lift off his neck. Good. The quiet authority he had put into his words appeared to have registered. As he tied the shirt around Ong Chu's head, gently securing the jaw to the skull, he could see the Baggage Master attending to his compatriot's face. He noted with some satisfaction that they were talking to each other in Thai. Christians two, Lions one. He lifted Ong Chu gently to his feet.

"Let's get you back to camp, slowly does it."

"Lead on, Colonel. I'm right behind you." So, Max thought, he's trying to regain the initiative which means he knows he'd lost it. They set off with Ong Chu leaning heavily against Max's shoulder. After a few yards he seemed to gather his strength and bore his own weight. The track began to narrow and Max eased past the Sherpa.

"I'll lead, you just watch out for yourself." With frequent looks back over his shoulder to ensure that Ong Chu was right behind him, he picked a careful path along the track. This time their footfalls were audible, Ong Chu's more so as he tended to shuffle a little. From time to time, a hissing noise escaped from his lips and Max guessed that he must be in considerable pain.

Checking back, Max could see the Baggage Master following behind Ong Chu, his rifle held at the port position. He wondered what the Thai thought they could do in their current predicament that warranted keeping the rifle ready for use.

The moon came up as they slowly retraced their steps back to the camp site but the clouds repeatedly obscured the thin, cold light. Max's mind juggled with the various permutations of their situation. So long as the Thais had weapons – and he must now assume that there were probably others – they held the whip hand. But up here in the Himalayas they were far from being on their home territory and not only were they dependent upon the Sherpas to guide them through the mountains and porter their equipment but they were now in a prohibited area, liable to be arrested by armed police or Nepal Army patrols. At least, he comforted himself, he wouldn't have to do much explaining as to why he was outside the area of their trekking permits.

"Stop here." The command cut through the night and his thoughts. There was an exchange between the two Thais and then the radio operator came up and brushed past them, disappearing down the track.

"Where's he going?" Max asked shortly.

"Quiet please, Colonel. There will be no talking from now." It was difficult to tell how close to the camp they were, especially because their rate of progress had been much slower on the return leg than on the outward journey. But Max reasoned that if the Thai was afraid that their voices would forewarn of their arrival, a gunshot would be even more unequivocal. He gambled on it.

"I shall talk as much and as loudly as I damn well want to. If you want to shoot, go ahead, that will sound the alarm for sure."

The Thai walked towards him until he stood between Max and Ong Chu.

"That is correct, Colonel." Max congratulated himself quietly. Round two to Devlin. The thought had barely enjoyed a second of satisfaction before he collapsed onto the track, momentarily paralysed by the pain from his right kidney. His mouth worked as silently as a goldfish as his lungs sought for the air that refused to enter. His mind, working with detached precision, told him that the Thai had used the metal stock of his rifle in a vicious lateral strike. The silent isolation of the pain was broken as he threw up and perspiration stood out on his face. His body gave an involuntary shudder and he spat to clear his mouth. Through the miasma of pain and nausea, the Thai's disembodied voice clung to his brain like refractory chewing gum.

"We shall continue in silence."

Getting back to his feet proved more difficult than he had anticipated. He felt an arm under his own and turned to see Ong Chu bending over him. He'd taken his hands away from supporting his already swollen face and the effort of helping Max was obviously increasing the pain so that his eyes screwed up and tears formed at the corners. Max made the extra effort and forced a smile.

"Thanks, old friend, look after yourself. I'm OK." The words were uttered with difficulty. To distract himself, he checked the head sling, tightening it a little to provide sufficient support and ease the pain.

Walking sent pains shooting up his spine and down his right leg but he was determined to get Ong Chu back to camp now. His mind resumed its unsuccessful attempts to make sense out of the situation. For the life of him, he could not see what the Thai thought he could achieve once they were back in the camp where the Sherpas far outnumbered them. He presumed that the radio operator had gone on ahead to prepare some sort of reception but it was beyond him to imagine just what that would be.

A dull thud from behind him was followed by a terrible scream of human pain that didn't stop but lowered into a series of slightly lower pitched screams. His own trauma had slowed Max's reactions and by the time he turned his head sufficiently to look back towards the sounds, the screaming was accompanied by a bubbling sibilance that emerged from the Baggage Master's wide open lips. Max's eyes took in the salient features even as his mind linked them all together.

The man's right arm had been completely severed from his shoulder but appeared to be held inside the sleeve of his padded jacket which was still held on by an inch or two of fabric at where the armpit level would have been had there been an armpit. His head rolled slowly back on his neck and the Thai collapsed in slow motion; as he did so, Max saw Nyima standing behind the crumpling figure, his *kukri* raised high above and outside his right shoulder. By the time that Max's mind had collected itself sufficiently to send a signal to his voice, his hoarse shout was too late.

"No! Nyima, no!" The sharp steel of the heavy blade cut deep into the cervical vertebrae causing a curiously dead sound which Max's mind converted into a ringing reverberation. The force of the blow toppled the dead man's body forward.

The only noise he could hear was the stertorous sound of canvas being dragged over a rough surface. It took a little while for him to recognise that it was his own breathing. A tiny corner of his mind, high up above the jumble of conflicting emotions and broken trains of thought, formulated a perceptive commentary which Max converted into words.

"What a terrible fucking mess."

The Baggage Master's bloodied corpse was left out of immediate view beside the track. Max supported Ong Chu back into the camp whilst Nyima gave them an account of what had brought him onto the scene.

"I saw him slip out of his tent after you, though I didn't identify what he was carrying until he was part way down the track. I think he had the extending stock folded up until then. I was watching when he attacked Ong Chu but there was nothing I could do then because he had that HK-53 and I was too far away to get close enough to creep up on him. When he said that bit about people falling off mountains, I knew he'd killed Laptsering." He nodded to himself. There was a pause before he added.

"So, I killed him."

There it was then, Max thought. To the Sherpa it was a simple human equation. The words were devoid of emotion, as if all he'd done was squashed an errant mosquito. Max's mind was a mad firework display of thoughts racing off into the void and disappearing, one hard on the trail of another, each burst of light leaving a reinforced darkness. He could not bring himself to criticise Nyima; he'd done what Max had felt like doing and now it troubled him that he could even think of sitting in judgment on the morality of it. As against that, he now had a dead foreign member of his expedition and the circumstances of that death would call for massive explanations, even if they hadn't been in a prohibited area. He was still struggling to discern a way through this maze of seemingly unanswerable complications when figures loomed up out of the darkness.

"Are you alright, Saheb?" He breathed a lot easier when he recognised Deepraj accompanied by several Sherpas.

I'm OK. But Ong Chu needs a doctor." He clapped the Gurkha on the shoulder. "It's good to see you...but what's happening in camp?"

"The *Siam-ko* Saheb has been shouting at the other clients. He asked me to try and find you." He looked at Ong Chu's bandaged face as he spoke. "What's happened, Saheb?"

"I'll explain everything to you later. Let's get back to camp first then you can organise a stretcher party and bring them back along this track." Max interrupted himself. "No. On second thoughts..." He turned to Nyima. "You take the stretcher party back and pick up the Baggage Master."

"Huzoor." The big Sherpa was unnaturally quiet. Max decided that he was probably experiencing delayed shock. The best antidote would be activity but he'd have to get a mug of hot sweet tea with a shot of rum in it into him first. He turned his attention to Ong Chu. Using one of the Maglights the Sherpas had brought with them, he carried out a cursory examination of the damaged jaw. The swelling was already quite pronounced. Feeling gently along the jaw line with his finger tips he confirmed what he'd suspected: the jaw was dislocated and was probably fractured on the right maxilla. Rather than spell out the extent of the damage to a man who was already in enormous pain, especially because he knew that he hadn't the skill to relocate the jaw and thereby relieve him of much of it, he sought refuge in words of comfort.

"We'll get you fixed up, old friend." He smiled encouragingly while wondering whether he was managing to conceal the lack of confidence he felt.

"Let's go." He led off back down the track.

It took little time to reach the camp. Max gave Ong Chu a shot of pain killing morphine and bound his jaw in a more comfortable crepe bandage. Having settled him as best he could he confronted the Professor.

"I'm afraid that your colleague, Mr. Rangsimaporn, is dead. I've sent out a party to recover his body." As he spoke, he watched the Professor's face; the eyes definitely registered when he said the man was dead but it was impossible to say whether they expressed anything other than a measure of surprise.

"How did he die?"

"By the look of him, I'd say he was killed by someone wielding a kukri. I also found this..." Max pulled the HK-53 out of the bag he had stored it in. "...next to his body. Even in Nepal a man may defend himself with a knife against another with a Heckler & Koch number 53 model sub-machine gun. There seems to be a very obvious explanation." The Professor stared at him, his face still a mask of his feelings. Max ploughed on.

"One of your research assistants," he said the words with heavy sarcasm, "as you doubtless know by now, had his cheek laid open by me. This, after he smashed *Sardar* Ong Chu's jaw with a karate chop. It goes without saying that I can't understand what an academic expedition into Buddhist art of all things requires a team of what I judge to be professionally trained soldiers all presumably armed with similar state-of-the-art firearms and a high-tech satellite transceiver which has to be operated clandestinely." He kept his voice steady though the process of outlining the catalogue of contradictions fuelled his anger. "You've made a fool of me and I hold you responsible for both deaths. Now I want an explanation and," he shook the rifle in the Professor's face, "I don't want any more hogwash, just the unvarnished truth."

The Professor stood silently but now he averted his eyes from Max's face. A bird suddenly twittered inappropriately and the Professor appeared to have come to a decision. His lips were firmly compressed as he looked Max straight in the eye.

"Colonel, I think I made a serious error by not confiding in you." He paused, speaking slowly as though choosing his words with care. "I cannot express my present feelings adequately but I am desolated to think that my mistake has caused all this loss of life, this...madness." He held his hands a little apart, as though holding an invisible box, it was an eloquent gesture of despair. "Perhaps, as I explain, you will understand why I did what I did and then you may find it easier to," he paused, fishing for the words with his hand, trying to turn them out of the air, "understand, if not to forgive." He looked down at the ground and when he looked up again, Max saw that he had donned the old authoritative coat but his words retained their note of apology.

"I have some medical training, may I examine Ong Chu?" Anxious though he was to hear the explanation, he was doubly concerned for the Sherpa. He nodded and led the way to the Sherpa's tent. There was barely sufficient room for all four men inside. The air reeked of rum as Deepraj tried to trickle the spirit into Ong Chu's barely open mouth. His face was drawn with lines of pain and the sweat beads stood out, defying the bitterly cold night air. Ong Chu's eyes, already responding to the morphine, rolled towards Max in a silent question.

"The Professor wants to examine your jaw, he may be able to help." The look of distrust persisted. "It's OK, truly."

The inconsequential thought occurred to Max that he hadn't really noticed how small and slender the man's hands were. The Professor gently felt along the jaw line and up into the maxilla on each side. It reminded Max of a motor mechanic he'd once seen, both men's hands moved over their respective charges with the deft assurance of one who had designed and engineered them. The Professor spoke whilst looking at Ong Chu.

"The jaw is dislocated, probably fractured on the right side too. Most of the pain is from the dislocation." His hands remained on Ong Chu's face but he turned his head to speak to Max.

"I would like to put it back, if you'll permit."

Max looked at Ong Chu. The decision was the Sherpa's, not his. But he knew that he was in no condition to think clearly for himself. He indicated the Professor with his head. "I think he knows what he's doing, I'd let him go ahead if I were you." The injured man's eyes closed and Max wondered whether the morphine had put him to sleep. Seconds later his eyes opened and he gave an almost imperceptible forward movement of his head.

"Alright. Go ahead. He's had a shot of morphine so he'll cope with any additional pain." The Professor re-arranged the makeshift pillow whilst he talked softly to Ong Chu, telling him what he was doing. Max watched his fingers as they felt their way over Ong Chu's face then, with a minimum of movement, the jaw was suddenly relocated.

"The soft tissue damage will still cause a dull pain for a while but the worst of it should be over now. I think the fracture may only be a hairline job but it's a case for x-ray examination and a professional maxillo-facial surgeon. He'll have to be evacuated." Max's appreciation for the skilful remedial attention was counteracted by the didactic manner in which he spoke of the evacuation. The humility of their earlier exchange had already evaporated and it seemed as though the man had conveniently forgotten that he was the author of Ong Chu's condition. He looked at Ong Chu, saw that his eyes had closed and that he was breathing steadily. He told Deepraj to keep an eye on the Sherpa and motioned to the Professor for them to leave the tent. Once outside, he stood up.

"May I remind you that we are presently in a prohibited area, that we've deliberately evaded the police at Hatia, our permits don't allow us to be here, our Nepalese liaison officer will be searching for us so the balloon has probably gone up already. You talk of evacuation as though all we have to do is whistle up a helicopter just like flagging down a taxi!" He was aware that his voice was rising and he took a grip on himself.

"Ong Chu is my responsibility, not just as my *Sardar* but as an old friend and brother-in-arms. You and your colleagues are also my responsibility, including that dead psychopath out on the track…and I still haven't heard what all this is about but I have a bad feeling that I'm not going to like it, whatever it is." The Thai actually seemed to shrink as Max berated him.

"I'm very sorry, Colonel."

"It's a bit late for apologies." Max indicated the fire and as they walked towards it he asked one of the Sherpas to bring them some coffee. He'd already decided to send Ong Chu down to the nearest landing strip and fly him out to Kathmandu. If – and it was a very big if – they were allowed to continue with the project, he would be desperately short of key personnel at this juncture but he needed to put Ong Chu in the care of someone capable of forcing his way onto the first available flight. That meant Nyima. Added to which, it would put physical distance between the big Sherpa and the dead Thai. The whole job had suddenly become a monster salvage operation, salvage the situation, salvage the expedition and not least to salvage his own reputation through it all. For the first time since the Thai had been killed, he became aware of the throbbing in his side. He looked around for someone to get some rum put into his coffee but the area suddenly looked deserted. Christ, he thought, the Sherpas could be putting their heads together and calling a halt of their own volition. With Ong Chu effectively out of the picture and Nyima having compromised his own position, there was no appointed leader. In the extraordinary position they found themselves in it was not impossible that one of the young hot-heads might start getting bloody-minded. The Professor broke into his thoughts.

"Colonel, I..."

"Just hang on a moment will you, sir." Max called out for Nyima. He couldn't afford a power vacuum. A few moments later the big Sherpa's figure appeared, his silhouette outlined against the yellow light of the Coleman lamps, momentarily lost in the shadows until he entered the warmer halo of light around the fire.

"Take over as *Sardar* for the time being and think about your suggestions for a deputy."

"Huzoor."

"Tell all our Sherpas that I'm discussing the situation with the *Siam-ko* Saheb now and I'll come over and tell them everything as soon as I've finished. Remind them that we are still a team and that the first rule of the mountains is that we keep working as a team. They're all my responsibility and it's my job to decide how we deal with the problem." He emphasised these last words lest there be any doubt in anyone's mind who was in command. "I'll also work out how we keep you out of trouble with the authorities." He added for the Sherpa's own peace of mind.

"Huzoor." Nyima managed a trace of a smile but his previous impassivity had given way to obvious anxiety. All the Sherpas were Nepalese and as such needed no permits to roam wheresoever they wished across the Himalayas. Nyima, on the other hand, had killed a man, a foreign visitor, and Max was in the most unenviable position of all, a foreigner without a permit, responsible for leading a party of unauthorised foreigners into a prohibited region and accounting for the death of one of his Sherpa employees and a foreign client. The alternatives were equally unattractive. Whoever it was that had coined the phrase 'between a rock and hard place' could never have imagined a dilemma more apt than that which he now faced. Stop, go on or turn back, each was as untenable as the last. He sank down onto a camp chair and was reminded of the damage to his kidney.

"I detect a hint of trouble from the Sherpas, Professor, but they'll most probably stay in line for the time being."

"I'm afraid this is all my fault. I ought to have confided in you earlier and taken my chances." Whatever confidences he had not been entrusted with, Max felt that this was the understatement of the year.

"What you mean, is that you lied to me and now you regret that you underestimated the people you were dealing with."

"No...well, yes." Even now, Max thought, he's being selective with the truth.

"But if you'll hear me out, you will see that I would have had to reveal my real purpose eventually."

"Eventually." Max invested the word with a mixture of frustration and contempt.

"I told you that my interest lay in the treasures of Buddhist art. This was a deliberate half-truth." He paused and looked directly into Max's eyes before turning to face the fire.

"You will recall that when the 14th Dalai Lama fled from Tibet in 1959, there had been little time in which to prepare. His Holiness was both spiritual and temporal leader of Tibet and so it was essential for all the principal leaders to abandon the country so as to form a government-in-exile around him. It was equally essential to find a place from where the resistance of the Tibetan people could be organised and where the authorities in Beijing could neither control His Holiness nor make it look as though he was under their influence. The Lhasa cabinet decided to remove the Dalai Lama's Treasury. They knew that it would be plundered by the Chinese and would certainly not be used for the benefit of the Tibetan people. Equally, they were realistic enough to appreciate that it would take very considerable funds to educate world opinion and to compel the Chinese to renounce their illegitimate claim to Tibet as an integral part of the PRC." There was an intensity about the way in which he spoke which made Max reappraise him.

"However, the physical safety of His Holiness dictated that the whole operation be carried out virtually as soon as the decision had been taken." He paused and turned his face towards Max with a wry smile. "Making every allowance for their lack of administrative skills and their cultural fatalism, they were at least two centuries behind the times." His face changed, a frown creasing the gap between his eyebrows.

"And there were traitors to the cause, even then." He turned to face the fire again.

"Speed and expediency militated against carrying the gold and jewels of the Treasury, so only a part was taken at that time. The remainder, which, incidentally, was by far the greater part, was left behind in the care of trusted abbots in the monasteries between Lhasa and the Indian-Nepal border. The Chinese got wind of this after the flight of His Holiness, which is why so many monasteries were reduced to rubble."

"Don't tell me." Max interposed, a note of incredulity in his voice. "You're here to collect the balance?" The Thai nodded.

"Yes, I am charged with the responsibility of collecting the balance, as you put it."

"Well, not with my help you're not, Professor or whatever you are. I'm in enough trouble with the Nepalese government as it is. I'm certainly not risking a lifetime in a Chinese prison." The extraordinary account he had been given was little short of flabbergasting and he was furious at the realisation that he'd been conned into compromising himself irretrievably, short of a miracle.

"This is where we turn back and you take the blame for everything, especially the two deaths." What nettled him was that the man could have believed he was gullible enough simply to fall in with his plans. Even now, he sat there waiting for Max to exhaust his anger on cloth ears.

"Our plan does not involve entering Tibet, we rendezvous with the party bringing the Treasury at a location on the Nepal side of the border, about one day's march from here. The information that we received over the satcom was that our Tibetan friends will make the rendezvous by nightfall tomorrow."

"So your clandestine communications have all been about making this meet?"

"Exactly."

The wind changed direction and blew acrid smoke into Max's eyes, making them smart. As he rubbed them, he thought how appropriate it was, smoke blown into his eyes, secret messages and some sort of treasure trove. It was the stuff of adventure writers, fictional creations of smoke, mirrors and deceptions except that he had been tricked into becoming a part of something that would demonstrate yet again that the innocent bystander is the customary sacrifice in all such enterprises. His anger had not abated.

"But why all the violence?" He didn't wait for an answer. "It was one of your men who killed young Laptsering, wasn't it?" It wasn't a question but an assertion seeking confirmation. The Professor nodded defensively.

"I'm profoundly sorry about that, as I am about the injury to Ong Chu."

"Your apologies, profound or not, won't bring him back nor will they mend Ong Chu's jaw." He wiped the smoke tears away with his sleeve. "Research assistants!" He spat the words out with loaded sarcasm. "Where'd you get them from, some Thai drug lord's private army?"

"With your knowledge and experience, Colonel, you know that a task of this nature requires men with special skills. Those who planned the enterprise had to anticipate trouble but I confess that I never for a second thought they would be used against people on our own side."

"Perhaps that's because you didn't tell us or them that we were all on the same side." Max cut in. The Professor met Max's anger with a soft apologetic tone, conveying the impression that he was distancing himself from all the distasteful events. He was no longer telling his story to the fire but looking directly into Max's eyes.

"I know, I know." He admitted quietly. "As you more or less guessed, my men are Thai Marines. They were on a special forces training course at Fort Lauderdale when they were approached and each one volunteered to join the expedition. Unhappily, like so many of their kind, they react first and think second. In truth, the blame is entirely mine. I failed to brief them adequately and I compounded this mistake by failing to tell you the true purpose of the operation." Whilst speaking, he had put his right hand into a pocket of his jacket and produced a well worn string bracelet of little *mane* stones which he was manipulating through his fingers, turning the bracelet like a flexible wheel. Max noted a slight change in his voice, as though it had acquired a genuine dimension of sincerity over and above the more formal note of apology.

"The simple truth is that I could not be sure that you would agree to mount the operation if you knew its real purpose. I was under enormous constraints of time and I badly needed your help. I admit that I deceived you but I had always intended to reveal the truth once you were committed."

"With your predilection for accuracy, I think 'compromised' would be more appropriate, don't you?" Max didn't even try to hide the bitterness now. He could see no possible way of squaring his position with the Nepal Government, this would be the ultimate kiss-off. The only remaining question was whether he could salvage a profitable outcome out of the shambles. If the story about the Thai marines and Fort Lauderdale was true, it probably meant that there was an American finger in the pie, most probably CIA. That spelled money. Whether you called it compromised or committed it amounted to much the same thing. Right at this moment in time, he had the Professor over a circumstantial barrel. What had been sauce for the goose could equally serve for the gander.

"If, and I emphasise that word *if*, I go on from here, I will never have a future in Nepal. My utility to you was always premised on my somewhat unique qualifications but they will now become redundant. I would need a redundancy package to compensate for my loss."

The change in the Professor's attitude was as fundamental as it was sudden.

"You were on the verge of bankruptcy when we approached you. You had no future in Nepal and little demand for your unique qualifications," he said the words slowly to strip them of value, "anywhere else. You grabbed at our offer because you had no choice."

The words and the tone in which they were delivered were calculated to rob Max of his self-respect and he felt that they had almost done so, almost but not quite. The Thai had forgotten that both of them were on opposing horns of the same dilemma: either they both got off together or they would both be skewered. The words of his company commander at Sandhurst all those years ago came back to him: "Always profit from your mistakes."

"Double the total contract price and add on a US$250,000 success fee," he paused and smiled, "or we turn back in the morning and I hand you over to the Nepalese authorities." The Professor's face changed yet again, losing its hard edge and slipping into a satisfied smile.

"Agreed."

Max had a niggling feeling that he'd won the battle and lost the war.

Kumbakarna Himal

87°18' East 27°48' North

Gojo retracted the telescopic aerial, closed the fan-like sections of the dish and packed them away. His fingers were still numb from their brief encounter with the penetrating sub-zero wind and he hurried to put his gloves back on. The dull crunch of boots in the snow caught his attention and he looked up to see Topgye striding towards him, the fur flaps on his hat frozen rigid at such an angle to his head that for a moment they looked like horns.

"Contact?"

"Yes, chief. They'll rendezvous with us as arranged in," he pulled his coat sleeve back and checked his watch, "27 hours."

"Good. Come and get some tea inside you." Topgye turned away and thrust his great bulk into the wind, making his way towards the ice cave where the rest of the party was sheltering.

Gojo slung the bag containing the communications equipment over his shoulder and followed in the wake of the big man, letting him break the force of the wind. Inside the cave, everyone was bent over their individual bowls of scalding yak butter tea. Gojo drank two before he began to feel remotely human again. They had used the smokeless chemical blocks to heat the tea but it was miserable not to have a real fire to warm themselves by. Still, he thought, the women and children took it all in their stride. He wondered whether his five years of study in China had softened him, away from his people's natural hardiness. Looking at the men and women around him, their cheeks reddened by the searing cold of the winds off the Changtang, their conversation typically good-natured but a little subdued by their situation, he wondered what would become of them all. Even if they could return to Kham, they would still have to construct convincing accounts of their whereabouts to the officials. More likely, it seemed to him, they would be compelled to flee to one of the refugee settlements in India where they'd spend the rest of their days. He upbraided himself, mentally, for his pessimism in taking it for granted that their homeland would not be freed in their or his lifetime. Yet, was this now what they were fighting for? And if it was a hopeless cause, what was he doing wasting his life on it? Not for the first time, he pondered the dilemma, whether to remain and fight for the land he loved, enduring the ever increasing regulations imposed on them by the Chinese and their cruel sanctions or join the exiles, free to follow his religion, close to His Holiness but far away from the soil of which he was such an integral part? Perhaps events had already foreclosed his options. Stepping out of his reverie, he walked the few paces to where Topgye was and hunkered down beside him. Speaking softly over the bowl of his tea, he said,

"Chief, you said that we had crossed over into Nepal as we came over the pass. Does that mean we are safe from pursuit by the PLA now?"

The reply did not come immediately. The big Khamba slurped his tea noisily and wiped his mouth on the sleeve of his sheepskin lined overcoat.

"In the past they have followed us for as much as two days' march into Nepal. After the Nepal Army decided to hunt us down after their own trouble in Mustang, the PLA were content to leave the Nepal side of the border to them." He turned his head and looked Gojo in the eye. "But I'm assuming that they'll come after us themselves." He looked around at the others, the heat of their bodies combined with that of the animals filled the cave with a pungent smell of old sweat and rancid butter. "You saw their spotter plane and that was three days ago. Pity we didn't bring a Stinger, I'd have had that bloody bird out of the sky before you could say Mao Zedong." He grinned but his face grew serious again as he continued. "We may have travelled just that bit too fast for them but…?" He left the sentence in the air. Yishi had been listening to their exchange.

"They may have asked the Nepalese to get us, now we're over the border?"

"They probably have but that won't stop them from pursuing us themselves, especially if they even guess at what we're doing and…" He looked at each of them in turn. "My gut instinct is that they have." He thumped his belly for emphasis. "I feel that we're in for a fight but we have to deliver our package, no matter the cost." He lifted his eyes up, scanning the faces of the men, women and children. "It's time to send the women and children on a separate route." His gaze found a sturdy middle-aged woman who was stirring butter into a bowl of tea and called out to her.

"Choden-la?" She looked up and smiled at him. "Take the women and children by the old route to Chyamtang. Take all the yaks and leave as soon as you can." She nodded without interrupting her stirring. He spoke to Gojo. "Tell Tashi-la to get ready and you are responsible for the child."

"Chief." The young man was momentarily taken aback by this instruction. He had always assumed that Topgye himself would assume responsibility for the boy. But he felt a prick of excitement just to know that he had been chosen for this task.

"Yishi. You pick three or four men and give us 10 minutes' start, then follow. If you catch sight or sound of pursuers, don't engage them if you can avoid it, send a runner to warn us and keep your distance. Dump all the unnecessary loads and sort out the fittest ponies, let the women take everything they can." He put a hand on Gojo's shoulder.

"Speed is what matters now. We have to try and outrun them. Transfer the Treasury to the mules and load everything else onto the yaks. We will carry our weapons, ammunition and some *tsampa*, tea and butter. Your pony is well-tempered and a sure-footed little bugger. Make a double saddle for Tashi-la and the child and you ride hers."

They stood up as Topgye's instructions were carried out. The level of noise from the conversation fell away as people busied themselves with their tasks. Gojo was about to walk away when Topgye's hand fell on his shoulder.

"Once the shooting starts, get Tashi-la and the child into safety and stay out of the firefight so as not to draw attention to yourselves."

His dark eyes levelled into Gojo's. "I know you want to get into the fighting but I chose you for this work because of your education and training. Yishi and the rest of us are good for fighting and killing but you have it all up here." He tapped his forehead. "Take the radio equipment with you and if we get separated, make the rendezvous without us. Choose two men for back-up and if all else fails, leave them as your rearguard and slip away."

"But Chief," Topgye raised his gloved hand, palm outwards, cutting him off in mid-sentence.

"The safety of the child is your only responsibility, there is none greater. You will not fail." It was said with such solemnity that it silenced Gojo. Topgye let his eyes crinkle into a smile and punched the younger man in the chest.

"Get on with it."

As he walked towards his pony, his mind struggled with his emotions. To be put in charge of the child was a rare honour but it was also a frightening responsibility. As a geurilla fighter his responsibilities had been to himself and latterly the men under his command. His rational mind told him that Topgye had put him in charge of the child because, apart from the chief himself, he was the best trained to see the operation through to a successful conclusion. But he couldn't escape the niggling worry that he was being removed from what would be the mother of all fights if it came down to it. Did it mean that Topgye harboured doubts about his courage? He shrugged off his doubts, there was no time for the luxury of self-analysis. He unstrapped his saddle and began to make up the double saddle for mother and child.

"See, here is the man who will guide us safely over the mountain and make sure that you do not fall off the pony." She pointed at Gojo as she spoke to the little boy who was gripping the folds of her heavy *bhaku.* Gojo looked up from where he was crouched over the saddle that he'd put on the ground. He smiled at the boy, his little cheeks were chapped red from exposure to the harsh, icy wind but what struck Gojo most profoundly was the serenity in his face, the calm grey eyes that were incongruous in one so young. No matter what his feelings were about himself, those eyes conveyed utter trust. He experienced a curious, paradoxically unconfusing set of emotions; a sudden inner strength that infused his whole body and a feeling of humility in the face of this child's faith. He beckoned to him to come closer as his ungloved hands worked skilfully to make up the double saddle.

Tashi Yangzom looked up as she sensed someone looking at her. There was a brief moment, a quick shaft of a secret shared as Topgye Sey nodded towards her then turned away to shout encouragement to his men.

Lhasa

General Fei Yisheng was a good party member but he detested the garrison commissar's public self-reproach sessions. Self-reproach was inimical to his metabolism. Nonetheless, at this particular moment, an inner voice prevailed on him, arguing that he was indeed at fault. His patience, gossamer thin at the best of times, was now in shreds. Naturally, the majority of the responsibility lay with factors outside his control; the replacement staff officer who went in such fear of him that he did nothing rather than do anything wrong – that misbegotten son of a whore ex-district commander at Shekar-Tingkye who had committed several units to the search and whose rear communication link was 'malfunctioning', obviously deliberately, placing them beyond recall. Yes, he fulminated to himself, as he numbered them off in his mind, factors beyond his control.

He lifted his eyes a fraction and looked out through the far window. A corner of the Potala Palace, its long poled prayer flags, like the broken teeth of a vertical comb, fluttered, sending prayers to heaven as these stupid, superstitious and primitive people believed. Even as he condemned them yet again, it occurred to him that there was a particularly sharp edge to this corner of the Potala and it pointed more or less directly into his window. How was it that he had failed to notice it before? He would have to close off that window and have a mirror positioned on the external wall to throw the image back if the *feng shui* was not to dog him. There was most definitely some bad feng shui about this whole business. He refused to countenance the thought that he had been outfoxed by the Khambas. He had directed the search and destroy units to cover the highest passes into Sikkim, Nepal and even as far west as India. Past experience had taught him that the Khambas always took the highest passes where their mounted and foot skills were a match for regular infantry. He had been convinced that this would be their choice, even more so when the report came from Kharta Shika that there had been a sudden shortage of meat and futher enquiry revealed that a large number of yaks were unaccounted for. So confident had he been in his ability to outthink these filthy nomads that he had not made a contingency plan for the Pepti Pass, even though it was closer to Kharta Shika than Tsanga where he had concentrated the available units in the area. But his intuitive skills told him that this was no ordinary gang of roaming Khamba cut-throats. His long fingers sought out the criminal intelligence report from Chushar and as he read through it again, he spread out the faxed copies of the identification papers and took a magnifying glass to the almost useless photographs. The quality of reproduction was dreadful but he was looking for one particular face which, when matched with the height, weight and distinguishing features on the ID papers would confirm what he now believed to be the case. This one…he compared the shape of the face with his control data, true there was no moustache and the head was shaved like a monk, not drawn back in braided plaits, but the shape? He checked off the height, it was a match. One forefinger tapped the faxed photograph, it was him, the murderer Topgye Sey, the one they called 'the Fox'.

Again he looked up and in the same moment, averted his eyes from the inauspicious corner and its provocative bunting; if this terrorist and the scheming monks were acting in concert, it was counter-revolutionary, not mere banditry. The disquieting notion that he would be called to account for his acts and, perhaps even more, his omissions, cast a deep shadow in the far corners of his deepset mind. Beijing would have to be advised and his enemies among the cadres would ensure that a scapegoat was found in Lhasa. The sigh that escaped from his lips sounded like an inner tube being deflated under water. He would have to go on the offensive in anticipation.

Part way through drafting a signal to HQ military intelligence at Beijing, the timorous staff officer slipped into the room, as self-effacing as if he'd eased his shadow under the door. He coughed.

"Comrade General?" Fei ignored him and continued to write. The officer advanced a few more paces into the room and tried again.

"Comrade General," he paused, then in a moment of rare courage, carried on. "The Nepalese Consul-General is here." He quickly added as an afterthought, "As you requested."

Absorbed as he was in the top priority task of protecting his own, not inconsiderable skin, yet Fei Yisheng found time to admire his own exquisite calligraphy. He wrote in classic ideographs, eschewing the ugly modern practice of using the modified characters. To be interrupted from two such tasks by a man whom he detested in order to talk to a man he despised was altogether too much. He motioned with his head, a sign almost imperceptible to the uninitiated but well understood by his permanent staff officer. The temporary incumbent waited upon the General's orders. Almost five minutes slipped by before the staff major screwed up enough courage to try again.

"Comrade General," he paused, hoping that he might receive some small sign that his presence was acknowledged. None was forthcoming. He cleared his throat and said tentatively.

"The Consul-General of Nepal is waiting outside in the ante-room."

The great head raised itself just enough for the eyes to engage with those of the junior officer.

"Several minutes ago I indicated that you should show him in. It seems that your eyesight is on a par with your staff work." The eyes were lowered beneath the downward tilting brow and the pen resumed its intricate path across the paper.

In the ante-room, Ishwari Raj Sharma drew on the cigarette held with the filter protruding between his index and middle fingers. An orthodox Brahmin, the tobacco was not supposed to touch his lips, apart from which, like so many of his ilk, he was a nicotine addict. He had a fully developed sense of the proper order of all persons and that sense was acutely offended. That he, the Consul-General should have to wait outside the office of a man who was not even the Governor of the Autonomous Region, was an affront to his dignity, and to that of Nepal too, he added as an afterthought. The man was a slayer of sacred cows, a repugnant idolator, devout in his worship of himself, as untouchable as the *chemi* who emptied his cess pit. He took another drag on the cigarette and let the smoke curl deeply into his lungs before exhaling softly through his part opened lips. Unlike the governor, General Fei never used the telephone, simply summoning him into his obese presence. It was, he was quite sure, a deliberate technique, adopted to remind the Consul-General of his true standing and that of his country. His hand shook a little in anger as he pressed his lips against the middle and index fingers, keeping his mouth clear of the proscribed leaf whilst permitting him the necessary relief. As the smoke rose towards the ceiling, Sharma's imagination fancied it saw a malevolent black Bhairab slowly eviscerating the great mound of flesh, the bulbous head and face exhibiting that intensity of terror and pain which only the Hindu pantheon of gods could exact.

The sound of the door opening broke his fantasy.

"General Fei will see you now, Mr. Sharma." Even the words of invitation nettled the Nepalese, treating him as though he was some indigent petitioner. He rose and entered the General's room through the open door, the cigarette still smoking in his cupped hand. He was walking towards the desk when he suddenly noticed that the only vacant chair in the room was against a wall, some distance away. He turned his head, intending to indicate to the staff officer to bring the chair over for him but was only in time to see the door close, leaving him alone with the General.

The sound of the chair's feet scraping against the floor made him turn back to face the desk where, to his asonishment, Fei was actually on his feet, his palms pressed together fingers pointing upwards in the traditional Nepalese greeting.

"Namaste, Consul." Sharma was so taken aback by this unexpected greeting that in his automatic response he pressed the lighted end of the cigarette between his palms and had to restrain the impulse to cry out.

"Namascar, General Saheb."

"I must apologise." The General indicated the distant chair. "Major Liu is new, has yet to learn his duties." As he spoke he pressed the bell push under his desk which brought the unfortunate staff officer back into the room within seconds. Sharma's extensive knowledge did not embrace Mandarin but the tone of the General's voice needed no translation. The effect, moreover, turned the Major's face an unhealthy shade of jaundiced grey as he scurried across the room to bring the chair comfortably close to the desk and then obsequiously bowed himself out of the room.

"Most regrettable, most regrettable." Fei proffered a lacquered box of cigarettes which Sharma declined. They were, his keen eye observed, the distinctly inferior Chinese brand.

"Consul, this matter of the Khamba criminals has becomed a subject for further collaboration between our countries. Recently he has murdered unarmed officials sent to offer them pardon and offer of re-education and re-integration into community." He paused to test the Nepali's reaction to broaching the subject without the customary diplomatic courtesies. Sharma's only real advantage was his fluency in the English language, particularly in the light of the General's habitual linguistic errors. He preened himself in his mind as he rehearsed the polished phrases with which he would respond. He did not believe a word of the alleged offer of a pardon and he knew well what re-education meant in the Communist vocabulary. He played along with a measure of feigned dismay.

"Your lamentable experience is what we learned of them when they fomented political unrest in Mustang." He shook his head knowledgeably.

"Now, I regret to informed you, a band of Khamba criminals have cross over into Nepal by Pepti Pass." He pushed an open map across the desk and a long forefinger tapped out the point so that Sharma could identify the Pass. "Their leader is very dangerous criminal, Topgye Sey." He paused and looked straight into Sharma's face. "It is in interests of Nepal and the People's Republic of China to put end to her activities. I'm sure Nepal Government don't want her making trouble in Nepal or jeopardised warm relations between our countries, specially in difficult times, isn't so?" Irrespective of the wrong tenses and gender, the attempt at friendly words belied the unmistakable message behind them. Sharma maintained a dignified control over his irritation at the implicit reference to the precarious political climate in Kathmandu.

"We would not wish to harbour such a man at any time, General. Now is no more difficult than any other save that during a period of social reconstruction, the focus of the peoples' minds must not be distracted." Sharma launched into his standard polemic about the overthrow of the farce of the so-called 'constitutional monarchy' and its spurious claims to democracy. The platitudes rolled glibly off his lips as he extolled the irreproachable virtues of the new regime. Nevertheless, it was a source of constant irritation to him that, more often than not, Fei was better informed about events in Nepal than he was. He had sent several despatches to the ministry of foreign affairs about the grave disadvantage under which he laboured because they sent him no internal intelligence reports on the current state of affairs.

"Yes, yes." General Fei was as familiar with Sharma's political haverings as he had been with the contents of the late Chairman Mao's little red book. In essence, he thought, there was little to choose between them. He let the man talk himself to a standstill, he didn't understand half of what he said anyway, not that any of it mattered. He interposed after what he considered sufficient time for the man to finish his polemic.

"Your nearest infantry unit is Purano Gorkha Regiment." His finger traced a path on the map to Taplejung. "About several days' march away." The effort of leaning so far forward made his voice wheeze. "Too far away to catch her. You must use parachute soldiers quickly." By way of explanation he pushed forward a geophysical weather overlay. The whorls and arrows meant nothing to Sharma but he said,

"I understand." What he did understand was that both he and his government were being treated as though they were puppets, obliged to dance in accordance with the strings pulled by Lhasa and Beijing. He decided not to be drawn into any further discussion of a situation in which he was so hopelessly disadvantaged. If any action was to be taken, he had sufficient information to pass on to his superiors in the Singha Durbar. For now, he decided to shelter behind the protective barrier of diplomatic protocol.

"I shall convey your words to my government, General. Of course, until I receive the Governor of the Autonomous Region's formal written request, any assistance that I could afford would be entirely unofficial." He managed a confidential smile. "Naturally, in the light of our excellent relations, I shall do my utmost to ensure that there is total co-operation. But you will understand that my informal request will not carry the weight that these circumstances," he waved his hand across the map, "indicate to be necessary." He pushed his chair back and rose to leave. General Fei's bulk began to move as though he too would get to his feet.

"Please." Sharma waved him down with an eloquent sweep of his palm. "Don't incommode yourself, I can see myself out." He wondered whether the General had genuinely intended to stand up, probably not, he decided. Leaning back in his chair, his hands flat on the desk, Fei nodded.

"Please give greetings to Brigadier-General Karki when you sended unofficial request." The reference to the commanding officer of the Nepal Army Airborne troops and the slightest of inflections on the words 'unofficial request' were not lost on the Nepali. He raised his hands in salutation, turned on his heel and walked out of the room.

Outside the ante-room, the sentry came to attention as the Consul stepped into the corridor. Acknowledging the salute with a slight nod of his head, Sharma walked purposefully towards the head of the stairs leading down to the ground floor. His mind was seething and he felt the urge, habitual in a devout Hindu, to bathe himself clean of the verbal excrement to which he'd been exposed. There would be no 'unofficial request'. If and when the official request came through from the governor, it was highly likely that the code book would be temporarily mislaid, always assuming that the communications officer had not been incapacitated by another of his woefully untimely fevers. The Chinese, he was well aware, poked fun at the incompetence of Nepalese officialdom. Well, let us live up to our reputation, he decided. For the first time since entering the Chinese military cantonment, the fine, dark features of the Brahmin's face registered a degree of genuine pleasure.

Coincidentally, General Fei was indulging himself in a small measure of self-congratulation. Now that he was satisfied that no Nepalese troops would be deployed in the target area for several days, he felt safe to get the commander-in-chief of the Autonomous Region's military command to authorise hot pursuit of the Khambas across the border. The Fox was about to lose his brush. The slender fingers lay at rest across the silent keyboard of his map covered desk.

The Rendezvous

The RV was in the same re-entrant as Honggaon but further north. Whoever had chosen it had a sound knowledge of geurilla techniques. The approach from the south was by way of a perilously flimsy looking rope suspension bridge and the route in from the north was a narrow twisting track, so narrow he noted, that at some visible points the slightest error would probably send man or beast straight down the open side of the ice face. But it was also a track that could be held by one man. He pointed back to the south side of the bridge.

"I suggest that the Sherpas stay on that side and only you, me and your people cross onto this side to make the contact."

Despite the freezing cold, beads of sweat were forming on the exposed part of the Professor's forehead. He had negotiated the swaying bridge with obvious trepidation and Max found some grim satisfaction to note that there was at last something to disturb the man's equilibrium.

"You'd better wipe that sweat off your face and get some more cream on or you'll get frostbite."

"Yes, thank you." The Thai dug into a pocket of his down jacket and fished out a small face towel. "I agree with your suggestion, very practical." He mopped his brow and took off a glove to rub some UVA cream on. The keening wind blew some of the fur lining of his hood so that it stuck to the freshly applied cream. He looked around their position. "I think we need some shelter from this biting wind."

"I'll get the Sherpas to find us somewhere, probably up in those rocks, there ought to be an ice cave or two." He pointed to above where they stood where the snow face seemed fissured with shadows. Nyima had joined them as he was talking and Max gave him instructions to find suitable shelter on both sides of the bridge. Max was thankful that he'd changed his mind about sending the big Sherpa down with Ong Chu, he was an excellent *sardar.* After the Professor had revealed the true purpose of the expedition, Max had retailed the story to both Ong Chu and Nyima. After his jaw had been re-located, though still in considerable pain, Ong Chu had been able to speak and it had been his insistence that Nyima stay on as *sardar*, explain the situation to the Sherpas and inform them of the extra money Max would give to every man who volunteered to accompany them on the last stage of the journey. Nyima had done a great job, emphasising that they were all Buddhists and that they would be doing something of direct assistance to His Holiness the Dalai Lama. There had been no defectors. Whatever his shortcomings had been, Max now saw him as a tower of strength. He established a base camp on the south side of the bridge and soon had the kitchen tent up and buzzing with preparation of a hot meal. The Thais posted two men as lookouts behind a low snow berm that they constructed on the northern side and from where they had a long view of the approach track. As night fell, they settled in to wait for the party from Tibet.

Max decided to eat with the Sherpas. It gave them an opportunity to quiz him about the clients and the extraordinary business of the Dalai Lama's Treasury. Despite the recent sobering events they exhibited their customary thirst for knowledge, plying him with questions, most of which, he was amused to note, dealt with how much it was all worth? Along with their incredible steadfastness on the mountains they had a venial streak of the mercenary in them which tended to put a monetary value on so many aspects of life. In the army, Max had felt a sense of disappointment when he encountered the attitude but his experience in the business of running a mountaineering organisation had altered his perspective. It was all a question of balance: the Sherpas marketed their skills to the highest bidder, how were they to put an appropriate value on those services unless they had a broader grasp of economies beyond Nepal? Nevertheless, he found some wry amusement that their interest in the Treasury was significantly greater than the religious cause that it was intended to serve. That aside, the departure of Ong Chu under such bizarre circumstances had shaken them and he had felt it important to reassure them.

He ate with relish, the staple high altitude food of unleavened millet bread, potatoes and *dhall* always seemed a hundred percent tastier than the same dish eaten back in Kathmandu. They huddled together to share what little warmth there was, giggling and ribbing each other. After a while, one of the young Sherpas began to play a bamboo flute and a hush fell over them as the plaintively sweet notes seemed to hang in the eerily frozen night air. The melody was an old Sherpa folk song and the flautist's extraordinarily pure notes were a pure joy to the ear. As the melody sweetly rose and fell, Max got up and walked out of the warmth towards the bridge. Far below, he could hear the murmuring of the glacial waters as they flowed swift and strong. In the darkness, the bridge gave him an even greater sense of human frailty, its wooden cross members quivering and bending underfoot with a mischievious spirit of their own. He admitted to a sense of relief when he reached the far side and gave himself a penitent reminder not to relish the Professor's discomfiture.

The three remaining Thais sat huddled around their cooking stove, exacting what psychological warmth they could from its thin blue chemical flame. The two Marines got to their feet as Max approached them but he waved them back onto their camp stools. They shuffled themselves around to make some room beside the Professor and Max hunkered down beside them.

"Well, we're here. There's nothing for us to do but wait."

"Yes." The Professor pulled back the elasticated wrist band of his Parka and checked his watch. "I estimate another two hours or so, provided they made good time and had no difficulties." The heavy quiet of the Himalayan night was threaded by the distant notes of the flute. It was, Max felt, an atmosphere in which a man might reveal his inner thoughts in the security that they would only exist in this harsh elemental environment and never be exposed to the analytical light of day. Whether it had this effect upon the Professor he knew not but he broached it without any prefatory remarks.

"You don't have to tell me if you don't want to but are you genuinely a professor?"

The Thai's face registered a hint of a smile.

"I'm Professor of Oriental languages at the University of Bangkok." Well, Max wondered, is that it?

"How did an academic such as yourslf come to be mixed up in," he sought unsuccessfully for the right words and ended up with a lame, "all this?"

"You may well wonder." He indicated his mug and one of the Marines lifted the kettle off the fire and poured out some tea. The unshielded light struck his features and Max could see that the hint of a smile was still there.

Sutape Disanawat Sukhum had a sense of the ethereal, as though the here and now were in a temporary suspension and his words and deeds, even his thoughts, existed in a curious vacuum from which they could not be removed. He genuinely liked the Irish ex-officer even though he was irritated by his tendency to anger when his plans were interrupted. The man had an uncanny faculty for empathising with Asiatics which he found uncharacteristic of most Caucasians, most of whom tended either to patronise or despise. Despite both an inherent disinclination to confide his inner thoughts to others and the dictates of his mission, he felt an overwhelming need to reveal himself to the man, not, he chided himself, to unburden his soul but to speak openly for once. The inhibitions of the clandestine operation sent out warning signals but there was a quality in the Himalayan darkness that compelled him to override them. He stole a quick glance at Devlin's face and saw again the odd combination of strength and compassion; he saw also a dimension of loneliness for which he could ascribe no cause. When he spoke, he looked directly into the small blue flame of the stove.

"What, you are asking yourself, is a Thai professor of linguistics doing with a bunch of specialist forces meeting up with the Dalai Lama's Treasury in the Nepal Himalaya?" He gave a dry chuckle at the incongruity of the skeletal picture he had painted, then continued.

"For me, the beginning of the story is that I am, in reality, only half-Thai, though that is my formal citizenship. My father was Tibetan." He felt rather than saw the slight movement of Devlin's head at this disclosure.

"You may recall, with your very considerable knowledge of this part of the world, that prior to 1956, Tibetan merchants used to travel down through India and Burma to Thailand and sell their goods as far south as Singapore. My father was one such. A wealthy man by our standards, he made the annual caravan. On one of his journeys he met my mother in Thailand and they were married within the month. After that, she accompanied him on his travels." In his mind, he pictured them as he always did, the images slightly unfocussed, as were the photographs which were all that remained of his memory of his parents.

"I was born in 1953 and as soon as I was two years old, my parents took me with them on the trading journeys. By the time I was five, I had acquired a child's command of the languages of the countries through which we passed, hence my lifelong interest." He paused and inhaled deeply. The memory was undulled by the passage of time and it still hurt.

"We were in northern Malaysia or the Malayan Federation as it was then called, in the State of Ipoh. The deep jungles of this part of the country concealed the base of operations of the Communist terrorist Chin Peng, the commander of the Malayan Communist Party Forces. The Communist terrorists or CT's, as they were commonly called, waged a campaign of terror as they fought to take over the whole of the Federation. Villages that refused to co-operate with them were singled out for terrible retribution. Usually the village headman would be dragged from his attap hut at night, disembowelled and left to die in the main street. By the time the village awoke, the dogs and the carrion crows had been at their ugly work and the remains would be black with shit-flies." He paused again and screwed his eyes up into slits as he told the story that he had never before recounted to a comparative stranger.

"It was my parents' grave misfortune to be staying with such a headman when the CT's came. The headman's son was about the same age as myself and as a special treat, we had been allowed to sleep in a tree-house a few yards away from the hut. Little Yusuf and I were awakened by the noise and watched in paralysed fear as the CT's dragged our parents out and left them in the middle of the village. Yusuf began to vomit as they cut open his father's belly and I held his mouth shut so as not to give away our position." He paused and breathed in and out slowly, regaining control over his emotions.

"There are still nights on which I smell the vomit in my nightmares." He felt his mouth go dry and the corners of his eyes tightened but he fought against the urge to let the tears come.

"For the Communists, you see, the ends always justify the means." He felt the Irishman searching for words but he knew, himself, that no words could articulate adequately the expression of commiseration that others felt at such times, nor, in fairness could one expect others to do so. Such events were not for vicarious sharing. He gave a short sigh. "I was left with my maternal grandparents on the caravan's return journey. My Tibetan relations provided funds for my education and upbringing and I travelled freely between my two homelands until the Chinese overran Tibet and closed the borders." He turned to look at Devlin and the Irishman's eyes met his.

"That event acted as a catalyst for my split allegiance and brought home to me the debt I owed to my Tibetan family. I got in touch with His Holiness' representatives and offered them the dubious value of my services." He searched the other's face to see if he could discern an understanding of what it was that motivated him, his apparent readiness to accept calmly the deaths and injuries of others. He knew that his hostility to the Communists was dangerously single-minded but his efforts to present an outward appearance of academic disinterest did have the effect of modifying his instincts. Without quite knowing why, it had become important to him to gain the approval of the Irishman. His nerves were on edge now that they were so close to bringing the operation to a successful conclusion. He had taken Devlin a fair way into his confidence. But the next few hours would put them all to the test, especially if the handover couldn't be effected smoothly. The Irishman's initial reaction augured well.

"Yours is a fascinating story, Professor. I think I see where you're coming from now."

Max understood a great deal more than he had before and he fought down a sense of deep irritation that he had been kept in the dark for so long. It was difficult to assess how he would have reacted had they confided in him from the outset, it was easy to judge it all with the wisdom of hindsight and tell himself that he wouldn't have touched it with a barge pole. Against this rational analysis there was an inner voice that admitted that he would probably have taken it on in any event. He faced himself with the fact that he was sitting here now because the Professor had made it financially worth his while, so didn't that make him a pure mercenary? At least the Thai was following the dictates of his religious beliefs and philosophy. Where, he asked himself with a sense of emptiness, were his beliefs, his philosophy? A lapsed Catholic who had flirted with the religions of Asia as and when they suited him, but apart from a firm belief that there was a divine power into which all these theosophical movements connected, he had neither the conviction nor peace of mind enjoyed by the adherents of any one of those movements. It struck him that he envied the Thai's sense of dedication. Despite his Tibetan roots, it couldn't be much fun abandoning the comfort of an academic life in Bangkok to freeze his arse off on top of the Himalayas, saddled with the massive responsibility he'd accepted.

The next two hours slipped by as the two men found mutual topics of interest. The two Marines sat stolid faced, occasionally talking quietly to each other or checking and re-checking their weapons. After an hour, they got up and exchanged places with the two sentries behind the snow berm. The men they replaced reported back to the Professor then lapsed into a companionable silence as they sipped the steaming mugs of consommé heated over the little chemical Tommy cooker.

As the time for the RV drew closer, the conversation became more stilted, watches were checked and re-checked and the Marines stood up stretching their muscles and loading and unloading the 5.56-mm cartridges into the magazines of their HK-53's, worried that they would freeze up in the sub-zero temperature.

Max found himself in a curious situation: though he was the leader of the expedition, they had reached the point at which logically the Professor was in command. As against that, their disposition was manifestly a military one and as such the ex-professional soldier was the man whom circumstances dictated should take control. The dilemma resolved itself in his mind on the basis that the safety of the party was still his responsibility.

"Professor, I think it would prudent for one of your Marines to scout up along the track for about 10 to 15 minutes."

"Agreed." The response was immediate. Max looked at one of the Thais and gave him his orders. The man reacted without hesitation, raising his weapon in salute before turning and moving quickly out along the track.

"I'm grateful." The Professor acknowledged. "This is much more your line of country than mine and these men respect you." Max nodded whilst registering doubts about the credibility of the last statement. As he got to his feet, he thought he heard a sound from the direction of the track. He put one hand on the Professor's arm to caution silence whilst he turned his head sideways on to their front, easing back the hood of his Parka to free his ear.

"*Tuck*!" This time they all heard it as they strained their eyes into the darkness. The figure of the Marine he'd sent out to scout the track came into sight around a bend, followed by a series of muffled shapes of men and animals. Max stood back to let the Professor get on with his business.

The discipline of the Tibetans was good, he observed. Sentries were posted and men moved about with a sense of quiet purpose. He counted 25 heads and about twice that many animals.

"Colonel!" The Professor called to him from a small knot of people standing close to the bridge. They fell silent as he walked up to them. The Thai was facing a tall, bulky Tibetan with features that looked seriously lived-in.

"Topgye-la, this is Colonel Devlin. We owe him a great debt of gratitude for enabling us to make this meeting." He spoke in Tibetan and Max wondered if the newcomer realised that he understood what they were saying. The Professor turned to Max and spoke in English.

"Topgye Sey is the leader of the Khamba forces, a great and courageous patriot, devoted to the service of His Holiness." Max brought his gloved hands together to make *namascar* and the Khamba responded similarly before extending his hand and grasping Max's forearm firmly.

"I have heard of you, Devlin-la." He spoke in Tibetan and Max smiled in acknowledgement. "We know you as a friend of our people and our cause." He uttered the words with a solemnity that Max found a little embarrassing.

"But you are a very famous man, Topgye-la." The Tibetan was still grasping his forearm. He managed a wry grin. "They say that you are the thorn under the Chinese saddle," he paused, then added, "and you have given the Nepalese government a hard time."

"Mustang?" The lower half of the Khamba's face was occupied by grinning teeth.

"Mustang." Max felt the enormous strength of the man's grip through the padding of his jacket and clothing as Topgye leant back and roared with laughter. Max found himself taking to the man. He indicated the bridge.

"We're camped on the far side. I suggest we cross over and discuss our plans there." The glow from the Sherpas' cooking stove was just visible.

"Yes. My men will stay on this side for tonight. We'll move the loads over in the early morning." He turned and called out into the gently undulating body of men and animals.

"Gojo!" Max saw a younger man break away from the indistinguishable mass and hurry across to them. "Bring Tashi-la and the child across the bridge to the far side." Max was surprised to learn that there was a woman, even more so a child, amongst these heavily armed Khambas. It struck an incongruous note amidst the slung AK 47's and bandoliers of ammunition.

"Forgive us for a moment, Colonel." For all his formidable size and rough manner he was not lacking in courtesy as he drew the Professor aside. Max walked over to the access point to the bridge and watched a couple of Khambas make their way across with some shapeless bundles. A minute or two later he recognised the one called Gojo leading a small child by the hand followed by a figure slim enough even in the heavy winter clothing to be a woman. Gojo was holding a torch in his free hand and he paused a moment to let the woman catch up with them. The light from the torch swept momentarily over her features and Max saw that she was young. It was more than enough for an adult using both hands to cross the bridge safely and Max felt impelled to offer to assist but he was pre-empted by the Khamba who led his charges onto the bridge without hesitation. Feeling a bit like a child watching a trapeze artist at a circus, he stared in admiration as the young man guided woman and child surely across the gently swaying lattice work. He waited until they reached the other side before stepping onto the bridge himself. As he shuffled gingerly across the narrow foot boards he pondered on the puzzle of the presence of the woman and child. Search his memory as he would he could not recall ever hearing of a Khamba battle group travelling *en famille.* Still, he reflected, times changed and circumstances too. Perhaps Topgye Sey had decided to bring his family out to safety. Now, he laughed silently to himself, there *was* a notion. However else one described their present situation it was stretching belief to describe it as safe.

"How much does Devlin-la know?"

"Only about the Treasury." Topgye listened intently as the Professor gave him a brief account of the events that had marked their journey to the RV.

"What about the return and exit plans now? It looks as though we have real problems."

"I know." The Professor nodded agreement. He knew that the original plan for traversing Nepal and entering India was now unlikely to succeed. Far too much attention was already going to be focussed on the expedition's members. Try though he might, he had not been able to conceive of an alternative plan as yet. He raised his hands, palms uppermost in a gesture that spoke volumes.

"I'm working on it...but my options are severely limited." There was a moment's silence as both men stared vacantly at each other, their minds preoccupied with the dilemma they now faced.

"I think you should tell him. He's a resourceful man, we depend on him for his knowledge and contacts...we can't fight our way out of the country."

"You really think he should be told?" The Professor's face was creased with doubt and he studied the Khamba's face for any sign of hesitation.

"His burden is heavy and we have to trust him." He paused a moment before continuing. "Someone will have to be the scapegoat... the Nepalese will blame him, not you. He's always been a friend of our people, isn't he entitled to know the cause he serves?"

"Mm...perhaps you're right." The Professor was acutely conscious of the personal cost to the Colonel and despite the arrogant attitude he'd adopted towards the man when he'd jibbed at going on to the RV he was sympathetic towards him, indeed, he reflected, he both liked and admired him. Still, he agonised, was any price really too high to pay when the cause was so great?

"I'll sleep on it tonight. We can consider it in the morning with our minds freshened by sleep."

"If you say so." The Khamba was reluctant to leave the matter in abeyance. He was accustomed to making critical decisions and relied substantially on his intuitive senses to guide him. They'd served him well and kept him one step ahead of his enemies for all these years. He respected the teacher, as he thought of him, but his instincts drew him towards the white soldier in whom he recognised a kindred spirit. That spirit engendered trust. He walked away from the Thai and spoke critically to one of his men who was not carrying his weapon. The high tones of Tibetan abuse crept slowly down the scale as his anger wound slowly around the errant man, rooting him to the ground on the last, deep-throated grunt. The man's face registered a grin of embarrassment before he turned and loped back towards his machine-rifle.

Topgye spat expressively after him before continuing on his tour of the encampment.

Max stepped off the ice plateau and suddenly felt himself falling, he tried to reach out but his limbs were too heavy and wouldn't respond as he tumbled down and down in a noiseless drop broken only by a voice calling insistently.

"Saheb! Saheb!" He felt a pull on his shoulder and in that instant he was awake. Deepraj was shaking him with one hand and holding out the satcom handset with the other. "It's Jamsung Saheb."

Max's dream fuddled brain took a second or two to register. He looked at the face of his wristwatch, 5.33, then took the handset.

"Jamsung?"

"Max...I have a message from your policeman friend." The reception was thin but audible.

"Go ahead."

"Orders have been issued...arrested." Static mush drowned the middle part of the message.

"Say again, all after issued." He waited for the swell of the static to subside.

"Orders issued for you and your party to be arrested." Max felt a chill that had nothing to do with the mountain temperature.

"Shit!"

"Say again?"

"Sorry, I was just reacting to your news."

"OK. Understood."

"What about my friend, can he help?" The reception was awash with waves of mush and the only words he caught were 'military jurisdiction'.

"Have the orders been issued to the army and not the police?"

"Correct, I say again, correct." Max cudgelled his brain for constructive thoughts.

"Can you find out the name of the nearest brigade commander?" It was a long shot but he might just be someone he knew.

"...try. One more thing..." Max cursed the satcom. It was the most expensive piece of high-tech communication equipment available on the open market and it still performed like a bloody old army radio set.

"Say again, all after 'one more thing'."

"...Khambas heading in your direction...my information...PLA in pursuit." There was a pause that appeared to have nothing to do with interference, then Jamsung's voice came over clearly. "What the hell's going on?"

One thing was absolutely certain, the situation was far too complex to start explaining over the radio link. Moreover, whatever the inwardness of all these factors, the consequences for Max personally were dire.

"Trouble, I say again, trouble."

"Understood."

"Keep morning and evening schedules until further instruction."

"Roger." Jamsung's voice came over strong and clear. He added. "Good luck, Max."

"Thanks. We'll need it. Out." He handed the satcom back to Deepraj.

"Reception poor, Saheb?"

"Too bloody right..." His ungenerous views on the quality of the reception were interrupted by the unmistakeable sound of a short burst of semi-automatic firing. As he struggled into his down jacket, Max ordered Deepraj to tell Nyima and the other Sherpas to stay down, then he cursed the long laces on his boots as he missed out most of the loops and wound them around his ankles. There was more firing now. On his hands and knees, he pushed his way out of the tent and the freezing dawn air made his eyes water temporarily. The bridge was out of sight around a bend in the mountainside and though the gunfire sounded as though it came from the direction of the bridge the noise was bouncing off the steep ice slopes creating double and triple echoes. Keeping close in to the exposed rockface beside the track he ran towards the bridge. There was quite a little firefight going on now in a disciplined sort of way. No long bursts of automatic fire but controlled exchanges, the contrasting tones of 'tung-ki-tung' that he associated with professional soldiers rather than the absurd magazine-emptying bursts favoured by small time crooks and big-time film producers. He permitted himself a grim smile, despite this unfavourable development, he felt the old sense of comfortable familiarity with combat.

As the angle of the track altered sufficiently to give him a view, the sight that met his eyes presented oddly. He caught the muzzle flash of firing coming from behind a bluff of rock at the northern extremity of the track on the far side of the bridge, though he could not make out any figures. Happily, he had sited their encampment out of the potential line of fire from the far side, otherwise they would have been fatally exposed. Behind their snow berm, the Thais and a couple of Khambas were in firing positions, their weapons pointing in the direction from where the firing was coming but without sight of a visible target. As he took all this in, several Khambas came up from behind him and flattened themselves against the rock face. Max quickly pointed out the source of the gunfire and the man beside him changed places with a Khamba carrying a powerful sniper rifle. Max put a restraining hand on the man's arm and pointed towards the track between the berm and the hidden rifleman. A figure was crawling, belly-down, along the track towards the bluff of rock. Just short of it, the figure paused, rolled over on his back and pulled his hands apart in a sharp motion. Next minute, he slowly lobbed something high into the air, over the bluff so that it fell on the side farthest from where he lay. The sharp 'thwang!' of the explosion reverberated around the mountains and loosened the snow and ice above the track immediately to the north of the bluff.

The firing ceased.

There was no movement for about one minute then, one of the Khambas next to Max rolled out of cover to the left, well within the arc of fire of anyone still hidden behind the bluff. Drawing no fire, he got slowly to his feet. As he did so, the grenade thrower stood up and leaning back against the mountainside, shuffled slowly towards the bluff until he could peer around it. Next minute he was out of sight around the far side of the bluff only to return moments later wearing a large grin.

It didn't need a military genius to guess that they had been 'bumped' by an advance Chinese patrol. Even if the patrol's procedure had been defective so that no one had survived to report back, Max was convinced that the sound of the gunfire and the grenade exploding would have carried sufficiently to advertise their presence and position to the main combat unit. Nyima trotted up to him to report.

"We're breaking camp, almost finished." He cocked his head towards the northerly portion of the track. "Chinese?"

"Has to be." Max thanked his lucky stars that he'd retained Nyima, the big Sherpa was proving to be worth his weight in gold. "Good work." He clapped him on the shoulder. "As soon as the gear is packed get the boys to start moving down the track for about 15 to 20 minutes then hold up until I reach you."

"Huzoor." Max looked back across the bridge which was now swaying with men loaded down with packs heading towards them.

"Detail off six of the boys to help the Khambas get their stuff across to this side." Nyima gave an affirmative flick of his head and headed back down towards the overnight camp. Max felt a touch on his elbow and turned to find the Professor standing beside him.

"What was that you were saying earlier about this being much more my line of country?"

"Colonel, if you please." His face actually looked worried Max registered as the Professor waved towards the southern end of the bridge where Topgye was just stepping down, an enormous load carried on his shoulders. They both trotted over to the bridge.

"Leave that stuff here, some of the Sherpas will shift it for you. I've detailed six of them to help your men get the remainder of the kit across." The Tibetan uttered an appreciative grunt, lowered his load to the ground and chuckled.

"We should do this more often, Colonel, our men work well together!" Max's smile of reply concealed his deep misgivings about their situation. He was beginning to feel like the filling in a Sino-Nepalese sandwich and the only thing that seemed certain was that even if the bread was discarded, he'd be devoured. He turned to the Professor.

"The success of any joint operation depends on clearly defined objectives and absolute confidence between the respective commanders." He let his eyes shift from the Professor's face to the Khamba's and then back to the Professor. For once, the Thai would not hold his eyes but looked away towards Topgye. The Khamba's face was a study in weathered inscrutability. If the Professor had been looking for some sort of response there, there was none. Max had an intuition that in some as yet undefined way, he actually had the whip hand. For immediate purposes, it was a question of priorities.

"Candidly, I think I'm being used...for some private agenda you people have." He saw the Professor's mouth begin to open and cut him off short with a peremptory wave of his hand. "Whatever it is, it'll have to wait. We have to get both groups away from here smartish. My guess is that that little excitement was just a forward scouting party, the main Chinese unit will be on us any minute." He paused momentarily. If he disclosed his own dilemma he would probably lose the edge that he felt he had over them. Even as that thought entered his mind, he saw the paradox, if anything he'd established his authority by setting a yardstick of candour.

"I think I should tell you that just before the attack, I received a message that the Nepalese authorities have instructed the military to arrest me."

The Khamba's face was now scrutably grim and the Professor's brow furrowed in obvious anxiety.

"My suggestion is that we move the whole party to somewhere relatively safe and defensible from attack by the Chinese. The deeper we go into Nepalese territory, the less inclined the Chinese will be to follow and equally, it should cramp their style if they know they're near any Nepal Army unit." He paused and gave a short deprecatory laugh. "At this stage, even a Nepalese gaol presents a less disquieting prospect than a Chinese bullet." He'd been tempted to add 'up the arse' but thought better of it.

"I imagine you'll have somewhere in mind that will meet our purposes Topgye-la?" The Khamba removed his hat and began rubbing his hand backward and forward across his shaved head. He mumbled incomprehensibly to himself for a few seconds then his eyes seemed to quicken.

"Shadung. There is a Nepali-Bhotia village, a winter village really, about one day's march from here. I've been sheltered there before. It's unlikely that there'll be anyone there at this time of the year and it will provide us with shelter. It's all low-built stone houses recessed into the mountainside, good defensive positions."

"Right. Shadung it is." Indecision, Max felt, was the last quality they needed. Nor, by the same token did they want command by committee.

"Talk to my Sherpa *sardar,* the pair of you can guide us. We can't spare the time to bring the ponies and mules over the bridge, leave 'em where they are. Once your men and kit are across, we'll have to cut the bridge. Travelling on foot with all this gear, we'll need to buy every spare minute we can."

The march to Shadung was even more arduous than Max had anticipated. The Khambas were all tough but they looked strained and tired. The Sherpas were all mountain fit but beginning to show occasional symptoms of the stresses of their situation. No one complained but it was an uncharacteristically silent group of men who kept up the cracking pace, exacerbated by the thin air at this altitude. After they had been going for about an hour, Max quietly relieved the Professor of his rucksack, overcoming the man's protests with little fuss.

Nyima and Topgye took it in turns to set the pace from the front, dropping back occasionally to encourage the less resolute.

Gojo had hung a mass of equipment from his belt and carried the little boy on his shoulders. From time to time he joked and played the fool and the child's peals of laughter sang out over the heads of the sweating men, making them smile. Wherever the width of the track permitted, Max walked with the young woman between himself and the Professor. She insisted on carrying her own load to the dismay of the Khambas, but she proved obdurate amd shouldered what must have been a 30-pound pack, striding along with the best of them.

There was little breath to spare for conversation and Max took the opportunity to observe her closely in the enforced silence. Once or twice he looked across at her to find her regarding him with a wisp of a smile at the corners of her eyes and mouth. On these occasions she didn't look away in the feigned embarrassment commonly adopted by so many coquettish Oriental women, her look was open and direct, yet far from a brazen 'come hither'. Max began to feel that he was being assessed in some way other than ordinary human or physical terms and for inexplicable reasons it disturbed him. He surprised himself that it took so long to realise that her eyes were extraordinarily beautiful. Perhaps, he thought, it was the serenity in them that had that effect upon him. Apart from a brief acknowledgement when he offered her his hand at one or two places where the ground underfoot became treacherous, no words passed between them. He realised that he was actually hoping that she'd give him the smile that her face held barely concealed. Bloody fool, he chided himself, behaving like some anxious teenager. But there was a quality about her that overrode the absurdity of his emotions at this time and place and he had to force his mind back onto the overwhelming problems that he now faced.

The pace was unrelenting. As the hours passed, each person became more or less isolated in their individual endeavours to keep up. Despite the bitter cold, Max's inner layer of clothing was soaked in sweat. Had it not been for the Goretex outer wear, he would have run the risk of hypothermia from the winds that knifed across their bodies and felt as though it was abrading their faces. At 10.30 he called a halt for a quick meal. The smokeless briquettes were soon tantalising them with heat that only served to boil the water and even that was frustrating as the altitude delayed bringing it to the boil. Forty-five precious minutes were consumed before they resumed the march.

Shadung was typical of the high altitude Tibetan culture villages of two-storey dwellings built in stone. In the dark, it was hard to determine what condition they were in, not that they were overly concerned about it after a 15-hour forced march on three hours' sleep.

"We're in luck." Topgye's resilience seemed limitless. "Three of the houses are still occupied but the village headman is a bit nervous." He made a quizzical expression and then grinned. "Whether he fears us or the Nepalese authorities, I can't tell. But we'd better watch him in case he thinks of covering his arse by warning the local military."

"Perhaps we should leave him in no doubt about which side his bread is buttered?" Max threw out the suggestion trusting that the Khamba would know how to implement it. Topgye's face registered agreement coupled with a hint that it was not without its humorous aspect. His nose twitched.

"These people are dirt poor and their houses filthy."

Max's high regard for the Tibetans generally did not extend to their standards of personal or domestic hygiene. The observation that Topgye had just let drop meant either that he was a most uncommon Tibetan or that they were due for imminent exposure to mind-boggling conditions.

They conferred quickly about quartering their respective parties and Topgye made his immediate defensive dispositions. The overall plan had the Sherpas in a rough inner sanctum with the armed Khambas deployed in a semi-circular configuration, their backs to the mountainside. Topgye had the courtesy to seek Max's approval for his deployment and received a swift nod. Max had never conducted military operations under such conditions, the nearest equivalent he realised to his amusement had been the mountainous Radfan of Yemen. If you treated the snow as though it were sand, much the same principles appeared to apply. If they ever got the chance, it would be fascinating to quiz the Khamba chief on his tactical philosophy.

They entered the ground floor of the headman's house and climbed to the first floor by way of a wooden ladder that rose almost vertically, disappearing through a space in the darkness above their heads. Max led the way. As his eyes came level with the upper room, his first impression was that the entire space was pitch black save for the dull glow from a fire giving off the unmistakable aroma of yak dung. The mildly acrid smoke entered his lungs and he had to bend low to avoid the greatest concentration of smoke that hung beneath the rafters. As he stepped forward, he felt rather than heard a crunching under his boot; almost simultaneously he saw that the floor appeared to be moving. As his eyes began to adjust to the gloom, he realised that the floor was carpeted in wall-to-wall cockroaches. He felt his stomach heave and he turned to get back down the ladder.

Unfortunately, by this time, the others were pressing hard behind him. He managed to gasp out.

"Go back! Back down! Go back!" This had little effect other than to bring those following behind him to a halt.

"We can't stay here, it's seething." His brain struggled temporarily for the right words and Tibetan and Nepali vocabulary fought for dominance. His words had failed to have the electrifying effect upon them that he felt the situation demanded. The rising nausea gripped his imagination at the thought of being enveloped in the vile things, their sensors waving in front of them like a blind predator's sticks.

"Go down! Get back down the ladder!" Whereas his initial command had been singularly ineffective, the tone of his voice and the force of his body as he physically pressed them back began to yield results, albeit slowly. There was a certain amount of bemused mumbling but they retreated and allowed Max to force his way out of the house and into the suddenly welcome night air.

"Nyima!" Max's voice sang out through the stillness that was only gently broken by voices murmuring as they went about their tasks. Moments later, the tall Sherpa emerged from halfway down the central thoroughfare. Topgye suddenly materialised beside Max and paused as he tried to light a pipe.

"I'm sorry, Colonel-la. But I did warn you." He gave a soft chuckle and returned to sucking on his pipe whilst holding a Zippo lighter to the bowl.

"It's not your fault…but wild horses won't drag me back inside these houses." His arm swept wide, embracing the village. "Lice, fleas, ticks, even leeches don't bother me much but cockroaches…especially armies of them." He threw his arms up in a gesture of despair. "That's why I always make it a rule to pitch camp outside village boundaries." He paused, reflecting on the fact that the object of seeking shelter here had been primarily for the protection of the stone walls against gunfire and their tents would not only afford no protection whatsoever but, on the contrary, would draw down fatally effective fire.

"Saheb?" Nyima's arrival coincided with that of the Professor and left no time for further prevarication.

"I'm going to pitch a few tents at the southern end of the track for the Sherpas." He looked towards Tashi and the boy and nodded in their direction. "I'm sure we can accommodate you as well…if you wish." He was irritated with himself for that little moment of hesitation. His natural inclination was to offer her as much comfort as he wanted for himself but he realised that his gesture might have been misinterpreted, after all, presumably she had been travelling with the Khambas for some time, and when all was said and done, she was a Tibetan, even though he doubted whether she would have been content to put up with the disgusting conditions in the house. His train of thought was broken by the Professor.

"Is it wise for us to remain here tonight?" He addressed the question to both Max and Topgye. Both men looked at each other and Max spoke first.

"You may be right...but everyone needs a rest and some food, preferably hot." He looked at Topgye enquiringly. "What d'you say, we brew up and let everyone get an hour or two's rest? We can have a council of war while the men prepare a meal."

"Saheb?" Max felt a hot mug thrust into his hand as he spoke. With that amazing capacity of English and Gurkha soldiers for conjuring up a mug of tea in jungle, desert or mountain, Deepraj had the immediate answer to fatigue.

"I heard that British soldiers marched on their tea, just like we Tibetans, now I see what it meant." Topgye's face wore an expression of admiration.

"Will you join me?" Max raised the steaming mug. "British Army tea, hot, sweet, strong and...," he was about to add the habitual 'just like we prefer our women' when he thought better of it, "...and life giving!" He grinned at them and offered the mug to Tashi. Whatever their customary mores, there was no way he was not going to prefer their solitary female companion. She accepted it gracefully, blew on it and bent down to give the boy a sip. He drank it carefully, his eyes never leaving Max.

"It tastes funny." That notwithstanding, he began to sip noisily at the brew, giving them all cause for amusement.

In minutes they were seated on packs in a temporary bivouac beside a house that had the mountainside for its back wall, nursing their respective mugs of British Army and Tibetan tea and alternately sipping on the dark rum that Deepraj had brought along in a water canteen. Topgye unfolded a map and Gojo shone his torch onto it.

"We're here, right?" He looked to Max for confirmation and got a quick nod.

"Right now, I don't think you are in any more danger from the Nepal Army than we are?" He checked again for agreement.

"Agreed."

"We must expect the PLA to be hard on our heels. Having knocked the bridge out, they'll have to follow us on foot and we've left a few extra obstacles in their path to slow them down."

"How'd you do that, no one seemed to fall seriously behind?"

"I left a small rear party to cover us and add to their difficulties. They'll join us here."

"So we have to await their arrival in any event."

Topgye shook his head and then looked quickly in the Professor's direction. Max felt sure that he caught a barely perceptible shake of the Thai's head. When he looked back at the Khamba's face, he wondered whether it was just his imagination that read a momentary unease.

"We have the task of getting the Treasury and my people to safety…that means India. My expertise is limited to the border areas and I have reached about the limit of my knowledge. Colonel-la, we have to put ourselves in your hands for this next part of the journey." He raised his hand as he saw Max begin to interrupt. "I know. I know that you are in personal danger too but," he smiled enigmatically, "that puts you on an equal footing with us, so we have a common purpose, no?"

Max gave a grunt of recognition to the uncomfortable truth of this analysis. He blew onto his tea, causing the liquid to ripple gently and the steam to dart out, like a frightened banshee into the bitter night air before scurrying back to the safety of the mug.

"OK. This is the way I see it. One thing is certain, we can't move a group of about 60 people through Nepal unnoticed, especially when half of them are Tibetan. In ordinary times I might have been tempted to try it at night but these aren't ordinary times and all they need to do is deploy a couple of battalions of hill troops and we're dead." He paused. "And I'm not speaking figuratively. In view of the Nepal Government's current relations with China, we have to anticipate a large scale response." Topgye nodded silently.

"The bulk of the Army are not political but we will be painted as an external threat and that doesn't involve political loyalties, only the basic job of a soldier."

As he spoke, Max was looking into the faces of both the Professor and Topgye, trying to read what was really there. His instinct told him that the Professor was still holding out on him despite their current predicament. He decided to keep to himself the long shot that he might know the local military commander and by the same token, he decided to say nothing of his arrangement with Hans Fischer. He wasn't about to abandon them but he had an itch that he couldn't scratch, an uncomfortable sense that they would readily abandon him once he had served their purpose, whatever that was. He turned his attention to Topgye.

"Whatever happens, you and your Khambas will have to make a run for it. I don't know whether you'd planned to go to India but that's your safest destination. But hampered by the Treasury and on foot, frankly I don't think you'll make it. The Sherpas are both in their own country and on their own terrain." He stopped to let this sink in so that they could draw their own conclusions. As he had come to expect, the Professor was very quick on the uptake.

"So you're suggesting that we could move the Treasury undetected if we can get the Sherpas to take it?" He frowned in concentration. "Can your Sherpas be trusted…it's a fortune?'

"Does a wise man entrust his wife with his best friend? They're only human…but these men have never cheated me and they are Buddhists too. How much of a choice do you have?"

"True, true." He spoke slowly as he digested the idea. "What, they keep the Treasury until they can move it over the border after things cool down?"

"I think you should put it to Nyima."

There was a pause whilst each thought his thoughts. Topgye took a deep breath and began to speak.

"I agree. Besides, there is another far more important decision… the child and Tashi-la."

"Topgye..." The Professor started to interrupt him but he held up his big hand, palm outwards towards the Thai.

"No. This is my decision." He turned to face Max. "The safety of the child and his mother is the only thing that truly matters. They must reach Dharmasala…whatever the cost. My life and that of my men are insignificant in comparison. Your idea is good, Colonel-la. To travel without the Treasury is to free ourselves of a great burden."

Max's mind raced with possibilities as to why the child and his mother could be more important than the Treasury but he kept it to himself and concentrated on the logistics.

"If you reduce your party to half its size or even less, we might just stand a chance of fooling the Nepalese. If we travel south, we're running to meet the danger. What about going east into Sikkim?"

"You say we. Does that mean that you'll come with us?" There was a note of cautious optimism in the Professor's voice. Max wondered whether he'd been imprudent. To travel together with them was to flirt with almost certain trouble, trouble on an even larger scale than he already faced, even if it made any sense to start comparing his fate in either eventuality. Entering Sikkim without a permit was liable to result in detention in India if he was caught. His ace in the hole was Fischer, if he could be persuaded to fly him out or to the southern border and relative safety. He felt a light touch on his arm.

"Please take us, Devilin-la." She said it softly but she was not smiling in the way that he had hoped for earlier nor was she pleading yet there was something in her expression and the tone of her voice that made him forget all his careful calculations. He found himself nodding acquiescence.

"Alright." This time she did smile and his world seemed to shrink, as though nothing existed outside the parameters of that smile. When she spoke he barely recognised the words though he heard the sounds.

"His Holiness will be forever in your debt."

"That's OK," he mumbled almost incoherently. Topgye's voice dragged him back into harsh reality.

"We should get the Sherpas on their way tonight. My guess is that in 8 hours or so they'll be safe from the Chinese and one more group of Sherpas without any foreigners would not be noteworthy."

"Agreed. Let me get Nyima over and we can discuss it with him together. Meantime we'll set up a temporary camp outside the village and get the Sherpa cooks to work on a hot meal for everyone." He looked towards the Professor.

"I suggest your Marines hold themselves in reserve. I don't imagine they speak Tibetan and they'd get under Topgye's feet." The Khamba chief nodded.

"I'll deploy half my force on the approach and in defensive positions in the village. The other half will relieve them after they've eaten." He turned and beckoned his deputy with his head. "Gojo!" The young Khamba closed up on their group.

"Stay as close to the little one as lice in your hair." He grinned but it was more a reassurance than an attempt at humour.

It was nearly midnight before Nyima bade Max the traditional farewell between friends.

"*Pheri betaünla* Huzoor."

"*Asah chha*." Max's expression of hope carried more than a hint of a prayer as they gripped each other's forearms. Seconds later he was watching the tall Sherpa swing quickly down the track after the main party. The words stuck in his mind, 'until we meet again' should perhaps have been 'if we meet again'. He was not given to premonitions or the myriad superstitions that dogged the lives of the hill people with whom he had lived for so long. But as a pragmatist he rated the prospects of a successful flight as thin to improbable and their chances of being shot by the Chinese as distinctly short odds. Standing alone on the track, dwarfed by the great mountains, he had a momentary sense of his insignificance which was magnified by the sudden awareness of his isolation. Other than Deepraj, he was now more alone in the Himalayan wilderness than he had ever known and the sense of loneliness was reinforced by the knowledge that he had become a fugitive.

He stared out across the stark moonlit landscape, the snow reflecting the light so that the rifts were black shadows that hid the demons the Sherpas always sought to propitiate. His mind turned back to Deepraj. The Gurkha's unswerving loyalty and resourceful skills made him the most indispensible Man Friday, but he was no confidante, no Jeeves. Max had learned to treasure what he characterised as his 'unmarital' status, a situation he had retreated to with the conviction of a convert after his volcanic affair with Shooja in Malaysia. The emotional wounds had been long in healing. His mind's eye conjured up the beautiful woman's face but it dissolved into Tashi's.

How long he stood there before the crunch of snow underfoot brought him out of his trance he didn't know, save that it felt like an age. As he turned to look and made out who was there, his heart gave an unmistakeable trip. She was speaking softly to Gojo, so softly that he couldn't catch the words. She walked towards Max leading the little boy by the hand, Gojo remained standing where she had spoken to him.

"Devilin-la." The inability to conjoin the 'v' and 'l' fell sweetly on his ear. "Forgive me but I would like to speak to you alone for a little." Max felt a bizarre sense of awkwardness that he could not offer her a seat. He spread wide his arms taking in their surroundings and let his face convey an unspoken apology for the lack of amenity. But what struck him as most incongruous was how, in this remote, desolate mountain fastness she managed to carry an aura of gentle femininity that belied her undoubted powers of endurance.

She laughed lightly, dismissing his concerns before her face grew serious.

"Topgye Sey has confided in me that he has absolute trust in you to help us." Again Max found himself responding silently with a dismissive wave of his hand. She continued.

"There is something that he wants you to know but he has given his word and the Teacher will not release him from it."

Max nodded gently. His instinct for self-preservation demanded that he have the full picture. It troubled him that the Khamba chief felt unable to confide in him, he had trusted the man, instinctively. Now he felt his anger towards the Professor and his unrelentingly secretive manner. It was as though he was making Tashi break ranks and his protective feelings towards her fuelled that anger.

"Perhaps it would be best if I insist that the Teacher tell me himself?" He adopted her description of the Professor.

"Please." Her hand was on the back of his as she spoke. He turned his wrist to let his fingers close around hers, squeezed gently to reassure her and released his grip.

"Let's go and find him."

The Professor was sitting beside a smouldering fire of yak dung, his eyes closed in apparent sleep, as were Deepraj and two of the Marines. Max assumed Topgye was in the village with his men. Though they made little sound as they approached, the Professor started awake, his face registering concern.

"What is it?" His expression seemed to relax as he caught sight of Tashi and the boy. He patted the bundle on which he was sitting, inviting them both to join him. Tashi shook her head slightly and remained standing beside Max, her face revealing nothing of her thoughts. Max stood opposite the Professor across the embers that glowed in harmony with the rise and fall of the wind. He spoke softly but with some determination.

"I think there's something that you ought to have told me, Professor." The Thai's eyes flicked across to Tashi then down as he seemed to take in the presence of Dondhup standing beside her, her arm hugging him protectively against her side. His gaze held on the child's face as he held his silence.

Max pondered whether or not to exonerate Tashi from the responsibility for speaking out of turn and explain that she had not disclosed anything other than the fact that something of significance was being concealed from him. But the man's track record for opacity dictated that he leave him guessing the extent of any revelation that Tashi may have made. Max had the distinct impression that the Professor was genuinely struggling with himself but he also sensed that he wouldn't – or couldn't? – bring himself to lie to her face. Perhaps, after all, he intended to withdraw into what he perceived to be a dignified silence. Searching for some clue as to the man's intentions, Max looked into a face of unreadable detachment, still looking towards the child yet his eyes had lost focus.

"Well?" Max prompted more peremptorily. More seconds elapsed then the Professor's eyes re-focused yet his face appeared to have acquired a measure of calm. He looked directly into Max's eyes.

"Please, sit down." He spoke in his unaccented Tibetan. Max was minded to continue to stand but as he glanced towards Tashi she gave him the slightest of nods and they both found space on an empty bundle to the Professor's right.

"I would be right, wouldn't I, that in your opinion the risks and indeed the sacrifices have been excessive when seen against our objective?"

"That's a fair assessment." Max leaned forward, his elbows resting on his knees, his hands on either side of his face. "And they continue to be." The older man's head dipped very slightly in acknowledgement.

"What I am about to tell you is a secret shared by only seven men." He paused and inhaled deeply before expelling the air slowly between his teeth. "You will become number eight."

"There is no great magic in numbers. A secret shared is a secret lost."

"True, but you wouldn't disagree that the fewer the numbers, the greater the security?" His eyes followed Max's as he shot a look at the Marines.

"My little force know only that we come for the Treasury...and they speak no Tibetan." He raised his voice and called Gojo over from where he hovered in the background.

"Find Topgye-la and ask him to join us here."

"But the chief ordered me to remain with Tashi-la and the child."

"Do as I say." The tone of voice brooked no opposition. "Tell your chief that these are my instructions and come back with him." The young Khamba shifted his weight from one foot to the other, clearly hesitant about whose orders to follow. Tashi resolved his dilemma.

"Please follow the Teacher's request. We will be safe here." He raised his hands in a prayer of salute, then loped away towards the village.

"You may recall, Colonel, that after their seizure of Tibet in 1950, the Chinese tried to exercise their suzerainty over Tibet through His Holiness the 14th Dalai Lama, at first directly and then when he would not co-operate, indirectly. After the flight of His Holiness in 1959, they seized on the Panchen Lama as their puppet. At first he acquiesced, then when he recognised the Chinese for what they were, he was imprisoned in Peking for 17 years. The Chinese know that they have to exploit our religious leadership in order to clothe their naked colonialism in the trappings of legitimacy and, most especially, to control the great mass of the Tibetan people through the medium of our religion. So, despite their ideological hatred for all formal religious movements, they know that if they can bend our religious leaders to their command, they will acquire the key to the hearts and minds of the Tibetan people. It is essential to grasp the significance of the influence of the *trulku,* the reincarnations of previous Lamas throughout Tibet and the Chinese have done so. To this end, when in 1995 His Holiness recognised Gandun Nyima as the reincarnation of the Panchen Lama, the child...he was only six years old...was taken into custody by the Chinese authorities and has never been seen since. Soon afterwards, Peking announced the recognition of another child as Panchen Lama. Then, in 1997, someone whom you would probably cast in the role of kingmaker, the 6th Reting Lama, died. Peking was quick to appreciate the potential of a Reting Lama schooled in their ways, and announced that it had appointed a new Reting Rinpoche. Traditionally, though the Chinese abolished the office of Regent in 1950, it has always been the Reting Lama who has acted as Tibet's Regent during the minority of the Dalai Lama." He paused and picked up a half-burned twig with which he began to trace indecipherable figures in the snow beside him.

"The key to the political absorption of Tibet into the People's Republic of China is to acquire control over our spiritual leadership... we are a spiritual rather than a temporal people. Despite every evil step that they have taken, including the mass abduction of thousands of Tibetan children and their 're-education', to use the Communist vernacular, in the Chinese mainland, the heart of Tibet is still our religion. So long as our unequivocally supreme spiritual leader is free, that heart remains Tibetan, unconquered and unconquerable." The fierce passion with which he spoke these last words drove home to Max that the Professor was, truly, his father's son. Nor could there be any doubt about where his loyalties lay. It dawned on him that what he had previously perceived as a measure of ruthlessness was the product of a driven desire to prove his utter commitment to his forefathers.

"Some four years ago, the spirit of Tibet fell into greater jeopardy than we have ever known." His eyes held Max's and his voice became so soft that he could only just catch the words.

"His Holiness the 14th Dalai Lama died of a coronary embolism."

"I..." Max's surprised exclamation was stifled by Tashi placing her hand on his arm to indicate that he should not interrupt.

"It was immediately obvious that if the Chinese were to learn of this before the discovery of the 15th reincarnation, they would put forward a false figure of their own choice. The crisis only deepened with the discovery of the reincarnation of Rinpoche, had they been able to seize the child you can well imagine the potential for evil-doing. A false claimant would have created doubt and confusion sufficient to enable them to introduce their own certainty into the spiritual vacuum; at its lowest it would have divided the Tibetan people, whereas kidnapping the true re-incarnation..." His voice fell away and he opened his palms in a gesture that conveyed the limitless potential for controlling first the infant Dalai Lama and through him his followers and their spiritual well-spring of motivation.

Max's mind raced with the revelation itself and its ramifications. He was genuinely staggered that the secret of the 14th Dalai Lama's death had been so closely guarded for so long. The enormity of the dilemma facing the Tibetan leadership was only equalled by the unparalleled security they had achieved in a community, like so many movements in exile, riven with competing interests and personal jealousies. But as he digested this, the disclosure that they had already found the 15th Dalai Lama fed a notion that swiftly assumed massive proportions. Why else would this bizarre assortment of people be where they were, when they were.

"And the reincarnation..." It was his turn to search the Professor's eyes steadily, insistent on being told the truth, even if he had already guessed the answer.

"The 15th Dalai Lama?" Even as he asked the question his eyes slid across the fire until they focussed on the child.

"*Kundun* Dondhup Yangzom." The Professor spoke the words with reverence and bowed his head gently towards the little boy. For Max there were innumerable questions but most of them would have to wait. For now, two matters impacted on him, neither of them of great consequence in the great scheme of which he had become an unwitting participant but he needed to know, for himself. He turned his head to look at Tashi and spoke softly.

"You are the mother of the 15th Dalai Lama?" She nodded and her smile was infused with a mixture of maternal pride coloured by a quiet awareness of her role in the history of these transcendental events. Max knew that he shouldn't ask, it was pointless, probably discourteous and certainly untimely, nevertheless he had to know.

"And..." He was about to say 'your husband' but thought better of it. "The child's father?" He watched her face cloud over a little and she hesitated before speaking.

"He was a kind and wise man, a physician who worked tirelessly for the people of our province. He always gave freely of his time and energy...too freely," she added, her lips set in a small tight line.

"There was an epidemic. He begged the Chinese to allow him access to the research laboratories of his old university in Shanghai but they refused him. He struggled on tending to his patients and spending every other hour trying to isolate the virus that was claiming so many lives. One day he succumbed to it himself." She lowered her eyes and stared at her closely knit hands, then looked up and smiled at her son.

"I'm so very sorry." Max felt rather than heard the inadequacy of his words. He had replied in a direct translation and it had failed to convey the sense of comfort with which he had wanted to imbue the words. She gave a little flicker of a smile by way of acknowledgement.

The Professor was speaking again but only part of Max's mind was listening as he spoke of the search for the reincarnation of the Dalai Lama, the auguries, the manifestations, the tests and the eventual confirmation by the Reting Lama that the child was, indeed, the true reincarnation.

What consumed Max's heart and mind was a sense of desperate futility. He knew now, with a certainty that he could not account for, that he had fallen in love with the widow of a Tibetan national hero and, even more impossibly, the mother of the 15th Dalai Lama.

Shadung

The first explosion brought them to their feet straight out of the exhausted sleep into which most of them had fallen. The second was unmistakably a mortar shell and Max registered it as a hit on the village. So much for the rear party's obstacles, he thought to himself. He didn't know just how good the Khambas were in a geurilla role, though he suspected that they had developed strong survival skills. But against well-trained mountain warfare troops with modern weaponry he didn't rate their chances in a stand up engagement, especially if the PLA were prepared to use mortars, even in foreign territory. He now found himself in the unenviable position of being on the edge of a sophisticated fire-fight, unarmed, without troops of his own, dependent upon a weird combination of Khamba geurillas who were not under his command and Thai Marines who answered to an academic, with his mobility shackled by the urgent need to protect a woman he had fallen in love with, not to mention the infant Dalai Lama. In other circumstances he might have been able to see the comic side of his situation and laugh out loud but the paramount need to reassure Tashi and Dondhup lent his expression a grim determination.

"We're quite safe here for the moment." He hoped that his voice carried the conviction that he wasn't too confident about in himself. What now troubled him was the command structure. Command should always gravitate to the one best able to cope with the particular circumstances faced by a group and he had no doubts whatsoever who that person was. It was a relief when the Professor hurried up to him and asked.

"What should we do?"

"Get the hell out of here with as little essential baggage as possible." Communications suddenly assumed vital importance.

"If you don't have a radio link with Topgye, send one of the Marines back to the village to make contact and get him back here for a few minutes. We need a plan and we don't have one." He contained his irritation at their lack of preparation, partly assuming some of the blame. The Professor reacted promptly and despatched one of the Marines. Max looked over at Gojo.

"Have your people got a mortar in your equipment?"

"No." The Khamba looked taut and anxious. Max had the distinct impression that he wanted to be back in the village with his men.

"Your job is the most important of any of us." He gave a swift sideways glance in the direction of Tashi and the child.

"Right now, we have Topgye and the others between us and them." Or however many of them were surviving the mortar attack, he thought grimly as he walked quickly back to a vantage point from which to observe the village. He kept his eyes on the slope beyond the village, looking for a tell-tale flash. The throaty 'gloot' of a mortar fired from close range would not be identifiable as to location as the sound bounced off the mountain walls. Max guessed that the PLA would be using the portable Russian M-37 with its 82-mm shell. There was no indication of either kind. The crash of the mortar shells exploding was now augmented by automatic rifle fire. He pointed at the Marines.

"Are you ready to go?" They nodded and hefted their Bergens onto their backs.

"Right. Straddle the track ahead of us, 20 metres up and as far off the track as the terrain allows. Eyes up but make a positive identification before opening fire. Clear?" A chorus of "Sirs!" acknowledged his orders without hesitation and they loped off up the track. Max had been hoping that by now Topgye would have sent a message back to him. That Gojo had not arrived was worrying. An explosive plume of dirt and snow no more than 75 metres away confirmed his earlier suspicion that the mortar fire was creeping towards their position. He shot a look at the Professor.

"We're getting out of here, now!"

"But..." The objection, whatever it was, was cut off.

"No but's. If you want to stay, go ahead. I'm taking Tashi and the boy as far away from this as I can." A thought suddenly occurred to him and he added.

"Have you got the dead Marine's arms and ammunition in your equipment?"

"It's in the yellow container." He indicated with his arm but jumped a little as another shell exploded a little closer to them. Max turned to Deepraj.

"Got your kit on?" He grinned approvingly as he noted that his question was unnecessary, the Gurkha was hefting what looked like Tashi's backpack.

"Bring whatever arms and ammunition you can find in that box." Deepraj dropped the backpack and ran over to the yellow container. At that moment, Max caught sight of Gojo loping towards them, the skirt of his heavy sheepskin overcoat flapping as the wind lifted them like drunken sails. His chest heaving from the exertion he began to speak even before he reached them.

"Topgye says he's pinned down...the mortars...says he'll hold on...you go." Even as he was speaking, Max began to rethink his immediate plan. He checked his watch, 5.40, the early light of dawn would soon be on them, removing yet another line of defence as the darkness lifted. He changed his mind.

"OK, Gojo, carry the little one on your back."

"We're ready, Devilin-la." Tashi materialised beside him and picked up her pack from where Deepraj had dropped it. She had another, smaller one, hung over one shoulder. Up close, Max could see the tenseness at the corners of her eyes.

"Great." He smiled encouragement. A curious madness seized him as the barrage of dirt, rock and snow crept towards them, above all else he wanted to hold her face in his hands and kiss her. He shook his head, still smiling.

"No. I'm Max, Tashi, Max...got it?" A half-smile plucked at her mouth and lifted the corners of her eyes fractionally but it was more than he had hoped for against the fear that was still evident in the drawn skin across her high cheekbones. He bent down and lifted Dondhup as he gestured with his head for Gojo to turn around.

"Now, my small friend, you'll see the fireworks from higher up." The boy's face peeped out from the fur lining of his headgear, curious but not registering fear. Max turned away as he heard Nyima's voice calling him.

"OK, Nyima, listen." He pointed at Tashi and Gojo. "Take them with you and your boys and trek for one hour then rest up. If I don't join you within the next hour, go on without me. Get the child and his mother to Namche Bazaar and then arrange for their passage to India, at any cost. Take your instructions from Tashi-la." He turned to face her directly.

"You'll be safe with Nyima and the Sherpas, you can trust them." She reached out, laying her hand on his forearm and gripping it firmly.

"You will join us?"

"Of course. Now get going." He reached around and put his hand on the small of her back, gently propelling her towards the track. Gojo lifted the small pack off Tashi's shoulder and hefted the boy into a more comfortable position on his back. Tashi looked back at Max over her shoulder.

"Join us quickly." Max nodded and smiled, waving the little party on its way.

The battle noise from the direction of the village was creeping disturbingly closer and he looked up at the sky, noticing the darkness softening around him.

"Saheb." Deepraj held out what a brief examination revealed to be a Ruger AC-556F sub-machine gun together with four fully loaded magazines in a light webbing belt pouch. Max unfolded the stock and checked the action.

"Shall I keep this?" The Gurkha tapped the sling of a HK-53 that he had slung over his shoulder.

"Damn right you better."

In the flurry of preparations, he had not appreciated that the Professor was still there. As he locked a magazine into position and cocked the action, he spoke quickly.

"Follow Nyima's group up the track for about 10 minutes and find yourself a comfortable spot to wait for us." He waved towards the Marines who were spread out in a defensive arc facing the village.

"Have you got a weapon yourself?" By now, Max had decided that no one could be taken at face value. The Professor unzipped his Bergen, reached in and dug out a Glock 23 self-loading pistol.

"Mmm. I hope you know how to handle it." He had been half-hoping that he'd have a HK-53 that he could swap for the Ruger. If the PLA soldiers got close enough for the sub-machine gun to be effective, it would probably be all over.

"I'll send one of the Marines back to accompany you. Get out of sight and give us 15 minutes to join you. If we haven't shown up by then, get moving down the track to meet up with Nyima's group. The reality is that none of this kit...," he tapped the Schmeisser, "...will avail us if we get trapped." He cocked his head in the direction of the village. "That lot sound as though they've enough equipment to start a war. You'd better get going." He softened his last words marginally out of a residual respect for the man, despite the cumulative sense of anger that blamed the Thai for letting him walk into this situation blindfold to the truth. Without waiting to see whether his orders were obeyed, Max struck out for the village with Deepraj, collecting the Marines en route.

What was left of the village was in smoking ruins. Bodies lay around indiscriminately in positions totally inimical to subsisting life. Some were readily identifiable as Khambas, others were obviously villagers, especially the women and to his disgust he counted five children, their little limbs akimbo, raggedy heaps of inanimate clothing, split skin, bones, blood and hair. It rekindled deeply buried memories of similar excesses he had been confronted with in Afghanistan and Kosovo and the recollection did nothing to blunt the revulsion he was experiencing now. His eyes quartered the ground as far as he could see for any sign of life. Nothing. In the same moment that he registered that resistance had ceased, the firing also stopped. His instinct for self-preservation triggered warning signals in his brain which was screaming at him to get out. Experience dictated that the cessation of the mortar bombardment would be the time for the Chinese soldiers to advance on the village. The dawn light was now upon them. Unless the Chinese were psychic, he could pull out with the Marines and make good their escape. He looked back at their escape route and the dismay was like a punch in the stomach. What he had failed to see in the darkness was that the south-running track was fully exposed to anyone in the village for nearly 200 metres.

"Move out now! Go! Go! Go!" He pushed Deepraj ahead of him and grabbed at the nearest Marine, pulling him back and out of the village. They ran quickly but they were weighted down with their packs, weapons and ammunition. Max looked back over his shoulder to check on the Marines behind him.

"Close up! Close up!" Pointing ahead to the beginning of the exposed section of track he shouted his orders to the two Marines nearest him whilst on the run.

"You two get into position and cover the rest of us until we reach where the track bends around out of sight." He waved his arm and stabbed at the end of the exposed section. "There! Got it?" They had reached the start of the exposed section and the two Marines dropped into firing positions, adjusting themselves to give a good arc of fire. Max cut the air towards the track with his free hand and shouted at Deepraj.

"Go!" As the Gurkha shot off along the track the remaining Marines were hard on his heels. He addressed the two men in firing positions.

"As soon as you see me drop out of sight, you two follow like bats out of hell! Don't open fire unless the Chinese fire at us. We'll give you covering fire." He didn't waste another second. These men were professional soldiers and knew the drills. He spinted up the track, his chest brusting and an agonising stitch yanked at his right side as he reached what he estimated to be the halfway mark. He sent a variety of prayers to an unseen god that the Chinese would advance cautiously through the village and give them the minute or so that they needed to get clear.

God had turned off his hearing-aid.

He heard the smack of bullets above his head and snow and rock chips rained down on him as he hurled himself around the corner and out of line of sight. Drawing deep painful breaths, his eyes were momentarily unsighted by the glaze of effort as he turned and crawled back to a vantage point from where he could assess the situation. Looking back over his shoulder he yelled at the Marine nearest to him.

"Covering fire! Give them covering fire!" He yanked the Ruger into a firing position as the Marine threw himself down beside him, his HK-53 held forward as he sought a target. Max felt the thud of another Marine beside him as the first one opened fire with short sharp taps.

The two rearguard Marines were sprinting strongly, slightly bent forward, their boots hammering against the packed snow of the track as a curtain of rock chips and snow advanced inexorably on them from behind. It sounded like a type 62 RPD.

"Rapid fire!" He shouted the order as he opened up with the Ruger, even though he had no target. He yelled at the approaching Marines.

"Run! You buggers, Run!" The second Marine in line jerked his head up as the rock and snow began to rain down on him seconds before the unseen soldier dropped his aim, hosing the bullets onto the target and smashing the Marine up against the mountainside like flotsam on the shoreline.

Max searched desperately for a give-away sign of the unseen gunner's position, his brain stubbornly telling him that there couldn't be a flash eliminator fitted to a firearm that could produce that stream of fire yet still seeing nothing.

The remaining Marine was now no more than 30 feet from them and his mates were screaming encouragement at him. When the first bullet struck him, Max saw the surprise register on his face a second or so before he fell forward sprawling hard onto the track so that his body bounced once before settling. What happened next was so unexpected that Max was slow to react, too slow and too late.

As the Marine's body hit the ground, one of the men beside him cried out.

"Chai!" In the same instant the Marine was on his feet, running towards his fallen comrade. Max's cry of 'No!' was too delayed by far. Max watched the surreal drama acting itself out on the narrow track in front of him. The rescuer got the fallen Marine onto his back in a fireman's lift and started back towards the bend. It seemed for an incredibly suspended moment of time that the firing had ceased to allow the man to be recovered. Max's mind snatched at the nanosecond of hope that someone on the Chinese side had a soldier's sense of honour and that just...maybe...they would be permitted to save their wounded.

The first shots probably hit the already dead or wounded man, though the force of the impact jolted the running Marine before his knees buckled and he staggered on a for a few paces before suddenly standing bolt upright, the dead Marine slipping off his shoulders as the top half of the would-be rescuer's face simply left his head.

Max fought down the nausea that welled up in his throat.

"Go!" What he'd intended to be a shout came out more like a croak but no one needed an explanation. The three of them ran back down the track. After a few minutes, the pace, the altitude and their respective loads began to tell on them. Max felt as though his knees had divorced themselves from his motor muscles and every step was a leaden effort. Ahead of them, the track narrowed until it squeezed between a cleft in the rock. Max strained his eyes to see through the dancing haze which veiled his pupils, he thought he'd caught sight of a slight movement in the cleft but he dismissed it as a trick of the light and his own physical endeavours.

The sound of a mortar shell exploding behind them but well back, closer to the village, spurred them on to redouble their efforts to reach the rock cleft. As they entered it, it transpired that it was a short rock corridor which gave them a brief but no less welcome sense of security.

As they reached the far end of the corridor, the Professor emerged from the shadows to their right.

"Colonel?" Max lurched to a halt, brushing hard against the snow covered face of the mountainside which, in turn, dislodged some snow that fell on his head, the icy particles moistening his lips as he dragged the thin air into his lungs.

"Where are the others?"

"Dead." Max shook his head, not up to providing a blow-by-blow account at this juncture. As if to underscore the point, another explosion from the northern side of the track reverberated off the surrounding mountains and Max thought he detected the sound of a snow slide. He looked at Deepraj.

"If we're lucky, they'll bring down a rockfall onto the track or, better still, blow half the bloody track away."

"The luck's not with us on this trip, Saheb." The Gurkha's face showed nothing of his feelings but Max recognised in his words that intuitive sense of fatalism innate in so many hillmen. Nor, he admitted to himself, could he argue with the historical accuracy of the observation. In any event, he wasn't about to trust to that fickle-hearted lady. He ordered the Marine who had accompanied the Professor to take up the rearguard position. Looking up and back towards where he guessed the Chinese would be, he noted that any decently equipped mountain warfare troops could traverse gaps in the track that contoured the mountainside. At best, it would only delay them a little.

"Re-load and make safe." He fished out a fresh magazine and exchanged it for the empty one as Deepraj and the Marine who had fired his weapon did likewise. Max had a slight feeling of guilt that nagged him into saying something which would add to his earlier cryptic announcement.

"They were brave men, good soldiers, Professor…and they died in a great cause." There was a momentary flash of what he read as appreciation in the Thai's expression. He looked away, gave another long look backwards then gestured Deepraj to take the point.

"Let's go."

They had set off at a cracking pace but after about a quarter of an hour Max had to tell Deepraj to slow down to accommodate the Professor. His face ran with sweat and his breathing became laboured.

"Sorry, Colonel." His apology came out as a wheeze. Max nodded a quick acknowledgment but the fact was that at this reduced rate of march, their pursuers would almost certainly gain on them.

"Take your pack off." After a momentary hesitation, the Thai shrugged himself out of his Bergen. To Max's relief, one of the Marines picked it up and hefted it over one shoulder. He smiled at the man.

"We'll take it in turns." The Marine managed a grin and set off again. With his load lightened, the Professor made better time but he still couldn't maintain the pace that Max tried to set and they had to make frequent adjustments to their rate which also broke their rhythm. He fretted inwardly but there was nothing for it but to allow the Professor to make the best time he could. Several times Deepraj turned and looked back wearing an expression that clearly said 'If we keep on at this rate, we're mincemeat.' The Professor's frequent mumbled apologies served only to heighten the sense of frustration. Max repeatedly checked his watch to measure their progress. It was a little over an hour and a half before Deepraj's curt tones broke the silence.

"We're here."

'Here' turned out to be a rock strewn piece of ground about 60 square metres in area, at the base of a rock fault that created a natural 'chimney' running almost vertically up the face of the mountain to what looked as though it was some sort of plateau, 30 to 40 feet above their heads. Max quickly retraced his steps to assess the visibility of the platform from the approach route. As he'd suspected, the fault itself was out of the line of sight but the bulk of the ground at its base was visible from a distance of some 50-60 metres. He cast around him for a concealed lying-up position with a line of sight up the track. There was precious little cover and not much prospect of one man holding off the PLA in a Thermopylae type of tactic. Nonetheless, it was an essential move. He ran back to the platform and Gojo stepped forward to meet him.

"I've done a reconnaissance ahead of us. The track continues contouring the rockface for about another 200 yards then it emerges into the side of a broad based ravine with a river running through it. Once we're into the open land of the ravine, there's no cover until we pick up a track on the far side of the river. We'll be very exposed."

"How long d'you think it'd take us to cross over and make cover on the far side?"

"An hour? Maybe an hour and half? It depends on how much time it takes us to cross the river." He shook his head, discouraged at their poor prospects.

"It won't work." Max's lungs were expanding painfully as the cold air was sucked in. He waved a hand around the platform despondently.

"This is no defensive position and anyway, we can't hold off a regular PLA unit, not with all the kit they're carrying. Equally, we can't risk crossing the river, we'd be cut down long before we found cover. Our only hope is to evade them until nightfall, then we may be able to slip deep enough into Nepal to discourage them from following us any further. But..." he gave a slight indication of his head in the direction of the Professor.

"He's not in any condition to make a run for it and though Tashi-la is fit, someone will have to carry the boy."

Gojo nodded emphatically. Max stepped into the base of the chimney and studied the formation. It was uncomfortably wide at its base but narrowed quickly before continuing on up for about 30 feet in a more or less regular gap between the opposing rock faces. Still looking up the chimney, he called Deepraj over.

"Have we got about 40 feet of climbing rope?"

"I'll look." The Gurkha unravelled a length of thick nylon cord that was tied to the heavy frame which bore his equipment, rough measuring it across his chest as he did so.

"About 35 to 36."

"It'll have to do." Max made his mind up, this was their escape route.

He beckoned over the Marine who had carried the Professor's pack. The man was dependable. Together they retraced their steps back up the track for a short distance.

"Re-arrange some of these rocks to give yourself an observation trench. If you get a Chinese soldier in your sights, don't wait for him to fire, shoot first. Don't give them an opportunity to fire on us. I'll call you back as soon as I have everyone but your mate off that platform. When he calls you, you'd better come running like the clappers." The Marine acknowledged his instructions with a silent lifting of his weapon.

"One more thing, grab your spare ammunition and thermal blanket out of your pack, I'm afraid you'll have to lose the rest of your kit." The Marine did as he was told and Max hefted the framed Bergen over one shoulder.

"You have to keep our back door shut tight…but you'll have the quickest exit." He pointed back to the platform and then up towards the plateau above their heads.

"OK, sir." The Marine managed a quick smile as he caught the drift of Max's words, then started on building his trench. Max had an uncomfortable transposition of the words 'trench' and 'grave' in his mind but pushed it away as he concentrated on getting the rest of his plan carried out.

"Tashi-la?" She looked up expectantly, the anxiety still drawing the contours of her face in taut lines.

"Quick as you can, pack one load with the absolute essentials for yourself and Dondhup. We're going to leave most of our baggage." He instructed the others to abandon their packs, taking only the bare essentials with them. To Deepraj, he said, "We'll take one tent, 12 emergency ration packs, the medical bag and the satcom phone." He turned to the remaining Marine and Gojo.

"Take these packs about 150 metres down the track…," he pointed to the south, "…and dump them. Let's hope that the Chinese think we've abandoned them for the sake of speed. OK, now listen up, everyone." He outlined the basic plan quickly.

"Whilst I make the first ascent, Deepraj will show you how to climb, using the rope to support yourself…but don't worry." He noticed the anxiety in the faces of Tashi and the Professor. "We'll be hauling you up from the top." He turned to Deepraj. "You follow me, carrying Dondhup, then Tashi." He smiled encouragement at her. "You, Professor, then Gojo, lastly the two of you." This, to the Marine.

"If we come under fire, you'll have to cover your chum so that he can get back here, then the two of you get your arses up the chimney. The base is wide but you'll have the rope to get you into the throat." The Marine nodded quickly. Slipping the coiled rope over his head, Max stepped into the base of the chimney and took one last look up it. To Deepraj he said.

"Give me a stirrup, then I'm onto your shoulders to get me into the throat." The Gurkha cupped both hands and leaned forward, taking Max's weight. The lower end of the throat was slightly wider than Max had calculated and he found himself fully stretched, his back against one wall and both legs straight out, lodging him firmly against the opposing rock walls. Shifting the bulk of the pressure onto his left leg, he inched the right boot up a little and using his gloved hands on the wall behind him, pushed his body up a few inches. Repeating the manoeuvre with alternate boots, he made a few feet. About a quarter of the way up, as he slid his back up he could feel a sudden loss of tension as he seemed to press back into a concavity, he felt himself slipping and slammed one foot into the far wall to put a brake on his descent. His back slid down lower than his feet and for a panic-striken second he thought he was going into a dive. His hands searched desperately through the fabric of his gloves for an irregular feature in the rock face behind him against which he could he could get some purchase. Just as he felt himself reaching the critical angle at which he'd lose the tension that held him between the two faces, the fingers of his left hand felt a thin rib of projecting rock and he pressed his palm against it in a jolting thrust that tore at his shoulder. He winced at the sharp pain as the shoulder muscles screamed…but it held.

Sweat dripped into his eyes, stinging them. He shook his head to divert the beads of perspiration and took a deep breath. The incident had drained him, momentarily and he remained frozen, his eyes virtually level with his toecaps, telling himself that the physics of his position were hopelessly wrong, knowing that he had to correct it promptly but wondering where he would find the strength to do so. Not for the first time, his mind began to play word games with him. 'God is in his heaven and all's well' transmuted itself into 'Heaven and all heavy', the meaningless phrase repeating itself in his brain. He couldn't look down, knew that he shouldn't in any event and instinctively looked up. The top of the chimney appeared tantalisingly near yet far. He closed his eyes and as if on cue, Tashi's features swam against the back of his eye lids, he saw the anxiety, her hands cupping her jaw, slender fingers reaching up towards those high cheekbones, her expression when they had parted company back at the village, did she genuinely care? How much could he read into it?

"Saheb?" Deepraj's worried voice floated up from the ground, snapping him out of his reverie.

"OK. I'm OK!" He managed, the words belied his situation, but a fall now would probably dash their slim hopes of survival. He gritted his teeth and despite the feeling that it was a retrograde move, he released the tension on his right leg and lowered it until it was beneath the line of his buttocks. Levering himself carefully, he inched his position back into correction. Now he studied the rock face above and behind him as best he could, intent on avoiding the depression that had cost him precious time and energy.

Now that he was balanced, he resumed his ascent, stomping each boot against the opposite wall and sliding his back up, aided by his hands. The Ruger gradually moved across his chest until it slid off and hung underneath him. The minutes seemed to tick by, inconsiderate of the effort he was making. He determined not to look up for at least five consecutive moves, then lengthened that to 10, setting himself a series of minor challenges to narrow down the focus of his endeavour.

It dawned on him that his knees were now closer to his chest, the chimney narrowing and he abandoned counting moves and looked up. The lip of the chimney was no more than three feet above his head. He could feel his legs trembling with the effort but he ignored it as the sense of achievement forced adrenalin around his system. It was short lived.

No sooner had he rolled over the lip of rock and lay flat on his back in the snow, drawing down great lungfulls of frozen air, relishing the precious moments of respite than the sound of gunfire shocked him into action. He searched desperately for anchorage for the rope and enjoyed the first bit of luck that he'd encountered for days. The top of the chimney had a miniature haff-like feature around which he looped one end of the rope, dropping the free end down. Within seconds it went taught and he watched the loop as it took the strain of Deepraj as he came up the chimney in a series of hand pulls and thrusts with his boots. It occurred to Max, too late, that he ought to have secured the rope around him and then looped it over the rock but there was no time for that now. The gunfire had increased and become an exchange, the echoes reverberating around the surrounding mountains.

Dondhup's fur-capped head came into view and Max kneeled down beside the lip and pulled the little boy up and off Deepraj's back.

"Huzoor." The Gurkha managed a gasp of appreciation before rolling over the edge. Max removed the loop from the rock and secured it around his waist and over his shoulder before bellowing down the chimney.

"Tashi...now!" As he was bracing himself as best he could, Deepraj joined him and grabbed onto the line. They felt the weight stretch the rope taut and both men began to haul it in, Max walking backwards, his back taking the major strain. Their combined efforts had Tashi sprawling in the snow beside the lip of the chimney in less than two minutes. Max waved her towards Dondhup as he ran forward and lowered the rope again. The rate of firing had increased and Max's sense of anxiety notched up several rungs as he heard the unmistakable crump of a hand grenade. The Marine's firing trench was unlikely to afford him sufficient protection if the grenade was lobbed behind him. As if to prove his calculation correct, the two-way firing stopped only to start again a moment or two later but this time the sounds came almost directly up the chimney. Max guessed that the remaining Marine had opened fire from the rock platform itself.

"Professor...quick!" He yelled down the chimney. The chatter of the firearms increased and he guessed that Gojo was also returning fire.

The line went taut as the Professor started up. Almost simultaneously, he heard the Professor shout but he couldn't make out what he said other than hearing Gojo's name.

"Crump!" The sound of the explosion was carried up the chimney.

"Move it man! Move it!" Max could no longer hear the automatic sound of the Marine's HK-53 but the metallic bite of Gojo's Kalashnikov was still detectable. As they strained to pull the Professor up, they both heard the sound of a man's screaming and the Kalashnikov fell silent.

"Come on, Deepraj, pull the bugger up!" The load began to move as they strained to get him up quickly but it felt unresponsive and Max's fears were reinforced when he heard low moans rising up the chimney.

"Hang on! You're almost there." He shouted encouragement to the limp weight that clung to the rope. The veins in Deepraj's temples bulged and his own arms felt as though they would crack under the strain. In silence they heaved, hand over hand, pulling the dead weight tantalisingly slowly until they got him up to the rim and Deepraj grabbed him under one arm and unceremoniously bundled him over the rim, the manoeuvre causing the Professor to cry out in pain.

"Christ!" Max cursed under his breath. All they needed now was the Professor's cries to give away their position. They dragged him as gently as possible away from the chimney top and Tashi knelt beside him to give him support. Looking back at the rim, the crushed snow all around it caught his attention. He fell to his knees and eased the remaining snow and compressed ice away from the edge. Freshly falling snow or ice particles would be tell-tale signs of their position.

"I think he's badly wounded but I daren't examine him any closer, he's already moaning." Deepraj whispered. Max gave a grim nod of acknowledgement and hurried over to the Professor, putting one hand to his mouth and gesturing downwards with the other. The Thai's eyes were dull and his face screwed up in pain but he gave a move of his head in recognition of Max's message. Putting his mouth close to the Professor's ear, Max spoke softly.

"I want to move you away from here. We're exposed and I need to take a look at your wound. Can you keep quiet if we carry you for about 100 metres or so?" The pain filled eyes blinked slowly and he gave the slightest of nods.

"Good man." Signalling with his hands, Max indicated to the others that they should move in the direction of the mountainside, some 200 metres behind them. Cradling the Professor in a makeshift chair of their linked arms, they carried him slowly over the virgin snow carpet, Max's hair standing up at the back of his neck as their boots crushed the snow and each step precipitated a low moan that the Professor was obviously trying his best to control.

The sounds of shouted orders funnelled up the chimney, making them seem even closer than they were and lending a desperate energy to their exhausted limbs. The further away they got from the mouth of the chimney, the faster he felt able to move. Tashi strode purposefully ahead of them, dragging Dondhup along, his little legs snagging in the drifts of snow. She stopped for a moment, then turned and waved them forward encouragingly. Whatever she had found by way of a resting place, Max decided they would accept without hesitation. He could only guess at Deepraj's condition but he knew that he was reaching the end of his abilities to carry the Professor's dead weight much further.

It was a concavity in the mountainside with a short overhang. Not much in real terms but palatial in their desperate circumstances. They left the Professor in Tashi's care whilst they trudged back to the chimney to recover their packs. Retracing their steps to the temporary shelter neither man spoke but Max gave Deepraj a look that conveyed both appreciation for his efforts and a silent prayer of hope that this ploy would work. The Gurkha squeezed a grin out of his tired features and Max offered up a silent prayer of thanks for the steadfastness of this enigmatic hillman. As he began to undo the Professor's down jacket, his eyes fell on the face of the God-child and he was strangely moved by the extraordinary serenity in a face whose features were, as yet, not fully formed. If someone was to watch over them, could it be this little 4-year-old boy with the deep, dark eyes of a Bodhisattva?

Kathmandu

The office of the commanding officer of the Airborne Forces reflected the man. Minimal furnishings, standard issue desk and chair, three Army-issue easy chairs around a coffee table that owed more to utility than fashion, four telephones and a hat stand. The walls, in the space not occupied with maps and aerial views of Nepal and its immediate neighbours, were hung with elaborately silver-framed photographs of the man standing together with the military commanders of other countries and one or two minor heads of state. The careful observer would have noted that there was a remarkable balance between east, west and 'uncommitted' nations' representatives. Only one of the several flies on the wall would have known that the photographs were always rearranged so that the most prominent position was accorded to the country of the commander's visitor.

One wall, in particular, bespoke his multi-national military background, beginning with a photograph of a young officer cadet receiving the sword of honour at Dehra Dun Military Academy, the first and only Nepalese to do so; another was of Staff College colleagues at Camberley in England, senior staff officers at their farewell dinner in Leningrad, Paratroop Course graduates in Haifa and, most recently, the Joint Services Staff College at Beijing. Brigadier-General Karki was a committed soldier, a man who owed his remarkable success to his single-minded commitment to himself. In fairness, second only to this top priority was his loyalty to his country, a factor which foreign military attachés vying for his ear, frequently overlooked. Fortunately for Nepal, as the General saw it, he viewed with messianic conviction the confluence of national and personal gain.

Had he enjoyed an education which included the works of Shakespeare, he might well have wished a plague upon the house of Bhandari. As he had not, he wished them unending bouts of diarrhoea. With the star of Beijing currently in the ascendant, he had carefully cultivated a close rapport with the chief of security for Tibet. The Nepalese Consul-General's signal had arrived on his desk far too late for Nepal Army paratroops to be deployed effectively. If the Khamba geurillas were inside Nepal, it would take two brigades with air support to guarantee their elimination, a force not currently at his disposal. The stinking Khambas would melt into Nepal's *Bhotia* communities living in the high Himalaya and become indistinguishable. The weather militated against dropping paratroops into the mountains and the political climate dictated that the only troops wholly loyal to the current government should not be deployed to a region too far distant from the capital lest they were needed at short notice.

His eyes wandered over the map of the area seeking a solution, the words of his old Staff College mentor whispering in his ear: use the terrain, let it inform your strategy.

He picked up a large meteorological talc overlay and aligned it carefully over the map. Dr. Kawasaki of the UNDP was one of the small band of Asian experts that he had used his influence to persuade the government to retain. The Japanese weatherman was totally apolitical and his forecasting uncannily accurate.

The Khambas' infiltration point and the mountains to east and west of it were now under a heavy snowfall which was blanketing the area to a north-south depth of some 20 miles from the Tibetan border. South of the snow-line, the monsoon was shown as medium-to-heavy and increasing. The one factor that gave him comfort was that whatever made life difficult for the searchers, including the pursuing PLA unit that he assumed to be operating there, would be doubly so for the Khambas until they could reach their kith and kin in the lower reaches of the mountains.

"Your car is waiting to take you to the Security Council meeting, General Saheb." He had been so involved with his thoughts that he'd not heard his Brigade Major enter the office.

"You've seen this signal from Lhasa?" It was more an impatient commentary than a question since everything passed over the BM's desk before reaching him. The Major nodded, screwing his sun-burned wheaten features into an expression that the General had seen on his own face when shaving. It was uncanny the way these two men grew more alike each day. Physical resemblance apart, they shared the same exclusive interests and he valued his subordinate's political judgment.

"That shitty Consul-General will have to be replaced at the earliest opportunity. We can probably neutralise the Khambas but not as quickly as General Fei wants us to, especially because he wants us to interrogate them."

"What about the Rai *burro*?" The Major glanced quickly into the adjoining room then closed the door behind him. It was unlikely that there were secret police agents in the Airborne Forces HQ but highly probable that Army HQ was well infiltrated. He lowered his voice.

"DIG Maniprasad Rai could well swing the armed police behind him, they have a heavy concentration of hillmen amongst their junior officers and NCO's. If he did, any move he made would probably be during the monsoon when we can't deploy our helicopters to maximum effect. He's ex-Army and can think like a soldier. At worst he could run interference against us." He paused for a moment before adding.

"But I don't suppose you were proposing to do the job yourself?"

The General gave a wolfish grin.

"No, I'm not. You are." Momentary incomprehension clouded the Major's features before his eyes noted the talc over the map and he put two and two together.

"On attachment to Purano Gorkha?"

"Precisely. I'll tell the chief of staff that he can have a small recce group of paratroops under command to his favourite infantry regiment. He'll be so puffed up at getting some of our men back into a traditional role and under command that he'll readily commit Purano Gorkha to a search and destroy mission."

"And if we meet up with the PLA unit, they'll observe our paratroop flashes and badges."

"You don't miss a trick." The General picked up his cap and swagger cane.

"I'll take Sardhoj to the council meeting. Put a stick on three hours alert and do the staff work in readiness." He walked across the room, letting the Major open the door for him, standing briefly to attention.

The Security Council meeting was already underway when General Karki arrived. He slipped into his seat and bowed a silent apology to the president whose small, thin figure barely occupied the large gothic looking chair at the head of the conference table. The old man nodded acknowledgement with his rheumy eyes, almost indistinguishable from the large liver spots on his wrinkled face. The game, as Karki thought of it, was noisily afoot. Each council member lied glibly, littering their speeches with their fanatical adherence to revolutionary ideals whilst plotting their personal advancement to positions of greater financial influence. The president, like a devout Brahmin's white umbrella, sheltered the opaque, fly-blown logic from exposure to the heat of critical analysis.

The foreign secretary's sing-song voice rose above the undisciplined clamour, his old-fashioned high honorifics and courtly grammar barely registering in the Paratroop General's conscious. The soldier was carrying out his own appreciation of the opposition. Aside from the president and foreign secretary, there was the commander-in-chief whom he rated as a witless relic of the old nepotism; additionally there were Harihar Bhandari, the chief cadre of the Armed Students whom he had privately labelled as an odourless fart, and Shere Shumsher, the Bhandari faction's lap-dog appointee as inspector general of police. The real forces to be contended with were the two deputy inspectors of police.

From behind his permanently worn dark glasses, he studied the Mongol features of Maniprasad Rai, trying to read the unreadable. Suddenly the previously inscrutable face moved as the DIG began to speak. Within seconds he heard the foreign secretary mention Honggaon, a village he knew to be directly in the path of the Khambas. The meeting had his full attention.

"True, it's a matter of course to detain anyone who violates the terms of their trekking permit, though in the case of Colonel Devlin I believe that there must be some sort of reasonable explanation."

"What you believe is completely contrary to the facts!" Harihar Bhandari's voice was heavy with sarcasm to the point of rudeness. General Karki quietly relished the animosity between the rival groupings. The president pushed his Nepali hat back on his head in a gesture of tired frustration.

"What facts are these, Bhandari-ji?" His tone was friendly.

"The fact that his party deliberately avoided the police post at Honggaon, that they contrived to leave their liaison officer behind, that they have not been seen since their presence was reported north of Honggaon in a prohibited border area and the fact that they are obviously spies!" Flecks of spittle had gathered on Bhandari's lower lip and now flew across the table with the vehemence of his final words, landing like diseased bubbles on the paper before him. The foreign secretary raised his hand to stem the flow of vitriol.

"As to your last fact," he lingered on the word with the disdain of a school master reproaching a wayward pupil for a grammatical howler, "you are well aware that the Colonel was investigated frequently during his years in Nepal and there was never a whisper of anything clandestine about his activities. The members of his group are the accredited nationals of a country without whose generous assistance we would have no international air links. As I understand him, the DIG is merely cautioning some diplomacy in the official handling of the Devlin group." He paused for the remaining members of the council to digest his words and to allow Bhandari to reflect on the wisdom of pursuing his personal vendetta. General Karki respected the man's professionalism.

Turning slightly to face the president but keeping his eyes on Bhandari, the foreign secretary continued,

"My advice, Huzoor, is to leave the present orders for the detention of Colonel Devlin's party as already issued. They should be detained, brought back to Kathmandu and required to provide a full explanation."

"Devlin and the other foreigners should be tried as spies." Bhandari interjected without waiting for the president's response.

"I agree your suggestion." The president looked directly at the foreign secretary, ignoring Bhandari. A fly settled on his liver spot mottled hand but he ignored that too.

"Now, what about these Khamba insurgents?" General Karki was reminded that despite his advanced years and an appearance of decrepitude, the old man's mind was still sharp. He wondered whether the foreign secretary had briefed him before the meeting. He tried to read the notes that lay on the table in front of the president but had to stop when the commander-in-chief began to speak. He outlined current military deployments, rambled discursively about the weather and rival demands on potential internal trouble spots. Karki recognised the signs; as usual, the man was demonstrating that he was nothing more than an over-promoted clerk. The president gave a short impatient wave of his hand which unsettled the fly.

"This is a job for the Paratroops eh?" He turned to face General Karki as he spoke.

"My staff have examined the pros and cons of deploying airborne forces in this area." The General wished he'd brought a map with him, it would have made his task easier, none of the council's members knew a contour from a concubine. "Regrettably, we have concluded that paratroops cannot be used to maximum operational effect in this terrain." He watched as a frown of incomprehension began to cross the president's brow.

"Given the time and weather factors, the best that we can suggest is that a detachment of paras be put under command of Colonel Pashupati Thapa who commands the *Purano Gorkha* battalion closest to the infiltration point. Acting in a conventional role, they could be used as his reconnaissance unit." He looked towards the C-in-C.

"With your permission, sir, I propose seconding my Brigade-Major to liaise with Colonel Thapa. After all," he smiled confidentially, keeping his eyes locked on those of the C-in-C, "this is really a classic job for well-trained mountain infantry."

There was a distinct narrowing of the C-in-C's bulbous eyes as he registered the fact that Karki had already planned the military response to the Khambas including sending his No.2 as his eyes and ears. He could still veto the plan if he wanted to but if he did so now, it would look as though he didn't have a grip on his own house. The paratroop general continued to smile at his commander. It was too early to force his hand, especially during the monsoon when mobility was vulnerable to the whim of the weather. If his plan was rejected he might have to reconsider his options but he was counting on the C-in-

C's innate lazyness coupled with his preference for anything which involved *Purano Gorkha.* The response, when it came, surprised Karki by its political adroitness.

"Colonel Thapa will need more than a handful of paratroops if he is to carry out this task successfully. I can give him the eastern division Tope Khana in an infantry role. The gunners will be delighted to leave their heavy equipment behind for a change." He turned towards Bhandari.

"Perhaps Bhandari-ji could spare two cadres of his young warriors?" The whisper of a smile at the corners of his mouth was completely lost on the ASO commander as he leaned forward in his eagerness to demonstrate his co-operation.

"The Biratnagar Brigade will be put at Colonel Thapa's disposal."

"Excellent! Excellent!" The C-in-C turned the glimmer of a smile on, full beam. "I think that disposes of the immediate problem. I will put Colonel Thapa in overall command and promote him temporary Brigadier." He flashed a little triumphal smile at the paratroop general who nodded his acquiescence. So many private agendas, so many overblown egos to be massaged, Karki thought to himself. The president signalled the end of the meeting and the council members began to talk amongst themselves and to their advisors sitting in the row behind them. General Karki's adjutant leaned forward and spoke into his commanding officer's ear.

"Bhandari hates Devlin. He even tried to have him murdered by *goondas* when he was in Kathmandu before he left on his expedition. This operation will be used as a cover to get the job done properly." Karki caught Bhandari's eye momentarily and smiled across the table. He spoke softly, still smiling,

"He can do what he wants to, for our purposes. It could even be to our advantage to have Colonel Devlin dead and the responsibility laid at Bhandari's feet. By the time it's done, the recriminations will add to the confusion and help to create the right atomosphere for us to take full control." His eyes surveyed the other occupants of the room, revising or confirming his assessments of people whom he regarded in the main as corrupt windbags or light-weights on the political make. Apart from the president, whose age and deeply ingrained democratic principles militated against trying to win him over, the only man with intellect and political skills was the foreign secretary. If he could be won over, he would be a powerful ally, especially against New Delhi and Beijing. The Indians would do their utmost to foment civil unrest in order to retain their influence over Nepal's affairs and the Chinese would fight to retain this toehold in the subcontinent. When the time was ripe, he would approach him.

The buzz of conversation grew louder and the C-in-C was talking to him now, his tiny mind obsessed with matters of little consequence. Karki listened with one ear whilst the better part of his mind continued to plan his coup. Removing the Bhandari faction, disarming the Students and ensuring they were held responsible for the political assassination of Colonel Devlin. He allowed himself a second's reflection on the death of a man for whom he held a grudging respect. No matter, when all was said and done, he was only a foreigner anyway and it was a small sacrifice for the greater good of Nepal.

0°10' East 0°8' North

Max realised his mistake too late. It was starkly elementary but he had overlooked it. If the Chinese were to be led to believe that they had crossed the river it could only have been by sprouting wings. Beyond the river there was a snow field, a pristine blanket without sign of human tracks.

"Shit!" He whispered to himself. Now he realised that he was hoist with his own petard of cleverness. If he hadn't dumped the extra backpacks part way along the track, they might have been persuaded that Gojo and the Marines were the last of the party. There was no other option, they'd have to make a run for it.

As if on cue, the Professor winced in pain. One look at his face was enough to make him realise that there was no way the man could move under his own steam. The leaden futility of their predicament cramped his mind. He looked up into the sky in an involuntary quest for inspiration and the gods of the mountains heard him. A snow flake fell on his upturned face, then another and another. He reached out and grabbed Deepraj's arm.

"Snow! It's snowing!" It was a jubilant whisper. He clenched his fists as if he could grab a layer of it and pull it down around them. A whispered prayer urged on the elements. "Come on my darlings, snow us in!"

The Gurkha's face registered a small crack of pleasure as he grasped the significance of Max's jubilation.

The snow *Bhairabs* responded to his imprecations and the flakes grew larger and denser with each passing second until visibility was down to a bare six feet. Max tugged at Deepraj and they both scrambled over to Tashi.

"This will hide any tracks in less than five minutes. It could even cover the equipment we abandoned further down the track. The bloody Chinese are probably playing it very cautious, that track is precarious and there could be more ambush sites on the far side of the rock corridors." He spoke in Tibetan and then Nepali. Tashi and Deepraj nodded their understanding in turn.

"We can make a temporary snow shelter here and attend to the Professor. Then we'll try and move on after dark." He said nothing about the Thai's condition, they had enough to worry about without adding his conviction that the man would not survive. He put his mouth close to Deepraj's ear.

"D'you think you could get our tent up?" The Gurkha said nothing but crawled towards the equipment.

"You two keep warm until we get you some better shelter." Max smiled at the mother and son then moved over to where the Professor lay, the snow already mantling him as he lay in a fetal position, unmoving. He felt for a pulse and found it weak and irregular. His pallor was grey but Max attributed that more to the cold. The blood stained clothing around his abdomen was barely visible through the cellular blanket of snow. It was obvious that the combination of shock and loss of body heat alone threatened his prospects of survival, irrespective of the nature of his wounds. They had to get him under cover and stabilised. All that assumed that they remained undetected by the Chinese, and that carried no guarantee.

"How is he?" Tashi sank down onto her knees beside him.

"Bad." Max replied softly. He pointed towards the tent that Deepraj had almost finished erecting. "We have to get him inside." Taking hold of him under his armpits, Max began to drag him bodily over the snow. Despite the care he took, the Professor's lips, taut with supressed pain, parted to emit short gasps. Tashi lifted aside a fly-sheet and cradled the Professor's head as Max and Deepraj manoeuvred him inside.

The crackle of gunfire startled them and Max and Deepraj's eyes met in a silent question.

"I think they're covering their advance down the track."

"*Hola.*" The Gurkha's cautious response reflected both their concerns.

"Get the kit in." Max gestured with his head and Deepraj crawled out of the tent, reappearing moments later with their rucksacks. There was a deadly futility to the task of attending to the wounded man and the added frustration sapped Max's energies. He had neither the skills nor the equipment to undertake anything more than a rudimentary fix for the wounds and exposing them in these temperatures would probably put paid to the man's prospects of survival.

"Have we got a thermal blanket?" He looked up briefly as Deepraj began to unstrap one of the packs. Together, they carefully wrapped the Professor in the metallic sheet which had saved so many victims of mountain accidents.

The light softened as the snow lay ever more thickly over the roof of the high altitude tent. The only sounds were those of their breathing. The cold was eating into their minds more powerfully than their bodies. Thin trails of steam rose from their nostrils, pumped by hearts that still raced in fear.

As if to remind them of the precarious position, the gunfire chattered again, this time magnified a little.

"I think they're in the rock corridor south of the chimney base." His words were intended to give comfort to Tashi and the child. She gave a tiny flick of her head, half-acknowledgement, half-incomprehension. The steam generated by his words dissipated slowly upwards. She was still cradling the Professor's head. Despite the fact that it was bad practice for someone with obvious internal wounds, Max trickeld a little brandy from his hip flask into the corner of the Professor's mouth. He gave a short cough and his eyelids fluttered then opened.

Max put his finger to his lips to signal the need for silence but the man's eyes were not properly focussed. Leaning forward so that his softly spoken words could be heard, he gave a quick rundown of their situation then leaned back a little to see whether it had registered.

"Sorry…" The word was forced out between the tightly drawn lips. Max leaned forward again.

"Don't worry. We're as safe as possible here. We'll rest up awhile then get you evacuated to a hospital." The Professor's eyes gained focus for a moment and their message was that he understood that his position was hopeless and Max's words no more than anodyne comfort. His lips began to move but there was no sound. Even allowing for the temperature, his pallor had worsened and Max didn't have to be a doctor to know that his patient was slipping away from him. The Professor's eyes closed again and Max looked at Tashi and shook his head gently. She removed her right hand from its glove and began to stroke the dying man's forehead.

In the eerie silence of the snow covered tent, the lyrical sounds of a small voice chanting a Tibetan prayer grew gently in intensity. Max looked up to see Dondhup kneeling beside the Professor, his palms placed together in the attitude of prayer with his serious little face appearing to hang suspended over his fingertips.

"Trust you." The words, barely more than a whisper but rising above the sound of the prayer, made Max look down. The Professor's eyes were open and focussed on Max's face with a burning intensity as though they held his total life force.

"Take Dalai Lama…to Dharmasala…" The words died but the eyes continued to bore into Max's. Suddenly the Professor's gaze shifted until it fell on the face of the one for whom he had made his personal sacrifice. In the strange half-light of the tent Max watched as the pain that had etched its presence into every line and surface of the Professor's face yielded to a serenity that was totally incongruous to their surroundings. The child's features appeared to lose their innocence, acquiring a gentle wisdom that Max had sometimes thought he'd detected in the face of Buddhist statuary.

There was no actual moment that Max could identify as death, more a growing awareness that the soul had departed for another incarnation.

Max unzipped the door flap and pulled it carefully aside. The snow had banked itself up to about two feet and formed a wall. He peered through the thick veil as it continued to fall heavily, swirling into his face. He felt ambivalent about breaking the wall down, on the one hand, it provided excellent camouflage just in case the Chinese did climb up onto their plateau, on the other, if it continued to rise, it could bury them alive. There was no telling for how much longer the snow would continue to fall. He opted for concealment until the snow reached roof level. Leaning back a little he zipped the door closed.

"Max?" The sound of her voice gave him a momentary fillip. She crawled across to where he was crouched by the door, carefully picking her way so as not to disturb the sleeping figures of Dondhup and Deepraj.

"What are you going to do now?" It struck Max that even the lightest of whispers was capable of carrying emotion, but he wondered whether it was conveyed more by the anxiety that drew her face. Impulsively, he took her arm and tucked it under his.

"When the others wake up, we'll have something to eat and drink."

"No." She shook her head and her hair brushed lightly against his temple. "I mean can you get us to Dharmasala?" This was the 64-thousand dollar question and one he couldn't answer. He smiled, enjoying her closeness but anxious to give her some reassurance.

"First we have to find a way out of here, once I'm sure the Chinese have gone back." She continued to frown.

"The thing is, I don't think this plateau we're on leads to anywhere. That means we'll have to go back down the chimney and follow the track we were on." His words, he could sense, were giving her no comfort at all.

"Look." He dug into his down jacket with his free hand and pulled out the map. Pulling his mitten off with his teeth, he unfolded enough of it to reveal the area in which they were. He had no idea whether she could read the map but he knew that psychologically distances appeared shorter and it would give her a feeling of practicability.

"Here, hold this." He switched on his torch and gave it to her to illuminate the map. His forefinger tapped softly on where he reckoned their position to be.

"We're here." He traced back to the border to give an idea of relative distances. "This is where you crossed into Nepal." He ran his finger back down to their position and then slowly traced a route south towards the Nepal-India border. "That's the nearest exit point for us." She was pressed against him as she followed his explanation. He pressed her arm more firmly against his side and she didn't resist.

"We'll have to skirt around the villages and travel by night. Once we're over the river, I think we'll be safe from the Chinese but we'll have to keep out of the hands of the Nepalese authorities." He turned to look into her eyes, his words were of reassurance but his feelings were a strange mixture of physical yearning and a desire for something else he couldn't put a name to; her respect? Probably, but in his heart of hearts he admitted that he wanted to be wanted. By her.

"It'll be a bit difficult but we'll do it." He couldn't help wondering whether you could really love someone if you looked into their eyes and lied. But there was no alternative, he had to bolster her hopes, keep her morale high if they were to make it safely out of the mountains, let alone reaching the border. He was rewarded by a softening of the tension in her face.

"It's far." The bald statement, made without the tension, was a commitment rather than an objection. This had to be the smallest group of people he'd ever had responsibility for yet it posed far greater problems than any before. The fact that the Nepalese authorities would now regard him as an illegal only added to the enormity of the burden. The ultimate complication was his emotional involvement. Accustomed to shutting in his most private thoughts and feelings, she was prising open his defences as he experienced a need to share his thoughts with her. It was as though he was breaking faith with himself.

"Yes, it's a fairly long way but..." He paused, the new desire to share fought with the old habit of self-containment. "I have an emergency plan that may save us having to make the journey on foot." The frown reappeared.

"A friend may be able to fly in and pick us up, then..." He made a motion of flying his hand up into the air. Even as he did so he wondered whether she would think he was quite mad. Despite her remarkable self-assurance and relative sophistication, he hadn't the slightest idea whether she'd even seen an aeroplane. He could have saved his doubts.

"Can a helicopter fly at these heights?" She shook her head. "Not in these conditions, I'm sure." He smiled, she was way ahead of him.

"No, not a helicopter, a small aeroplane that can take off and land in short distances. But you're right, I don't know how far down we'll have to go before he can reach us and he'll have to wait for the snow to stop." He found it hard to concentrate, her forehead touched his cheek as she bent over the map and the natural scents of her hair and skin filled his sinuses.

"Look here." He struggled to contain himself now. It felt like it had as a choirboy trying to stifle a laugh in church, somehow the the desperate gravity of their situation only heightened his desire for her. He ran his finger over the map which was balanced on her knees, pointing to an area west of Lamobagar Gola and north of Yakua. "I think there's an abandoned airstrip just about here. If I'm right, we could get there in about three days, travelling at night, provided the snow stops." In fact he calculated that they could probably do it in two night marches but he allowed a margin for the unforeseen.

"I'll contact the pilot tonight and find out if it's practicable."

She took off her mittens, took his hand between her palms and began to restore the circulation. "You mustn't leave your fingers exposed, you will get the black finger." He had not heard the expression before but since it accurately described frostbite, he simply nodded acquiescence. He was fascinated by her hands, the fingers were long and slim yet her hands were small.

"Thank you." It was hopelessly inadequate but he said it with a depth of feeling that he had not felt for too long.

The rustle of movement as Deepraj stirred in his sleep made him pull his hand away. He wondered whether his frozen face was capable of blushing but she looked him straight in the eye and laughed softly and he caught the humour of their circumstances.

"I'll make some tea." She turned, brushing against him as she did.

"No, Tashi. We need some soup, we've had nothing to nourish us for several hours and I don't know when we'll get another opportunity." He shook Deepraj out of his slumber.

"Brew up some beef broth on the Tommy cooker and see if we've got some of those concentrated trekkers biscuits." The Gurkha rubbed his tired eyes.

"I'm dying of hunger, Saheb."

"Aren't we all?" Max echoed. Reaching for his pack, he dug into one of the pockets and pulled out a large bar of Hershey's chocolate, broke off some for each of them and passed it out.

"Once you've got the soup on the cooker, let Tashi-la watch it while you and I check our equipment." He snapped back the elasticated wrist cuff of his down jacket and checked on the time. There were four hours to go before the next communication schedule. He wished he'd arranged an emergency contact schedule. Too late for that now. Knowing that she wouldn't understand their conversation he broached something he'd forgotten to ask when they had dragged the Professor's body out earlier and given him a shallow snow grave.

"Did you salvage everything useful from the Professor Saheb's kit?"

"Huzoor." There was, Max had to admit, a world of reassurance in the Gurkha's one word of respectful acknowledgement. Here they were, almost totally dependent on a high-tech communication device and hoping to arrange an air-lift by one of the most sophisticated aeroplanes ever designed. Yet, whichever way it went, it would be human endeavour which would be in greatest demand for the immediately foreseeable future.

By 6.30 that evening the snow had started to ease off. An hour later, Max stood outside the tent and punched in the numbers. The sky was an impenetrable black and he had his head thrown back as if he could see the signals pulsing their way up to the ionosphere. It took three or four re-dials before he connected to a ringing tone at the far end. No one picked up. He let it ring until the automatic cut-off killed the connection.

Deepraj looked at his watch but kept his thoughts to himself.

Max checked on the battery. It showed about half its capacity. He made a mental note to conserve it. They had no means of re-charging it and the spare battery had been in the packs they'd abandoned on the track. He checked his watch and pressed the re-dial button.

This time it rang twice before he heard it picked up.

"Jamsung? It's Max. Can you hear me?"

"Max? Yes. What's your situation?

"Pretty bloody awful." He was going to have to pin point a position and he was counting on the Nepalese being unable to hack into the satcom line.

"We need the emergency evacuation plan. Ask our friend if he can make a landing in the area 27:40, 87:15, got that?" There was a slight pause and he pressed the phone closer to his ear in an instinctive clutching at the distant voice.

"You mean the old Mingmo strip?" Max wished that he could have hugged his old partner.

"Yeah, the abandoned one...can he tell if it's still usable?" Pleasure quickly dissipated as the signal began to break up.

"Jamsung! You're breaking up. Can you hear me?" There was a surge of power and the reply came back loud and clear.

"Depending on the weather and your friend. I'll arrange it. When can you make the RV?"

"Three days, d'you hear me? Three days."

"I'll confirm at next schedule."

"Great!"

"How many in your party?"

"Four."

"Destination?" Max realised that his thinking had been so short term that he'd only thought as far as getting them out of the mountains.

"Not yet decided." The signal began to break up again. He picked his words with economy. "Want to leave it open."

"...friend's flight plan..." Max caught the gist.

"OK, OK. Tell him..." His mind scrabbled for a sensible destination and came up with nothing. Crossing the Indian border was out of the question, they'd risk being shot down by IAAF pilots doing their Top-Gun number. The all-weather airports within Nepal would be too open for them to escape detection.

"Tell him to fill his tanks."

"Say again?" Jamsung's voice was weak.

"Full tanks, fly on full tanks."

"Roger." Deepraj tapped Max's arm and pointed to his watch.

"Jamsung?"

"Yeah?"

"Our situation is pretty desperate, OK?"

"I know. Save your battery. Call you next schedule."

"Thanks."

The contact with Jamsung lifted Max's spirits. He ran over their immediate plan with Deepraj once again, more to satisfy himself that there was no greater number of flaws in it than he'd already appreciated but now he felt his voice tinged with enthusiasm. Next he went over it with Tashi but this time he spoke slowly, choosing his words carefully so that Dondhup could follow the plan.

"Deepraj is going to go down the chimney to make sure that there aren't any Chinese still around. Even if they're still there, they'll have no reason to suspect a solitary Nepalese, after all, it's his home." Dondhup's face lit up in a smile that recognised the basic logic. Moreover it was the fact. They'd worked out a simple code of signals. If the Chinese were in their path, he'd sing a few bars of a particular folk song then find somewhere not too far distant to pass the night before doing another reconnaissance in the morning. On the other hand, if he was satisfied that it was safe for them to leave the plateau, he'd sing a different song.

"Right. You two stay out of the cold until I get back." He wanted to give Tashi some physical reassurance but he held back, half-raising his hand in a gesture that told them to stay but managing also to convey a message of confidence.

Back at the top of the chimney, they tied opposite ends of the rope around themselves.

"Good luck, *Burho.*" Deepraj grinned at Max's choice of words. Nepalese men regarded themselves as 'old' when they reached 40 years of age, even when they were physically virtually in their prime. Max had never addressed him in this fashion before but now it seemed an appropriate way to express both appreciation and respect.

"Everything'll be *tic-tac*, Saheb." Yes, Max thought, it'd better have to be bloody *tic-tac* or they were all likely to be drop-dead. He put onc hand on the Gurkha's shoulder. Customs and courtesies were incongruously different. If Deepraj had been a Sherpa, they'd have shaken hands but the old military *kaida* held them back from such familiarity.

"I'll be off, then, Saheb." With the nonchalence of a man setting off on an afternoon stroll, Deepraj lowered himself over the rim of the chimney, waiting until Max had taken up the slack in the rope. Seconds later he was part way down. Save for an occasional muffled slither of fabric against the rock face and one low grunt, the descent was silent.

The rope went slack, then two short tugs and he knew that his one man recce patrol had reached the bottom. They'd agreed on a half-hour's initial reconnaissance provided that the immediate area was free of Chinese troops. If they were still around, it would take him that much longer to get back to the chimney without arousing suspicion.

A chill wind was blowing and Max pressed himself into the snow trench he'd created for himself, wishing he'd brought his sleeping bag with him to retain body heat during his vigil. Peering down into the black hole he could see nothing at all. He turned his head so that he could catch the slightest sound but after two minutes he pulled his ski cap back down, covering his ear. Exposing it to the steel-wire whine of the Himalayan winds risked losing it to frostbite. He rubbed it vigorously to restore circulation and then suffered a wicked burning sensation as the blood was restored to the capillaries. He had to make an effort not to scratch it raw. The effort made him sweat a little but the wind iced the beads of perspiration. He pulled his hood back over his head, noting how the exposed fur of the lining had frozen rigid.

After what he reckoned had been about 20 minutes he checked the time. The luminous dial mocked him, only seven minutes had elapsed. He changed his mind about burrowing into the snow, stood up and began to walk about, waving his arms up and down to fight off the creeping cold that could send him into a terminal sleep. Just moving around was painful but he persisted. He devised a simple routine of walking around for three minutes before he lay down beside the chimney for four minutes.

He was about to get to his feet for the third time when he thought he detected a noise at the base of the chimney. Aware that he was ready to grab at any excuse not to get up, he discounted it.

There it was again, only this time it was unmistakably a human voice.

"*...yo tara matra t'hoina, joon poni kasaideunla.*"

Thank god, it was the right song. He fed the rope down until he felt it pulled on. In a combination of pull and climb, Deepraj made it to the top of the chimney and lay flat on his stomach breathing heavily. After a minute or so he recovered his breath and struggled to his feet, brushing the snow off his trousers. He wore a contented smile.

"No one's about, Saheb. The snow's unmarked in both directions, so they could have continued on south down the track or have turned back. I can't tell."

Max offered him his hip flask and while the Gurkha sipped on it, he considered the news. They were well into Nepalese territory here. There was an even chance that the Chinese had concluded that the fugitives were all accounted for. It depended on how precise their intelligence had been. Equally, even if they had been pursuing a child, there was no way they could tell whether one of the victims of the carnage at Honggaon wasn't their target.

It was a delicate balance between the need to move and the demands of safety. The wind seared across his face, momentarily blinding him with its chill. They had to get down to a lower altitude, at this height and in these conditions they'd soon perish. The decision dictated itself.

"OK. We'll strike the tent and take our chances on the track."

The going was slower and even more tiring than he'd bargained for. The track itself was buried under a foot of snow and in places there were drifts as much as six or seven feet deep. Their legs ached from the monotonous repetition of lifting them high enough to clear the surface then plunging into the icy mousse of snow. The plan had been for Deepraj to take the point a short distance ahead of them, just in case they met up with anyone searching for them but breaking the path had proved such an exhausting process that they had abandoned caution and took it in turns. Max's plan of march was also jettisoned; instead of trekking for two hours and resting up for 20 minutes, they had to take a break every half hour, especially when first Max, then Deepraj were struck by fierce cramps brought on by the unaccustomed high-stepping action and loss of body salt.

After three hours of painfully slow progress through the unnaturally silent, snow-blanketed landscape, he decided that they needed some sustenance to keep their morale up. Two of the precious smokeless fuel briquettes heated up a mixture of snow and beef concentrate and they huddled together, sipping at the steaming mugs.

"D'you think we've avoided the Chinese, Saheb?" Max was superstitious about making any optimistic assertions but he also felt the need to encourage his little band, particularly the Gurkha who was carrying a heavier load than any of them. He blinked affirmatively.

"Probably." He translated for Tashi's benefit and noted the slightly quizzical expression on her face when she replied.

"Really?"

"I can't tell." He felt the irritation in his voice and immediately regretted it. Smiling, he added, "If I was searching for you, I'd never give up." She made a little moue and shook her head slightly.

"You're avoiding the question." It was like a game of truth or consequences. He took a sip of soup to buy a moment or two before answering.

"You're right. I don't know. My logic tells me that we'd probably have bumped into them by now if they'd continued down the track.

The same reasoning suggests that they probably wouldn't want to penetrate too deeply into Nepalese territory and risk an accidental clash with a Nepalese Army unit or, at best, cause a rift in fraternal relations. But...," he gave a little frustrated wave of his mug. "I don't have much experience of the Chinese mind. I only know that if Dondhup escapes, there'll be an incredible loss of face. So, if I was commanding the pursuit party, I'd be worried about my future."

"For someone who says he doesn't know the Chinese mind, I think you've got it absolutely right. That's why I'm doubtful whether we've shaken them off. Our best hope is that the PLA who are pursuing us haven't been told who their quarry is. That, too, is a very Chinese way of doing things. Everyone is kept in the dark." Max looked at the serious face, the fatigue and anxiety that tugged at the corners of her dark eyes and saw only a sharp mind concealed behind a beauty that defied definition.

"So, really, you agree with me? They're in the dark." He waved an all embracing arm around them. "We're in the dark, like so many blind creatures groping our way through this cold, cruel landscape." She shook her head.

"Uhuh. They may be blind but you," she pointed at him and then at Deepraj with her mug, "you two are on your own territory." He gave a quiet laugh, nodded and then translated for Deepraj's benefit. The Gurkha's eyes creased into a smile.

"I have no eyes but I lead..." He began the old Nepali nursery riddle.

"A walking stick." Max completed and they both grinned.

"Come on, pack up, we have to press on." He drained his mug and handed it to Tashi. Provided they didn't lose their way whilst skirting around the villages or fall down some hidden crevasse, his most pressing concern was how quickly Nepal Army units would reach the area and start to comb the mountains. Even with their poorer standard of training, Nepal Army Gurkhas were still competent soldiers. He was counting on their staff work being of a much lower quality than the abilities of the troops. It was a calculated risk that they wouldn't search at night and standard procedures would probably mean piqueting the track and quartering patrols in the villages. If they positioned listening-posts around the villages, there was a very high risk of detection, even by skirting wide around them, a time and effort manoeuvre that was exceedingly costly in any event. He'd have to judge to a nicety just when to abandon this particular orientation and strike across country to find an alternative route to their destination. One thing was for sure, it was going to take all of the three days he'd allowed and probably then some. All this was based on the presumption that Hans Fischer *would* come and that he'd be able to get in and out of the old airstrip. The 'if's' repeated themselves in his brain like an empty mantra, slowly, keeping in step with the rhythm of his boots crunching into the snow as he stepped into the gaping holes that Deepraj had broken.

A line of pain ran across the back of his neck and transmitted itself into his shoulders; he shifted Dondhup's weight a little in a futile effort to earn respite for his aching muscles.

They had studied the map again before setting off and adopted Deepraj's suggestion that they strike off west, cross the low saddle that they had been contouring and pick up a parallel track that would take them southeast of Honggaon even though by dawn they would be uncomfortably close to Hatia. He turned the options over and over in his mind. The further south they progressed, the lower they would be, the more oxygen there'd be in the air and the temperature would be higher. As against these enticing attractions, the easier their path so the greater the risk of being caught. Time moved inexorably against them and their provisions would barely last them the three days, even if eked out.

"Tuh!" Deepraj gave a tired grunt as Max bumped into him. He turned round slowly and Max saw that his eyes were thin slits in his drawn, grey face.

"I'm all in, Saheb."

"I know. Take a break." He let Dondhup half slide, half fall down, then made the boy exercise his numb, stiff limbs. All of their nerves had been battered to shrieking point over the past 24 hours. They'd have to draw on their hidden reserves of resilience if they were going to last the course. One instinct told him to make as much progress as possible on this first leg of the journey, another warned him that in their present condition they were liable to make a mistake and that could prove fatal. He thought aloud as both men sucked the thin air into their hungry lungs.

"D'you think we could find a cave within...," he brushed his sleeve back to look at his watch, "...the next two hours?"

"Possibly." The Gurkha shrugged exhausted shoulders. They were both bent forward like a couple of old men. "Probably." He managed a tired grin.

"Right. We keep our eyes peeled for a cave. But if there's a formation that'll give us some shelter to pitch the tent, we'll settle for that."

The Gurkha managed a grunt of acknowledgement before handing one of the packs to Max and then signalling Dondhup to get ready to clamber onto his back.

"This reminds me of carrying the six-inch mortar and base plate in Helmand Province." Max was about to add that at least he wasn't liable to be blown up by a roadside IED when he remembered that, unlike Helmand, they were liable to be shot at by both the Nepal Army and the PLA.

"You wish you were back in the battalion?"

"Nahh!" Deepraj shook his head and pointed up the hillside. "There's no place like home."

Max found the energy to chuckle, then, making sure Tashi was ready, he began the steady mind-sapping task of breaking a path up the snow encrusted hill.

It took nearly an hour and a half of relentlessly exhausting trudging before they settled for a semi-adequate refuge. It was no more than a rock cleft, so formed that a combination of overhang and slip left a tall but narrow niche into which they squeezed themselves out of the reach of the glacial wind's whip-wire punishment. Max's hopes of finding some dried yak dung or lichen to burn were disappointed. In a moment of rash extravagence, he committed three of the fuel briquettes to the dual task of turning snow into hot water for their meal – a task they performed admirably – and thawing out their deep frozen marrow, an objective beyond the powers of the little blue and yellow flames that danced with coquettish impudence.

Deepraj involved Dondhup in helping him to pack the open aspect of the cleft with a low wall of packed snow. Tashi was busy brewing a none-too-sweet smelling concoction, the principal constituents of which appeared to be chicken bouillon and Tibetan tea block. Max caught her eye and wrinkled his nose disapprovingly.

"We must economise...*and* it's nourishing." She spoke reproachfully, taking his expression of distaste seriously. He hunkered down beside her and put his hand on her shoulder.

"I know, you're right. In these conditions it's...," he stopped himself involuntarily, suddenly aware of an unintentional play on words, "...a feast fit for a king." He looked towards Dondhup and she followed his gaze, then she caught the gist of it so that when he laughed, she smiled and shook her head in a gently reproving way. He scooped up a handful of snow with his bare hand and added it to the pot. Without any warning he heard her click her tongue at him then she rapped his knuckles with the ladle.

"Agh!" He let out a little gasp of pain and drew his hand back sharply. Though it had only been a playful knock, his hands were in a delicate balance between being part-electrified with pins and needles and part numb. It was like a dentist's needle into an unanaesthetised gum. Taken aback, she looked worried and taking his hand in both of hers, she drew it towards her face and breathed on it, gently massaging sensation back into the swollen fingers.

Through the fatigue and cold and the pain, he sensed an animal magnetism coupled with an overwhelming desire to protect her. He had the sudden urge to take her head between his hands and brush her lips with his. He sought for meaning in the pressure of her fingers against his and he searched her eyes, hungry for some sign that his feelings were reciprocated. She gave a half-smile, pressed his hand and maintained the pressure all the while looking him straight in the eye. He curled his fingers around her small hand and she didn't resist. In that moment, brief and innocent to the casual observer, he knew that everything he sought in a woman was right there beside him; in her strong sensitive hands, her eyes that laughed silently, the soft warm lips that said so much in so few words and the rakish angle of her fur-lined Tibetan hat, perched like a brocade flower pot with furry ear flaps over her lustrous black hair.

"Mama." Dondhup pulled gently on his mother's arm. "See what we made." The little face that had worn such a grave mien when reciting prayers for the Professor was now indistinguishable from any 4-year-old eager to show off his achievements. He pointed towards the snow wall and Tashi clapped her hands together appreciatively. Max wondered at the child's ability to switch between his two utterly different personalities and yet there was no doubting that aura of something indefinably different about him.

"Uncle?" Now he looked at Max, seeking his approval. Max smiled, with any other boy of his age, he'd probably have high-fived him but somehow it seemed inappropriate and anyway it was highly improbable that Dondhup would have had a clue as to what it was all about.

Minutes later they were sipping tentatively at the hot concoction, fighting tiredness and allowing the scalding liquid to work its way through their circulations. Both Tashi and Dondhup's eyelids were closing involuntarily and he chattered to them, forcing them to respond and so to stay awake. He instructed Deepraj to zip together the two largest sleeping bags and then lay the other two on top, then they all climbed in to share the heat of their combined bodies. Max permitted himself an inner chuckle as he organised their sleeping arrangements with Tashi and Dondhup sandwiched between Deepraj and himself so that she lay next to him. Not that their advanced state of fatigue nor the layers of clothing were conducive to even the most restrained of passion but their bodies necessarily formed together like malleable pieces of a jigsaw. He pressed himself against her and experienced a thrill of happiness and anticipation at her firm response. Hardly had he snuggled himself into the folds of her body, his face pressed lightly against the nape of her neck, the scent of her hair and skin in his nostrils than he fell into an exhausted sleep.

Tashi worked her free arm round behind her until she found his hand, then she pulled his arm gently around her and laced her fingers into his.

25,000 Feet Above Sea Level

Hans Fischer was worried. The little aeroplane lurched and bucked violently against the invisible currents of air that alternately plucked at it then rejected it as the Himalayas' dangerous pockets sucked and blew indiscriminately. Occasional sightings of the moon disclosed a malevolent blue banshee that played a wicked game of cat and mouse with him behind the floss of nets through which the all too fragile aircraft cut a path. He shivered and massaged his eyes, alternately, before checking his instruments again. To all intents and purposes he was flying blind and the muscles of his stomach were cramped tight. It's OK to be frightened, he comforted himself, that's what keeps me alive. Unless some of this cloud lifted, he would have to turn around and try yet again tomorrow. Not that he relished that prospect either with the level of security now that much higher and the civil aviation department demanding more and more detail of his flight plans. They were bound to get even more suspicious if he persisted in trying to fly in these conditions. Allowing for the head wind that he had been battling with ever since leaving the Kathmandu Valley and provided that his calculations were accurate, he ought to be about 5 minutes from Mingmo now. The cloud was impenetrable, no matter how hard he strained his eyes. He checked the altimeter yet again, reminding himself that he had made the adjustment for the appropriate pressure before deciding to risk descending another 500 feet.

He wondered, not for the first time, what would be in Max's mind as he waited for a sight of the aircraft, assuming, he cautioned himself, that he was still there. Jamsung had told him that he'd spoken to Max the day before yesterday and he had been expecting Hans yesterday. Abandoning the attempt the previous night, he had been unable to get confirmation from Jamsung that Max knew of the change in plans. Still, he reflected, compared to conditions 18 hours ago, tonight was like taking chocolate from a baby.

The thick cloud began to break up, whipping past the cockpit window as if on rubber bands. He squinted at the stark terrain, jagged snow peaks that pointed up at the aircraft's soft underbelly as if, like a magnetic force they could draw it down into the black depths into which the moonlight could not reach. He was searching for a signal fire or coloured smoke flare but nothing stirred on the shattered checker board below and ahead. It struck him that Max might well not have any signal flares and there wouldn't be much in the way of kindling at these altitudes, yet he desperately needed something to help him assess the strength and direction of the prevailing wind. One error up here and he was likely to join that select band of Himalayan adventurers who had made a descent of a major peak without having first climbed it.

Mingmo had been a fair-weather landing strip and even at those times of the year it had never been a popular destination amongst the Nepalese pilots whom Fischer respected as second to none in their flying skills in the Himalayas. Even before the STOL aircraft had come into service, the ancient Dakotas were coaxed in and out with peerless skill until the law of averages demonstrated that that very skill had lulled the airline administrators into believing that the pilots' accounts of scraping in and out by the skin of their teeth were little more than *braggadocio*. Then it had taken one aircraft and 10 lives to close down the strip. Even allowing for the skis on his superb little machine, Fischer knew that what he was attempting to do was certifiable.

He brought the little craft down another 500 feet, sacrificing manoeuvrability for better visibility. He peered through his side-screen searching for the lighter strip of darkness which would be the snow field known as Mingmo. He saw it before he actually recognised it for what it was. There was no sign of a flare or signal fire. As he started his turn to bring him in on the windward approach, the false valley between the two adjacent ridges created wind sheer and his body tensed up as he physically held the aircraft in balance. The runway looked even shorter than he had measured it on his aerial map and with the entire strip cast in shadow, he couldn't even tell if there were any stray rocks that had found their way onto the narrow shelf and now lay hidden beneath a thin veil of snow. The darkness seemed to mesmerise his eyes, pulling him down. He realised that it would demand a substantial slice of luck over and beyond his skill to land the aircraft safely, let alone take off in the thin air with a full load. Right now, he realised, was the moment to abandon the enterprise. It was doomed.

They screwed their eyes up, seeking out substance where there was only the tantalising drone of the aircraft's engine. Even now, Max felt torn between caution lest it was a Nepal Army spotter plane and the instinctive desire to wave, shout, do anything to attract the pilot's attention. He erred on the side of caution, knowing all too well that their morale, all that had kept them going for the last 48 hours, would be devastated by disappointment. Equally, he knew that Hans would be looking for a signal flare and a wind indicator and he had to measure out his obligations to the Swiss. His mind did the calculations yet again; the weather argued against it being a Nepal Army pilot, only the senior officers had the necessary skills to handle the STOL in these conditions and most of them had been good friends to whom he'd passed on the occasional lucrative private charters. He hoped that they would find any excuse not to fly on such a mission rather than seek him out. On the plus side, the timing and precise location together with the engine noise all argued in favour of Hans's Pilatus Porter. The weather looked as though it was deteriorating again, was unlikely to improve over the coming weeks and most telling of all, they had finished their last stock of food 18 hours ago. He turned towards Deepraj.

"Shall I light it Huzoor?" The Gurkha's eyes were bloodshot with fatigue, he'd barely slept more than an hour in the last two days. Max took another look up into the clouds, wondering whether Hans would see the smoke of some cast-off clothing they'd heaped over their last two briquettes of fuel.

"Light it."

Fischer blinked and unscrewed the knurled locking nut on the side window so that he could look directly into the night. He was almost sure he'd seen a mustard glow. He screwed his eyes up against the wind as the mountains invaded his cockpit, lowering the temperature dramatically. There! There it was again and now he could just make out a threadbare sleeve of smoke like an emaciated ghost inviting him to his own destruction.

Whatever else the wind might do, right now it was blowing precisely in the right direction. It was make your mind up time and his professional pride made the decision. Every sense and muscle was tuned in to the fabric of the aircraft and he talked to it as though it were alive.

"Come on *liebchen,* you're so beautiful." He winced as a rogue gust dealt him a mighty sideswipe to the fuselage, lifting one wing suddenly and causing his feet to scrabble at the pedals for a second before he felt the headwind come up under the belly of the plane supporting him as he evened out and hauled back on the engine speed. The stall warning buzzer erupted into his ears as he felt the skis touch the surface and start to plane. He put the engine into reverse thrust and watched the end of the runway rushing towards him, too fast.

"*Sei mir gut, sei mir gut, liebling*!" He urged between clenched teeth as the little aircraft slid forward before, almost imperceptibly, the drag of the engines began to slow it down. Despite the freezing temperature, beads of perspiration stood out on his forehead as he gunned the engine a little to begin the short taxi back to the far edge of the airstrip.

There was no time for introductions as Max bundled them into the aircraft. He gripped Karl's hand and the expression on his face said it all. As the Swiss turned his attention to the runway, it began to snow again, this time in earnest. He completed his run to the limit of the field as Max was buckling Tashi and Dondhup into their seats. The noise of the engine filled their ears as he opened the throttle to maximum, he turned around and gave them all a grin which was intended to instil the confidence that he didn't share. Max gave him a thumbs-up. Dondhup sat next to a window and stared out, his eyes wide with wonder. Deepraj put one arm around the boy's shoulders and received a quick smile of appreciation. Max held Tashi's hands in his and she closed her eyes as the little aircraft began to move forward, oh so slowly. The snow whirled past Dondhup's window and he pressed his face against the perspex. Max felt Tashi tremble as they rushed forward, the windscreen wipers swung and thudded only to reveal a blackness which he could not penetrate from where he sat. The muscles across his back and neck were stretched taut and the joints in his limbs set hard. He pressed her hands then wondered whether it was more for his own comfort than hers. It felt as though they weren't accelerating fast enough to reach lift-off and he knew that the airstrip simply fell off the edge of the short plateau. There was a fractional change in the pitch of the roof and he pressed his boots hard against the floor feeling for the vibration of the skis. They were airborne.

Within minutes, the little aircraft was flying as level a course as the winds and air pressure would permit. He undid his seat belt, pressed Tashi's thigh firmly and went forward. Deepraj was already snoring and Max marvelled at the old soldier's facility for snatching sleep at the drop of a hat and in the most extraordinary of circumstances. He eased himself into the co-pilot's seat and clapped Fischer on the back.

"Bloody marvellous! God, you were a sight for sore eyes."

"You and I have lived in Nepal for too long." Fischer gave Max a quick sidelong glance. "We are both completely mad but I am crazier than you. I asked myself as I was coming here, Hans my friend, why are you flying through a Himalayan snow storm to rescue a crazy Irishman who is also a wanted criminal?" He shook his head in disbelief at his own actions. "Here." He pulled a flask out of the net pocket beside him and thrust it towards Max.

"Real French cognac, laced with Nepalese coffee!"

Max gestured towards the back of the cabin. "Women and children first." He poured some of the deliciously aromatic liquid into a plastic mug and made Dondhup sip a little. The boy coughed and Max thumped his back. He reached for the mug and began to gulp it down with the same relish that most children of his age reserved for a strawberry milkshake. Max waggled an admonitory finger at him and grinned as he eased the mug out of the child's hands. Tashi insisted that Max drink first then he let her nurse the mug, warming her hands and trying to co-ordinate drinking with the breaks in the turbulence.

"Max?" Fischer called him forward. "Where do you want to go?"

"That depends on what you can tell me. What about Meghauli?" He'd racked his brains over their next move. In their present condition they were in no fit state to make a run for it. What they needed most immediately was a safe place to rest-up and recoup their strength. The Jungle Lodge offered both isolation, comfort and security. Before they'd left Kathmandu, Jamsung had confirmed that the nucleus of the old permanent staff still remained there during what had once been the closed season. Now they were there to guard against poachers, watch over the elephants and maintain the place pending a return to normal.

"Impossible!" Fischer gave a derisory laugh. "The field is waterlogged and these are snow skis, not water skis." There was no point in pressing him, if he said it couldn't be done, that was definitive.

"Alright then, I think it'll have to be Kathmandu."

"Kathmandu?" Fischer gave him a look which suggested that he seriously doubted his sanity. "Kathmandu?" He repeated.

"D'you still park this contraption of yours in the royal flight hangar?"

"Yes, but it's now called the presidential flight."

"Same difference. It's the closest building to the perimeter wire. I hate to ask any more favours of you but would it be possible to create a small diversion on the airside of the administration block?"

"You mean could *I* create a diversion?" There was a note of sarcasm in the question.

"Well, I don't suppose there'll be anyone else around that I could ask." Max grinned back.

"I think my arrival at this hour of the night on an unlit runway will create some unfriendly interest. I could take offence, you know how touchy we German-Swiss can be."

"Yes, but don't overdo it and get yourself arrested." Max counted on there being either a ladder or more likely a short mobile boarding stair that could be manhandled. "I'll need about 7 or 8, say 10 minutes maximum. Could you be diverting for this long?"

"I've just performed a miracle and now you want me to make a fool of myself in public!" He shook his head in mock disbelief then fell silent for a few moments. When he spoke, the gravity in his tone rose above the noise of the engine.

"You know they'll shoot you if they get a chance?" He looked into Max's face to see whether his words had registered.

"As bad as that?"

"I don't know what you've been up to but the word is that you're wanted, more dead than alive." He gave a grim laugh. "I think you've screwed up Sino-Nepal relations from what little I've been able to gather." His face relaxed a little.

"Well done!" He laughed aloud.

"Silly bugger, that wasn't my intention." Max felt a bit lightheaded, amused at the revelation and unable to view it seriously.

"Well, whatever you intended, the government is making a lot of friendly noises towards the Chinese but they're not having much success, so they've found a scapegoat." He looked straight at Max. "You."

"Won't that earn me some powerful friends amongst the opposition?"

"Are you mad?" He slapped his forehead. "No, I've already decided you're a crazy man, now you want me to think you have nothing left inside?" He tapped his temple with a forefinger. "Everyone in Kathmandu is looking after number one. Remember, whenever there is turmoil, it's always the foreigners who are to blame and you are some convenient foreigner. So, don't trust anyone."

"I trusted you and you came through like the darling man you are."

"Yah. But if it's my neck or yours, don't count on me." It was said lightly but Max wondered whether there was a hint of truth in it. He reproached himself for even allowing the thought to cross his mind. Hans had risked his life to pluck them out of the mountains, there was a limit to what one could ask of anyone, friend or no.

"I haven't time to give you the full story, that'll have to wait until we have a long evening and equally long drinks. Right now I'm deeply indebted to you for saving all of us."

"You can repay me sometime." Fischer glanced down at his watch then peered out at the mountain peaks that marked their path like giant stalagmites on a slalom course across the top of the clouds. Ten minutes to landing."

"Assuming that I can get us out of the airport perimeter wire, we'll hide up beside the Golf Club Building. Can you get a message to Jamsung, tell him to come and pick us up as quickly as possible."

"What about the curfew?"

"Shit! I'd forgotten." Max smacked his forehead with his palm. "OK, tell him not to break the curfew but to come at the earliest minute possible. We won't be able to hang around the Golf Club after about 6.30, there's bound to be some lunatics eager to smack balls before breakfast."

Suddenly the clouds broke away in front of them and the lights of the Kathmandu Valley spread their magic like a tapestry of fireflies. Fischer didn't even call up the control tower which he could see was in darkness. Minutes later they touched down with the lightest of bumps and Max's heart beat quickened.

"Keep your heads down." He spoke quickly above the roar of the reverse thrust. There was no point in taking the risk that a zealous security guard or dozing airport worker would notice that the aircraft was carrying passengers.

The taxiing lights illuminated the interior of the darkened hangar then swung out again as Fischer manoeuvred the aircraft so that his door faced away from the open side of the building. He cut the engine and the stillness of the night enveloped them until he swung the door open and gradually the monsoon nightsong of crickets, cicadas and frogs throbbed its way inside.

"Go now while I do my post-flight checks." Fischer spoke softly. Max put one hand on Deepraj's arm.

"Go and recce the perimeter fence, we'll wait inside." The Gurkha eased himself out and dropped to the floor with only a gentle thud before disappearing into the night.

Max reached out and grasped Fischer's hand firmly. "Bless you."

"Good luck, crazy man. Go!"

Max beckoned Tashi and Dondhup forward, indicating with his hands that he'd go first. He dropped to the ground and then steadied Tashi as she came out of the door facing towards the interior of the cabin. Hans lowered Dondhup into Max's arms and the three of them hurried deep into the shadow at the rear of the hangar. Max blinked his eyes furiously to adjust to night vision. They watched in silence as Fischer locked up his aircraft and walked out of the building. He stopped on the apron immediately in front of the hangar entrance and lit a cigarette. Blowing smoke into the air he gave a little wave of the hand holding the cigarette and ambled off towards the administration block.

Max's eyes began to adjust and he looked around for a mobile stair. A movement close to the edge of the hangar entrance struck his peripheral vision and his head swung round. Seconds later, Deepraj materialised beside them and whispered into Max's ear.

"There are some empty oil drums stacked up against the inside of the wire. We can get over easily but..." He gestured towards Tashi with his head. "They'll have difficulty, her *bhaku*.... and it's a long drop on the other side."

"That's OK." Max had special knowledge about Tashi's clothes, in particular that she was wearing his spare longjohns so that a momentary gathering up of the skirt of her *bhaku* would not pose a problem. He turned to Tashi and explained the plan. It involved descending the chain link perimeter fence slowly rather than dropping to the ground and risking a twisted ankle or worse. She gave a gentle upward twist of her head, acknowledging that she could cope.

The sound of raised voices in the distance signalled the start of Fischer's diversionary tactics.

"Let's go." Max took Dondhup's hand and motioned Deepraj to lead the way. On reaching the fence, he decided to supervise the operation whilst standing on the uppermost drum. Tashi climbed up with surprising agility and he guided her over the top and watched her make her way down the other side, clinging to the linkage and pressing her boots against a convenient vertical stanchion. The rest of the operation was accomplished with relative ease, Deepraj carrying Dondhup on his back for the climb down. Max cast a grateful eye up towards the low cloud base which insulated them from the moonlight and deepened the welcoming shadows. They made their way across the adjacent fairway and onto the macademised first tee of the Nepal Golf Club. Making their way down towards the main road, they concealed themselves next to a storm culvert whilst Deepraj ran lightly across and disappeared into the grounds of the clubhouse. Minutes later, he re-appeared and beckoned them across. A door stood open and Max looked enquiringly at Deepraj who tapped the hilt of his *kukri*.

"I used the key." They grinned at each other and he bundled Tashi and Dondhup inside. With a quick look towards the airport and the road, Deepraj gently closed the door. Inside there was an all-pervading smell of dust and sweat but it was dry and comparatively warm and they sank onto the floor exhausted. The old soldier's maxim came to him with a winceing pun, 'An' if yer knows a better 'ole, go and lie in it'.

Max walked towards the frontier post, arm in arm with Tashi, holding Dondhup's hand. They all laughed with sheer relief as the sun shone down on them and there were no border guards on duty. Freedom was theirs for the taking. Then from close behind them they heard the sound of a vehicle approaching at speed, Max looked back over his shoulder and saw that it was an army Toyota jeep. He ignored it and told Tashi to keep walking. The jeep overtook them and stopped 20 yards or so in front of them but on the Nepal side of the frontier's drop-arm barrier. Still they walked on as uniformed men jumped out of the vehicle and a dark-skinned Thakuri superintendant of border police walked back towards them. Max felt the panic sending blood behind his eyes as he cast about for an escape and could think of none. He felt the sweat stand out on his forehead and a hollow feeling spread from his stomach up into his diaphragm as though it was closing off his airway. He was no longer aware of whether or not they were moving.

"Colonel Devlin." He had his hand on the pistol that hung from his belt and Max saw that the flap was undone. Yet there was a curious note in the voice, neither question nor statement. He spoke again.

"Colonel Devlin." The words were spoken softly, enquiring and slightly muffled. It suddenly struck Max that he was coming out of a dream but the voice was real. Now the panic was doubled, first there had been the nightmare, now an awful reality was replacing the nightmare as he opened his eyes and made out the dim figure of a man wearing a uniform cap, either police or army. His mouth was dry but his skin broke into a nauseous sweat. The officer must have noticed him stir because he stepped even closer to the window from which Max was supposed to have been keeping watch.

"Huzoor, I'm Lakpar." He paused a moment, then added as if to reassure. "Huzoor, Ong Chu's *bhai,* Lakpar, you remember me?"

The thoughts rushed through Max's sluggish mind one tumbling over another. First there was the blessed relief then there was the silent vote of thanks to Jamsung for a bright idea for rescuing them followed by concern that Jamsung himself had not come.

"Yes, yes, of course, Inspector Lakpar, it's good to see you. I didn't recognise your face in this light." He beckoned him around the corner and stepped over to the door and opened it. Lakpar walked in and Max waved an arm towards the others.

"We're all here and ready to leave." He tried to inject a little humour into his voice as he took in the sight of the three figures now sitting bolt upright. He rubbed his fingers through his hair, fully alert now though his eyes ached. A quick look at the luminous dial of his watch showed that it was well over an hour since he'd relieved Deepraj. Something, he couldn't say what, sensed that Lakpar's arrival was not all good news. He plunged in.

"What's up?"

"Both Jamsung and Fischer have been arrested."

"Shit!" This was a multi-dimensioned disaster that heightened the vulnerability.

"Why?"

"I have a cousin-brother in the armed police. He told me that they only intended to arrest Jamsung, apparently the General wanted him brought in by the regular police but the DIG Saheb delayed acting on the orders whilst he tried to get a message to Jamsung to warn him." Max held his hand up signalling that he wanted to interrupt.

"You mean DIG Maniprasad?"

"Yes, the Colonel Saheb's friend."

"Well, who's this General who wanted to arrest Jamsung?"

"General Karki, the Airborne Forces Commander." Max could make out that there was a puzzled expression on the young man's face which was suddenly replaced by comprehension.

"Of course, the Colonel Saheb has been out of Kathmandu." He paused and his voice took on a sober timbre. "General Karki has declared martial law. He is now in charge of Nepal."

"So, the police were forced to arrest Jamsung?"

"No, he was arrested by Paratroops. They have been arresting people all over the Valley, including all the members of the last government."

Max smiled grimly. "Well, that's a good start, especially if it included that little rat Bhandari and his bastard relations." Lakpar's face registered a brief smile but it was quickly replaced with a look of anxiety.

"It may not be so good after all, we know that some of the Paratroops were trained by the Israeli Mossad and some of their methods are as barbaric as our ancestors."

"What's the role of the police in all, this?"

"We've been ordered to assist the military government. The IGP has ordered us to carry on with our normal duties."

For Max, it was the revolution nightmare all over again except that this time there were very few foreign diplomatic missions in the capital, the foreign press was represented by local stringers and they weren't going to jeopardise their cosy numbers with email despatches that could be traced back to them as individuals. Not that Max blamed them. There was a savage dimension to the Nepalese psyche, one which the tourists and diplomatic corps were never allowed to see. No, the eyes of the world were not upon Nepal, this paratroop general and his officers would have as free a hand as the SLORC government of Burma. Just to complicate matters further, he was a wanted fugitive nor was he free to slip out of the country alone and unnoticed, he was bound to a woman with whom he was in love and the 4-year-old 15th Dalai Lama. He was also physically and mentally drained.

Fear, undiluted, pumped adrenalin into his fatigued system. One thought dominated his mind, to get the hell out of their present location, quickly and then find a way out of the country before all his options were cancelled. Instant flight also meant abandoning his friends to the less than tender mercies of the military government but he had to face reality, and reality was bloody frightening and just around the corner.

He ran the options through his mind as he chivvied the others into readiness to leave. His options were seriously circumscribed. Anyone with whom he could hope to hide out was likely to be under surveillance. In these first days of the revolutionary regime, the government would have its hands full containing any potential opposition so that ought to cut him a little slack. One *buckshee* foreigner and a refugee Tibetan mother and child would not merit distracting from the primary objective of imposing an iron will on a people whose history was chequered with autocratic rulers anxious to make an example of anyone foolish enough to challenge their authority.

"When did General Karki seize power?"

"Early yesterday morning." Judging by past experience, the first two or three days would be the time of maximum confusion, presenting them with their best chance of benefiting from the general ignorance and fear that would be rife. The corollary to that was that it would also be the time when the revolutionary regime was most trigger-happy. But, he reminded himself plangently, beggars could not be choosers.

"What about your *dai*, Ong Chu?" Max chided himself for his oversight.

"He's at my house, we didn't want to take any risks. He's ready to travel with you if you want him to." Max nodded thoughtfully. A hint of encouragement tinged Lakpar's voice as he added. "My wife is preparing some hot food for you all, we expected you'd all be starving." The thought of a hot meal cheered Max.

"Can you get us through the checkpoints?"

"Unless the paratroops stop us, yes." That was it then.

"If you can't talk us through a para check-point, you'd better be prepared to crash the barrier. With us on board you'll be a marked man." Lakpar gave a slight inclination of his head, acknowledging the truth of this observation.

"OK. Let's go to your place."

With Max, Tashi and Dondhup hidden underneath a tarpaulin in the back of the jeep and Deepraj in the passenger seat the journey was uneventful, for which mercy they were profoundly grateful. Lakpar's house had once upon a time been a lodge in which a Rana Maharaja had kept one of his mistresses in the grounds of his palace. Now its high compound walls and tall cedars afforded them shelter and privacy from prying eyes. The reunion with Ong Chu was a curious mixture of warmth and relief coloured with anxiety. His jaw was sufficiently recovered for him to be able to talk albeit he looked and sounded like a fifth-rate ventriloquist. Lakpar's wife plied them with pork *mo-mo's* and she fussed over Dondhup whilst keeping up a lively conversation with Tashi. The affinity between their languages enabled them to communicate without difficulty. The sudden domesticity lulled Max into a false sense of security. The temptation to rest up here, delaying their departure for a day or two, was almost overwhelming. He fought against what he knew was weakness born of his exhaustion. Time was now of the essence, the military coup had yet to be consolidated and it took little imagination to foresee one or more possible scenarios in which counter-revolutionary movements would attempt to move against General Karki. Any coup initiative had to maintain its momentum and this demanded decisiveness at all levels of command. The innate divisiveness that was such a feature of the multi-ethnic, many tongued peoples of Nepal, allied to the near anarchic philosophy that democracy had ushered in, meant that no regime, consensual or otherwise was safe. There was danger abroad in the shape of trigger happy paratroopers but there would be many policemen who, pressed into the service of the coup leaders, would want to keep their options open. Max allowed himself a brief inner laugh as he coined a phrase that encapsulated a plank of his strategy: in a coup, cash is king.

The germ of an idea began to take shape in his mind and he let himself relax under the influence of the food and drink. He questioned Lakpar closely about the extent of the General's control but as he had anticipated, his knowledge was limited to the immediate environs of Kathmandu and Patan. There were only two roads leading out of the Valley to the south, the original short one over the Tribhuvan Rajpath to Birgunj and the much more popular but longer route via Pokhara to Bhairawa. The former was by far the most tortuous and vulnerable to monsoon landslides, the latter less fissile and marginally less demanding on a driver's skill and concentration. He reasoned that the longer route would necessarily have more check posts and their prospects would deteriorate exponentially as his powers of concentration diminished. As against this argument, he knew that, given no undue interruption, he could reach Birgunj in just over 4 hours. All this assumed that he had a vehicle to drive. He caught Ong Chu's eye.

"Where's the Range Rover?"

"In the workshop at Tahachel. It's ready, Jamsung had been going to collect it today." Max was irritated and snapped back.

"What's wrong with it, it was perfectly alright before I left?" He was about to cite the Nepali saying, *Bhadur ko hat ma nariwal phutchha*,[1] but he stopped himself in time. Deepraj slapped his forehead with his open palm.

"Oho! Huzoor, I forgot to mention it, the brakes needed attention, they were pulling to the right. I asked Jamsung Saheb to have it checked."

"But it can't have taken this long?" Max's temper was on a short fuse even though as he spoke he knew that he was being petty-minded. Without particularly good grace, he added, "Well, never mind now, let's hope that the workshop hasn't broken something else." Lakpar spoke quietly.

"If you're thinking of driving over the Rajpath, the workshop is ideally located. I can probably get you through the city to Tahachel, but from there you'd be on your own." He sounded dubious. Max nodded.

"I don't want you putting yourself and your family at any greater risk, you've already taken too many chances for us."

“"It's nothing, Huzoor, you're family." At any other time Max would have hugged the man but he was deeply troubled by the ill-fortune that he was visiting on all his friends. He forced himself back to the decision making process. He checked the time, if they were to leave after dark he still had a few hours to make his plans.

"How are you going to get through the check posts?" Ong Chu's anxiety made the question sound accusing. Right question, pity about the timing, Max thought. He was less than confident of his proposed solution and he hesitated before exposing it to the cruel light of day.

"I think that if Deepraj and I wear military-style uniforms and we sound authoritative enough…" His voice trailed off as the expressions of incredulity informed their faces.

"None of the army units drive white vehicles, nor do the police." Lakpar shook his head speaking softly as though he had thought that Max would have known this. Max's tetchy response reflected the paucity of his solutions.

"Well, who do?" Even as he said it, the answer flashed straight into his mind. Before they could respond, he answered his own question.

"The World Health Organisation!" A possible hurdle baulked his enthusiasm for a second. "Are they still here?" Lakpar's grin was faster than his tongue.

---

1 'Even coconuts break in the hands of a monkey.'

"Oh yes. The head of the WHO office is a *Chinya.*" Well, now, Max reflected, there's a pretty coincidence, as if he wasn't in deep enough shit with the Chinese, now he was going to impersonate a Chinese WHO official. If this went wrong, he'd probably be extradited to Beijing and shot. Nonetheless, it was essentially sound as a strategy for getting them through the checkpoints, indeed, it was probably the only way they'd do it. His mind raced with ideas to flesh out the plan.

"Paint, can we get some blue paint?" He turned towards Ong Chu.

"Blue?" He shook his head slowly. "No, but we have some black."

"It'll have to do. Can you get hold of one of those WHO circulars we used to hand out to trekkers? It has the logo on it?" Ong Chu nodded.

"We won't have time to paint individual logos onto the doors of the Range Rover. We'll just make one of those cut-out transfers then we can just paint straight over them and we'll stick one on the bonnet too." As he thought it through, the mechanics of the scheme took shape. He gave them a list of requirements and set a timetable. He turned to Lakpar.

"Can you get enough petrol to fill your tank?"

"Yes, the pump at Police HQ is for police and military use only, all the other petrol stations have been closed down."

"We'll siphon your tank into the Range Rover, that should just about get us to the border." As he went over the plan with them, he was relieved to note that there was no dissenting voice.

In the event, it took longer than he had allowed for but when he stood back and surveyed the results of his handiwork, he got a kick out of the effect. The artwork on the WHO logo had been subject to a measure of artistic licence but he wasn't anticipating any close scrutiny and he was satisfied that it would certainly pass muster in the dark. In fact, he indulged himself in a little self-congratulation, everything from the lipsticked blotches on Dondhup's face and arms to the makeshift nurse's cap and cloak that they had fashioned for Tashi and the best touch of all, a stethoscope that Lakpar had 'borrowed' from a police surgeon's office, were all calculated to enable them to survive anything short of a very close inspection.

Leave-taking had been necessarily brisk and Max insisted that Ong Chu remain behind. No one else was to pay the price for all this folly unless their presence was absolutely essential to the escape plan. He had agonised long and hard over jeopardising Deepraj any more. There was nothing to connect him with any of the events in the mountains and he could simply melt into the background. No sooner had Max broached the subject than Deepraj assumed a look that signalled a total breach of faith. The Gurkha had given a dry spit of disgust.

"How'll you manage on your own?" To add force and more than a hint of disparagement, he'd added, "You're all foreigners!" He knew just how this would dismay Max whose fluency in Nepali frequently enabled him to pass himself off as Nepalese in the dark.

"You need him, Max, you just can't do it alone, not with the child." Ong Chu had spoken quietly but in a voice that brooked no opposition. With a sigh of anxiety coupled with relief, he'd let them overrule him. It was axiomatic that he needed the Gurkha but calling on his loyalty to this extent was a demand far beyond the call of their relationship.

"I'm really happy to have you with me." The words were inadequate and Deepraj gave a short, disparaging 'Tuh!' But as he turned away, Max could have sworn that he saw him grin at Ong Chu.

The road started the incline that warned him that they were approaching the checkpost at Thankot. Even in normal times, driving over the Rajpath after 22.00 hours had been prohibited. In the old days, Max used to send someone up to the checkpost during the day to pay the road *cess* and a healthy dollop of palm grease for the barrier official who would have to get out of a warm bed to open the road. By that hour, the police post further up the road would have been deserted, all the officers fast asleep. This time, he knew he'd have to busk it.

"Shall I stop here, Huzoor?" The barrier was some 30 yards ahead of them and Deepraj slowed the vehicle down to walking pace.

"No. Drive right up to the barrier, but when you stop leave the engine running. Remember, we're in a hurry." He grinned at the Gurkha. "The doctor Saheb says that anyone coming in contact with our patient has to have an immediate injection."

Deepraj followed the instructions and jumped out of the vehicle almost as he applied the brake. Running up the stone stairs outside the *cess* official's office-cum-quarters, he banged loudly on the door. Max was relieved to note that there were neither soldiers nor police officers manning the barrier.

A grumpy voice from within demanded to know who it was. Deepraj adopted his best parade ground manner and kicked the door impatiently. A protesting voice could be heard as the bolts were drawn and a resentful figure clad in an overcoat thrown hastily over sleeping apparel emerged onto the verandah where it commenced kicking awake an even more resentful bundle of rags before turning round and slamming the door closed behind him. The watchman grumbled his way to the barrier where he kept up a running commentary of complaint as he undid the padlock and swung the barrier pole up.

Deepraj strode back, slammed the driver's door shut and accelerated through the barrier and up the road.

"So far so good." Max said to no one in particular. Half turning in his seat, he told Deepraj, "Same drill with the police." They were on top of the police post before they realised it. Paradoxically, it wasn't showing any lights and appeared to be totally unmanned. It just didn't make sense that the exits and entrances to the Valley would be unguarded by the coup commanders. He tried to put himself in their shoes. In these early stages, it would be essential to insulate the local population from the soldiers manning the checkposts and guarding the key points. The police would be under the command of the military and on what little he knew of the situation, even if all the army units in the Valley were deployed, the soldiers would still be in a significant minority. This meant that the paratroops would have to enforce their control with ruthless discipline. It would be absolutely vital to foster an atmosphere of abject fear if they were to command the obedience that they could not enforce by sheer weight of numbers. By all accounts, this General Karki was no fool, he'd be acutely aware that every key point had to be manned by soldiers loyal to himself but on what Max knew of the Nepal Army's order of battle, there would be precious few paratroops to spread over all the critical points. He'd be forced to deploy other, non-para, units, perhaps those whose commanding officers had thrown in their lot with him. In which event, the least sensitive positions could be manned by ordinary infantry regiments. It all made logical sense but Max found himself hoping that their luck would not desert them at this juncture and he wondered, in a blasphemous moment which, if any, of their respective god's: Hindu, Buddhist or lapsed Catholic, was watching over them. Let it not be paratroops.

As they rounded the bend he saw a knife-rest barrier and the outline of typical Gurkha hats that told him that his ecumenical prayer had been harkened to.

"Approach them slowly." He turned to check that Tashi was awake. Touching her arm, her head started up off her chest, her face, framed by the nurse's cap, full of anxiety.

"Don't worry, we're just coming to an army checkpoint. Let them see Dondhup's face." He squeezed her arm gently and she responded, wrapping slim fingers around his wrist. He turned his attention back towards the checkpoint. One soldier was waving his torch at them whilst another had his rifle pointed straight at Deepraj. Now, everything depended on the confusion that Max had bargained for. Deepraj let his window down and the torch bearer spoke to him.

"Where's your pass?" The tone was peremptory but Deepraj responded with equal authority.

"We don't need a pass."

"Without a pass, no one's allowed on this road."

"Oh lad!" Deepraj sounded avuncular as he warmed to his task of the senior NCO lecturing a new recruit. "You must be very wet behind the ears, diplomatic personnel don't need passes, if you don't know that, go and check with your guard commander." There was a note of impatience in his voice and he could see that the sentry was wavering.

"Our orders…"

"Your orders don't include standing in the way of United Nations personnel." He'd identified the regiment and knew that they were regularly posted to UNFOR detachments around the world. "Stand clear lad, we're on very urgent business, look." He tapped the side of the door with his fingers and the torchlight swung down onto the logo. Max's nerves were strung tight, the muscles across his shoulders taut, was it going to work? He'd toyed with the idea of making up false identification documents but they simply hadn't had the time or the wherewithal. The sentry with the rifle now decided to get in on the act, he lowered the muzzle a little and came closer.

"What's up?"

"He says they don't need a pass, says their diplomatic." He flashed the torch around the interior of the vehicle. The two soldiers began to discuss it amongst themselves, their voices too low for Max to be able to catch what they were saying. Deepraj pitched in again.

"We're in a hurry, OK?"

"Wait. I'll call the Lieutenant Saheb." Torchlight walked off towards a house that perched beside the road with a 5,000-foot drop for a back garden.

"Shall I crash the barriers?" Deepraj whispered softly.

"No." It was too soon to cast caution aside. They had the bulk of the journey ahead of them and doubtless more such checkpoints to negotiate, there was simply too much road on which to be stopped.

"This lieutenant may speak English. I'll talk to him if he does. Just lean back in your seat and insist that you're carrying out your orders." Minutes dragged by like a cripple. The remaining sentry walked slowly around the Range Rover and peered inside when he was abreast of the rear passenger door. The sound of voices caught Max's attention and he could make out a hatless figure striding purposefully towards them. As he reached the door, Max could see that they had caught themselves a young second lieutenant. He had a typically western hillman's face, almost certainly a Gurung. That spelled patience, courage and less encouragingly, stubbornness. The lieutenant spoke to Deepraj.

"Who are you?"

"Ex-Sergeant Deepraj Rai, Number 2113, now working for UNDP Saheb." Max was amused to note that Deepraj was using the old soldier routine and had promoted himself into the bargain.

"Do you have an authorisation?"

"No, Huzoor, I was just detailed off to drive the doctor Saheb. I work in the general duties pool, Huzoor." Deepraj was sitting to attention in his seat. They had worked out a simple cover story that would be impossible to check out quickly. The lieutenant leaned against the driver's door and peered inside.

"Who are these people?"

"The doctor Saheb and the nurse are from WHO." Deepraj's pronunciation of the World Health Organisation was almost incomprehensible. The officer looked straight at Max.

"What is your name, sir?" Max felt a flutter of hope at the word 'sir'.

"Dr. Maxwell, I'm part of the WHO infectious diseases team in Kathmandu, Lieutenant. We have a very sick child here." He gestured towards the back seat. "I have to get him to India immediately, we couldn't even wait for a flight out." He hoped that the man would ask more about the child's condition.

"Please give me your passport." The lack of a pass could be explained, lack of a passport could not. The bluff had to be played to its limits. He started to pat his pockets as if searching for the passport.

"Really, Lieutenant, I must object to this delay, every minute counts...it isn't just the child, we could be on the verge of a major epidemic, it could infect the majority of the inhabitants of the Kathmandu Valley...not just those in contact with him." The officer took a step backwards and craned his neck to get a better view of Dondhup. Max's passport was inside a red leather holder and it was one of the old-style Irish passports, pre-dating the standard EC design. He thanked his luck stars that he had long ago stopped using all his middle names, now the document bore only a Christian name and a surname. The trick was to get the lieutenant to concentrate on reading it as Devlin Maxwell, in that order, something which he could sustain so long as the red leather jacket was not peeled off to reveal the correct order of words on the front.

"What's the matter with the child?" A note of caution had crept into the man's voice and he still stood back a little from the door, as he reached forward for the passport. Max held it firmly with the front page open as the lieutenant's fingers closed over it.

"We've made a provisional diagnosis of bubonic plague." If the whole car had burst into flames, the officer could not have sprung back any faster.

"Arey-oh!" No sooner was the exclamation out of his mouth than his hand dived into his pocket, pulled out a handkerchief and held it to his face.

"It's the old cracked water pipes and people's insanitary habits you see, Lieutenant..." Max let his words fall away as though nothing more needed to be said. The officer nodded as though his head would fall off.

"We have to get him to our WHO research facilities in Patna in order to identify the particular culture and," he added a forlorn note, "if we are to save this little one."

"Of course, of course." The lieutenant walked backwards as he waved them on.

"Let them through, hurry up!"

"Thank you, Lieutenant." Max waved a hand in salute as Deepraj engaged the gear and weaved through the staggered knife-rest barriers. Waves of relief washed against the muscles in his neck that were tensed like rocks. He slumped back into his seat, all energy drained. Tashi and Deepraj spoke simultaneously.

"What did you say to him?" He told them and they both laughed, though their laughter had more than a touch of hysteria in it and they fell silent.

The motion of the car climbing through endless hairpin bends soon had a soporific effect on him.

"Wake me up in half an hour and I'll take over." He was tempted to add 'and for Christ's sake don't you fall asleep at the wheel' but thought better of it.

"Huzoor." Max had a clear picture of the Gurkha's face, drawn grey as he stared out through the windscreen into the differing shades of darkness that clothed the Himalayan foothills. Then he fell asleep.

The Tribhuvan Rajpath
0030 hrs

Shaken out of a muggy, sweat-filled sleep, momentarily it was reminiscent of being woken for a pre-dawn stand-to in Belize. The same child-like craving to turn over and let rude reality ebb away beyond the edges of sleep, the same almost obscene sense of duty that had once demanded that he lead by example was now second nature, command resilience. He sat up and stretched his cramped limbs, suddenly aware that it was both cold and clammy. He looked out through the Range Rover's wraparound windows at the view that confirmed what the fall in temperature had already announced; they were going over the top of the first mountain range. Only another 70-odd kilometres of narrow hairpin bends.

"Where's the coffee?"

"Who knows?" The surly response was indicative of the fatigue eroding Deepraj's customary respectful attitude. As he turned round in his seat he saw that Tashi had anticipated him and was unscrewing the cap of the Chinese-made vacuum flask, letting the musky sweet aroma of the whisky laden coffee steal under their noses.

"Pull over here, *Burho.*" Max chided Deepraj gently, characterising him as 'an old man' was a playful way of reminding him that they were all deeply fatigued. Yet the strain seemed to have set into the Gurkha's face in a fixed expression of concentration and he didn't respond as Max had intended. Both men got out and walked around the vehicle, stretching tired, aching muscles. Tashi leant out of her window, a steaming plastic mug in her hand.

"Coffee...doctor?" She laughed lightly. He took it gratefully and handed it over to Deepraj who grunted but registered some satisfaction.

"How do you expect to earn if you don't work?" He tossed the Nepali proverb at him and was rewarded by the beginnings of a grudging smile, the gesture of a silent toast and a noisy slurping as he sucked the coffee down.

"We have another cup for the relief driver, here." She handed over a second mug. After a moment or two the combination of coffee, whisky and words appeared to do the trick.

"I'm really bushed, Saheb."

"I know you are, you old bugger. I'll drive from here on. Get your head down, recline the seat right back, I'll only wake you if we run into another road block." Deepraj shook his head.

"No, Huzoor, one hour each."

"We'll see." Max wasn't going to argue the toss. "This coffee could do with some more sugar."

"It needs more whisky...*Bahun's* piss."

The Range Rover swung sweetly around the endless hairpin bends as Max drove as fast as the tortuous road and the hollows over the monsoon culverts would permit. His fatigue was secondary as he felt the powerful engine responding to his tight control. Yet again he was thankful that he'd opted for the manual gear box. Touching the brakes as he steered into each bend and accelerating out of them, the familiar rush and roar rhythm of the V8 engine was therapeutic. The sky was well hidden but the night air that rushed in around the wind deflectors and into the open window smelled of rain. That, he confided to himself, was an added factor that he could well do without. In the absence of random patrols or intermediate checkpoints which he calculated as unlikely, given their limited available manpower, he ought to have a clear run through as far as Chisapani Garhi between the two mountain ranges that separated the Valley from the plains.

From time to time the telephone poles swung back and forth, in places the cables swooped down negligently low enough to touch. They carried the landline link from Kathmandu to the towns in the flatlands of the Terai and he toyed with the idea of cutting the cables but dismissed it after he reasoned that it would bring out a repair party from either or both ends of the line and, in any event it would be a futile exercise because the military radio network would remain unaffected.

The tyres scrunched into gravel as he took a corner too wide and too fast. Out of the corner of his eye, the deeply dark, unfenced drop beside him seemed to draw the offside wheels towards its gaping maw. He blinked his eyes fiercely, shook his head and rolled his shoulders alternately as he pushed away the sleep. Then her hands were on his shoulders, kneading the aching muscles at the base of his neck and across the top of the scapula. He stretched his head backwards like a contented cat, her fingers, sensuous but strong, squeezed and probed, dissipating the tension.

"Thank you." He spoke softly so as not to disturb Deepraj. "Talk to me." He needed to stay awake but he needed to explore her mind too. This was the first moment of relative intimacy that they had shared since their nights on the mountains. He began to wonder whether there wasn't some pre-ordained rule of fate dictating that they would never be truly alone together. He suspected that she might well believe in some such nonsense. For now, their minds and bodies tensed to the slightest alien sound or movement that signalled an intrusion into their stolen privacy. She reached inside his shirt with one hand, brushing the hairs on his chest with her fingertips whilst she traced the back of his ear with her other hand. He felt the blood rising in him, the warmth generated by her spontaneous physical expression of caring.

"How long will it take for us to reach the border?" He felt her breath on his ear and gently rubbed against her face with his head. The question was simple enough to answer in terms of time and distance, even making allowances for his fatigue. No, the imponderables were the prospects of bumping a roving patrol, let alone their chances of successfully bluffing their way through the next checkpoint, particularly once they were exposed to the light of day. None of which even considered the possibility that anyone would be actively searching for them. He struggled with the dilemma of whether or not to tell her the unvarnished truth about the potential hurdles before them or shrug them off as obstacles only there to be overcome? Mentally, he wandered ahead on the road, visualising the barriers, the questions, his responses to each situation.

"Max-la?" Her voice took on a worried note.

"Mm? Oh, sorry my love." He knew that if he made light of it she would see through it and suspect that the situation was even worse. Could it get any worse, he wondered? No, the real dilemma was whether or not to share his anxieties with her because he loved her or to put up the pretence of the strong silent knight who would protect her against all evil.

"You're so tired." It was a cop-out but there was nothing to be gained by pretending anything other than what she could see for herself.

"Yes. True. But I've driven over this road many, many times. At night it is quietest and Deepraj will drive part of the way, so I'll get a rest." He had no intention of letting Deepraj drive provided that he could stay awake. The Gurkha was a good, steady driver but most of all Max wanted speed.

"We should reach the border in just under three hours from now." He let his eyes wander for a fraction of a second to the dashboard clock.

"But it isn't opened until 6am, so I'm hoping that we can simply sneak across." In fact he had given precious little thought to how they would cross into India. He imagined that the official border crossing would most probably have been closed because of the coup and he held out little hope of their charade about WHO and the plague surviving cynical immigration officials, let alone military personnel. In taking each hurdle as it presented itself, he had deliberately ignored the last fence. He reached up and brushed her hand with his. Her fingertips found his lips and traced them lightly. God in heaven! That he should find love in such circumstances, where even their small acts of tenderness had to be found amidst flight. To be sensually aroused whilst throwing his little party around bends that turned back on themselves again and again, with a 6,000-foot drop one side and an equally hazardous 3-foot deep monsoon drain on the other was sheer madness. He misjudged the next bend and had to wind the steering wheel furiously to correct it, they were all thrown around in their seats.

"I'm sorry, I distracted you." Tashi had been thrown against the door pillar, he had felt her hands slide away from his face. He wanted to reach out for her but dared not take his hands off the wheel.

"Are you alright?" He enquired solicitously.

"Yes." She laughed lightly. "It's like a wild horse!" It suddenly occurred to him that she may never have been in a 4-wheel off-roader before.

"You've not travelled on mountain roads like this before?"

"Oh yes!" She laughed again and he thought how amazingly musical it sounded.

"On horseback, not one of these wild animals!" He chuckled with her. Deepraj stirred, adjusting his sleeping position slightly. The intriguing capacity of Gurkha soldiers to sleep in the most curious of positions had never ceased to amaze him. Irrespective of the position, they seemed to have a natural faculty for falling asleep at any time and in the most bizarre places, a skill that the British soldier had to acquire with practice.

All of a sudden it struck him that Tashi was unnaturally quiet. He looked back in his rear view mirror and noticed that she looked strangely pre-occupied. He risked a quick glance as he asked, "Is something wrong?" She lifted one arm weakly and pointed to her stomach.

"I think I'm going to vomit."

"Put your head out of the window and take deep breaths, go on." He encouraged her. His concern for her was tinged with a wry sense of the bizarre, here was a woman who had survived high Himalayan passes pursued by murderous Chinese, battled with sub-zero snowstorms and a hair-raising flight across the Roof of the World in a tiny aircraft only to suffer from car sickness in the most luxurious 4×4 ever made.

"Look in that basket of food that Lakpar's wife gave us, see if there's a lemon in there and some salt, it's the best remedy, suck on a salty lemon." He continued to take quick glances at her whilst negotiating the 'straight' stretches between bends. After a while she flopped back in her seat and a little while later he saw her tentatively suck on half a lemon. Their eyes met fleetingly and he could see that she no longer looked so pale.

"Alright?" He reached back and squeezed her knee with his left hand. He looked again and she nodded with her eyes closed. There was little more that he could do for her since stopping the car would only give her temporary respite and trying to balance out temporary discomfiture against the consequences of getting caught was not an option open to him. Neither course held any attractions. A few minutes later she looked as though she'd fallen asleep and he felt a flood of relief.

The inevitable sense of drowsiness threatened to overcome him again and he gripped the steering wheel tightly then released it suddenly several times over, making his body go rigid then relax by turns. Every device he'd ever used was thrown into the battle to stay awake at the wheel and keep the vehicle on the road heading towards freedom. He didn't want to think of it in terms of hours and minutes, that was beyond appreciable contemplation. He began to sing quietly to himself, composing different melodies to the words of *The Lobster Quadrille* from Alice in Wonderland.

Army Headquarters Kathmandu

Hans Fischer was furious, partly with himself for getting into this mess and partly with his captors for disregarding his diplomatic status. He was also anxious to find out precisely what they had arrested him for. It defied reason that it had anything to do with Max because he was sure that his erstwhile passengers had made good their escape from the airport, unless...? If they'd been caught and the truth beaten out of them? He doubted whether Max would have given him away but the young woman had a child, always an easy point of leverage, there was the potential flaw in his defences. With that realisation the fear came back and hit him with sickening immediacy.

The vile stench of old and fresh human faeces and the penetrating stink of urine so polluted the air that even with his handkerchief covering nose and mouth the smell clung to his nostrils and filtered down, contaminating his lungs. His head ached and it was all he could do to stop himself from throwing up, either because of the stench or, more likely, because he was afraid. His cell had no light other than the short carpet of low-voltage light that crept in under the door and reflected against the indeterminate liquid on the floor, as to which he did not want to investigate any further. Ever since he had been pushed roughly in and the door slammed behind him he had not moved for fear of coming into contact with the sources of the overwhelming smell. They'd taken his watch so he could only guess at the time.

How long had it been now, two hours, three? He was, he realised, rapidly becoming disoriented. Perhaps, he reasoned, because his life was ordinarily governed by instruments for measuring everything from time to distance to atmospheric pressure to speed he was more vulnerable to being broken down by this kind of psychological torture. Whether in theory that was so or not, he knew that in reality it was working, especially as the anger evaporated, displaced by naked fear. Try though he might to rationalise his situation, blind panic came at him out of the darkness and strangled each constructive thought that forced itself out of his mind.

Drops of sweat formed along his forehead and trickled down, smarting his eyes and he wiped them away with his sleeve. His only hope, he told himself, was to shelter behind official indignation and demand to speak to his head of mission. Even that prospect offered little promise of relief, Wen Zhaoyun was a paid-up member of the central committee of the Chinese Communist Party whose primary loyalty was to Beijing. The CCP would never have allowed him to take up a UN post unless they could be sure that he would put the PRC's interests before anything else. In this present confusion, they would expect him to collaborate with the coup regime until they had worked out their own agenda. These plangent thoughts were interrupted by the sound of approaching footsteps which halted outside the cell door. He heard a bolt slide back and the dim orange light of the low-voltage bulb hanging threateningly from the ceiling invaded the cell so that he had to squint.

"Come!" The figure in the corridor was peremptory, the voice gave nothing away. Relief at leaving the filthy hole was overshadowed by a dread apprehension of what was to come next. In all his years in Nepal, from time to time he had been told horror stories of the treatment of political prisoners. Even people arrested for minor offences were subjected to a mandatory beating. He decided to start his strategy early.

"There will be much trouble because of this. You can't arrest a United Nations official!" The uniformed figure walked on, ignoring him and he lapsed back into silence as they wound their way along the corridor between patches of darkness and indiscriminately positioned naked light bulbs. His gaoler suddenly stopped and he nearly stumbled into him. They were in front of a curtained doorway. The gaoler pulled the curtain aside and motioned him to enter.

"Come in, Mr. Fischer." The room was lit with fluorescent tubelights and Fischer had to hold his hand up to his eyes for a moment before he adjusted to the brightness. Varnished plywood furniture, the hallmark of high taste in a government office, signalled that he was in a senior official's room. Behind the desk with its customary coating of dust sat three uniformed figures. In the far right-hand corner, a fourth figure sat in shadow.

"Why were you at the Tibetan's?" The tone was hostile, the words more an accusation than a question. Fischer looked around for a chair and the same voice jumped in.

"You will stand, Mr. Fischer, you are not the great foreign Saheb now." Heavy sarcasm was injected into the word 'Saheb' and Fischer's slender hopes were further bruised as he realised that this man was a xenophobe as well. Slender though it was, he knew he had to stand on what little dignity he could muster.

"No sir, I am just a United Nations official who has served in Nepal for many years. You have no right to treat me in this way. I insist that I am released and my head of mission informed." His throat was so dry that there was only just enough air to complete his sentence. The officer who had first spoken looked towards the figure seated in the far corner then rose to his feet and walked around the desk towards Fischer.

"Do you think that Ambassador Wen will approve of you assisting a man who is wanted for criminal offences in your host country, do you?" Fischer knew that his chief was so obsessed with 'face' that he would probably ignore anyone except whoever was acting as foreign secretary and then he'd probably talk in tangential Chinese allegories. A fat lot of good that would do anyone. What really troubled him was the knowledge that they appeared to know what he'd been doing. He decided to call their bluff.

"I don't understand what you are talking about. I go to a restaurant to eat and suddenly I am grabbed by some gorillas in some sort of uniform, I don't know what they were, then I am thrown in a disgusting cell. Is this the way to treat a UN officer?" His anger was genuine and leaked through the fear. The interrogator appeared to be unimpressed by this protest.

"What have you told your *Chef de Mission* about yesterday's flight?" He rolled the title around his mouth, relishing his facility with the language. Fischer began to wonder whether there was sufficient residual sophistication in the man to establish a sensible rapport. He'd not mentioned Max by name and that slender thread of hope was worth clutching at. Moreover, the log for the previous day had not been completed so that there was no actual record of where he had flown. The problem was that he'd not got around to working out a story to cover the flight, now he had to invent one on the spot. He temporised.

"That there was a lot of turbulence."

"Yes, that's why I want to know what made you take such risks?" The officer sat on one corner of the desk, his arms folded. He tapped the insignia over his breast pocket.

"Paratroops make it their business to know about flying conditions."

"Then you'd know that it was nothing unusual for an experienced pilot in these mountains." There was a long pause as each man measured the other. Fischer rehearsed silently what he was going to say then, quite abruptly his interrogator changed tack.

"I want you to prepare to take off for a reconnaissance flight." He glanced at his watch. "In an hour, an hour and a half." Fischer's sense of relief nearly made him smile. Once back in the air, he would be in control. But, instinctively, he knew that it would be a mistake to jump at the opportunity.

"I'm seized for no reason, stuck in a filthy hole, my watch, my wallet, everything taken away from me and then you expect me to be some sort of airborn jockey, is this a joke?" He expostulated.

"You are now under military law, Mr. Fischer." He waved down Fischer's objections.

"We have your chief's authorisation to charter your aircraft for matters of vital national security. So," he gave a thin smile, "you will cooperate, just like everyone else, for the good of Nepal." His tone changed from the curt military to a more amicable manner and he motioned towards a chair, inviting the Swiss to sit down.

"You have worked in Nepal for a number of years, three consecutive tours, isn't it?" He continued without waiting for a reply.

"I expect you would like to continue to do so?" Fischer's mind was a jumble of emotions as fear was doused with hope and the unanswered questions hung like dry washing on a line. There were no windows in the room and the dampness and stairs he'd been bundled down made him feel sure that it was subterranean, yet insects still threw themselves suicidally against the naked fluorescent tube. He'd registered his official protest and now he was being offered an out, not that there was any choice in the matter and he knew with absolute certainty that he would do anything rather than return to that stinkhole. But a reconnaissance flight? He wondered where Max was now? The ex-soldier was a born survivor even though it seemed to be at the cost of everything that he'd ever achieved. What the hell? He reasoned. He'd risked his neck for an old friend for old times' sake, now, self-preservation was a powerful and necessary instinct.

"Where do you want to go?" There was a palpable change in the room's atmosphere and a trickle of sweat ran down the small of his back.

"You'll be taken to the airport and I will join you there. You will not need to file a flight plan." The officer slipped off the edge of the desk and began to talk to the other two seated behind it. Fischer knew he was being dismissed and became aware of another uniformed figure standing beside him. He felt that he had to maintain his stance of aggrieved UN official so he continued to sit. One of the officers who had sat silent throughout the exchanges flicked his eyes towards Fischer and the interrogator looked over his shoulder.

"You will leave now, Mr. Fischer." He looked at the man standing next to the pilot and pointed towards the door. Fischer decided to chance his luck just once more.

"What about my watch, I need it if I'm to fly?"

"Yes, yes." The hand waved imperiously at the door and he instructed the escort to return Fischer's personal belongings to him.

In the corridor, his escort beckoned him to follow. They appeared to be retracing their steps and he began to feel a sense of unease, wondering if, perhaps, he had misunderstood the situation. He spoke in Nepali to the back of the man.

"I'm going to the airport, yes?"

"Huh." It sounded affirmative but in his current frame of mind Fischer was disinclined to accept anything at face value.

The steel quarters on the escort's boot heels rang against the stone-flagged floor and the Swiss pondered the apparent paradox of experiencing claustrophobia in this huge building when a tiny cockpit gave him a sense of endless space. They climbed up narrow wooden stairs out of what he had rightly assumed to be the cellars of the building and then up a further two flights of stairs until they were walking along a covered verandah that hung precariously around each face of a central courtyard, its sides open to the night air. He inhaled deeply, washing out the toxic memories of the cell's stench. Inclining his head slightly, he could just look up into a clear night sky and smell the freedom he had come so close to losing.

They reached the end of the verandah and abruptly started to descend, sending his anxieties into freefall again, the staircase so dark that he had to put one hand on the wall to feel his way down. The acrid aroma of urine rose up, a sure indication that they were reaching the foot of the stairs behind which the lazy and improvident took their relief. He bumped into the escort and stepped back a pace. His eyes were only part adjusted to the gloom but he could make out a pair of double doors one of which was slightly ajar allowing some dirty light to filter through the ubiquitous door curtain.

"Wait here." The escort gave a short wave of his arm then pulled aside the curtain and pushed in through the open door. Alone for the first time since leaving his cell, Fischer's curiosity got the better of him and he eased the flimsy fabric to one side to give him a view of the interior of the room. The obligatory dirty light bulb suspended from threadbare wiring threw its ugly glow onto a scene that brought the bile rising into his throat and made his scalp feel as though it had shrunk against his skull. What was tied to a wooden chair was, or looked like, a man. What should have been the head flopped forward lifelessly onto a naked chest that was pockmarked with red raw eruptions some of which were slightly rimmed with dark blood. The face had been beaten to a distorted pulp yet retained sufficient of its underlying features for Fischer to be able to recognise to whom it had once belonged. He took it all in as he recoiled in horror from the torn clothing, urine and faeces that pooled around the base of the chair. He felt his legs giving way beneath him and he gasped as he lost his breath and his pulse accelerated in a frenetic tom-toming. He closed his eyes but he couldn't shut out the picture that seemed to be burnt electronically across his optic nerves. Even as the waves of nausea ebbed backward and forward in his throat, his mind kept repeating manically, 'Jamsung was such a fastidiously clean man'.

The Tribhuvan Rajpath

Max had been on the point of waking Deepraj when the rain suddenly began to rush down on them. What had begun as a light shower had progressed into a relentless deluge that drubbed against the roof and washed in sweeping waves across the windscreen. At first he had welcomed the cooling effect on the tense humidity that had taken a toll of his concentration, but such was the weight of water that the roads were soon awash, the culverts flooded and what had been quiet fresh water rivulets trickling from ledge to ledge down the crevices in the mountain wall had been transformed into prodigious waterfalls that cascaded in torrents onto the road from where they bounced over the edge into the open abyss. The force of each successive torrent pushed the Range Rover towards the open edge of the winding road and Max had to try to gauge accurately the right speed and angle to drive through them, the angry water punching against the side of the vehicle like the breakers of a wild sea.

On one of the longer stretches of straight road he glanced into the rear view mirror. She looked as though she was in an exhausted sleep. He was dying for a cup of coffee but he knew they couldn't afford to stop, especially because the rain was slowing him down. He couldn't recall ever feeling so utterly drained both physically and mentally, if only he could rest his eyelids for just a moment or two, surely one or two seconds would be alright he assured himself. The rigid disciplinarian within him fought against this heresy, it was a weakness that had to be overcome. He set his mind to the task of devising physical contortions which would promote a more active circulation and interrupt its inexorable downward trend to sluggishness. Rolling his head, he dropped it forward onto his chest then back onto his shoulders, then flexed his arms and shoulders in an arrhythmic pattern. He found it mildly amusing to wonder what anyone so misbegotten as to be on the road at this ungodly hour would make of his manic actions? Then, he reasoned with himself, by any normal standards he would have been certified as 'Doolally pip' from the time that he'd knowingly signed up to this whole enterprise. There was another wonderful expression, it had been coined by the white soldiers of the old Indian Army. In pre-Independence days there had been a military psychiatric hospital at Deolali. The 'Paddies', 'Jocks' and 'Tommies' with their habitual distortion of Indian place names had re-named it 'Doolally' and then added the military acronym "PIP", standing for "psychiatric-in-patient". His mind reached well across the Indian border and yet he was still struggling with the problem of how they were to cross over the few yards of no-man's land that separated Nepal from India. Logic insisted that there had to be a thousand crossing places along the 600-plus mile frontier but equally, he knew that they could hardly wander along some sort of parallel track looking for a convenient footpath that struck off at 90 degrees in the hope that they would fetch up on the right side of an invisible line. Their luck had held up so far since the murderous mayhem at the hands of the PLA but how far was it safe or prudent to push it? A detailed plan, that most basic of military prerequisites for any operation whether small-scale or involving divisions even armies, that's what they needed, no more of this head down and trust to the fates. What was that line from the song in *Guys and Dolls*, 'Luck Be A Lady Tonight'? Yes, now he had it 'Don't breathe on some other guy's dice'.

No dice tonight. He dug into the numbed recesses of his mind seeking inspiration but met only the black conveyor belt that ran, glistening, beside him on the endless winding road. The rhythmic 'tud-tud' of the windscreen wipers was a mesmeric percussion behind the rich, throaty rumble of the big engine as he tried to edge above the 25-miles an hour that the contours confined him to. He threaded the big vehicle around the corners with metronomic regularity of speed and movement that swung him gently first to the left then to the right. He rounded a wide angled bend and watched the road stretch out for a luxuriously inviting 200-yard stretch of straight downhill gradient. Now, he consoled himself, now he could afford to let his eyelids slide down for those precious few seconds' relief. The warmth seeped gently upwards, joining his eyes to the rest of his eased limbs and back and he felt himself smile.

The steering wheel wrenched his hands violently and he swam upwards out of the enveloping depths as jacketed danger signals struck into his fuddled mind rolling back the duvet. One eyelid, marginally lighter and less resistant than the other rolled up sufficiently to fill him with the terrifying image of the vehicle rolling towards a deep gulley where white water dashed against an old fall of rocks. Both eyes were wide open in shock as he smashed his foot into the brake pedal and tore at the steering wheel, yanking the heavy vehicle away to the left. For a gut-wrenching moment the response seemed too slow to hold them back, slower even than his reaction. As he lost sight of the edge of the road under the bonnet he instinctively stamped on the accelerator and heard the wheels spin and whine momentarily before the scrunching signalled that they had bitten on a solid surface and the Range Rover teetered before rocketing violently towards the rock wall on the nearside. He brought it to a juddering halt, the motor still running and his hands shaking.

"What happened?" Deepraj was pushing himself upright.

"I fell asleep. God! I'm sorry, everyone." He'd spoken in English but the words needed no translation. The Gurkha clicked his tongue against his palate and shook his head slowly. Max felt Tashi's hand on his shoulder.

"Let Deepraj drive for a while...why don't you?" It was said with compassion rather than criticism and Max felt doubly guilty. He muttered an apology in Tibetan and flicked his head towards Deepraj to take over. He slipped out of his door and leaned against the side of the vehicle, his face upturned so that the rain washed over it. He rolled his tongue around his lips, tasting the cold drops and trying to come to terms with his obstinate pride that had nearly brought them all to their graves without any assistance from the Chinese or the Nepalese. He shook his head and climbed in on the passenger side. Adjusting the rake of the seat, he lay back with his eyes closed and tried to ignore the movement of the vehicle. He was a bad passenger at the best of times and the sleep that had dogged him so tenaciously over the previous hours now eluded him. He ascribed it to being too exhausted. Opening his eyes, he thought that the sky had started to lighten a little. He looked at the dashboard clock, ten to four. On the basis of time alone, he judged that they would probably reach Hetaura in another half hour. As an industrial zone it would probably be reasonably well guarded against saboteurs and the political 'free-thinkers' from the border area.

"What are you doing?" He enquired irritably as he felt the vehicle rock suddenly.

"Lighting a cheroot, Huzoor." The answer was delivered in an offhand, bland manner. 'Bland' was not the word that Max would have chosen to describe what smelled like dried buffalo turds but which Deepraj smoked with some relish.

"Must you smoke those disgusting things?" He asked wearily.

"Huzoor." It was one of those cleverly respectful answers, neither an acknowledgement nor an apology but a succinct response that he had learned to recognise when the Gurkha had a fixed idea from which he would not be shifted.

"We may all be killed driving over the side of the mountain or being shot at but I really don't want to die of poisonous fumes."

"Huzoor." It was clear that the malodorous practice was not to be interrupted. Max gave up and shut his eyes again.

They drove on to the undulating hum of the engine and Max turned his mind back to finding a solution to the problems that waited ahead of them. The steady thrum and the unbroken predictability of the altered whine as Deepraj changed gears through each turn reminded him that the Gurkha was a competent if unspectacular driver. Weren't these the very assets that made him so indispensable he asked himself? All-round competence and steady dependability. Too often, he acknowledged, he took the man for granted yet where would he be if the Gurkha hadn't been there, as reliable as a Swiss chronometer, over the past weeks? Right at this very minute he could get out of the vehicle and walk off into the hills, just another indigenous face among millions, yet he continued to risk his own security needlessly. Max's eyes strayed towards the driving seat. Sitting bolt upright at the wheel, his naturally wheaten complexion now darkened by the sun and snow of the mountains, he was the archetypal hillman, tough, loyal and as Max had learned over the years, idiosyncratic.

"Tired?"

"Huzoor." Deepraj kept his eyes on the road. How, Max pondered, was it possible to get so many differing inflections into that one word. This time it was a shared confidence that also conveyed that no offence had been taken at Max's irritable chiding. He closed his eyes again and tried to sink back into the seat.

"It's stopped raining, Huzoor." He opened his eyes to a curious grey-green colour wash as the incipient dawn moved in to occupy the sky. He raised his seat and looked out for the next road marker. By reference to the time, he estimated that they were no more than 20 minutes from Hetaura and the configuration of the road confirmed this as it slid down in ever widening loops towards the tributary of the Rapti river, the waters in full spate, seething and tearing down its swollen bed, sweeping the debris of uprooted trees and boulders and the occasional plank of wood or corrugated sheet of GI from a flimsy hut built too close to the water margin. Not unlike the four of them, he mused philosophically, picked up and dashed by a tide of fate over the Himalayas down towards the Gangetic plain like so much flotsam and jetsam. And yet he did not believe in notions of fate or Deepraj's *kishmet* or Tashi's *dharma*. Respect? Surely he respected it and the belief that others had in it but he could not accept that there was an inevitability in the course of one's life. It flew in the face of his firmly rooted conviction that every man held the bulk of his destiny in his own hands so that no matter what the fates had in store for you, ultimately the decisions and the consequences were one's own. All of which, he conceded grimly, meant that he'd clearly made a bugger's muddle of his life to date. Perhaps, those that followed their *dharma* drew strength from the very inevitability that it imposed? Yet, he wondered, if that were so, why was it that the Tibetans traditionally consulted the various oracles of state before they took any important step? Presumably, their great religious leaders involved in this extraordinary business had done so and there had been a prodigious confluence of favourable auguries before they had allowed His Holiness to embark upon this perilous enterprise. He looked back at the little figure stretched out on the back seat, his small shaven head resting against Tashi's thigh, his first inclination had been to laugh a little cynically at the notion that this perfectly normal, happy child could be revered as the reincarnation of the Dalai Lama, yet despite himself he did sense an emanation of something serene when he studied Dondhup's face. His thoughts slipped back to the auguries, perhaps it would all resolve itself happily for this reincarnation of Chenrezig, no matter what the exigencies of Nepalese politics, the Buddhist community within the country was far too powerful a religious force for the coup leaders to confront with impunity. But as for himself, he could not see that any such auguries would embrace an eminently expendable lapsed Catholic. He shook his head in momentary self-disparagement, he did not want to begin to analyse the significance of these potentially enormous events upon himself. After years of futile searching, in a manner inconceivably beyond imagination, he had happened upon a woman whom he instinctively loved and who echoed that love in a wholly uninhibited way. So many fates held in his inadequate grasp.

As they neared Hetaura, he felt that the options were shutting down. It was only fair to offer Deepraj a decent escape route, an opportunity to look after his own interests.

"Deepraj, my friend, I think it's time for you to leave us."

"Huzoor?" The response was uncomprehending.

"Leave, split, bugger-off, escape. Get safely away, now." There was a lengthy pause whilst the Gurkha stared ahead, reading the road. Without turning his head towards Max, he said.

"Why? Huzoor."

"Because this is not your problem, it's my responsibility. If we get caught, you'll be in the deepest trouble because you're Nepalese. I'm just a meddling foreigner and I don't think that Tashi-la and the child will come to serious harm. But I won't be able to help you, come to that, I won't be in much of a position to help myself. You can bale out now and no one will be any the wiser. Lie low or slip out to your relations in Darjeeling and wait until the great *tamasha* blows over. I've got enough gold on me for you to buy yourself a good plot of land and farm it successfully." He'd not wanted to make it sound so mercenary and added hurriedly.

"After all the years that you've been with me, it's the least I can do for you."

The Gurkha took his eyes off the road for a second and looked at Max, anxiety creased the corners of his eyes. He turned back to face the road, the thoughts trudged through his mind at a snail's pace.

"I've never farmed. My father's not a farmer. I'm a *Lauri*[1] not a bloody farmer." He changed gear angrily as they swung into a corner. Once around the bend and into the straight he seemed to have calmed down a little.

"What will the Colonel Saheb do?" He managed to inject the question with the disdain that a nanny would have for a recalcitrant child that had indicated a desire to leave the nursery.

"It's *pagal*!" He tapped his head, indicating the universal sign of madness. Max found himself suppressing a laugh as he digested what Deepraj obviously regarded as self-evident stupidity that he could ever manage without the Gurkha's indispensable services. There was, moreover, a certain finality in the manner in which he'd spoken. Whether it was weakness, tiredness or the realisation of the simple truth of the words, a baldly stated but succinct summary of his situation, he neither knew nor cared but he accepted the response. Maybe he hadn't really tried hard to persuade the man to quit but common decency had dictated that he give him the opportunity, *sauve qui peut*. He was conscious of a sense of foreboding that only grew as he struggled with the problems that lay ahead.

His ears quickened as he thought he detected the sound of an aircraft.

"Can you hear something?" He stabbed his finger up towards the sky. Deepraj lowered his window and leaned sideways.

"Aircraft."

"Thought so." Now he listened attentively to the sound of the engine. It was a small plane, no doubt about that. As the sound grew in strength, even though it was concealed from them by the cloud base, he became convinced that it was the Pilatus Porter. There was only one such aircraft currently in operation. What the hell was Hans Fischer doing overflying the Rajpath at this ungodly hour? None of the explanations that he thought of had a favourable interpretation.

A rabbit darted out immediately in front of them then shot off down the road. Without a moment's hesitation, Max accelerated after it. The rabbit stuck suicidally to its course as the vehicle gained on it

---

1 An expression used by Gurkha soldiers to describe themselves, derived from the 18th century practice of Gurkhas to serve in the Army of the Sikh Rulers who were based in Lahore, hence 'Lahori'.

second by second until suddenly it swerved off and was swallowed up in the camouflage of rock and scrub.

"We're just like the rabbit…except we can't do the disappearing bit."

"Huzoor."

"Sure as night follows day, they'll get us at Hetaura."

"Huzoor." The mechanical repetition nettled Max's tattered patience.

"Parrot!" The brittle atmosphere was eventually softened by Tashi's quiet probing.

"Isn't there any other road to the border?"

"Not until we reach Simra, about halfway between here and the border itself." He shook his head despondently. "And we still have to get through Hetaura, down this road. There's just the one bloody road to the border, we're on it, so are they." So sure was he by now that they would not be able to finegle their way through the inevitable road block that he felt close to despair. He pulled up against the side of the road, killed the engine and reached back for the map in the overhead net.

"Let's look at this map again." He signalled with his hand for Deepraj to get out and dismounted himself. Outside, he laid open the map on the bonnet. Deepraj lit another of his evil smelling cheroots and Max felt a pang of guilt at the realisation that the Gurkha had gone, uncomplaining, without his customary addiction. They studied the various shades of brown and green that coloured both the paper and their movements. He found it distracting to be at odds with the man. It was difficult to make an apology in terms that fitted their circumstances. There was no direct equivalent in Nepali for the English word 'sorry', the only expression that even approximated to it was an overly self-abasing begging for forgiveness.

"*Ek eis tehra.*" He used the old regimental form of addressing him by the last four digits of his army number. "Is there any rum left?"

"Enough."

"Tashi, can you pour us some coffee?" She nodded and busied herself before handing out two mugs. The aroma floated up at them, its muskiness accentuated in the crisp early morning air. Max took the silver flask out of Deepraj's hand and poured an equal amount into each mug. He grinned at him.

"*Khau-unh, eh?*" He took a sip and then handed it to Tashi before turning back to the map.

"Look." He pointed to their position. "If we go on, we'll be stopped for sure, probably about here, near the old road *cess* barrier." He tapped at a point marginally further south. "But if we abandon the Range Rover here, just before the junction with the Jhawani road, and go on on foot, we could skirt around the likely road blocks and rejoin the main Birgunj road near the Kharra Khola bridge. From there we could probably hitch a lift."

Deepraj measured the distance roughly with his finger.

"It's only about two or three miles but it'll take us three or four hours. Does Saheb think that they're up to it?" He flicked his head towards the interior of the Range Rover. Max was about to remind him that they'd accomplished far more in the debilitating snows when he glanced again at Tashi and saw in the daylight the fatigue etched into her finely drawn features that had been concealed in the darkness. She registered that they were talking about her and slid out onto the roadside. Max took her arm gently and explained what he had in mind.

"D'you feel up to more walking, this time you'll likely have the sun beating down on you?" Her dark eyes closed the gap between them, turning his attention away from the tiredness that tugged obdurately across her high cheekbones. She inclined her head a little to one side and gave him the smile that warmed his soul.

"You lead, we'll follow."

Five minutes later, they abandoned the Range Rover, leaving it out of sight from the road, part way up a rocky water-course overhung with ferns and greenery. Max looked back once more in the direction of the vehicle as they climbed up into the tree clad high ground to the east of the road. Another, highly moot decision. For a man with no fixed and firm deity to importune, he found himself back with the superstitions of his early childhood. He rubbed his hand against a smooth stone and touched the bark of a tree and heard his grandmother's voice in his ears.

"Isn't yer man the lucky little divil?"

Army Headquarters Kathmandu

General Karki was moderately pleased with himself. Twelve hours into the operation and all was relatively under control. What was even more satisfying was that Devlin and the Tibetans would also fall into his hands, shortly. Essentially they were a Chinese problem and once handed over to General Fei, the Chinese would resolve it in their own inimitable way. Nepal would be freed of a potentially embarrassing encumbrance and Beijing would be obligated towards the new regime. As the whole enterprise would be carried out in secrecy, New Delhi would have nothing to criticise and he would have kept his two meddlesome neighbours off his back. No international press parasites with their absurd notions of western human rights and no diplomatic repercussions. All in all, a successful outcome from which he would profit.

The ex-lieutenant colonel had proved an ingenious and determined opponent, qualities which he would have admired had it not been for the disproportionate amount of time, trouble and manpower that he had been compelled to divert to put an end to the man's potential for troublemaking. The outcome had to have been inevitable once the Airborne Forces commander had seized control though it had taken longer than he'd anticipated. Indeed, had it not been for their good fortune in pressing the Swiss UNDP pilot into service for the reconnaissance flight, even now they might have eluded capture. Bubonic Plague! That had been a smart ploy, no wonder the thick-skulled hill soldiers fell for it.

He looked at his watch, 04.50 hours. The Range Rover would be approaching the Hetaura checkpost shortly and he would be freed of all these irritants. Politics and religion, an explosive mix that professional soldiers did well to avoid at all costs. It was essential, he reminded himself unnecessarily, to dispose of Fischer. A pity, he reflected, such a skilful pilot. Nevertheless, 9 years flying around the Himalayan peaks was really tempting providence too far. The man chosen to bale out of the aircraft would enjoy some unique parachuting experience.

The intercom light flashed on and he toggled the 'receive' switch.

"I've checked the unit at the Hetaura checkpoint; it's a platoon of armed police under a para' *Sub'dar.*"

"Good."

"I took the added precaution of having the barrier moved back down the Rajpath so that it would not be visible from the northern approach until they were virtually on top of it."

"And this *Sub'dar* understands that I want them taken alive?" The General's adjutant chuckled lightly.

"He doesn't think much of the armed police, asked if it mattered if the prisoners got a bit damaged!"

Hetaura
06.25 hrs

"*Sub'dar* Saheb." The paratroop radio operator called him over to the set and handed him the microphone and spare headset.

"The Brigade Major wants to know what's happening."

"What's up?"

"Who knows? He sounds angry, started to give me a message then stopped and told me to call you to the set."

Subadar Lieutenant Thapa had all the arrogance of a member of an elite unit coupled with a liberal measure of over-confidence born of accelerated promotion. Now he enjoyed the special fruits of power engendered by an independent command. He'd set up the road block as instructed and deployed the crappy armed policemen, then waited for the foreigner and the Tibetans to fall into his custody. The trouble was that they were now two hours overdue according to his instructions and a tiny shadow of doubt edged itself into a corner of his narrow mind.

"Hetaura leader speaking."

"They haven't reached you?"

"No, Huzoor." He heard the Major swear.

"Well, has *anyone* passed through your position?" The impatience and sarcasm conveyed itself forcibly through the earpiece.

"A number of men and women, all vouched for by the local *Mukhia,* Huzoor." There was a lengthy pause broken once by the distant sound of voices over an open 'send' switch.

"The fugitives should have reached your position at least an hour ago at the latest. Have you enough men to send out lateral patrols over a map square?"

"These men are not field trained, Major Saheb, but I can do a limited local sweep on both sides of the road."

"Roger. Extend up to your maximum and advance to contact. Tell your radio operator to change to airborne frequency and maintain an open watch. Out."

Half an hour later, Thapa's advance patrol discovered the abandoned Range Rover. The Brigade Major took the message in the helicopter shortly after takeoff. It was one of those beautiful early mornings during the monsoon season when the clouds lift off the peaks, exposing them in sharp contrast against stonewashed blue skies as they protrude in all their glistening unreality from billows of soft white meringue snuggling around their bases throughout the Himalayan range. He could see Annapurna and Machhapuchre to the west and the wasp waist wisp spume that joined Everest to the ether in the east. Paradoxically, it gave him a benign sense of omniscience rather than omnipotence, almost a humbling sensation. The feeling of being suspended in a powered bubble was heightened each time the pilot tilted the rotor arms tipping them forward in their seats, body weight straining against the restraining belts. From this vantage point the problems that accumulated at ground level seemed to fall away, lost in the slipstream. The comfortingly heavy whirring drowned out most conversation so that each man was left alone to his own thoughts. Soon they would swoop low over the Terai in a series of sweeps that would reveal their quarry. Still, he reflected, this should not have been necessary. Devlin and the Tibetans had been within their grasp yet when the fingers uncurled, the fist had been empty. Overnight, he had become the second most powerful man in the country and in as many hours as it had taken to achieve this he could suddenly find himself returned to the status of a comparative nonentity or at worst be dead, not that there was much to choose between those two states now that the die was cast. He had brokered covert PLA support for the coup, knowing that they would need a counterbalance to the reaction from New Delhi. Beijing's support was critical to the success of General Karki's seizure of power but if they allowed these Tibetans to escape?

"Saheb." The pilot nudged him and pointed to his headphones. "Kathmandu Control." He slipped the headphones on and pressed the send toggle.

"Hunter One, over."

"Hunter One, message from Garuda control, stand by, over."

"Hunter One standing by, over." There was a pause and some mush before he heard the momentary buzz before the General identified himself with their personal code.

"Aerial this is KK. I say again, this is KK. I'm tired of these bastards, kill the quarry. Confirm, over." The Brigade Major frowned, this was a fundamental departure from what they had agreed. But this was neither the time nor the place to debate the issue. The General was not only his commander but the ultimate arbiter of life and death in the country. Still, his instincts warned him that it was a decision born of anger and he knew that he ought to counsel patience.

"Aerial? Do you read me, Aerial? Confirm!" The voice exploded over the airwaves. His reaction was conditioned by years of training.

"Aerial to KK. Confirmed, I say again, Confirmed." He listened but only mush came through the earpieces. Perhaps it was an illustration of just how astute a strategist the General was. He was suddenly acutely conscious of how exposed was his position. If ever there were to be a reckoning, there would be no witnesses to that order from his commander. He thought quickly then wrote on the message pad strapped to his thigh. He gave General Karki as the source of the order, entered the precise time at which the message had been received and designated the subordinate unit commanders to whom the order was to be directed for immediate action. He leaned back and handed it to the staff captain sitting behind him.

"Relay this message to Hetaura command." It was the best he could manage in the circumstances. As the Americans at Fort Bragg had habitually reminded him, 'Always cover your ass'. He turned his attention to the situation map that he had on the map board in front of him. From the aerial reconnaissance sighting in the early hours of the morning and allowing a short interval for a rest, the fugitives ought to have run into the Hetaura blockade by no later than 05.00 hrs.

They'd have difficulty making more than 3 to 4 miles an hour over this terrain, slightly faster if they'd found a higher ground track to the east. He calculated that they would be within a radius of two miles of Amlekhganj if they took the direct route to the border crossing at Birgunj. What if they'd taken a different route altogether? Devlin was devious and knew the jungle and savannah land around Chainpur to the west, he could have gone due west then struck off for Bihar opposite Rampur...or...the 30-mile-wide belt of jungle and elephant grass was excellent country in which to hide and run. Excellent, that is unless the hunter knew the country as well if not better than the prey. His early posting as ADC to the king when he'd been an ambitious young lieutenant had provided him with endless opportunities for *shikar.* Now the quarry would be the most challenging of all. He tapped the pilot on the arm.

"Can you raise Birgunj command control?" The pilot nodded.

"Signal them to scramble two more helicopters and put the whole flight under my command. I am assuming call-sign '*Shikar*-leader'." His eyes glistened at the prospect. What was power for if not to be used? He would have a sweep bigger and more effective than anything they'd ever seen. He'd drive them into a killing zone of his choosing with most of his flight in the role of beater. He sensed the adrenalin rising in anticipation of a manhunt that would make the old tiger *shikars* look tame in comparison. With a chinagraph pencil he drew a small circle on the map in the bow of the river south-west of Amlekhganj. This was where he'd let them exhaust their energies before driving them back onto their own tracks. It didn't call for highly-trained infantry, he would deploy armed police, game reserve rangers, *huggerum-buggerum,* armed or unarmed, anyone could be pressed into service as beaters.

Half a mile on the mountainside of the road to Amlekhganj a worn, grey wooden bullock cart pulled by two mud-stained bullocks moved along the road on a course as erratic and a speed as lethargic as the nature of the bullocks themselves. The sun burned down through the crystal clear air with laser-like intensity. Huddled against some odious smelling sacks on the wood planked floor of the cart, Max felt sick. He pulled the dirty cloth that he'd covered himself with away from his face, there would be little point in concealment if he had to throw up every so often. They had created two cramped tent-like cavities for themselves under the loosely draped pieces of cloth tucked between the tops of the sacks. He looked across towards Tashi, her eyes were closed but she opened them when he pressed his knees against hers. Never could it have been more accurate to say that the course of true love ne'er ran smooth; they had shared the most bizarre beds in their brief time together. His mind wandered off to an ideal bed of fresh, crisply clean cotton in a cool bedroom that looked out onto greenery that rustled in a slight breeze, his fingers traced slowly down her back and he laid his hand gently across the crease at the top of smooth buttocks…

The cart lurched through a particularly deep rut and the mental picture dissolved. The sudden movement let one of the pieces of hessian sacking drop, giving him a glimpse of Dondhup walking along beside the cart. It was some comfort that the little fellow had adjusted so incredibly well. With an old cloth tied round his head in a makeshift *pugaree* and a stick in his hand, he didn't merit a second glance. Max gave up any hope of sleeping. His mind was racing free of its governors as he analysed the permutations. The whole escape plan had degenerated into a series of kneejerk reactions which his rational forces insisted were no substitute for proper planning. Over every attempt to impose the order of analysis lay the emotive force of futility powered by a brain so tired that it resisted constructive thought. So much for the military mantra, 'Planning prevents piss-ups'. The mental pictures of the border that zoomed in and out of his mind's eye like a crazed telescopic lens were all guarded and patrolled for the entire 600 miles. Reason insisted that this simply could not be so but the fear of failure crabbed his reasoning faculties and snuffed out each flicker of an idea. Reason, like Jimminy Cricket, sat on his shoulder being ignored by his emotions. He made a conscious effort to relax and unballed his fingers from where they had buried themselves into his palms.

The cart lurched again and the *goru-gari wallah* hurled abuse at the bullocks. Seconds later, in a perfect imitation, Dondhup's voice repeated the abuse. Tashi sat up rigid, fear on her face but Max laughed quietly and told her what had happened. She sank back, covering her mouth instinctively to hide her own amusement.

Momentarily, his mind cleared and he stretched his neck left and right to ease the muscle spasm that had built up on either side of the brain stem. It was the multiplicity of imponderables that weighted him down, that and a dearth of intelligence that would have enabled him to select options by reference to risk criteria. He'd sent Deepraj on alone to scout ahead. On his own, he ran virtually no risk of being stopped any more than any other Nepali going about his business, coup or no. He checked the time, shouldn't he have been back by now? He half lifted himself and craned his neck so that he could see ahead around the stacked sacks. At a rough guess they were no more than a mile to the north of Amlekhganj. He daren't risk going into the town, even under this guise. He calculated that after another 20 minutes they'd have to abandon the bullock cart and wait for Deepraj to meet up with them just off the road. The countryside was barren and predominantly flat, affording almost nothing in the way of cover. He decided to offer the *goru-gari wallah* an additional inducement to stop until Deepraj returned. He'd been in two minds whether to trust the man, a Hindi speaker who claimed to be Nepalese but looked like a typical Bihari. Since the politicians had begun to flood the Terai with bogus citizenship certificates in order to purchase their poll results, it had become impossible to distinguish the genuine from the bogus. He called out to the man.

"*Aaj, kya din hei*?" The *goru-gari wallah* looked as though he was asleep, slumped with his head between his knees but he mumbled a reply.

"*Shukrabar.*" He turned and looked at Max, his remaining teeth flashing against the dark hue of his face. He cleared his throat and spat noisily before adding.

"*Burrah Bazaar.*"

For a moment or two, it failed to register in Max's brain, then the germ of an idea began to gather purchase against the shifting soil of fear and confusion. Of course! He punched his thigh as the realisation dawned on him, today was a major meat market, the cattle pens of Amlekhganj would be overflowing with water buffalo bound for the Kathmandu Valley's kitchens. And, he recalled with relish, they arrived from the south and left travelling north on the hoof, bringing motorised traffic to a standstill. He offered up a silent apology for the years of abuse that he'd meted out on jaw dislocating 'buff' steaks, his vilification of the poor dumb creatures as they ambled an eccentric course over countless miles of road, obstructing the progress of his vehicles. He smiled to himself and said quietly.

"Blessed are the bullocks for they shall enable us to inherit the Republic of India."

"Hah?" Queried the *goru-gari wallah.*

"*Kuch nei, kuch nei.*" Max shook his head, now smiling openly.

Deepraj had still not returned by the time that Max judged it prudent to proceed no further. The *goru-gari wallah*'s reluctance to wait was ameliorated by a sum which Max guessed was the equivalent of a month's income but he still managed to look insulted before he tucked the notes away in the top of his loincloth and squatted down beside the cart. Max decided to offer an inducement not just to pocket the money and still give them away. It didn't take a rocket scientist to realise that foreigners and Tibetans didn't choose to travel in this manner unless they were hiding from the authorities. He told him that when the Gurkha returned, he would get a bonus of 1,000 rupees. In the meantime, bullocks, driver and cart afforded them a measure of shelter both from the sun and unwelcome attention. The sun beat down on them and the air was dust dry. Tashi sat on the shaded side of the cart talking softly to Dondhup and Max decided to risk suffocation rather than discovery so he remained under the draped sack-cloth.

"Saheb...Saheb." The voice was insistent as was the hand on his shoulder. Opening his eyes was markedly against nature and as he did so, the glare made him shut them again quickly. He became aware of a shadow that momentarily blocked off the violent sunlight and peered out through half-open eyelids just as the reek of alcohol on Deepraj's breath hit him full in the face.

"Ugh! Where in God's name have you been?" His remonstration came out of his dry throat like a rustling croak. The drink appeared to have taken a disturbing hold on the Gurkha and Max groaned as he leaned or swayed forward, Max coluldn't determine which. When he spoke, Deepraj's voice was happily confidential though the words were a little smudged at the edges.

"Colonel Saheb, I've a plan." He announced, a wide grin across his face.

"Plan? All you seem to have is a gut full of *raksi*!" As he became more awake, so his anger increased. Deepraj, however, was not in the least bit troubled, the grin stayed fixed on his face and he leaned forward again, dropping his voice.

"Huzoor will see, I shall sort it out." There was a note of triumph in his voice but Max was only anxious to get a report on what lay ahead for them.

"What controls are there between us and the border?"

"Oho! Saheb, they're everywhere!" He spread his arms wide for effect. "Police, Nepal Army, I talked to them, they're looking for a *Gohra* and some *Bhotia!*"[1] For the life of him, Max couldn't understand how Deepraj could find it amusing to be the bearer of such unwelcome news.

"But, Huzoor, it doesn't matter...not even this much." He held up his thumb and forefinger trying to make as small a gap as possible, then put his hands on his hips and began to twirl around as he sang the old Gurkha soldiers' song about the Hill Station at Nainatal. He stopped mid-song and leant close to Max.

"*Gumi aiyo Relma, gumi aiyo Relma...*?" He paused and stared at Max, waiting for the penny to drop. Max's anger evaporated and a half-smile worked its way into his features as comprehension dawned. Nainatal, where the single track railhead ended in a *gumti* or turntable on which the engines were turned around for the return journey and, as he now remembered, Amlekhganj had a similar arrangement for goods trains coming up the single track from India. God bless Indian Aid for this contribution to countering Chinese influence, even if the rolling stock belonged in a railway museum. The message, of course, was clear, they would make their escape by train. Max nodded approvingly, there was a touch of genius in the idea.

"Well done!" He gave him a congratulatory thump on the back.

"The *gumti* isn't far from here and we don't have to enter the town. I've done a recce and there aren't even any guards, we can just slip into the yards through the fence which is broken down."

Max explained it to Tashi and watched the animated expressions of excitement on Dondhup's intelligent little face as he described the train and their plan. It wasn't as though they were about to catch the Orient Express from Platform No.1, they'd have to play it by ear. But

---

1 Literally, a white skin and some Tibetans.

there had to be a freight train moving down the line at some stage. For the first time since they'd bluffed their way through the checkpost at Thankot, he began to think positively about their prospects of getting out.

It took them nearly two hours of skirting around the edges of fields and walking through thin clumps of trees, all the time avoiding the main road and obvious tracks. Eventually they reached the railway terminus. There was an open sided wooden guard post beside the open entrance to the yards but no one was in it. Nonetheless, Max was chary about taking any risks at this juncture so they left Tashi and Dondhup sitting against the wall of an empty building a little distant from the entrance but from where they could observe anyone entering or leaving. He and Deepraj simply wandered in through the open gates and walked towards what looked like some sort of office. They could hear voices carrying on a desultory conversation but no one was visible. Deepraj seemed to know where he was going and so Max followed him as he moved quickly from a line of coal bunkers to a siding on which there were a dozen or more empty wagons. His hopes began to fade as there appeared to be no sight of an engine anywhere, just empty wagons and flats. Apart from two men who appeared to be carrying out desultory repairs to a bogey, the place was deserted.

"Where're the bloody engines then?" He whispered fiercely. Deepraj scratched the back of his head.

"I dunno. There should be one here." This statement of the obvious did little for Max's equanimity but he shook his head rather than get into a fruitless argument.

"Well, we can't just hang around here waiting for one to turn up. We'd best rest up outside the yards from where we can keep a lookout." Deepraj nodded. He appeared to have lost the alcoholic euphoria that had buoyed him up so much earlier. Outside the yards, Deepraj scouted around the empty building where they'd left Tashi and reported back that it seemed deserted but that there was a shaded portion of the flat roof from where they could keep watch without being seen.

It was not long before Deepraj's snoring provided Dondhup with an absorbing game: each time the Gurkha snored, the boy would tickle his nose with a chicken feather that he'd picked up along the way. This had the effect of making Deepraj rub his nose and interrupted the reverberation until he lapsed back into sleep whereupon the same process would be repeated. The child looked over towards Max and his mother and chuckled softly behind his hand. She wagged a disapproving finger at him but smiled as she did so. Moments later, she turned her attention to Max who lay with his head resting on her shoulder.

"Why don't you sleep? I can keep watch for the train."

"But you don't even know what it looks like." He challenged her softly.

"Yes I do, you've described it and if it has smoke coming from its chimney, how can I miss it?" He raised his hand and let it fall, acknowledging the force of her words.

It seemed like only seconds later that he started awake and felt her hand on his forehead.

"It's alright, you were dreaming?" He wanted to go on lying there with his head cradled between the crook of her arm and her lap, he couldn't recall ever feeling so cared for. There was a distant 'clank!' against a low susurration of steam.

"The train?" He asked needlessly.

"I think so." She nodded, her forehead slightly creased. She massaged his temples gently with her fingers. "There is a great tiredness within you." He pressed her fingers and she turned her hands around so that her fingers locked in his.

He forced his eyes away from her face and looked up at the sky. The sun was low and as he twisted around he could see rain clouds forming over the mountains behind them. He forced himself to his feet and stepped over to where Deepraj lay, keeping his body doubled over so that he could not be seen over the parapet. Then, stubbing his foot against the sole of Deepraj's boot he spoke in a low voice.

"*Ut! Ut*! We've a train to catch." He turned back to Tashi. "Stay here while we go and check it out but be ready to come immediately – and stay under this." He pointed up at the remains of a straw covering that extended part way across the flat roof.

As on the earlier occasion, they had no difficulty slipping into the yards, if anything there was even less activity and the thought crossed Max's mind that the railway was grossly underutilised as a means of transportation. The hissing and occasional clanking grunts of the steam engine dominated the air as they slipped around an assortment of wagons that bestrode the rails of the several sidings, all of which terminated in an aged and incongruously fragile set of buffers.

They peered around the corner of a loaded flat and Max's hopes took a downwards lurch, there, unmistakeable in its feral if dull magnificence stood the engine. It looked distinctly antedeluvian to Max's unversed eye, nowhere were the proudly burnished brass nameplates and fittings that he'd noticed on the Terence Cuneo paintings. This lumbering relic of a bygone era looked for all the world as though it was on its last set of wheels. But it wasn't the look of neglect that it wore with iron stoicism that troubled Max, it was the fact that though it was facing south, it wasn't coupled to anything and there was no activity to indicate that anyone had the intention of marrying it up to any of the lines of wagons in the immediate future. One man stood on the footplate, a dirty rag in his hand, wiping ineffectually at the nobs and levers in the cabin. Max whispered fiercely to Deepraj.

"Well, there's the engine, where do we sit?" Even as he said it he couldn't suppress the comic notion of Oliver Hardy scolding Stan Laurel, "Here's another fine mess you've got us into."

"The engine, Huzoor."

"Yes, I know it's an engine but what are we going to travel on, even if does run back to India?" His sense of exasperation quickly killed off the Laurel and Hardy image. He even wondered whether Deepraj may not have thrown off the effects of his recent alcoholic binge. "Don't you see, it hasn't got any wagons coupled to it."

"It doesn't matter." The Gurkha moved back and flattened himself against the side of the wagon which hid them from the engineer, if that was what he was.

"We'll ride on the engine." The very idea struck Max as sheer lunacy.

"What, you think the driver will give us a lift?" He couldn't contain the note of sarcasm in his response.

"No, Huzoor, my plan..." He paused for a second, obviously relishing treating Max to the brilliance of what must have been in his mind from the moment he'd first mentioned his 'plan'.

"...is that I'll drive the engine."

"You'll what?" But even as the lunacy of the proposition registered, so did the answer. He recollected that Deepraj's father was an engine driver on the Darjeeling Mountain Railway. As a boy he must have accompanied Deepraj Senior on the footplate many a time and doubtless been allowed to take the controls on occasion.

"Ahh..." He pointed his forefinger at him. "Your *Ba*?"

"Huzoor." There was a slow smile of pride in the man's face.

"But those Darjeeling engines are only toy size, this is a *pukka* job."

"They're all the same, small differences." He gave a dismissive jerk of his head and Max could see that if he persisted in his objections, he'd have a severe case of wounded pride. What the hell? He asked himself, they'd burned their boats or whatever the appropriate analogy was for people in their situation. What had appealed to him when Deepraj first mooted the idea was that it would probably never cross the minds of their pursuers to think of the railway as their escape route. He presumed that they were, even now, doubling security along the border and scouring the vast tracts of elephant grass which would have been a natural environment for a soldier to use to evade detection. No, the idea was so far off the wall as to be their salvation.

"OK, OK." He raised his hand and gave a small smile of encouragement to indicate that he'd withdrawn his objections. He gestured towards the figure on the footplate.

"What about him?"

"Salami." Max guessed that Deepraj had picked up this expression in Calcutta, it's message was clear no matter what word was used, 'bunce', 'grease', '*ghüs*', money spoke volumes in any language.

"Or, this." Deepraj tapped the hilt of his kukuri which Max suddenly noticed that the Gurkha was wearing suspended from his belt inside a cloth covered scabbard.

"No, buy him off." There were still a host of things that could go wrong between here and the border, not least of which was some complication involving a train coming in the opposite direction along this single line track. Deepraj may well be familiar with the controls on the engine but if there were signals, it didn't follow that he'd know their significance. An informed and even semi-willing presence on the footplate could prove invaluable. He checked his watch. In another

30 minutes or so, night would fall, question was, would the railway engine still be there?

"OK. You go and negotiate with the character on the engine. If he is the driver, find out if it's feasible to get to Raxaul before another train comes along. Offer him 5,000 rupees to take us there and let him raise you to as much as 20,000."

"But, Huzoor..." Max could see from the pained expression on the Gurkha's face that he thought Max was questioning his engine driving skills. He shook his head gently and held his hand up, restraining the interruption

"I know, I know you can drive...but let's try it my way first. If he agrees, so much the better, if not we'll have to take him with us anyway." Deepraj endeavoured to convey both a reluctant acceptance of authority and resentment at the expression of lack of faith in his abilities as an engine driver but what Max saw in his face was the look of a little boy deprived of the opportunity to show off a hidden talent. He was almost beside himself with frustration at this infantile display of petulance when they were running for their lives but he knew from long experience that losing his temper would only exacerbate the situation. He forced a grin and handed over a wad of rupee notes.

"Go on, sort it out, it's all up to you now." The look of wounded pride disappeared and all of a sudden, hoist with responsibility, the Gurkha was his old self. Max counted out some more rupee notes.

"Here's another 5,000, just in case." A look of disgust occupied Deepraj's face.

"That's half a year's wages you're giving him, Saheb."

"Yes, but it's a bloody cheap ticket out of this mess for us." With a slight shake of his head, Deepraj stuffed the extra money in his pocket, took a quick look around the back of the wagon to make sure that there was still no one else around, then strolled casually over towards the elderly steam engine.

When Max brought Tashi and Dondhup back to the waiting-up position behind the empty wagon, from the gesticulations and head movements it looked as though the negotiations were still in full flood but just at that moment he saw Deepraj look over towards where he was and hold his hand up in a beckoning gesture. Max turned and smiled at Tashi and Dondhup.

"Right, here goes. We're off for a train ride."

Deepraj met them halfway.

"He thought I was crazy until I showed him the money, then greed got the better of him but I'm not sure how trustworthy he is. Anyway, I gave him 5,000 now and told him he'd get another 5,000 when we reach Raxaul." He looked back towards the engine where the driver was hanging out of the open cab window staring at them. "We'll have to hurry."

"Well done!" Max waved away the balance of the money that Deepraj was handing back. "No, you keep it, you've earned it."

"Huzoor." There was a serene look on his face as he stuffed the notes back into his pocket. As they picked their way across the railroad tracks towards the engine, snorting and hissing like a bull waiting to enter the arena, some drops of rain began to fall on them. Max took a quick look up and saw that the dark clouds hung like overfull udders above them. He was almost fearful to look into the engine driver's face in case the man wanted to change his mind when he saw his oddly assorted cargo. When he did face him as they reached the engine's mounting step it was all he could do not to burst out laughing. The sheer incredulity on the man's features made him look retarded. His mouth slightly agape, he stood in shocked silence as Max greeted him. His eyes went from Max to Tashi to Dondhup and then back to the bundle of notes still in his hand, as if it was only the money that convinced him that this was all for real.

Max lifted Dondhup up onto the footplate first then swung himself up so that he could pull Tashi on board. He looked over his shoulder at the engine driver who was still standing motionless behind him.

"All ready to go?" He enquired as if they were about to embark on a joyride. The man looked at him then nodded slowly and wordlessly.

"Let's go then." As the engine driver turned away, Deepraj took Max's elbow and spoke quickly.

"He said that there's an upline freighter due out of Raxaul at 19.15." Max looked at his watch, it was 18.30. He called across to the engine driver.

"Well, let's get this bloody thing moving!" With one further, lingering look of curiosity in the direction of Tashi and Dondhup, he pushed his heavily oil-stained cap back to front and attended to the levers and dials behind him. With a mounting hiss of steam that startled mother and child, the great engine began to inch forward. Dondhup's eyes were as round as saucers and though he kept one hand clutching to Tashi's *bhaku,* he stood there mesmerised as the rain poured down and the engine began to pick up speed. A tarpaulin was draped loosely over the coal bunker at the rear of the engine and Max herded them both back towards its shelter. He had to shout and augment his words with hand gestures as the boiler sent up a series of great throaty coughs immediately followed by a ripple of lesser chuffing as it laboured for a response from the pistons as they drove the wheels over the lines. Tashi wriggled around on the coal to form a makeshift seat and then sat Dondhup down on her lap. Underneath the tarpaulin, with the dust and dirt of the road now clinging to their faces like a paste, they were almost indistinguishable from the coal. Max gave a grunt of satisfaction. Three men on the footplate of a solitary unscheduled railway engine was cause enough for comment. Add in a woman and child and they might as well have erected a neon hoarding to advertise their presence. Once through Amlekhganj, he felt that the balance of the run to the border should be relatively clear. If they got through.

Max noted with wry amusement that Deepraj was watching the engine driver closely, presumably refreshing his memory about the controls. The driver stood with his head out of the port window, his right hand on the steam controller. Max wedged himself in the opposite corner of the cab from where he could watch everyone. From time to time, the driver drew his head back into the cab and looked first at Max and then Deepraj, though in the darkness it was hard to discern what his expression might be. Nonetheless, Max couldn't help but feel uneasy, even though the man appeared to be keeping to his end of the bargain.

All of a sudden the rain began to beat down as though water had gone out of fashion, bouncing off the footplate and swirling around their feet. There was none of the 'clickety-clack' sound of carriage bogey's that Max had somehow expected to hear beneath their feet, just the chundering of the engine as it rolled effortlessly along the railway lines. He smiled to himself, it was not what one would describe as first-class accommodation but as far as he was concerned, this had to be the finest ride of his life.

The driver peered out through the glass porthole beside him, poked his head out from the cowling then swung back inside, the rain running off his face.

"Amlekhganj." As he said it, he adjusted the steam valve and reached for the brake lever.

"Why are we slowing down?" Max shouted at him.

"Speed limit."

Max looked to Deepraj for confirmation and the Gurkha nodded. Relaxing a little, Max tried to see out through the porthole on his side but the combination of rain and smoke only gave a vague impression of dim lights refracted through the water. Out of the corner of his eye he saw the driver reaching up over his head and almost simultaneously Deepraj's hand shot out and gripped the man's wrist.

"No whistle!" The Gurkha spat out the words.

"Regulations, we're approaching the signal box."

"What's the signal for 'proceeding through'?"

"Three long, two short."

"Is there a signal lamp for the track?" Max saw the surprise register on the driver's face as it became apparent that Deepraj was familiar with railway procedures. He paused for a second before he answered.

"The signalman uses a handheld lamp from his box."

"*Tik.*" Deepraj released the man's wrist. He rubbed it angrily before taking hold of the whistle cord. The shrill screams of the whistle overhead made Max's heart miss a beat. The driver moved across the plate to stand next to Max and lean out beyond the cowling. Seeing nothing from where he stood, Max hurried back to where Tashi and Dondhup sat, squatted down beside the boy and smiled into his little sunburnt cheeks, the eyes dancing with excitement.

"Good?" Max asked him. The boy nodded his head vigorously and pointed towards the whistle.

"Can we do that again?"

"Soon." Max laughed and looked into Tashi's eyes as he sought her fingers to lock for a reassuring moment.

"There's the signal." There was barely disguised relief in Deepraj's voice and Max turned round automatically. As they drew slowly alongside the signal box it struck him for the first time that the floor elevation of the box put the signalman marginally higher than those on the footplate so that he could see easily inside the cab. There was no point in trying to conceal himself now, better to behave naturally. The window beside the levers in the box was open and the signalman was leaning out shouting to the driver.

"Eh Ram! Where're you going?"

"Tell him Birgunj." Deepraj said just loudly enough for the driver to hear. "Go on, tell him, now!"

"Birgunj." They were past the window now but the signalman yelled after them.

"There's no scheduled down-line!" Again, Deepraj prompted the driver.

"Tell him it's an extra duty!" The driver gave Deepraj an angry look before leaning out and calling back to the signalman.

"Unscheduled duty!" He ducked back inside out of the torrential rain.

"Well done, *Bhai*." Deepraj spoke encouragingly. "That should clear us to Birgunj so let's get a move on." The driver gave him a sour look but did as he was told. As he opened the steam valve, he said to Deepraj, "You'll have to stoke the fire."

There was more than a hint of vengeance in his voice but the Gurkha grabbed the shovel without a second's hesitation, skilfully opened the door to the fire box with the blade end and took up a position straddling the plate between the coal bunker and the fire. Max was impressed and felt the need to impress on the driver that he was working for them, not the other way round.

"Can he signal ahead for them to stop us?" He jerked his thumb back towards the signal box.

"Could do," came the non committal reply.

"It's a straight single line between here and Birgunj, Saheb." Deepraj yelled as he drove his shovel into the heap of coal. "I don't think there's any switchgear on this side of the border either." He looked to the driver for confirmation as he shovelled coal onto the fire. The man looked back at him darkly.

"Well, is there?" Max prompted him sharply.

"No. But there are signals," he said sullenly.

"Ignore them."

"But..."

"Just do what I say, ignore them, if you want the rest of your money." Max let the words carry their own threat and saw Deepraj grin momentarily as he swung another shovelfull of coal across the cab. The engine was thundering along now, the smoke billowing back and occasionally eddying into the cab when a side wind caught them. Hot red sparks flew out of the chimney before they were extinguished by the rain and small particles of soot were mixed with the rain that fell on them.

"Listen, Huzoor, the rails are singing." Deepraj paused after throwing another load of coal onto the fire, the red glow from the open firebox reflecting the highlights of sweat and grime on his face and casting the rest in deep shadow giving him a demonic appearance. And yet, Max reflected, he was bent on an angels' errand, even if they were Buddhist angels.

The fruitlessness of the sweep had left the Brigade Major anxious and irritable. General Karki had left him in no doubt that he regarded this failure as totally unacceptable and he was acutely aware of the tenuous nature of his hold on power. Nightfall and the torrential rain had combined to make the aerial search a waste of fuel and resources and the pilots were all tired and complaining about unacceptably low levels of safety. Still he knew in his bones that Devlin would take advantage of all these conditions to slip through the net, no matter how tightly drawn and that meant keeping the whole squadron in the air ready to react instantly to the latest piece of information. He scanned the night sky searching for a break in the clouds and tried to persuade himself that what he saw was a thinning and lightening of the dark umbrella of cumulo-nimbus. The pilot was a lieutenant colonel, the best helicopter pilot in the Army. He was talking into his microphone. He glanced sideways at the Major.

"Birgunj Control." His tone was respectful, despite the difference in their ranks. Everyone knew where the true power lay under the new regime, the Major thought and wondered why the General hadn't promoted him immediately. He pressed one earpiece of the headset to his ear and identified himself.

"We have a report of an unscheduled railway engine heading for Birgunj, Huzoor."

"*Hut-terigar*!" He exploded in the cabin. What the…?

"One of the three men inside the cab looks like a *ghora.*"

"*Arey!*" The Major corrected himself in mid-thought. Why hadn't he thought of that? But who in his right mind would even dream of someone stealing a railway engine? Except this thrice-cursed foreigner, Devlin, his brain answered mockingly. He pressed the 'send' switch.

"Close the nearest units onto the Birgunj freight yard and block the line." Who cared if it turned out to be an innocent engine driver hurrying home? Something in his bones told him that this had to be Devlin. The timing was right, the method of execution imaginative enough and what *ghora*, other than a fugitive ex-lieutenant colonel fleeing Nepal, would be riding on the footplate of a steam engine at night in these conditions? As for the Tibetans, they might have been hidden though he had to concede that this could be a desperate diversionary tactic. But even if it was, their only identified target as at this minute was Devlin, so he had to run with it. He turned to the pilot.

"Take us due east, Colonel Saheb, until we hit the railway line at a point about halfway between Amlekhganj and Birgunj then turn and follow the tracks due south." He sat tensed up in his seat, his fists clenched tight shut.

"What ordnance are we carrying?"

"Anti-personnel and tracer."

He checked his map for the umpteenth time and tapped a point just under 10 miles from the border.

"Strike the railway line at Parmanipur, Colonel."

"Will do." He made a slight adjustment and spoke to the Major as he did so. "Do you want the gun cracked open for firing?"

"Certainly."

"And the rest of the squadron?" The Major had forgotten that wherever the Lieutenant Colonel went, his squadron would follow.

"Yes, yes. Tell them to be ready to fire when I identify the target." The Lieutenant Colonel passed the order on to the rest of his pilots as the gunner sitting behind them cocked the action on his MAG and spread the belt so that it would feed smoothly into the breech.

"What's our speed, converted into land miles per hour?"

"60-70." He did some rapid calculations.

"Any idea what speed the railway engine would be doing?"

"50-60 with his throttle fully open, I'd guess."

If he had calculated everything right, the train would reach the border in five or six minutes. If it *was* his quarry, he had precious little time left in which to act.

"Can you go any faster?"

"Sorry, no." The Major found himself grinding his teeth together as he willed the helicopter forward.

"There's the railway, now." The Lieutenant Colonel swung over to the right and the Major gripped the metal frame of his seat as the helicopter banked steeply. Suddenly he saw it and stabbed his forefinger at the plexiglass in front of him, his voice sounded unnaturally high.

"There! D'you see it?" The question was unnecessary, given the widening fan trail of smoke that the engine was leaving behind it.

"OK. Let's light it up with your searchlamp." The powerful halogen beam shot out, a silvered beam, alive with the rain caught in its glare. The pilot adjusted his approach at a slight tangent to the railway line so as to avoid the worst of the smoke that poured out of the stack. The beam crept forward until it struck the rear of the engine, the movement of the helicopter gave the light a bouncy characteristic and all he could see was one begrimed face before a hand came up and shielded the eyes from the searchlight's glare. He cursed as the beam slid off the engine and the smoke blanked his view. Tempting though it was just to blast off at whoever was in the cab, he needed to have a greater measure of certainty that this was his target. Supposing there were Indian nationals in the cab? 'Harey Ram!' Delhi would shit on Nepal from a great height. If he could just get a sight of the Tibetan woman and child that the Swiss pilot had been persuaded to tell them about, he would have a completely free hand.

"Can you swing wide and approach them sideways on?" The Lieutenant Colonel obliged and brought the helicopter in at an open angle from the front of the train but the smoke was still being driven down by the wind and rain, obscuring his vision of the cab.

"Get lower, I need to see under the smoke."

"I'm already below my safety level."

"Shit! We have to have a view of who's inside that cab."

The train was sliding past them, moving through the beam of light from the helicopter when a freak gust lifted the smoke for a second or two as they were broadside on. There! One, two, three men, their faces caught and held for a brief moment in the glare of the light, one dark with Indian features, one definitely Nepalese and the third distinctly European-looking.

"Right! Swing in behind and to one side of the engine, Colonel, and follow it so that it's in range of our gun." He spoke quickly into the microphone.

"Shikar leader to Birgunj Control." He looked at his watch, about four minutes to the blockade at Birgunj. The radio came alive in his ear.

"Can you give us ETA of quarry?"

"ETA four minutes, I say again, figures four minutes." He smiled towards the Lieutenant Colonel and wiped the sweat from his forehead with his neck-cloth. "We're in pursuit." He laughed out loud, a touch of hysterical relief in his throat. "They're about to reach the end of the line!"

The combined noise of the steam engine and the monsoon downpour deafened them to the sound of the helicopter. The first that they were aware of it was when its searchlight suddenly shot out like a laser over their heads then bounced back, blinding them as it probed the interior of the cab. Max had a nasty sensation of his skin shrinking against his scalp and a jackhammer thumping his heart. Deepraj yelled across the cab.

"Nepal Army?"

"Must be." Max screwed his face up in disgust. They were so near, what would the enemy do to stop them? Equally suddenly the searchlight was switched off and he shielded his eyes trying to spot the aircraft now that he could detect the distinctive 'whir-whir' of the rotor blades, but the blinding light had temporarily ruined his night vision. He took a quick look around the cab and immediately realised that the driver was panicking. His mouth was slightly open and he just stared out into the sky. God alone knew what he'd do when he snapped out of it. Max still didn't know how good a view of them the helicopter had managed to get but he called out to Tashi to keep down and not to look up.

"It's coming back!" Deepraj shouted. Squinting through the smoke and rain, he could just make out the shape of the chopper as it approached them at a tangent, sliding through the air on an invisible dolly.

"Snap!" The searchlight's beam struck out again, searching for them through the haze of smoke and pouring rain. This time, Max turned his face away smartly and closed his eyes down to slits. The light, he could still tell, held them illuminated as long as the pilot could maintain his course. It recalled the rabbit on the Rajpath but in their case there was no convenient gorse or scrub into which they could dive to escape being exposed to its glare. Now he had to factor in the prospects of some sort of reception committee or even some sort of barrier across the line. He took a quick glance at his watch, on his estimate, they were no more than 4 minutes from the border, at the most. The question uppermost in his mind was what steps would the Army take to stop them? Was this a pure chance sighting by a routine patrol or had the signalman at Amlekhganj reported the unscheduled train and some bright spark made the possible connection? The amount of notice that the opposition had had was in direct proportion to the preparations they could make to stop them.

The searchlight was doused again and this acted like a signal on the driver who sprang to life. The hiss of the steam brakes was the first indication that he'd invoked the small print on their tickets.

"What the hell's he doing?" Max yelled at Deepraj as the Gurkha knocked the driver away and released the brake control. The engine driver was witless with fear, wringing his hands and screaming out.

"Stop! We must stop!" Deepraj grabbed him by the front of his overalls and thrust a bundle of rupee notes in his face.

"You took the money, now drive the engine, you piece of shit!" The man's eyes seemed to roll up into his head and he put his palms together beseeching them to stop.

"Alright, now's your chance!" Max shouted at Deepraj and jerked his thumb at the controls. "Full speed ahead. We may have to smash our way through whatever obstruction they place across the lines." The engine driver looked on, his face a kaleidoscope of changing emotions as Deepraj took over the controls, disbelief turning to horror as he realised what was happening. The Gurkha pointed at the fire-box and shouted at him.

"Coal, plenty of it, now!" This was the final straw for the railwayman and he went berserk. Rushing at Deepraj, his arms flailing and thrashing, he tried to wrest the controls out of his hands. Max dragged him away but he continued to struggle with the violence of a madman.

"I won't go! I won't go!"

"Shut up and sit down!" Max tried to push the man to the footplate but this only incensed him more.

"I want to get off!" He reinforced this last cry by lashing out with his feet and one of his boots connected with Max's shin. Stung by the pain, Max spat at him through clenched teeth.

"You want to get off?"

"Yes, I want to get off!"

"Now…?" Too late, the man realised what he was agreeing to and tried to dig his heels into the wet steel footplate. With a heave that was powered by the pain in his leg, Max shoved him bodily off the engine and watched him roll down the mud embankment before he turned back to Deepraj.

"I hope you *can* drive this bloody thing or we're all done for."

"It's easy, Huzoor." The grin on the Gurkha's face showed that one man, at least, was in his element.

"Huzoor?" Deepraj turned towards Max.

"What?" The Gurkha pointed at the fire box.

"Coal *Marzie-hawas.*" This, Max decided, had to be the ultimate reckoning. Addressing him in the highest honorific, reserved for a member of the Royal Family, the ex-Gurkha Lance-Corporal was asking his Lieutenant Colonel to act as fireman and feed the fire with coal.

"You cheeky bastard!" Max couldn't contain the laughter as he reached for the shovel and began the none-too-easy job of keeping the coal on the shovel long enough to take two paces across the footplate as it rolled and heaved under his feet and then throw it into the open fire. He muttered to himself at the sudden reversal of roles but stuck to the job until the engine's new driver kicked the fire door shut and announced that it would suffice.

Max stood where the rain could wash the sweat and coal dust off his face for a few seconds then ducked under the cab's roof again.

"How far into India can we get this engine?"

"About 200 yards, then the lines change, Indian railways are broad gauge and we're on narrow gauge."

"200 yards?" That was a damn sight too close to the Nepal border for Max's comfort. He had visions of a Nepalese snatch squad coming across in the confusion and grabbing them.

"How fast are we going now?" He looked again at his watch.

"I don't know." Deepraj shrugged his shoulders. "60, 70 miles an hour?" Then he added. "But we'll have to slow down just before the border or we'll smash into the buffers."

"Don't slow down whatever you do!" Max shouted at him earnestly. "We'll jump off if we have to but don't slow down, that's what they'll be counting on." Deepraj stared at him for several seconds.

"*Pukka*?"

"Too bloody right, *pukka*!" The Gurkha gave Max a formal salute and turned back to watching his front. Max poked his head around the cowling and squinted through part-closed eyes. The buildings and lights of Birgunj swam illusively gently towards them. He stepped back into the coal bunker and showed Tashi and Dondhup how to brace themselves against the retaining iron panels using their small packs as cushioning for their heads. As he moved into the front of the cab and stood on the opposite side to Deepraj, the first buildings flashed by and he got the first genuine impression of the thundering speed at which they were travelling. The engine was responding to Deepraj's handling and Max felt nothing but admiration for this man who had been his largely uncomplaining soldier, servant and companion for almost 20 years. There was a certain magnificence in the way that he rode the footplate, astride a piece of machinery that must have been a 100-year-old, coaxing every ounce of speed out of it and Max felt a sense of pride in sharing this moment with him. Tenzing Sherpa had had his moment on the summit of Everest and whatever the outcome of this expedition, this had to be Deepraj's shining moment. Who could say which was the finer?

"Saheb!" The shout broke into his thoughts and Deepraj pointed forward. Max stuck his head around the cowling again. At this distance he couldn't make out what it was but it was a substantial blockage on the line and they were closing on it, fast.

"Ram it!" Deepraj gave a short hand movement of acknowledgement. As he turned his attention to the line ahead of them, Max could just make out figures and from their silhouettes he could tell that they were armed.

"Soldiers too, I think." He yelled across. Now the engine's own headlights illuminated the track and he could make out what looked like two 1-ton trucks, straddling the railway lines. There could have been something behind them too but if there was, it was concealed by the high canvas roofing. Now the obstruction raced towards them and he grabbed hold of an iron handrail with one hand whilst he wrapped his other arm around Tashi and Dondhup.

"This is it, hold on!" He braced himself as the engine roared forward. There was a recoil that nearly pulled his arm out of his shoulder as they smashed into the trucks, pieces of torn chassis and engine parts smacked into the sides of the engine and flew overhead, as the train, only fractionally checked in its headlong flight, in a series of explosive discharges discarded the remnants of the blockade that had been trapped against it. Shrieking and tearing, the steam engine punched its way forward as Max yelled, unnecessarily, "Keep it going, keep it going!"

"*Shabas*! Brilliant!" Max thumped Deepraj on the back. Every fibre of his body was urging the engine forward, any minute now and they would be over the border.

"Clang!" The smack of the bullet ricocheting off the cowling coincided with first one and then a second searchlight and he heard the unmistakeable chatter of automatic gunfire. He turned towards Tashi and yelled. "Get down! Get down!" Gesturing madly with his hand. Then he turned to the front and yelled 'Down!' at Deepraj. He was calculating that the Nepal Army would not physically pursue them across the border but they would probably continue to shoot at them until they risked hitting people on the Indian side. So, it was precariously balanced whether they would have time to jump after the shooting stopped but before they ran out of track. The rate of firing increased and he could see that they were using tracer in an attempt to hose onto the target. Bullets were clanging off the iron plates of the engine like a fairground shooting stall. He turned his attention back to Deepraj.

"Get down! That's an order!" His voice was hoarse and there was a note of desperation in it. The Gurkha waved him back.

"*Tik-chha* Saheb, I have to drive the engine." He grinned back at Max and gave a short wave of reassurance before being swallowed up in a sudden swirl of smoke that a side wind blew through the cab. Max heard the glass in the observation portholes smash onto the footplate, that meant that they were firing at them from the front as well as the rear. He took a chance, there was little choice in the matter, he had to know whether or not they had crossed over. Because they were firing from both front and rear, he doubted whether either gunner could depress the elevation low enough to make him a good target, crouched, as he was, close to the footplate and shielded fore and aft by the engine's iron plating. Nor could they fly too low for fear of getting in each other's field of fire. He bobbed his head around a side panel until he could see ahead. The 'No-man's land' sign flashed past him nanoseconds before the breath was knocked out of his body as he was smashed against the front of the cab and a red hot iron seared its way through his left shoulder. Even before the pain rendered him mercifully unconscious he tried to lift himself up with his left arm but nothing happened. He thought he told Deepraj to jump but his voice sounded as though it was trapped inside a hollow tin. There was a vicious 'Snap!' beside his right ear and then he neither saw nor heard anything.

He didn't see the high velocity round that scored the side of Deepraj's head, nor the second round that struck the Gurkha's thigh before he collapsed against the firedoor. Nor did he see or hear the bullet punctured engine, hissing and screaming as the dead weight of Deepraj's body pulled the brake lever down, bleeding steam and water drag its precious cargo through no-man's land until it struck and splintered the Indian buffers and lurched like an elderly drunk into the soft red soil of Bihar, the blood of the Irish Colonel and the Gurkha Lance-Corporal mixing with the coal that spilled onto the earth.

A company of Rajputana Rifles of the Indian Army cordoned off the wreckage and the Nepal Army units withdrew behind their border.

Dharmasala

"His Holiness's Government-in-exile is deeply indebted to the government and people of India for the generous hospitality that they have offered to us and our people for so long. Today, we are privileged to welcome the honourable minister for foreign affairs to our humble abode on this, most auspicious of occasions."

There was a brief scattering of applause led enthusiastically by the foreign minister's young aides. The air of expectation amongst this mixed audience of press, diplomats and several Hollywood stars who had identified with the cause of Tibet, made them impatient for their first sight of the 15th Dalai Lama.

Inside the marquee that had been erected to entertain the VIP visitors, it was hot and airless. Tashi dabbed at her face with the handkerchief that she had tucked into her woven silk apron. The dark blue silk brocade *bhaku* with the auspicious symbols picked out in a slightly darker hue and the contrasting fine cotton *hongchu* showed off her slim figure to perfection. She could hear the prime minister's voice now but she was not listening to his words even though she had mastered a little English.

"....sacrifice, laid down their lives for the freedom of our religion and our Tibetan way of life..."

The words hung lifeless on the leaden humidity of the afternoon. Stealing up at her, as if they crept in under the canvas walls, she heard Max's words, his voice.

"Don't count the cost, it's too high for you to pay, too high by far. Be content and rejoice that Dondhup is alive and has you to care for him. He will need your strength and wisdom in the years ahead."

Her thoughts drifted away to the precious two months that they had spent together in Mussoorie whilst she nursed him and Deepraj back to health. The *Kashag* had been opposed to her staying in the same cottage with him but she had given them her ultimatum, either they consent to her wishes or she would withhold her consent to Dondhup starting his formal training until he was 8 years of age. Her very real concerns for her son leant added force to her demands. But in her heart, she was irretrievably torn between her love and her sense of patriotic and maternal duty. She had discovered an unexpected ally in the old abbot of Shadung Monastery. He, it had been, who had silenced her critics with the suggestion that arrangements be made for them both to stay, incognito, at the VIP bungalow in Mussoorie attended by two deaf and dumb servants. It was, he had insisted, a very small part repayment of the incalculable debt that they owed to Colonel Devlin-la.

Max and Deepraj had been taken there not long after he had recovered from the extensive series of surgical procedures first to repair the broken bones and then fuse the severed tendons and nerves in his left arm. Despite the heat, she shuddered a little at the recollection of those first few nights when she would have to change the bed linen two or three times in as many hours as he lay there delirious, soaking them in sweat. It had been two weeks before he had ceased calling out the names of his dead friends. Even after he was through the worst and they had begun to make love, often he would sit out on the verandah, just staring at the distant hills and at those times she had known that the best she could do for him was to share his silence. He would speak when he was ready, she knew and she would be there to listen to his grief. He appeared to derive strength from accompanying Deepraj on his daily physiotherapy exercises, almost as though he could will the Gurkha to walk again. The first time he'd smiled was when Deepraj came out of the coma and asked for a cheroot. Then when it was apparent that her time with him was running out, her own sense of despair welled up in her and she reached out for him, her emotions scrabbling for purchase but sensing that he was slipping away from her.

Then there had been the gradual process of insulating himself from further hurt whilst she knew that he was still haemorrhaging pain. He'd begun to drink throughout the day and into the night. At first she had tried to make a joke of it and return the rum bottle to the glass cabinet but he either ignored her jesting or pretended he didn't hear. Yet no matter how much he drank, it appeared to have almost no effect upon him.

Only when they made love did she feel that he was wholly hers. Sometimes they were savage in their hunger for each other and they would cry out shamelessly. At other times their smiles for each other were soft and knowing, then she would lie cradled in the crook of his good arm and caress its strong muscles beneath the soft sun-bleached hair and wonder at the gentleness of a man with so violent a past. Often he would fall asleep and then she would watch over him, blessing the selfish seconds that were hers alone and she knew that his dreams were untroubled.

"Holy mother?" She was startled out of her reverie by the old abbot.

"Ahh..."

"You are thinking of the soldier." His voice sounded as tired as a cracked bell but he understood her and had shown her nothing but kindness and consideration. He had his hand on Dondhup's shoulder. She looked at her son, so different with his head freshly shaved and wearing the simple magenta robe. He had put on a little weight since their arrival when he had been thin and suffering from malnutrition. She feared that not only would she lose the man she loved but that this wonderful child with his zest for life and sense of the ridiculous would have his childhood stolen away from him. It was this fear that had been paramount in her mind. She sat on her heels and put her arm around a 4-year-old boy who would now carry the hopes and prayers of the Tibetan nation and she grieved for him too.

"Reverence, we have taken Devlin-la's spirit and left him an empty vessel." The old man put one hand on her head and the other on Dondhup's. The words were still with him though the best of the music had long departed.

"I once heard you singing the song of Sahle Aui. You remember the verse that Jatsun sang to her: Like the firmament, devoid of edge or centre. Let your mind meditate upon the vastness of Infinity."

Even as he spoke, her mind was wandering away to Max's last attempt to persuade the abbot to give his consent to their marriage. At that time the old man had seemed unyielding and totally unreceptive to their feelings as he constantly reminded her of her *dharma,* that it was written that she would guide her son so that His Holiness, in turn could guide his people. For his part, Max had sounded harsh and distant, the complete opposite of his true self. He was equally unyielding and would neither beg nor bargain, his pride had been dealt yet another grievous blow but he would not lower his shield and give the abbot a glimpse of the depth of the emotional wound. She had seen on his face what he had once characterised to her in a moment of anger as 'the implacable hatred of all priests for the dignity of what, for all their sophistry, they see only as the lust of men for women and vice versa but what we ordinary mortals know as love'. Then he had added with a shocking depth of bitterness,

"For it makes the meddling priest redundant, d'you see?" No sooner were the words out of his mouth than he'd wished them unsaid, the image of Dondhup lay between them. This time he said nothing but with a nod of respect towards the old man, he had turned and walked out of the room.

She, distraught, had fallen to her knees, the tears rolling uncontrollably down her cheeks. With Max no longer present, the abbot's facial expression had softened together with his voice and he had raised her up gently.

"I am not so heartless that I cannot feel the pain in your hearts. He is a good man, loyal and devoted to His Holiness and," he pressed her hand softly, "he loves you, but…" He let her hand drop from his and she saw the conflict in his face, a face that was suddenly grown terribly old.

"It is your path to tread as it has been mine." He lapsed into silence, telling his beads and then he began to incant a prayer that she could not hear.

She found him awkwardly trying to pack his bag one-handed, he'd been assured that the nerves would regenerate but it would take several months before he recovered the use of his left arm. Picking up a shirt, she folded it and packed it neatly, then one by one she packed the rest of the things that lay on top of the bed. She did it slowly, treasuring the touch of each garment that had been close to him. She could feel the fury and the sense of loss that struggled within him as she stood beside him, neither of them allowing a word of what they were feeling to escape. Then, unable to restrain herself any longer, she reached up with her arms, brushing against the safety pin of the sling that held the damaged arm against his left breast pocket. His one good arm wrapped her to him and she thought he would crush her. She buried her face against his neck and breathed in the scents of his skin and hair, then he released her and turned away.

"Deepraj!" The Gurkha limped into the room leaning heavily on a stick, he had refused to use a crutch.

"Huzoor." He stepped over to the bed and went to take hold of the bag but Max waved him away.

"Don't be a silly bastard, come on, let's go." He gripped the handles, his knuckles white against his tanned fingers and he walked towards the door in that slightly eccentric gait that she had noticed since his left arm was out of commission. He gave one brief glance back at her before he left the room. She felt the overwhelming emptiness squeeze the breath out of her throat as she thought she caught the gleam of a tear welling at the corner of his eye, then he was gone.

"*Namascar,* Huzoor." Deepraj was making *darshan* to her, his walking stick pressed between the palms of his hands and his head bowed down. She touched his head lightly and he looked up and gave her his best smile.

"Deepraj! Hurry up…it's a long way…I only have one driving hand." She felt rather than heard the bitter anger in Max's voice. The image of Deepraj's back passing through the door was distorted through her tears.

Moments later, she heard his jeep start up and the gravel spit as he accelerated drunkenly away.

[illegible] the touch of each [illegible] to him. She [illegible] of the [illegible] and the [illegible] rouged [illegible] that [illegible] he stood beside him, each of them allowing [illegible] of what they were [illegible] restrain herself any longer, she reached up with her arms, [illegible] one of the [illegible] that held [illegible] his left breast pocket. [illegible] and she thought he would [illegible] She turned her face against [illegible] and breathed in the scent of [illegible] Then [illegible] released her and turned away.

[illegible]

[illegible] against [illegible] fingers, and he walked [illegible] [illegible] He [illegible] before he left the room. She felt the [illegible] the corner of [illegible]

[illegible] pressed [illegible] head [illegible] and [illegible] gave [illegible]

[illegible] hard [illegible] rather than [illegible] through the door was distorted through [illegible]

[illegible]

Author's Note

How is it that an Englishman chooses Nepal and Tibet as the setting for the story? The seeds were first sown when I had the privilege to be commissioned into the 7th Gurkha Rifles, an experiencc that first drew me into a symbiotic relationship with the people of Nepal, never closer than when I married the beautiful, mercurial Bimala. Starting the first foreign law practice in Nepal, eventually I built what was described as 'the most beautiful house in Kathmandu'. *The Dharma Expedient* evolved as my own experiences broadened my perspectives. Serial rejection is the writer's norm hence Vajra Publications' decision to publish vindicated the original endorsement by Michael Sissons at A.D. Peters. Bonnie Chiang Collins has been a constant pillar of support and encouragement as well as my most invaluable advisor and I have been greatly sustained and guided by Scott Berry, my editor at Vajra, to whom much thanks. Special thanks go to Angel W. Lau without whose painstaking proof-reading my many and egregious errors would have been exposed. I have drawn on and been inspired by the people amidst and amongst whom I have lived in Nepal and the Nepalese and Tibetan communities in the hill town of Kalimpong, to many of whom I am indebted. Though the story will be classified as a political adventure, in truth it is a love story; the author's love for the country and multi-ethnic people of Nepal who inhabit what are called, with laughable understatement, the Himalayan 'foothills', investing them with their stoicism, sense of humour and gently seductive philosophy.

Counsel in the clouds is an autobiographical odyssey which goes to publication, dieu veult, in spring 2013, it traces the events that led to me living and practising as a lawyer in Nepal and provides one man's perception of the fascinating and extraordinarily diverse characters who peopled the Kathmandu Valley and influenced Nepal's destiny in the exciting mid to late 1960s.